MORIARTY PARADIGM

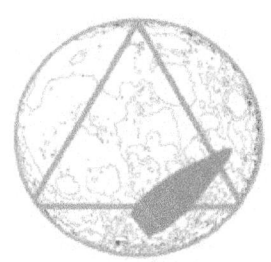

VALLIS TIMORIS

BY MIKE CHINN

INCORPORATING THE ORIGINAL TEXT OF

THE VALLEY OF FEAR

BY SIR ARTHUR CONAN DOYLE

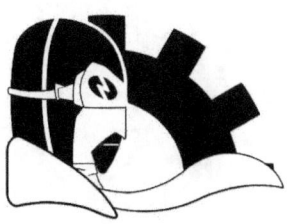

Fringeworks

To the memory of
the late, great Jeremy Brett

First published in Great Britain in 2015 by
FRINGEWORKS LTD
ISBN: 978-1-909573-24-6

Cover design: Adrian Middleton & Damon Cavalchini

Interior Artwork and Additional Design Elements: Darrel Bevan, Dover Pictorial Archive

Illustration of Lunar Mountains, from The Moon, by James Nasmyth & James Carpenter, John Murray Publishers, 1874.

Image of General Gordon taken from a carte-de-visite produced by Adams & Scanlan, 1884

Mike Chinn asserts his moral right to be identified as the author of this book.

The pastiche entitled 'Lunar Gordon Claims the Moon!' is based on the front page article of The New York Times, by John Noble Wilford, published on July 21st, 1969.

CONTENTS

FOREWORD

It was Conan Doyle's fault of course, but then so much in modern literature is. William Gillette, actor and writer, contacted Doyle while working on the script for a stage version of Holmes and asked if he might marry the character off. In a much-quoted reply (and prepare yourselves, Holmes fans because I'm about to quote it again) Doyle told Gillette "You may marry him, murder him, or do anything you like to him." For the next hundred and sixteen years (and counting) that's precisely what people have done.

Onscreen, on stage, on paper, Holmes and Watson have moved from one genre to another, one era to another, one gender to another…I suspect no other characters have proven to be quite so malleable.

I have an admission: I have yet to finish Mike's book. My fault entirely, work deadlines having crunched my time to a point whereby I either typed half-blind or typed nothing. It's my loss (as you will discover as soon as you get past my silly waffle and onto the real reason you're here) and one I shall rectify just as soon as it's far too late to be anything but a pleasure.

I wouldn't normally admit to such unprofessional awfulness but one of the reasons why is just too perfect an example to ignore: yesterday I completed final draft notes on a script in which Holmes and Watson team up with Doctor Who and fight aliens. I mean…talk about absurd. On this occasion it was partly Andy Lane's fault as well as Doyle's (I was adapting his original novel as an audio drama) but culpability aside…is there nothing these two characters won't get up to in the name of high adventure?

Mike puts them in another reality entirely, a steampunk-infused world where airships fill the Victorian skyline. He even dumps them on

the damned moon. Perhaps some Holmes devotees will twitch in their smoking jackets and tamp down their pipe tobacco with extra violence at such things. Let them, the joyless fools, because Mike knows what I suspect Doyle did back when his *laissez-fair* attitude started all this off (let's ignore his well-known dislike for the characters by that time in his career, I've a point to make and I'm not beyond twisting facts to make it): the trappings don't matter. It's all just window-dressing. What really matters is story and character. And Sherlock Holmes is Sherlock Holmes regardless of what celestial body he's standing on. John Watson, ever-loyal, the heart to Holmes' brain, is John Watson whether he rode into the Panjshir Valley on horseback or in the blazing ruins of a military airship.

So here you have the two men you know so well, know and, I presume, love (otherwise I can only imagine you bought the book due to a dirigible fixation and that's just strange). Relax, the vitals are taken care of, what remains, however improbable, is the icing on the cake. And sweet icing it is too…

GUY ADAMS, 2015
Spain

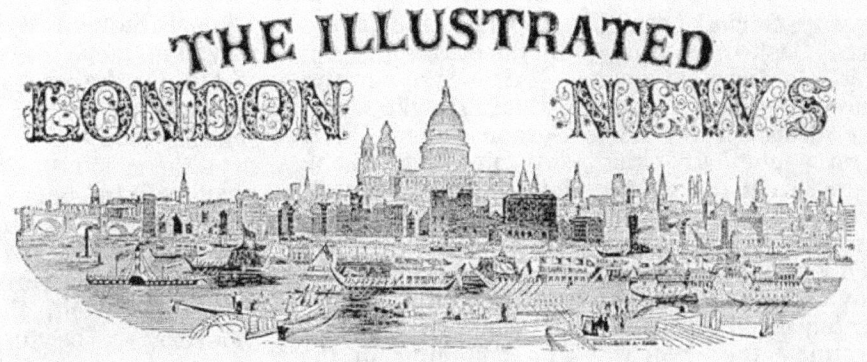

THE ILLUSTRATED LONDON NEWS

SPECIAL EDITION   SATURDAY 2ND JANUARY 1875   EIGHTPENCE

LUNAR GORDON CLAIMS THE MOON!

The first day of the year has dawned with the news that our great General, Charles George Gordon, has landed and walked upon the surface of Earth's moon, one week after being fired into space from the slopes of Mount Kilima-Njaro.

Major-General Gordon, along with one hundred members of the British Lunar Expeditionary Force, made his epic landing safely and smoothly at the last stroke of midnight on Friday, 1st January, 1875, in accordance with the primary chronometer situated at the Royal Observatory at Greenwich, with which the Expedition's own chronometers have been synchronised.

Previously known as Chinese Gordon, the 41-year old General of the Royal Engineering Corps, now dubbed Lunar Gordon by the general public, transmitted the following heliographic message to the Earth from aboard his flagship, the **HMSS Halley**, the first manned container ship to reach the moon. "Hello Greenwich, Major-General Gordon speaking. The Halley is grounded. We are on the moon."

The Halley, commanded by Captain Thomas Hawke of the Royal Navy was brought to rest upon a level, rock-strewn plain close to the western edge of the arid Mare Nubium, anchored to the lunar basalt less than a thousand metres from the descent site where more than a hundred ballistic torpedoes lie, launched from earth to the moon by the great Uhuru Gun situated upon the slopes of Mount Kilima-Njaro. However, instead of explosives these torpedoes, designed by Lancashire engineer, Robert Whitehead, contain the supplies with which Gordon's Expeditionary Force will build the first colony the be established on another world.

Eight hours after landing, Major-General Gordon opened the ship's hatch, stepped slowly down the boarding ramp and into a bleak new world. It was mid-morning, with the chill of long lunar nights behind him, and the sun high above the eastern horizon. Only the shadows of the lunar mountains protected him as he planted the first human footprint on the lunar rock and declared: "By the light of Earth, I claim the moon in the name of God, Queen and Empire."

These first steps onto the lunar surface came at five minutes past eight as the Hal-

ley's external cameras flashed, capturing Gordon's every move. As we await the despatch of the first photo-graphic plates from the moon, we must rely instead upon the heliographic relay whose messages have been eagerly watched and shared around the world, much to the awe and excitement of the tens of thousands of spectators gathered in the grounds of the Crystal Palace at Muswell Hill and a hundred more locations across the Empire

The surface is fine powder laid over rock," Gordon reported. "It adheres to my gauntlets like layers of fine coal ash."

After five minutes Captain Hawke joined Gordon outside their ship, planting the Union Flag and overseeing the mounting of cameras into the moon rock around the ship. Members of the crew joined them, jumping and bouncing in the lighter atmosphere as they conducted the first tests beneath the shadows of the lunar mountains.

Queen Victoria Offers Congratulations

During a break in setting up camp, a recorded message from Her Majesty Queen Victoria herself was played to the pioneers, and also to the crowds at home. In the message she said, "this has to be the most significant event in history."

"The moon is the jewel in the crown, eclipsing all others." The Queen told the pioneers, "because of what you have achieved, the heavens themselves are within mankind's grasp; and as you talk to us under the shadows of the moon, it falls to me to call upon the other great nations of the Earth to work together to bring a new age of peace and prosperity to the world."

PART ONE
TRAGEDY IN THE STEEL FORTRESS

I. THE WARNING

I drained my coffee—wincing at its strength—as I gazed down on an unusually quiet Baker Street: the early hour and winter cold allying to persuade all but the most hardy to stay close to warm hearths, if I had to guess. Although I would never admit to doing any such thing within the hearing of my old friend Sherlock Holmes, knowing only too well the rebuke which would follow. A vast shadow, cast by a watery Sun, flowed across the street; I glanced up as the silhouetted bulk of an aerostat—an internal flight to judge from its size; bound for the Hyde Park mooring masts by its height and bearing—drifted sedately overhead. At the time, I had no idea the vessel could be perceived as a harbinger, for it awoke stark memories which had yet to fade, despite the passage of more than seven years; a conflict of emotion. Even as I could admire the aerial behemoths which transported goods and personnel across the Empire with a despatch of which any sea-going vessel could only dream, there was a small part of me that feared them; the part which would forever be hanging in the blazing *HMAS Keane* up above the Panjshir Valley. Physically, I had escaped—along with many others—my wounds a minor, if persistent reminder of one of the Empire's less glorious moments; but spiritually...

I turned to replace the coffee cup on the breakfast table immediately behind me. Holmes had barely spoken a word since my arrival—summoned from my warm bed by a Teslagram—and I was beginning to fret. After my recent marriage I had urged my friend, at the request

of Clemmie—my new bride—to limit his intemperate demands for my assistance; predictably, he had paid little heed.

"I am inclined to think—" said I.

"I should do so," Sherlock Holmes remarked impatiently, cutting me short.

I believe myself to be one of the most long-suffering of mortals; but even I had to admit that I was more than a little annoyed at this sardonic interruption, coming close on the heels of my darkest thoughts. "Really, Holmes," said I severely, "you are a little trying at times." I brushed past my seated friend and settled in a plush chair by the fire, retrieving pipe and tobacco.

Holmes was too much absorbed with his own private thoughts to give any immediate answer to the remonstrance. He leaned upon a thin hand, an unsampled breakfast kipper pushed unceremoniously to one side, and he stared at the slip of paper which he had just drawn from its envelope. Then he took the envelope itself, held it up to the light, and very carefully studied both the exterior and the flap.

"It is Porlock's writing," said he thoughtfully. "I can hardly doubt that it is Porlock's writing, though I have seen it only twice before. The Greek ε with the peculiar top flourish is distinctive. But if it is Porlock, then it must be something of the very first importance."

The detective was speaking to himself rather than to me; but my initial vexation was extinguished by the interest which the words awakened.

"Who then is Porlock?" I asked.

"Porlock, Watson, is a *nom-de-plume*, a mere identification mark; but behind it lies a shifty and evasive personality. In a former letter he frankly informed me that the name was not his own, and defied me ever to trace him among the teeming millions of this great city. Porlock is important, not for himself, but for the great man with whom he is in touch. Picture to yourself the pilot fish with the shark, the jackal with the lion—anything that is insignificant in companionship with what is formidable: not only formidable, Watson, but sinister—in the highest

degree sinister. That is where he comes within my purview. You have heard me speak of Professor Moriarty?"

I sighed and lit my pipe. "I have heard you malign the Honourable Member for Cambridge on occasion, yes..." I tried to speak lightly, but was deeply disturbed at the recurrence of Holmes' peculiar mania. For too long he had been entertaining morbid fantasies of a corrupt mastermind at the heart of the Empire: a lynch-pin from which each and every ingenious plan or unsolved mystery hung. Moriarty was just one of many names he invoked at such times; but he was also the most prominent.

"You doubt me, Watson?"

"I do not doubt your sincerity." Though I did secretly wonder if Holmes' own genius did not hunger, on some level, for an opponent who was his intellectual equal. Someone to test his mettle: a Goliath to his Samson. All which beside, Holmes was notoriously dismissive of his own health when his remarkable brain was occupied: disdaining meals—as with that day's breakfast—sleeping little, if at all; and I knew only too well how physical neglect can lead to mental disturbance. I have had occasion to reprimand him, speaking more as his doctor than his friend, only to have my concerns swept brusquely aside with a word. "But the concept of a corrupt scientific mastermind, as famous among crooks as—"

"My blushes, Watson!" Holmes murmured in a deprecating voice.

"—I was about to say, as he is in the House of Commons, is more the staple of Penny Dreadfuls than our business."

"A touch! A distinct touch!" cried Holmes. "You are developing a certain unexpected vein of pawky humour, Watson, against which I must learn to guard myself." He barked a mirthless laugh and waved the single sheet of Porlock's note in a curt dismissal. "But in describing Moriarty as a criminal you are uttering libel in the eyes of the law—and there lies the glory and the wonder of it! The greatest schemer of all time, the organizer of every devilry, the controlling brain of a criminal and political underworld, a brain which might yet make or mar the destiny

of nations—that's the man! But so aloof is he from general suspicion, so immune from criticism, so admirable in his management and self-effacement, that for those very words that you have uttered he could hale you to a court and emerge with your year's pension as a solatium for his wounded character. Is he not the celebrated author of *The Dynamics of an Asteroid*, a book which ascends to such rarefied heights of pure mathematics that it is said that there was no man in the scientific press capable of criticizing it? Has he, through his many business concerns, not forged such inventions that the future of the Empire is ensured? Is it not down to him that Britain has laid claim to and set a colony—not two years ago—on the very Moon? Is this a man to traduce?" He slammed the note upon the table, rattling teacups. "Foul-mouthed doctor and slandered professor—such would be your respective roles! That's genius, Watson. But if I am spared by lesser men, our day will surely come." His eyes glowed with zeal.

I closed my own eyes, waiting for the fervour to pass. "But you were speaking of this man Porlock." I prayed that whatever the note contained it might distract Holmes away from such pathological fancies and focus his unique intellect on a solid problem.

"Ah, yes—the so-called Porlock is a link in the chain some little way from its great attachment. Porlock is not quite a sound link—between ourselves. I may not have correctly identified the man, but I have every reason to believe he occupies a minor role within the government itself."

I jerked upright, praying that I had misunderstood. "Porlock has government connections—?"

"Exactly, my dear Watson! Hence his extreme importance. Led on by some rudimentary aspirations towards right, and encouraged by the judicious stimulation of an occasional ten-pound note sent to him by devious methods, he has once or twice given me advance information which has been of value—that highest value which anticipates and prevents rather than avenges crime."

"Holmes," I persisted, "am I to understand that you have been actively bribing a member of Her Majesty's Government?"

Holmes favoured me with a languid stare. "A minor cog, Watson; a clerk; an under-secretary's under-secretary. But even so, adequately placed. I cannot doubt that, if we had the cipher, we should find that this communication is of the nature that I indicate."

Holmes flattened out the paper upon an unused plate. I arose and, intrigued despite my most grievous trepidations, leaned over him, staring down at the curious inscription, which ran as follows:

534 C2 13 127 36 31 4 17 21 41
DOUGLAS 109 293 5 37 BIRLSTONE
26 BIRLSTONE 9 127 171

I had expected a simple phrase, some words which would have meaning only to the sender and recipient—not this melodramatic jumble of numbers. "What do you make of it, Holmes?"

"It is obviously an attempt to convey secret information."

I bit back the equally obvious retort which rose to my lips: it would not do to provoke Holmes at this stage. "But what is the use of a cipher message without the cipher?"

"In this instance, none at all."

"Why do you say 'in this instance'?"

"Because there are many ciphers which I would read as easily as I do the apocrypha of the agony column: such crude devices amuse the intelligence without fatiguing it. But this is different. It is clearly a reference to the words in a page of some book. Until I am told which page and which book I am powerless."

"But why 'Douglas' and 'Birlstone'?"

"Clearly because those are words which were not contained in the page in question."

"Then why has he not indicated the book?"

"Holmes's thin lips twitched. "Your native shrewdness, my dear Watson, that innate cunning which is the delight of your friends, would surely prevent you from enclosing cipher and message in the same envelope.

Should it miscarry, you are undone. As it is, both have to go wrong before any harm comes from it. Our second post is now overdue, and I shall be surprised if it does not bring us either a further letter of explanation, or, as is more probable, the very volume to which these figures refer."

Holmes fell into watchful, brooding silence again and I could do nothing but return to my armchair and the morning newspaper, smoke my pipe and be thankful for the fire which burned heartily in the grate. The most recent lunar landings, by the United States of America and Germany, and the prospect of another by France before the year was out, greatly exercised the editorial page; such hawkish belligerence saddened me. I had seen too much of the reality of war to relish the thought of another; especially one fought in the airless wastes of Earth's closest companion.

Within thirty minutes Billy, the page, appeared with the very letter Holmes was expecting. The boy handed the missive directly to Holmes, giving a warm smile that was ignored as the man tore the envelope hastily apart. Billy departed with a careless shrug and wink in my direction; by now the boy was as well-inured to my friend's outward lack of courtesy.

"The same writing," remarked Holmes, as he opened the envelope, "and actually signed," he added in an exultant voice as he unfolded the epistle. "Come, we are getting on, Watson." His brow clouded, however, as he glanced over the contents.

"Dear me, this is very disappointing! I fear, Watson that all our expectations come to nothing. I trust that the man Porlock will come to no harm." He passed the letter across to me; I folded my newspaper and read:

"DEAR MR HOLMES,—I will go no further in this matter. It is too dangerous—I think I am suspected. I know I am suspected! After I had actually addressed this envelope with the intention of sending you the key to the cipher, I was visited—quite unexpectedly. I was able to cover it up. If he had seen the address, it would have gone hard with me. But even so I could sense his suspicion. Please burn the cipher message, which can now be of no use to you,

FRED PORLOCK."

Holmes sat for some little time twisting this letter between his fingers, and frowning, as he stared into the fire. "After all," he said at last, "there may be nothing in it. It may be only his guilty conscience. Knowing the delicacy of his situation, he may have read the accusation in the other's eyes..."

"The other being, I presume, Professor Moriarty."

"No less! When any of that party talk about 'He' you know whom they mean. There is one predominant 'He' for all of them."

"But what can he do?"

"Hum! That's a large question. When you have one of the first brains of Europe up against you, and all the powers of darkness at his back, there are infinite possibilities. Anyhow, friend Porlock is evidently scared out of his senses—"

"A situation in which you placed him, Holmes," I felt compelled to remind him; but I was ignored.

"Kindly compare the writing in the note to that upon its envelope; which was done, Porlock tells us, before this ill-omened visit. The one is clear and firm. The other hardly legible."

"Why did he write at all? Why did he not simply drop it?"

Holmes thought a moment. "Because he feared I would make some inquiry after him in that case, and possibly bring trouble on him."

"No doubt," said I. "Of course." I had picked up the original cipher message and was bending my brows over it. "It's pretty maddening to think that an important secret may lie here on this slip of paper, and that it is beyond human power to penetrate it."

Sherlock Holmes had pushed away his untasted breakfast and lit the unsavoury pipe which was the companion of his deepest meditations. "I wonder!" said he, leaning back and staring at the ceiling. "Perhaps there are points which have escaped your Machiavellian intellect. Let us consider the problem in the light of pure reason. This man's reference is to a book. That is our point of departure."

I brushed aside his sarcasm. "A somewhat vague one."

"Let us see then if we can narrow it down. As I focus my mind upon it, it seems rather less impenetrable. What indications have we as to this book?"

I responded even though I was certain the question was purely rhetorical; as was often the case I had become Holmes' sounding board. "None."

His thin lips twitched in a satisfied smile; already his mind was forging on like a chess-master three moves ahead of the board. "Well, well, it is surely not quite so bad as that. The cipher message begins with a large 534, does it not? We may take it as a working hypothesis that 534 is the particular page to which the cipher refers. So our book has already become a LARGE book, which is surely something gained. What other indications have we as to the nature of this large book? The next sign is C2. What do you make of that, Watson?"

I was forced to guess. "Chapter the second, no doubt."

"Hardly that, Watson. You will, I am sure, agree with me that if the page be given, the number of the chapter is immaterial. Also that if page 534 finds us only in the second chapter, the length of the first one must have been really intolerable."

"Column!" I cried.

"Brilliant, Watson. You are scintillating this morning. If it is not column, then I am very much deceived. So now, you see, we begin to visualize a large book printed in double columns which are each of a considerable length, since one of the words is numbered in the document as the two hundred and ninety-third. Have we reached the limits of what reason can supply?"

I scanned the cipher again. "I fear that we have."

"Surely you do yourself an injustice. One more coruscation, my dear Watson—yet another brain-wave! Had the volume been an unusual one, he would have sent it to me. Instead of that, he had intended, before his plans were nipped, to send me the clue in this envelope. He says so in his note. This would seem to indicate that the book is one which he thought I would have no difficulty in finding for myself. He had it—

and he imagined that I would have it, too. In short, Watson, it is a very common book."

"What you say certainly sounds plausible."

"So we have contracted our field of search to a large book, printed in double columns and in common use."

"The Bible!" I cried triumphantly.

"Good, Watson, good! But not, if I may say so, quite good enough! Even if I accepted the compliment for myself I could hardly name any volume which would be less likely to lie at the elbow of one of Moriarty's associates. Or for that matter," he dead-panned expertly, "a member of government. Besides, the editions of Holy Writ are so numerous that he could hardly suppose that two copies would have the same pagination. This is clearly a book which is standardized. He knows for certain that his page 534 will exactly agree with my page 534."

"But very few books would correspond with that."

"Exactly. Therein lies our salvation. Our search is narrowed down to standardized books which anyone may be supposed to possess."

The most obvious name sprang to mind: the grail for all travellers whether by rail or aerostat. "*Bradshaw*!"

Holmes tapped fingers to a pursed mouth. "There are difficulties, Watson. The vocabulary of *Bradshaw* is nervous and terse, but limited. The selection of words would hardly lend itself to the sending of general messages. We will eliminate *Bradshaw*. The dictionary is, I fear, inadmissible for the same reason. What then is left?"

Not *Bradshaw*, then— "An almanac!"

"Excellent, Watson! I am very much mistaken if you have not touched the spot. An almanac! Let us consider the claims of *Whitaker's Almanac*. It is in common use. It has the requisite number of pages. It is in double column. Though reserved in its earlier vocabulary, it becomes, if I remember right, quite garrulous towards the end." He picked the volume from his desk. "Here is page 534, column two, a substantial block of print dealing, I perceive, with the trade and resources of British India. Jot down the words, Watson! Number thirteen is *Mahratta*. Not, I fear,

a very auspicious beginning. Number one hundred and twenty-seven is *Government*; which at least makes sense, though somewhat irrelevant to ourselves and Professor Moriarty. Now let us try again. What does the Mahratta government do? Alas! The next word is *pig's-bristles*. We are undone, my good Watson! It is finished!"

He had spoken in jesting vein, but the twitching of his bushy eyebrows bespoke his disappointment and irritation. I sat helpless and unhappy, staring into the fire. A long silence was broken by a sudden exclamation from Holmes, who dashed at a cupboard, from which he emerged with a second yellow-covered volume in his hand.

"We pay the price, Watson, for being too up-to-date!" he cried. "We are before our time, and suffer the usual penalties. Being the seventh of January, we have very properly laid in the new almanac. It is more than likely that Porlock took his message from the old one. No doubt he would have told us so had his letter of explanation been written. Now let us see what page 534 has in store for us. Number thirteen is *There*, which is much more promising. Number one hundred and twenty-seven is—*There is*—" Holmes's eyes were gleaming with excitement, and his thin, nervous fingers twitched as he counted the words "—*danger*. Ha! Ha! Capital! Put that down, Watson. *There is danger—may—come—very soon—one*. Then we have the name *Douglas—rich—country—now—at Birlstone—House—Birlstone—confidence—is—pressing*. There, Watson! What do you think of pure reason and its fruit? If the green-grocer had such a thing as a laurel wreath, I should send Billy round for it."

I was staring at the strange message which I had scrawled, as he deciphered it, upon a sheet of foolscap on my knee. *There is danger may come very soon one Douglas rich country now at Birlstone House Birlstone confidence is pressing.* "What a queer, scrambling way of expressing his meaning!" said I.

"On the contrary, he has done quite remarkably well," said Holmes. "When you search a single column for words with which to express your meaning, you can hardly expect to get everything you want. You are bound to leave something to the intelligence of your correspondent. The

purport is perfectly clear. Some devilry is intended against one Douglas, whoever he may be, residing as stated, a rich country gentleman. He is sure—confidence was as near as he could get to confident—that it is pressing. There is our result—and a very workmanlike little bit of analysis it was!"

Holmes had the impersonal joy of the true artist in his better work, even as he mourned darkly when it fell below the high level to which he aspired. He was still chuckling over his success when Billy swung open the door and Inspector MacDonald of Scotland Yard was ushered into the room.

Those were the early days at the end of the '80's, when Alec MacDonald was far from having attained the national fame which he has now achieved. He was a young but trusted member of the detective force, who had distinguished himself in several cases which had been entrusted to him. His tall, bony figure gave promise of exceptional physical strength, while his great cranium and deep-set, lustrous eyes spoke no less clearly of the keen intelligence which twinkled out from behind his bushy eyebrows. He was a silent, precise man with a dour nature and a hard Aberdonian accent.

Twice already in his career had Holmes helped him to attain success, his own sole reward being the intellectual joy of the problem. For this reason the affection and respect of the Scotchman for his amateur colleague were profound, and he showed them by the frankness with which he consulted Holmes in every difficulty. Mediocrity knows nothing higher than itself; but talent instantly recognizes genius, and MacDonald had talent enough for his profession to enable him to perceive that there was no humiliation in seeking the assistance of one who already stood alone in Europe, both in his gifts and in his experience. Holmes was not prone to friendship, but he was tolerant of the big Scotchman, and smiled at the sight of him.

"You are an early bird, Mr Mac," said he. "I wish you luck with your worm. I fear this means that there is some mischief afoot."

"If you said 'hope' instead of 'fear,' it would be nearer the truth, I'm

thinking, Mr Holmes," the inspector answered, with a knowing grin. "Well, maybe a wee nip would keep out the raw morning chill. No, I won't smoke, I thank you. I'll have to be pushing on my way; for the early hours of a case are the precious ones, as no man knows better than your own self. But—but—"

The inspector had stopped suddenly, and was staring with a look of absolute amazement at a paper upon the table. It was the sheet upon which I had scrawled the enigmatic message.

"Douglas!" he stammered. "Birlstone! What's this, Mr Holmes? Man, it's witchcraft! Where in the name of all that is wonderful did you get those names?"

"It is a cipher that Dr Watson and I have had occasion to solve. But why—what's amiss with the names?"

The inspector looked from one to the other of us in dazed astonishment. "Just this," said he, "that Mr Douglas of Birlstone Manor House was horribly murdered last night!"

II. SHERLOCK HOLMES DISCOURSES

It was one of those dramatic moments for which my friend existed. It would be an overstatement to say that he was shocked or even excited by the amazing announcement. Without having a tinge of cruelty in his singular composition, he was undoubtedly callous from long overstimulation. Yet, if his emotions were dulled, his intellectual perceptions were exceedingly active. There was no trace then of the horror which I had myself felt at this curt declaration; but his face showed rather the quiet and interested composure of the chemist who sees the crystals falling into position from his over-saturated solution.

"Remarkable!" said he; "Remarkable!"

"You don't seem surprised."

"Interested, Mr Mac, but hardly surprised. Why should I be surprised? I receive an anonymous communication from a quarter which I know to be important, warning me that danger threatens a certain person. Within an hour I learn that this danger has actually materialized and that the person is dead. I am interested; but, as you observe, I am not surprised."

In a few short sentences he explained to the inspector the facts about the letter and the cipher—though I noted he omitted to mention the position his anonymous informant most likely held. Indeed, I could scarcely blame him: inviting as it did the full censure of the law. Porlock was reduced—in the inspector's eyes—to a simple, paid informant. MacDonald sat with his chin on his hands and his great sandy eyebrows bunched into a yellow tangle.

"I was going down to Birlstone this morning," said he. "I had come to ask you if you cared to come with me—you and your friend here. But from what you say we might perhaps be doing better work in London."

"I rather think not," said Holmes.

"Hang it all, Mr Holmes!" cried the inspector. "The papers will be full of the Birlstone mystery in a day or two; but where's the mystery if there is a man in London who prophesied the crime before ever it

occurred? We have only to lay our hands on that man, and the rest will follow."

"No doubt, Mr Mac. But how do you propose to lay your hands on the so-called Porlock?"

MacDonald turned over the letter which Holmes had handed him. "Posted in Camberwell—that doesn't help us much. Name, you say, is assumed. Not much to go on, certainly. Didn't you say that you have sent him money?"

"Twice."

"And how?"

"In notes to Camberwell post office."

"Did you ever trouble to see who called for them?"

"No."

The inspector looked surprised and a little shocked. "Why not?"

"Because I always keep faith. I had promised when he first wrote that I would not try to trace him."

"You think there is someone behind him?"

"I know there is."

MacDonald sighed heavily and leaned back in his chair. "This Professor that I've heard you mention?"

"Exactly!"

Inspector MacDonald smiled, and his eyelid quivered as he glanced towards me. "I won't conceal from you, Mr Holmes, that we think in the C.I.D. that you have a wee bit of a bee in your bonnet over Professor Moriarty. I made some inquiries myself about the matter—quite off the record and discrete, of course. There is not a man in Westminster who speaks ill of him. Even the merest suggestion rallies honourable men to his defence. He seems to be a very respectable, learned, and talented sort of man."

Holmes' lips twitched briefly. "I'm glad you've got so far as to recognize the talent."

"Man, you can't but recognize it! After I heard your view I made it my business to see him. At first our conversation was as you'd expect: the economy—both here and abroad—the growing tensions … then somewhere along the line it switched to a chat on eclipses. How the talk got that way I canna think; but he had out a reflector lantern and a globe,

and made it all clear in a minute. He lent me a book; but I don't mind saying that it was a bit above my head, though I had a good Aberdeen upbringing. He'd have made a grand meenister with his thin face and grey hair and solemn-like way of talking. When he put his hand on my shoulder as we were parting, it was like a father's blessing before you go out into the cold, cruel world."

Holmes chuckled and rubbed his hands. "Great!" he said. "Great! Tell me, Friend MacDonald, this pleasing and touching interview was, I suppose, in the professor's Westminster study?"

"That's so."

"A fine room, is it not?"

"Very fine—very handsome indeed, Mr Holmes."

"You sat in front of his writing desk?"

"Just so."

"Sun in your eyes and his face in the shadow?"

"Well, it was evening; but I mind that he had an electric lamp, and it was turned on my face."

"It would be. Did you happen to observe a glass display case, not unlike a bell-jar, upon the professor's desk?"

"I don't miss much, Mr Holmes. Maybe I learned that from you. Yes, I saw the glass dome—placed centrally, so not a visitor would miss it. I canna discern why, though: all it contained was a lump of polished, quite un-extraordinary rock."

"Not just a lump of rock, Mr Mac—and very far from un-extraordinary. There are but three other pieces on this world like it."

The inspector endeavoured to look interested.

"It is a lunar beryl, inspector," Holmes continued, joining his finger tips and leaning well back in his chair, "discovered on the surface of our solitary companion during the very first expeditionary landing on *Mare Nubium* on New Year's day in 1875; and returned in triumph with the world's very first selenauts."

The inspector's eyes grew abstracted. "Hadn't we better—?" he said.

"We are doing so," Holmes interrupted. My friend's talents are many and wonderful, but he would be the first to admit that prescience was not

one of them. Even so, his next comment was to be truer than he could have guessed at the time: "All that I am saying has a very direct and vital bearing upon what you have called the Birlstone Mystery. In fact, it may in a sense be called the very centre of it."

MacDonald smiled feebly, and looked appealingly to me. "Your thoughts move a bit too quick for me, Mr Holmes. You leave out a link or two, and I can't get over the gap. What in the whole wide world can be the connection between this lump of stone man, and the affair at Birlstone?"

"All knowledge comes useful to the detective," remarked Holmes. "There were three samples of lunar rock brought down, at the cost of a life and two minds. Once the scientists had finished poring over them, one piece was exhibited in the British Museum, a second placed on ostentatious display at the Pall Mall offices of the South Lunar Company, and the third was polished and mounted by Garrard—to be presented to Queen Victoria on the occasion of her Golden Jubilee last year. Although it is to my mind absurd to price such irreplaceable items, Christie's have placed a rough evaluation on the two displayed specimens at some forty thousand pounds—whilst Her Majesty's gift is quite rightly reckoned as priceless. Perhaps such sums may start a train of reflection in your mind."

For my own sake it certainly did; and the inspector began to look honestly interested.

"Then how could he buy—" I began.

"I may remind you," Holmes continued, "that the Professor's wealth can be ascertained in several trustworthy books of reference. Officially it is seven hundred thousand pounds; his parliamentary seat brings in nothing, of course."

"Then—"

"Quite so! He could afford such an item were it available, but since 1875 no similar gemstone has been discovered."

I quickly reached on obvious conclusion. "Stolen?"

Holmes clapped his hands. "Capital, Watson—you'll outshine us all yet—such was my original thought; but it would seem not. I have made

my own enquiries, and all three pieces of rock are indeed genuine: the very samples returned from the Moon."

"Then," I said thoughtfully, "there are more than three pieces..."

"Excellent! Of the three samples brought to Earth in 1875, it would seem the Professor has the fourth..."

The inspector was silent for a moment—then he burst into hearty laughter. "Ay, that's remarkable! Talk away, Mr Holmes. I'm just loving it. It's fine!"

Holmes smiled. He was always warmed by genuine admiration—the characteristic of the real artist. "But what about Birlstone?" he asked.

"We've time yet," said the inspector, glancing at his watch. "I've a cab at the door, and it won't take us twenty minutes to Victoria. But about this lump of stone: all questions of its authenticity aside, I thought you told me once, Mr Holmes, that you had never met Professor Moriarty."

"No, I never have."

"Then how do you know about his rooms?"

"Ah, that's another matter. I have been three times in his rooms, twice waiting for him under different pretexts and leaving before he came. Once—well, I can hardly tell about the once to an official detective. It was on the last occasion that I took the liberty of running over his papers—with the most unexpected results."

MacDonald leaned forward. "You found something compromising?"

"Absolutely nothing. That was what amazed me. However, you have now seen the point of the picture. It shows him to be a very wealthy man—or if not wealthy, a man with connections far beyond those of a humble MP. From his humble beginnings as a professor of mathematics he appears to have made some uncannily wise investments. Thirty years ago he began to make investments in several major works projects: Bazalgette's great clean-up of London's sewers, Pearson's underground railway and, of course, the Channel Tunnel. He is now a major shareholder in America's intercontinental railways and a member of the East India Company's Court of Directors. There is not an industry immune from his reach—electricity, mining, transportation. But how did he first acquire wealth?

He is unmarried. His younger brother is a station master in the west of England. His chair is worth seven hundred a year. And he owns a virtually priceless sample of lunar geology—if that is the correct terminology." He glanced in my direction, eyes twinkling. "I confess to ignorance in the area."

"Well?" I prompted after a moment.

"Surely the inference is plain."

"You mean that he had to have a great income in order to make those investments, and that he must have earned it in an illegal fashion?" said the inspector.

"Exactly. Of course I have other reasons for thinking so—dozens of exiguous threads which lead vaguely up towards the centre of the web where the poisonous, motionless creature is lurking. I only mention the peculiar piece of stone because it brings the matter within the range of your own observation."

"Well, Mr Holmes, I admit that what you say is interesting: it's more than interesting—it's just wonderful. But let us have it a little clearer if you can. Is it forgery, coining, burglary –where did the money come from?"

"I cannot be certain," my friend conceded, "but I have suspicions. Have you ever read of Jonathan Wild?"

The inspector scratched his cheek introspectively. "Well, the name has a familiar sound. Someone in a novel, was he not? I don't take much stock of detectives in novels—chaps that do things and never let you see how they do them. That's just inspiration: not business."

Holmes was dismissive. "Jonathan Wild wasn't a detective, and he wasn't in a novel. He was a master criminal, and he lived last century—1750 or thereabouts."

"Then he's no use to me. I'm a practical man."

"Mr Mac, the most practical thing that you ever did in your life would be to shut yourself up for three months and read twelve hours a day at the annals of crime. Everything comes in circles—even Professor Moriarty. Jonathan Wild was the hidden force of the London criminals, to whom

he sold his brains and his organization on a fifteen per cent commission. The old wheel turns, and the same spoke comes up. It's all been done before, and will be again. I'll tell you one or two things about Moriarty which may interest you."

"You'll interest me, right enough."

"I happen to know who is the first link in his chain—a chain with this Napoleon-gone-wrong at one end, and the corrupt web of blaggards, bureaucrats, businessmen, and bribe takers in between. His chief of staff is Brigadier Bastion Moran of the 1st Air Rifles."

It was a name with which I was well familiar: the paths of the Brigadier and I had crossed several times, most recently at a Mufti in Peshawar shortly before the Battle of Maiwand and all that followed. I remember him as no worse—and no better—than many of his class: indifferent and arrogant; whilst he would certainly never recall a simple army surgeon at all. But was he really as my friend chose to portray? Or was this symptomatic of the corruption Holmes perceived gnawing at all levels of society? "The son of the Lieutenant-Governor of India, Holmes?" said I, a little too sharply. "Surely not. There has never been so much as a whiff of scandal about the man."

"I should be amazed if there was, Watson. He is as aloof and guarded and inaccessible to the law as the Professor himself. What do you think he pays him?"

"I'd like to hear," commented MacDonald gruffly, clearly fallen under Holmes' spell.

"Six thousand a year. That's paying for brains, you see—the American business principle. I learned that detail quite by chance. It's more than the Prime Minister gets. That gives you an idea of Moriarty's gains and of the scale on which he works. Another point: I made it my business to investigate Moriarty's bank accounts, just the personal accounts he pays his household bills with, not the business accounts. In 1855 he opened a single account into which his meagre professional salary was paid. The following year he made significant personal investments from six different banks including Coutts, Barings and Rothschild. None of those

accounts even existed prior to 1856. Does that make any impression on your mind?"

"Queer, certainly! But what do you gather from it?"

"That he wanted no gossip about his past. No single man should know what he had. I have no doubt that he has twenty banking accounts; the bulk of his fortune abroad in the *Deutsche Bank* or the *Credit Lyonnais* as likely as not. Sometime when you have a year or two to spare I commend to you the study of Professor Moriarty."

Inspector MacDonald had grown steadily more impressed as the conversation proceeded. He had lost himself in his interest. Now his practical Scotch intelligence brought him back with a snap to the matter in hand.

"He can keep, anyhow," said he. "You've got us side-tracked with your interesting anecdotes, Mr Holmes. What really counts is your remark that there is some connection between the Professor and the crime. That you get from the warning received through the man Porlock. Can we for our present practical needs get any further than that?"

"We may form some conception as to the motives of the crime. It is, as I gather from your original remarks, an inexplicable, or at least an unexplained, murder. Now, presuming that the source of the crime is as we suspect it to be, there might be two different motives. In the first place, I may tell you that Moriarty rules with a rod of iron over his lieutenants. Moran's discipline is tremendous. There is only one punishment in their code. It is death. Now we might suppose that this murdered man—this Douglas whose approaching fate was known by one of the arch-criminal puppeteer's subordinates—had in some way betrayed the chief. His punishment followed, and would be known to all—if only to put the fear of death into them."

"Well, that is one suggestion, Mr Holmes."

"The other is that it has been engineered by an agent of Moriarty in the ordinary course of business. Was there any other disturbance, papers stolen or objects misplaced?"

"I have not heard."

"If so, it would, of course, be against the first hypothesis and in favour of the second. Moriarty may have coerced someone into engineering it, or they may have been paid so much down to have it managed. Either is possible. But whichever it may be, or if it is some third combination, it is down at Birlstone that we must seek the solution. I know our man too well to suppose that he has left anything up here which may lead us to him."

"Then to Birlstone we must go!" cried MacDonald, jumping from his chair. "My word! It's later than I thought. I can give you, gentlemen, five minutes for preparation, and that is all."

"And ample for us both," said Holmes, as he sprang up and hastened to change from his dressing gown to his coat. "While we are on our way, Mr Mac, I will ask you to be good enough to tell me all about it."

All about it proved to be disappointingly little, and yet there was enough to assure us that the case before us might well be worthy of the expert's closest attention. He brightened and rubbed his thin hands together as he listened to the meagre but remarkable details. A long series of sterile weeks lay behind us, and here at last there was a fitting object for those remarkable powers which, like all special gifts, become irksome to their owner when they are not in use. That razor brain blunted and rusted with inaction.

Sherlock Holmes's eyes glistened, his pale cheeks took a warmer hue, and his whole eager face shone with an inward light when the call for work reached him. Leaning forward in the cab, he listened intently to MacDonald's short sketch of the problem which awaited us in Sussex. The inspector was himself dependent, as he explained to us, upon a scribbled account forwarded to him by the milk train in the early hours of the morning. White Mason, the local officer, was a personal friend, and hence MacDonald had been notified much more promptly than is usual at Scotland Yard when provincials need their assistance. It is a very cold scent upon which the Metropolitan expert is generally asked to run.

"DEAR INSPECTOR MACDONALD [said the letter which he read to us]: Official requisition for your services is in separate envelope. This is *for your private eye. Wire me what train in the morning you can get for Birlstone, and I will meet it—or have it met if I am too occupied. This case is a snorter. Don't waste a moment in getting started. If you can bring Mr Holmes, please do so; for he will find something after his own heart. We would think the whole had been fixed up for theatrical effect if there wasn't a dead man in the middle of it. My word! It IS a snorter."*

"Your friend seems to be no fool," remarked Holmes.

"No, sir, White Mason is a very live man, if I am any judge."

"Well, have you anything more?"

"Only that he will give us every detail when we meet."

"Then how did you get at Mr Douglas and the fact that he had been horribly murdered?"

"That was in the enclosed official report. It didn't say horrible: that's not a recognized official term. It gave the name John Douglas. It mentioned that his injuries had been in the head, from the discharge of a shotgun. It also mentioned the hour of the alarm, which was close on to midnight last night. It added that the case was undoubtedly one of murder, but that no arrest had been made, and that the case was one which presented some very perplexing and extraordinary features. That's absolutely all we have at present, Mr Holmes."

III. THE TRAGEDY OF BIRLSTONE

Now for a moment I will ask leave to remove my own insignificant personality and to describe events which occurred before we arrived upon the scene by the light of knowledge which came to us afterwards. Only in this way can I make the reader appreciate the people concerned and the strange setting in which their fate was cast.

The village of Birlstone is a small and very ancient cluster of half-timbered cottages on the northern border of the county of Sussex. For centuries it had remained unchanged; but within the last few years its picturesque appearance and situation have attracted a number of well-to-do residents, whose villas peep out from the woods around. These woods are locally supposed to be the extreme fringe of the great Weald forest, which thins away until it reaches the northern chalk downs. The railway built a small station—for the first time providing Birlstone with excellent links to the capital, and access to the Sussex countryside for the city's masses—whilst a tethered aerostat line followed inevitably. A number of small shops have come into being to meet the wants of the increased population; so there seems some prospect that Birlstone may soon grow from an ancient village into a modern town. It is the centre for a considerable area of country, since Tunbridge Wells, the nearest place of importance, is ten or twelve miles to the eastward, over the borders of Kent. Only the terrible railway crash of 1878 cast a blight—albeit temporarily—over the area. A signalling failure caused a speeding train to plough into the rear of a stationary one; tossed high by the impact, two carriages had smashed through an aerostat support, dragging down the tethering cable above it. Many of the few passengers who had been fortunate enough to survive the initial horror died when a freight-laden

aerostat was plucked to earth, its mantle burst, and the toxic ammonia gas used for buoyancy billowed lethally across the countryside.

About half a mile from the town, standing in an old park famous for its huge beech trees, is the ancient Manor House of Birlstone. Part of this venerable building dates back to the time of the First Crusade, when Hugo de Capus built a fortalice in the centre of the estate, which had been granted to him by the Red King. This was destroyed by fire in 1543, and some of its smoke-blackened corner stones were used when, in Jacobean times, a brick country house rose upon the ruins of the feudal castle.

From the outside, the Manor House, with its many gables and its small diamond-paned windows, appeared to be much as the builder had left it in the early seventeenth century. Of the double moats which had guarded its more warlike predecessor, the outer had been allowed to dry up, and served the humble function of a kitchen garden. The inner one was still there, and lay forty feet in breadth, though now only a few feet in depth, round the whole house. A small stream fed it and continued beyond it, so that the sheet of water, though turbid, was never ditch-like or unhealthy. The ground floor windows were within a foot of the surface of the water.

The only approach to the house had originally been over a drawbridge, the chains and windlass of which were long rusted and broken. The latest tenants of the Manor House had, however, with characteristic energy, set this right, and the drawbridge was replaced by a steel construction composed of shutters which withdrew back into the building every evening and extended every morning. The latest electrical beam receivers were installed by Westinghouse-Tesla and a programme for wiring the house for electrical light drawn up. What was more, a great steel heart replaced the original basements and footings: a core bursting with heavy dynamos: some of which drove the new bridge, whilst the remainder engaged great metal struts which bodily lifted the entire Manor House several feet above the ground like a Malay longhouse. By thus renewing the custom of the old feudal days, as well as improving upon it, the

Manor House was converted into an island during the night—a fact which had a very direct bearing upon the mystery which was soon to engage the attention of all England.

The house had been untenanted for some years and was threatening to moulder into a picturesque decay when the Douglases took possession of it. This family consisted of only two individuals—John Douglas and his wife. Douglas was a remarkable man, both in character and in person. In age he may have been about fifty, with a strong-jawed, rugged face, a grizzling moustache, a distinct mane of white hair, peculiarly keen grey eyes, and a wiry, vigorous figure which had lost nothing of the strength and activity of youth. He was cheery and genial to all, but somewhat offhand in his manners, giving the impression that he had seen life in social strata on some far lower horizon than the county society of Sussex.

Yet, though looked at with some curiosity and reserve by his more cultivated neighbours, he soon acquired a great popularity among the villagers, subscribing handsomely to all local objects, and attending their smoking concerts and other functions, where, having a remarkably rich tenor voice, he was always ready to oblige with an excellent song. He appeared to have plenty of money, which was said to have been gained in the California gold fields, and it was clear from his own talk and that of his wife that he had spent a part of his life in America.

The good impression which had been produced by his generosity and by his democratic manners was increased by a reputation gained for utter indifference to danger. Though a wretched rider, he turned out at every meet, and took the most amazing falls in his determination to hold his own with the best. When the vicarage caught fire he distinguished himself also by the fearlessness with which he re-entered the building to save property, after the steam pumps on the local fire brigade's engine seized, leaving the venerable building to the flames' mercy. Thus it came about that John Douglas of the Manor House had within five years won himself quite a reputation in Birlstone.

His wife, too, was popular with those who had made her acquaintance; though, after the English fashion, the callers upon a stranger who settled

in the county without introductions were few and far between. This mattered the less to her, as she was retiring by disposition, and very much absorbed, to all appearance, in her husband and her domestic duties. It was known that she was an English lady who had met Mr Douglas in London, he being at that time a widower. She was a beautiful woman, tall, dark, and slender, some twenty years younger than her husband; a disparity which seemed in no wise to mar the contentment of their family life.

It was remarked sometimes, however, by those who knew them best, that the confidence between the two did not appear to be complete, since the wife was either very reticent about her husband's past life, or else, as seemed more likely, was imperfectly informed about it. It had also been noted and commented upon by a few observant people that there were signs sometimes of some nerve-strain upon the part of Mrs Douglas, and that she would display acute uneasiness if her absent husband should ever be particularly late in his return. On a quiet countryside, where all gossip is welcome, this weakness of the lady of the Manor House did not pass without remark, and it bulked larger upon people's memory when the events arose which gave it a very special significance.

There was yet another individual whose residence under that roof was, it is true, only an intermittent one, but whose presence at the time of the strange happenings which will now be narrated brought his name prominently before the public. This was Cecil James Barker, of Hales Lodge, Hampstead.

Cecil Barker's tall, loose-jointed figure was a familiar one in the main street of Birlstone village; for he was a frequent and welcome visitor at the Manor House. He was the more noticed as being the only friend of the past unknown life of Mr Douglas who was ever seen in his new English surroundings. Barker was himself an undoubted Englishman; but by his remarks it was clear that he had first known Douglas in America and had there lived on intimate terms with him. He appeared to be a man of considerable wealth, and was reputed to be a bachelor.

In age he was rather younger than Douglas—forty-five at the most—a

tall, straight, broad-chested fellow with a clean-shaved, prize-fighter face, thick, strong, black eyebrows, and a pair of masterful black eyes which might, even without the aid of his very capable hands, clear a way for him through a hostile crowd. He neither rode nor shot, but spent his days in wandering round the old village with his pipe in his mouth, or in driving with his host, or in his absence with his hostess, over the beautiful countryside in the Douglases MotoCar: a rattling steam-electric hybrid of some obscure manufacture which startled and amused the locals in equal part. "An easy-going, free-handed gentleman," said Ames, the butler. "But, my word! I had rather not be the man that crossed him!" He was cordial and intimate with Douglas, and he was no less friendly with his wife—a friendship which more than once seemed to cause some irritation to the husband, so that even the servants were able to perceive his annoyance. Such was the third person who was one of the family when the catastrophe occurred.

As to the other denizens of the old building, it will suffice out of a large household to mention the prim, respectable, and capable Ames, and Mrs Allen, a buxom and cheerful person, who relieved the lady of some of her household cares. The other six servants in the house bear no relation to the events of the night of January 6th.

It was at eleven forty-five that the first alarm reached the small local police station, in charge of Sergeant Wilson of the Sussex Constabulary. Cecil Barker, much excited, had rushed up to the door and pealed furiously upon the bell. A terrible tragedy had occurred at the Manor House, and John Douglas had been murdered. That was the breathless burden of his message. He had hurried back to the house, followed within a few minutes by the police sergeant, who arrived at the scene of the crime a little after twelve o'clock, after taking prompt steps to warn the county authorities that something serious was afoot.

On reaching the Manor House, the sergeant had found the steel bridge extended, the building settled firmly on its base, the windows lighted up, and the whole household in a state of wild confusion and alarm. The white-faced servants were huddling together in the hall, with

the frightened butler wringing his hands in the doorway. Only Cecil Barker seemed to be master of himself and his emotions; he had opened the door which was nearest to the entrance and he had beckoned to the sergeant to follow him. At that moment there arrived Dr Wood, a brisk and capable general practitioner from the village. The three men entered the fatal room together, while the horror-stricken butler followed at their heels, closing the door behind him to shut out the terrible scene from the maid servants.

The dead man lay on his back, sprawling with outstretched limbs in the centre of the room. He was clad only in a pink dressing gown, which covered his night clothes. There were carpet slippers on his bare feet. The doctor knelt beside him; one glance at the victim was enough to show the healer that his presence could be dispensed with. The man had been horribly injured. Lying across his chest was a curious weapon, a shotgun with the barrel sawed off a foot in front of the triggers. It was clear that this had been fired at close range and that he had received the whole charge in the face, blowing his head almost to pieces. The triggers had been wired together, so as to make the simultaneous discharge more destructive.

The country policeman was unnerved and troubled by the tremendous responsibility which had come so suddenly upon him. "We will touch nothing until my superiors arrive," he said in a hushed voice, staring in horror at the dreadful head.

"Nothing has been touched up to now," said Cecil Barker. "I'll answer for that. You see it all exactly as I found it."

"When was that?" The sergeant had drawn out his notebook.

"It was just half-past eleven. I had not begun to undress, and I was sitting by the fire in my bedroom when I heard the report. It was not very loud—it seemed to be muffled. I rushed down—I don't suppose it was thirty seconds before I was in the room."

"Was the door open?"

"Yes, it was open. Poor Douglas was lying as you see him. A bedroom candle was burning on the table. It was I who turned on the electrical lighting some minutes afterward."

"Did you see no one?"

"No. I heard Mrs Douglas coming down the stair behind me, and I rushed out to prevent her from seeing this dreadful sight. Mrs Allen, the housekeeper, came and took her away. Ames had arrived, and we ran back into the room once more."

"But surely I have heard that the bridge is retracted all night, and the whole building raised."

"Yes, it was up until I lowered it and re-extended the bridge."

"Then how could any murderer have got away? It is out of the question! Mr Douglas must have shot himself."

"That was our first idea. But see!" Barker drew aside the curtain, and showed that the long, diamond-paned window was open to its full extent. "And look at this!" He indicated a smudge of blood like the mark of a boot-sole upon the wooden sill. "Someone has stood there in getting out."

"You mean that someone jumped from the window and waded across the moat?"

"Exactly!"

"Then if you were in the room within half a minute of the crime, he must have been in the water at that very moment."

"I have not a doubt of it. I wish to heaven that I had rushed to the window! But the curtain screened it, as you can see, and so it never occurred to me. Then I heard the step of Mrs Douglas, and I could not let her enter the room. It would have been too horrible."

"Horrible enough!" said the doctor, looking at the shattered head and the terrible marks which surrounded it. "I've never seen such injuries since the Birlstone railway smash."

"But, I say," remarked the police sergeant, whose slow, bucolic common sense was still pondering the open window. "It's all very well your saying that a man somehow leapt from that window and escaped by wading this moat, but what I ask you is, how did he ever get into the house at all if the bridge was rolled back?"

"Ah, that's the question," said Barker.

"At what o'clock was it drawn in?"

"It was nearly six o'clock," said Ames, the butler.

"I've heard," said the sergeant, "that it was usually withdrawn at sunset. That would be nearer half-past four than six at this time of year."

"Mrs Douglas had visitors to tea," said Ames. "I couldn't move it until they went. Then I rolled it back myself and raised the house."

"Then it comes to this," said the sergeant: "If anyone came from outside—if they did—they must have got in across the bridge before six and been in hiding ever since, until Mr Douglas came into the room after eleven."

"That is so!" agreed the butler. "Mr Douglas went round the house every night the last thing before he turned in to see that those electrical lights not needed were extinguished. That brought him in here. The man was waiting and shot him. Then he got away through the window and left his gun behind him. That's how I read it; for nothing else will fit the facts."

The sergeant picked up a card which lay beside the dead man on the floor. The initials *VV* and under them the number *341* were rudely scrawled in ink upon it.

"What's this?" he asked, holding it up.

Barker looked at it with curiosity. "I never noticed it before," he said. "The murderer must have left it behind him."

Ames shook his head. "*VV—341*. I can make no sense of that."

The sergeant kept turning it over in his big fingers. "What's *VV*? Somebody's initials, maybe. What have you got there, Dr Wood?"

It was a good-sized hammer which had been lying on the rug in front of the fireplace—a substantial, workmanlike hammer. Cecil Barker pointed to a box of brass-headed nails upon the mantelpiece.

"Mr Douglas was altering the pictures yesterday," he said. "I saw him myself, standing upon that chair and fixing the big picture above it. That accounts for the hammer."

"We'd best put it back on the rug where we found it," said the sergeant, scratching his puzzled head in his perplexity. "It will want the best brains

in the force to get to the bottom of this thing. It will be a London job before it is finished." He charged up a hand-lamp, winding its handle for over thirty seconds, and walked slowly round the room. "Hullo!" he cried, excitedly, drawing the window curtain to one side. "What o'clock were those curtains drawn?"

"When the lights were switched on," said the butler. "It would be shortly after four."

"Someone had been hiding here, sure enough." The sergeant held down the lamp, and the marks of muddy boots were very visible in the corner. "I'm bound to say this bears out your theory, Mr Barker. It looks as if the man got into the house after four when the curtains were drawn, and before six when the bridge was raised. He slipped into this room, because it was the first that he saw. There was no other place where he could hide, so he popped in behind this curtain. That all seems clear enough. It is likely that his main idea was to burgle the house; but Mr Douglas chanced to come upon him, so he murdered him and escaped."

"That's how I read it," said Barker. "But, I say, aren't we wasting precious time? Couldn't we start out and scout the country before the fellow gets away?"

The sergeant considered for a moment.

"There are no trains before six in the morning; so he can't get away by rail. If he goes by road with his legs all dripping, it's odds that someone will notice him. Anyhow, I can't leave here myself until I am relieved. But I think none of you should go until we see more clearly how we all stand."

The doctor had taken the lamp and was narrowly scrutinizing the body. "What's this mark?" he asked. "Could this have any connection with the crime?"

The dead man's right arm was thrust out from his dressing gown, and exposed as high as the elbow. About halfway up the forearm was a curious brown design, a triangle inside a circle, standing out in vivid relief upon the lard-coloured skin.

"It's not tattooed," said the doctor, peering through his glasses. "I

never saw anything like it. The man has been branded at some time as they brand cattle. What is the meaning of this?"

"I don't profess to know the meaning of it," said Cecil Barker; "but I have seen the mark on Douglas many times this last ten years."

"And so have I," said the butler. "Many a time when the master has rolled up his sleeves I have noticed that very mark. I've often wondered what it could be."

"Then it has nothing to do with the crime, anyhow," said the sergeant. "But it's a rum thing all the same. Everything about this case is rum. Well, what is it now?"

The butler had given an exclamation of astonishment and was pointing at the dead man's outstretched hand.

"They've taken his wedding ring!" he gasped.

"What!"

"Yes, indeed. Master always wore his plain gold wedding ring on the little finger of his left hand. That ring with the rough nugget on it was above it, and the twisted snake ring on the third finger. There's the nugget and there's the snake, but the wedding ring is gone."

"He's right," said Barker.

"Do you tell me," said the sergeant, "that the wedding ring was below the other?"

"Always!"

"Then the murderer, or whoever it was, first took off this ring you call the nugget ring, then the wedding ring, and afterwards put the nugget ring back again."

"That is so!"

The worthy country policeman shook his head. "Seems to me the sooner we get London on to this case the better," said he. "White Mason is a smart man. No local job has ever been too much for White Mason. It won't be long now before he is here to help us. But I expect we'll have to look to London before we are through. Anyhow, I'm not ashamed to say that it is a deal too thick for the likes of me."

IV. Darkness

At three in the morning the chief Sussex detective, obeying the urgent call from Sergeant Wilson of Birlstone, arrived from headquarters in a worn and chipped dog-cart behind a breathless trotter—both of which, in a less rustic setting, would have replaced by something a little more in the modern vein. The local constabulary budget did not extend to any form of MotoCar: its officers would be forced to limp on in decaying vehicles until senescence loosened the purse strings. By the same token, the headquarters were not fitted with the latest Teslagram equipment, so he had sent his message to Scotland Yard from a First Class unit fitted in the guard's van of the five-forty train from Charing Cross . He was at the Birlstone station at twelve o'clock to welcome us. White Mason was a quiet, comfortable-looking person in a loose tweed suit, with a clean-shaved, ruddy face, a stoutish body, and powerful bandy legs adorned with gaiters, looking like a small farmer, a retired gamekeeper, or anything upon earth except a very favourable specimen of the provincial criminal officer.

"A real downright snorter, Mr MacDonald!" he kept repeating. "We'll have the pressmen down like flies when they understand it. I'm hoping we will get our work done before they get poking their noses into it and messing up all the trails. There has been nothing like this that I can remember. There are some bits that will come home to you, Mr Holmes, or I am mistaken. And you also, Dr Watson; for the medicos will have a word to say before we finish. Your room is at the Westville Arms. There's no other place; but I hear that it is clean and good. The man will carry your bags. This way, gentlemen, if you please."

He was a very bustling and genial person, this Sussex detective. In ten

minutes we had all found our quarters. In ten more we were seated in the parlour of the inn and being treated to a rapid sketch of those events which have been outlined in the previous chapter. MacDonald made an occasional note; while Holmes sat absorbed, with the expression of surprised and reverent admiration with which the botanist surveys the rare and precious bloom.

"Remarkable!" he said, when the story was unfolded, "most remarkable! I can hardly recall any case where the features have been more peculiar."

"I thought you would say so, Mr Holmes," said White Mason in great delight. "We're well up with the times in Sussex. I've told you now how matters were, up to the time when I took over from Sergeant Wilson between three and four this morning. My word! I made the old mare go! But I need not have been in such a hurry, as it turned out; for there was nothing immediate that I could do. Sergeant Wilson had all the facts. I checked them and considered them and maybe added a few of my own."

"What were they?" asked Holmes eagerly.

"Well, I first had the hammer examined. There was Dr Wood there to help me. We found no signs of violence upon it. I was hoping that if Mr Douglas defended himself with the hammer, he might have left his mark upon the murderer before he dropped it on the mat. But there was no stain."

"That, of course, proves nothing at all," remarked Inspector MacDonald. "There has been many a hammer murder and no trace on the hammer."

"Quite so. It doesn't prove it wasn't used. But there might have been stains, and that would have helped us. As a matter of fact there were none. Then I examined the gun. They were buckshot cartridges, and, as Sergeant Wilson pointed out, the triggers were wired together so that, if you pulled on the hinder one, both barrels were discharged. Whoever fixed that up had made up his mind that he was going to take no chances of missing his man. The sawed gun was not more than two foot long— one could carry it easily under one's coat. There was no complete maker's

name; but the printed letters *P-E-N* were on the fluting between the barrels, and the rest of the name had been cut off by the saw."

"A big *P* with a flourish above it, *E* and *N* smaller?" asked Holmes.

"Exactly."

"Pennsylvania Small Arms Company—well-known American firm," said Holmes.

White Mason gazed at my friend as the little village practitioner looks at the Harley Street specialist who by a word can solve the difficulties that perplex him.

"That is very helpful, Mr Holmes. No doubt you are right. Wonderful! Wonderful! Do you carry the names of all the gun makers in the world in your memory?"

Holmes dismissed the subject with a wave.

"No doubt it is an American shotgun," White Mason continued. "I seem to have read that a sawed-off shotgun is a weapon used in some parts of America. Apart from the name upon the barrel, the idea had occurred to me. There is some evidence then, that this man who entered the house and killed its master was an American."

MacDonald shook his head. "Man, you are surely travelling over-fast," said he. "I have heard no evidence yet that any stranger was ever in the house at all."

"The open window, the blood on the sill, the queer card, the marks of boots in the corner, the gun!"

"Nothing there that could not have been arranged. Mr Douglas was an American, or had lived long in America. So had Mr Barker. You don't need to import an American from outside in order to account for American doings."

"Ames, the butler—"

"What about him? Is he reliable?"

"Ten years with Sir Charles Chandos—as solid as a rock. He has been with Douglas ever since he took the Manor House five years ago. He has never seen a gun of this sort in the house."

"The gun was made to conceal. That's why the barrels were sawed. It

would fit into any box. How could he swear there was no such gun in the house?"

"Well, anyhow, he had never seen one."

MacDonald shook his obstinate Scotch head. "I'm not convinced yet that there was ever anyone in the house," said he. "I'm asking you to conseedar—" (his accent became more Aberdonian as he lost himself in his argument) "—I'm asking you to conseedar what it involves if you suppose that this gun was ever brought into the house, and that all these strange things were done by a person from outside. Oh, man, it's just inconceivable! It's clean against common sense! I put it to you, Mr Holmes, judging it by what we have heard."

"Well, state your case, Mr Mac," said Holmes in his most judicial style.

"The man is not a burglar, supposing that he ever existed. The ring business and the card point to premeditated murder for some private reason. Very good. Here is a man who slips into a house with the deliberate intention of committing murder. He knows, if he knows anything, that he will have a deeficulty in making his escape, as the house is surrounded with water. What weapon would he choose? You would say the most silent in the world. Then he could hope when the deed was done to slip quickly from the window, to wade the moat, and to get away at his leisure. That's understandable. But is it understandable that he should go out of his way to bring with him the most noisy weapon he could select, knowing well that it will fetch every human being in the house to the spot as quick as they can run, and that it is all odds that he will be seen before he can get across the moat? Is that credible, Mr Holmes?"

"Well, you put the case strongly," my friend replied thoughtfully. "It certainly needs a good deal of justification. May I ask, Mr White Mason, whether you examined the farther side of the moat at once to see if there were any signs of the man having climbed out from the water?"

"There were no signs, Mr Holmes. But it is a stone ledge, and one could hardly expect them."

"No tracks or marks?"

"None."

"Ha! Would there be any objection, Mr White Mason, to our going down to the house at once? There may possibly be some small point which might be suggestive."

"I was going to propose it, Mr Holmes; but I thought it well to put you in touch with all the facts before we go. I suppose if anything should strike you—" White Mason looked doubtfully at the amateur.

"I have worked with Mr Holmes before," said Inspector MacDonald. "He plays the game."

"My own idea of the game, at any rate," said Holmes, with a smile. "I go into a case to help the ends of justice and the work of the police. If I have ever separated myself from the official force, it is because they have first separated themselves from me. I have no wish ever to score at their expense. At the same time, Mr White Mason, I claim the right to work in my own way and give my results at my own time—complete rather than in stages."

"I am sure we are honoured by your presence and to show you all we know," said White Mason cordially. "Come along, Dr Watson, and when the time comes we'll all hope for a place in your book."

We walked down the quaint village street with a row of pollarded elms on each side of it. To our right, silhouetted against a metallic sky, the cables of a tethered aerostat system trailed across the country like the attenuated web of a vast spider, tracing the single railway line some hundred feet or so below it. Even as we approached the avenue's end, a train of dirigibles whirred above: buoyant whales, cargo pods strung from swollen bellies, straining against fore and aft mooring cables which plucked a strange melody from the running cable. Multiple impellers imposed an eerie chorus, underscored by the rhythmic beating of their condenser engines. It was both a comforting and daunting orchestration.

Marking the termination of the village's street were two ancient stone pillars, weather-stained and lichen-blotched, bearing upon their summits a shapeless something which had once been the rampant lion

of Capus of Birlstone. A short walk along the winding drive with such sward and oaks around it as one only sees in rural England, then a sudden turn, and the long, low Jacobean house of dingy, liver-coloured brick lay before us, with an old-fashioned garden of cut yews on each side of it. A single electrical receiving grid reared over its mossy roof. As we approached it, there was the extended replacement bridge and the beautiful broad moat as still and luminous as quicksilver in the cold, winter sunshine.

Three centuries had flowed past the old Manor House, centuries of births and of homecomings, of country dances and of the meetings of fox hunters. Strange that now in its old age this dark business should have cast its shadow upon the venerable walls! And yet those strange, peaked roofs and quaint, overhung gables were a fitting covering to grim and terrible intrigue. As I looked at the deep-set windows, the power mast looming over all, and the long sweep of the dull-coloured, water-lapped front, I felt that no more fitting scene—with its bizarre clash of ancient and modern—could be set for such a tragedy.

"That's the window," said White Mason, "that one on the immediate right of the drawbridge. It's open just as it was found last night."

Holmes lit a cigarette and blew out a long thin stream of smoke and I detected the unique odour: it was one of the Indian cigarettes he often brought to the countryside, supplied by Grimault of Paris. "It looks rather narrow for a man to pass."

"Well, it wasn't a fat man, anyhow. We don't need your deductions, Mr Holmes, to tell us that. But you or I could squeeze through all right."

Holmes walked to the edge of the moat and looked across. Then he examined the stone ledge and the grass border beyond it, using his lit cigarette as a pointer.

"I've had a good look, Mr Holmes," said White Mason. "There is nothing there, no sign that anyone has landed—but why should he leave any sign?"

Holmes flickered his familiar half-smile. "Exactly. Why should he? Is the water always turbid?"

"Generally about this colour. The stream brings down the clay."

"How deep is it?"

"About two feet at each side and three in the middle."

"So we can put aside all idea of the man having been drowned in crossing."

"No, a child could not be drowned in it."

We walked across the steel bridge, and were admitted by a quaint, gnarled, dried-up person, who was the butler, Ames. The poor old fellow was white and quivering from the shock. The village sergeant, a tall, formal, melancholy man, still held his vigil in the room of Fate. The doctor had departed.

"Anything fresh, Sergeant Wilson?" asked White Mason.

"No, sir."

"Then you can go home. You've had enough. We can send for you if we want you. The butler had better wait outside. Tell him to warn Mr Cecil Barker, Mrs Douglas, and the housekeeper that we may want a word with them presently. Now, gentlemen, perhaps you will allow me to give you the views I have formed first, and then you will be able to arrive at your own."

He impressed me, this country specialist. He had a solid grip of fact and a cool, clear, common-sense brain, which should take him some way in his profession. Holmes listened to him intently, with no sign of that impatience which the official exponent too often produced.

"Is it suicide, or is it murder—that's our first question, gentlemen, is it not? If it were suicide, then we have to believe that this man began by taking off his wedding ring and concealing it; that he then came down here in his dressing gown, trampled mud into a corner behind the curtain in order to give the idea someone had waited for him, opened the window, put blood on the—."

"We can surely dismiss that," said MacDonald.

"So I think. Suicide is out of the question. Then a murder has been done. What we have to determine is, whether it was done by someone outside or inside the house."

"Well, let's hear the argument," said the inspector, almost as if interrogating a suspect.

"There are considerable difficulties both ways, and yet one or the other it must be. We will suppose first that some person or persons inside the house did the crime. They got this man down here at a time when everything was still and yet no one was asleep. They then did the deed with the queerest and noisiest weapon in the world so as to tell everyone what had happened—a weapon that was never seen in the house before. That does not seem a very likely start, does it?"

"No, it does not."

"Well, then, everyone is agreed that after the alarm was given only a minute at the most had passed before the whole household—not Mr Cecil Barker alone, though he claims to have been the first, but Ames and all of them were on the spot. Do you tell me that in that time the guilty person managed to make footmarks in the corner, open the window, mark the sill with blood, take the wedding ring off the dead man's finger, and all the rest of it? It's impossible!"

"You put it very clearly," said Holmes softly. "I am inclined to agree with you."

"Well, then, we are driven back to the theory that it was done by someone from outside. We are still faced with some big difficulties; but anyhow they have ceased to be impossibilities. The man got into the house between four-thirty and six; that is to say, between dusk and the time when the bridge was rolled back and the house raised. There had been some visitors, and the door was open; so there was nothing to prevent him. He may have been a common burglar, or he may have had some private grudge against Mr Douglas. Since Mr Douglas has spent most of his life in America, and this shotgun seems to be an American weapon, it would seem that the private grudge is the more likely theory. He slipped into this room because it was the first he came to, and he hid behind the curtain. There he remained until past eleven at night. At that time Mr Douglas entered the room. It was a short interview, if there were any interview at all; for Mrs Douglas declares that her

husband had not left her more than a few minutes when she heard the shot."

"The candle shows that," said Holmes. He raised the aforementioned item and examined it briefly. "Why did Douglas have a candle when the house has electrical lighting?"

White Mason paused, his train of thought briefly derailed. "We shall have to ask." Then his mind returned to his original track. "The candle, which was a new one, is not burned more than half an inch. He must have placed it on the table before he was attacked; otherwise, of course, it would have fallen when he fell. This shows that he was not attacked the instant that he entered the room. When Mr Barker arrived the candle was lit and the lights were out."

"That's all clear enough."

"Well, now, we can reconstruct things on those lines. Mr Douglas enters the room. He puts down the candle. A man appears from behind the curtain. He is armed with this gun. He demands the wedding ring—Heaven only knows why, but so it must have been. Mr Douglas gave it up. Then either in cold blood or in the course of a struggle— Douglas may have gripped the hammer that was found upon the mat— he shot Douglas in this horrible way. He dropped his gun and also it would seem this queer card—*VV 341*, whatever that may mean—and he made his escape through the window and across the moat at the very moment when Cecil Barker was discovering the crime. How's that, Mr Holmes?"

"Very interesting, but just a little unconvincing."

"Man, it would be absolute nonsense if it wasn't that anything else is even worse!" cried MacDonald. "Somebody killed the man, and whoever it was I could clearly prove to you that he should have done it some other way. What does he mean by allowing his retreat to be cut off like that? What does he mean by using a shotgun when silence was his one chance of escape? Come, Mr Holmes, it's up to you to give us a lead, since you say Mr White Mason's theory is unconvincing."

Holmes had sat intently observant during this long discussion, missing

no word that was said, with his keen eyes darting to right and to left, and his forehead wrinkled with speculation.

"I should like a few more facts before I get so far as a theory, Mr Mac," said he, kneeling down beside the body. "Dear me! these injuries are really appalling. Can we have the butler in for a moment?" We waited for the poor, shaken man to appear. "Ames, I understand that you have often seen this very unusual mark—a branded triangle inside a circle—upon Mr Douglas's forearm?"

"Frequently, sir."

"You never heard any speculation as to what it meant?"

"No, sir."

"It must have caused great pain when it was inflicted. It is undoubtedly a burn. Now, I observe, Ames, that there is a small piece of plaster at the angle of Mr Douglas's jaw. Did you observe that in life?"

"Yes, sir, he cut himself in shaving yesterday morning."

"Did you ever know him to cut himself in shaving before?"

"Not for a very long time, sir."

"Suggestive!" said Holmes. "It may, of course, be a mere coincidence, or it may point to some nervousness which would indicate that he had reason to apprehend danger. Had you noticed anything unusual in his conduct, yesterday, Ames?"

"It struck me that he was a little restless and excited, sir."

"Ha! The attack may not have been entirely unexpected. We do seem to make a little progress, do we not?" Holmes glanced towards MacDonald who seemed to be exhibiting some restlessness. "Perhaps you would rather do the questioning, Mr Mac?"

"No, Mr Holmes, it's in better hands than mine."

"Well, then, we will pass to this card—*VV 341*. It is rough cardboard. Have you any of the sort in the house?"

Ames considered. "I don't think so."

Holmes walked across to the desk and dabbed a little ink from each bottle on to the blotting paper. "It was not printed in this room," he said; "this is black ink and the other purplish. It was done by a thick pen, and

these are fine. No, it was done elsewhere, I should say. Can you make anything of the inscription, Ames?"

"No, sir, nothing."

"What do you think, Mr Mac?"

The inspector's brows drew down in thought. "It gives me the impression of a secret society of some sort; the same with his badge upon the forearm."

"That's my idea, too," said White Mason.

"Well, we can adopt it as a working hypothesis and then see how far our difficulties disappear. An agent from such a society makes his way into the house, waits for Mr Douglas, blows his head nearly off with this weapon, and escapes by wading the moat, after leaving a card beside the dead man, which will, when mentioned in the papers, tell other members of the society that vengeance has been done. That all hangs together. But why this gun, of all weapons?"

"Exactly."

"And why the missing ring?"

"Quite so."

"And why no arrest? It's past two now. I take it for granted that since dawn every constable within forty miles has been looking out for a wet stranger?"

"That is so, Mr Holmes."

"Well, unless he has a burrow close by or a change of clothes ready, they can hardly miss him. And yet they have missed him up to now!" Holmes had gone to the window and was examining with his lens the blood mark on the sill. "It is clearly the tread of a shoe. It is remarkably broad; a splay-foot, one would say. Curious, because, so far as one can trace any footmark in this mud-stained corner, one would say it was a more shapely sole. However, they are certainly very indistinct. What's this under the side table?"

"Mr Douglas's dumb-bells," said Ames.

"Dumb-bell—there's only one. Where's the other?"

"I don't know, Mr Holmes. There may have been only one. I have not noticed them for months."

"One dumb-bell—" Holmes said seriously; but his remarks were interrupted by a sharp knock at the door.

A tall, sunburned, capable-looking, clean-shaved man looked in at us. I had no difficulty in guessing that it was the Cecil Barker of whom I had heard. His masterful eyes travelled quickly with a questioning glance from face to face.

"Sorry to interrupt your consultation," said he, "but you should hear the latest news."

"An arrest?"

"No such luck. But they've found his electric bicycle. The fellow left his bicycle behind him. Come and have a look. It is within a hundred yards of the hall door."

Holmes paused as we were about to leave the room. "One more thing, Ames: your master was carrying a candle, yet this house is electrically lit…"

The old man nodded. "The system is not yet fully functional, sir, and is liable to cut out unexpectedly. Mr Douglas was in the habit, last thing at night, to carry a candle and not trust in Westinghouse and Tesla."

Holmes pursed his lips, glanced briefly in my direction, and left the room of death.

We found three or four grooms and idlers standing in the drive inspecting a bicycle which had been drawn out from a clump of evergreens in which it had been concealed. It was a well-used Rudge-Whitworth, splashed as from a considerable journey, though its battery was clean and new. There was a saddlebag with spanner and oilcan, but no clue as to the owner.

"It would be a grand help to the police," said the inspector, "if these things were numbered and registered. But we must be thankful for what we've got. If we can't find where he went to, at least we are likely to get where he came from. But what in the name of all that is wonderful made the fellow leave it behind? And how in the world has he got away without it? We don't seem to get a gleam of light in the case, Mr Holmes."

"Don't we?" my friend answered thoughtfully. "I wonder!"

V. THE PEOPLE OF THE DRAMA

"Have you seen all you want of the study?" asked White Mason as we re-entered the house.

"For the time," said the inspector, and Holmes nodded.

"Then perhaps you would now like to hear the evidence of some of the people in the house. We could use the dining room, Ames. Please come yourself first and tell us what you know."

The butler's account was a simple and a clear one, and he gave a convincing impression of sincerity. He had been engaged five years before, when Douglas first came to Birlstone. He understood that Mr Douglas was a rich gentleman who had made his money in America. He had been a kind and considerate employer—not quite what Ames was used to, perhaps; but one can't have everything. He never saw any signs of apprehension in Mr Douglas: on the contrary, he was the most fearless man he had ever known; reckless, almost. He ordered the rebuilt bridge to be rolled back every night because it was the ancient custom of the old house, and he liked to keep the old ways up. The structural modifications—whereby the entire building was raised—well, that he put down to putting a modern slant on old ways; not that he particularly approved.

Mr Douglas seldom went to London or left the village; but on the day before the crime he had been shopping at Tunbridge Wells. He (Ames) had observed some restlessness and excitement on the part of Mr Douglas that day; for he had seemed impatient and irritable, which was unusual with him. He had not gone to bed that night; but was in the pantry at the back of the house, putting away the silver, when he heard the bell ring violently. He heard no shot; but it was hardly possible he would, as the pantry and kitchens were at the very back of the house and there were several closed doors and a long passage between. The housekeeper had come out of her room, attracted by the violent ringing of the bell. They had gone to the front of the house together.

As they reached the bottom of the stairs he had seen Mrs Douglas coming down it. No, she was not hurrying; it did not seem to him that she was particularly agitated. Just as she reached the bottom of the stair Mr Barker had rushed out of the study. He had stopped Mrs Douglas and begged her to go back.

"For God's sake, go back to your room!" he cried. "Poor Jack is dead! You can do nothing. For God's sake, go back!"

After some persuasion upon the stairs Mrs Douglas had gone back. She did not scream. She made no outcry whatever. Mrs Allen, the housekeeper, had taken her upstairs and stayed with her in the bedroom. Ames and Mr Barker had then returned to the study, where they had found everything exactly as the police had seen it. The candle was not lit at that time; but the lights were all turned on. They had looked out of the window; but the night was very dark and nothing could be seen or heard. They had then rushed out into the hall, where Ames had thrown the lever which activated the bridge machinery. Mr Barker had then hurried off to get the police.

Such, in its essentials, was the evidence of the butler.

The account of Mrs Allen, the housekeeper, was, so far as it went, a corroboration of that of her fellow servant. The housekeeper's room was rather nearer to the front of the house than the pantry in which Ames had been working. She was preparing to go to bed when the loud ringing of the bell had attracted her attention. She was a little hard of hearing. Perhaps that was why she had not heard the shot; but in any case the study was a long way off. She remembered hearing something like the sounds of a man in deep torment: a deep, anguished sigh followed by a sob; and then what she imagined to be the slamming of a door. That was a good deal earlier—half an hour at least before the ringing of the bell. When Mr Ames ran to the front she went with him. She saw Mr

Barker, very pale and excited, come out of the study. He intercepted Mrs Douglas, who was coming down the stairs. He entreated her to go back, and she answered him, but what she said could not be heard.

"Take her up! Stay with her!" he had said to Mrs Allen.

She had therefore taken her to the bedroom, and endeavoured to soothe her. She was greatly excited, trembling all over, but made no other attempt to go downstairs. She just sat in her dressing gown by her bedroom fire, with her head sunk in her hands. Mrs Allen stayed with her most of the night. As to the other servants, they had all gone to bed, and the alarm did not reach them until just before the police arrived. They slept at the extreme back of the house, and could not possibly have heard anything.

So far the housekeeper could add nothing on cross-examination save lamentations and expressions of amazement.

Cecil Barker succeeded Mrs Allen as a witness. As to the occurrences of the night before, he had very little to add to what he had already told the police. Personally, he was convinced that the murderer had escaped by the window. The bloodstain was conclusive, in his opinion, on that point. Besides, as the bridge was up, there was no other possible way of escaping. He could not explain what had become of the assassin or why he had not taken his bicycle, if it were indeed his. He could not possibly have been drowned in the moat, which was at no place more than three feet deep.

In his own mind he had a very definite theory about the murder. Douglas was a reticent man, and there were some chapters in his life of which he never spoke. He had emigrated to America when he was a very young man. He had prospered well, and Barker had first met him in California, where they had become partners in a successful mining claim at a place called Benito Canyon. They had done very well; but Douglas had suddenly sold out and started for England. He was a widower at that time. Barker had afterwards realized his money and come to live in London. Thus they had renewed their friendship.

Douglas had given him the impression that some danger was hanging over his head, and he had always looked upon his sudden

departure from California, and also his renting a house in so quiet a place in England—along with the modifications—as being connected with this peril. He imagined that some secret society, some implacable organization, was on Douglas's track, which would never rest until it killed him. Some remarks of his had given him this idea; though he had never told him what the society was, nor how he had come to offend it. He could only suppose that the legend upon the placard had some reference to this secret society.

"How long were you with Douglas in California?" asked Inspector MacDonald.

"Five years altogether."

"He was a bachelor, you say?"

"A widower."

"Have you ever heard where his first wife came from?"

"No, I remember his saying that she was of Dutch extraction, and I have seen her portrait. She was a very beautiful woman. She died of typhoid the year before I met him."

"You don't associate his past with any particular part of America?" prompted White Mason.

Barker shook his head. "I have heard him talk of Chicago. He knew that city well and had worked there. I have heard him talk of the coal and iron districts. He had travelled a good deal in his time."

"Was he a politician? Had this secret society to do with politics?" asked MacDonald.

"No, he cared nothing about politics."

"You have no reason to think it was criminal?"

"On the contrary, I never met a straighter man in my life."

White Mason: "Was there anything curious about his life in California?"

"He liked best to stay and to work at our claim in the mountains. He would never go where other men were if he could help it. That's why I first thought that someone was after him. Then when he left so suddenly for Europe I made sure that it was so. I believe that he had a warning of

some sort. Within a week of his leaving half a dozen men were inquiring for him."

The two policemen exchanged a look. "What sort of men?"

"Well, they were a mighty hard-looking crowd. They came up to the claim and wanted to know where he was. I told them that he was gone to Europe and that I did not know where to find him. They meant him no good—it was easy to see that."

"Were these men Americans—Californians?" asked MacDonald.

"Well, I don't know about Californians. They may have been Americans—from back east—though now I think on it, their accents were strange. Maybe like they were put on. But they were not miners. I don't know what they were, and was very glad to see their backs."

"That was six years ago?"

"Nearer seven."

"And then you were together five years in California, so that this business dates back not less than eleven years at the least?"

"That is so."

White Mason's bucolic features drew into a frown. "It must be a very serious feud that would be kept up with such earnestness for as long as that. It would be no light thing that would give rise to it."

"I think it shadowed his whole life. It was never quite out of his mind."

"But if a man had a danger hanging over him, and knew what it was, don't you think he would turn to the police for protection?"

"Maybe it was some danger that he could not be protected against. There's one thing you should know. He always went about armed: a large repeater pistol. It was never out of his pocket—all of his coats were tailored with an extra-large inside pocket to accommodate it. But, by bad luck, he was in his dressing gown and had left it in the bedroom last night. Once the bridge was back, I guess he thought he was safe."

"I should like these dates a little clearer," said MacDonald. "It is quite six years since Douglas left California. You followed him next year, did you not?"

"That is so."

"And he had been married five years. You must have returned about the time of his marriage."

"About a month before. I was his best man."

"Did you know Mrs Douglas before her marriage?"

"No, I did not. I had been away from England for ten years."

"But you have seen a good deal of her since."

Barker looked sternly at the detective. "I have seen a good deal of *him* since," he answered. "If I have seen her, it is because you cannot visit a man without knowing his wife. If you imagine there is any connection—"

"I imagine nothing, Mr Barker," replied the inspector calmly. "I am bound to make every inquiry which can bear upon the case. But I mean no offence."

"Some inquiries are offensive," Barker answered angrily.

"It's only the facts that we want. It is in your interest and everyone's interest that they should be cleared up." MacDonald paused a moment before proceeding. "Did Mr Douglas entirely approve your friendship with his wife?"

Barker grew paler, and his great, strong hands were clasped convulsively together. "You have no right to ask such questions!" he cried. "What has this to do with the matter you are investigating?"

The inspector was implacable. "I must repeat the question."

"Well, I refuse to answer."

MacDonald shrugged. "You can refuse to answer; but you must be aware that your refusal is in itself an answer, for you would not refuse if you had not something to conceal."

Barker stood for a moment with his face set grimly and his strong black eyebrows drawn low in intense thought. Then he looked up with a smile. "Well, I guess you gentlemen are only doing your clear duty after all, and I have no right to stand in the way of it. I'd only ask you not to worry Mrs Douglas over this matter; for she has enough upon her just now. I may tell you that poor Douglas had just one fault in the world, and that was his jealousy. He was fond of me—no man could be fonder of a friend. And he was devoted to his wife. He loved me to come here,

and was forever sending for me. And yet if his wife and I talked together or there seemed any sympathy between us, a kind of wave of jealousy would pass over him, and he would be off the handle and saying the wildest things in a moment. More than once I've sworn off coming for that reason, and then he would write me such penitent, imploring letters that I just had to. But you can take it from me, gentlemen, if it was my last word, that no man ever had a more loving, faithful wife—and I can say also no friend could be more loyal than I!"

It was spoken with fervour and feeling, and yet Inspector MacDonald was clearly not about to dismiss the subject.

"You are aware," said he, "that the dead man's wedding ring has been taken from his finger?"

"So it appears," said Barker.

"What do you mean by 'appears'? You know it as a fact."

The man seemed confused and undecided. "When I said 'appears' I meant that it was conceivable that he had himself taken off the ring."

White Mason interjected. "The mere fact that the ring should be absent, whoever may have removed it, would suggest to anyone's mind, would it not, that the marriage and the tragedy were connected?"

Barker shrugged his broad shoulders. "I can't profess to say what it means," he answered. "But if you mean to hint that it could reflect in any way upon this lady's honour—" his eyes blazed for an instant, and then with an evident effort he got a grip upon his own emotions "—well, you are on the wrong track, that's all."

"I don't know that I've anything else to ask you at present," said MacDonald, coldly. He glancing questioningly at White Mason and Holmes.

"There was one small point," remarked Sherlock Holmes. "When you entered the room there was only a candle lighted on the table, was there not?"

"Yes, that was so."

"By its light you saw that some terrible incident had occurred?"

"Exactly."

"You at once rang for help?"

"Yes."

"And it arrived very speedily?"

"Within a minute or so."

"And yet when they arrived they found that the candle was out and that the room's own lights had been switched on. That seems very remarkable."

Again Barker showed some signs of indecision. "I don't see that it was remarkable, Mr Holmes," he answered after a pause. "The candle threw a very bad light. My first thought was to get a better one. The room is wired for electrical lighting after all."

"And blew out the candle?"

"Exactly."

Holmes asked no further question, and Barker, with a deliberate look from one to the other of us, which had, as it seemed to me, something of defiance in it, turned and left the room.

Inspector MacDonald had sent up a note to the effect that he would wait upon Mrs Douglas in her room; but she had replied that she would meet us in the dining room. She entered now, a tall and beautiful woman of thirty, reserved and self-possessed to a remarkable degree, very different from the tragic and distracted figure I had pictured. It is true that her face was pale and drawn, like that of one who has endured a great shock; but her manner was composed, and the finely moulded hand which she rested upon the edge of the table was as steady as my own. Her sad, appealing eyes travelled from one to the other of us with a curiously inquisitive expression. That questioning gaze transformed itself suddenly into abrupt speech.

"Have you found anything out yet?" she asked.

Was it my imagination that there was an undertone of fear rather than of hope in the question?

"We have taken every possible step, Mrs Douglas," said the inspector. "You may rest assured that nothing will be neglected."

"Spare no money," she said in a dead, even tone. "It is my desire that every possible effort should be made."

"Perhaps you can tell us something which may throw some light upon the matter," White Mason asked her gently.

"I fear not; but all I know is at your service."

"We have heard from Mr Cecil Barker that you did not actually see—" Mason hesitated. "That you were never in the room where the tragedy occurred?"

"No, he turned me back upon the stairs. He begged me to return to my room."

"Quite so. You had heard the shot, and you had at once come down."

"I put on my dressing gown and then came down."

"How long was it after hearing the shot that you were stopped on the stair by Mr Barker?" enquired MacDonald.

"It may have been a couple of minutes. It is so hard to reckon time at such a moment. He implored me not to go on. He assured me that I could do nothing. Then Mrs Allen, the housekeeper, led me upstairs again. It was all like some dreadful dream."

"Can you give us any idea how long your husband had been downstairs before you heard the shot?" asked the inspector.

"No, I cannot say. He went from his dressing room, and I did not hear him go. He did the round of the house every night, checking that all unnecessary lighting was extinguished for he was nervous of fire—and I understand that electrical wiring may occasionally spark. It is the only thing that I have ever known him nervous of."

"That is just the point which I want to come to, Mrs Douglas. You have known your husband only in England, have you not?"

"Yes, we have been married five years."

"Have you heard him speak of anything which occurred in America and might bring some danger upon him?"

Mrs Douglas thought earnestly before she answered. "Yes," she said at last, "I have always felt that there was a danger hanging over him. He refused to discuss it with me. It was not from want of confidence in me—there was the most complete love and confidence between us—but it was

out of his desire to keep all alarm away from me. He thought I should brood over it if I knew all, and so he was silent."

"How did you know it, then?"

Mrs Douglas's face lit with a quick, brave smile. "Can a husband ever carry about a secret all his life and a woman who loves him have no suspicion of it? I knew it by his refusal to talk about some episodes in his American life. I knew it by certain precautions he took. I knew it by certain words he let fall. I knew it by the way he looked at unexpected strangers. I was perfectly certain that he had some powerful enemies, that he believed they were on his track, and that he was always on his guard against them. I was so sure of it that for years I have been terrified if ever he came home later than was expected."

"Might I ask," asked Holmes, "what the words were which attracted your attention?"

"The Valley of Fear," the lady answered. "That was an expression he has used when I questioned him. 'I have been in the Valley of Fear. I am not out of it yet.'—'Are we never to get out of the Valley of Fear?' I have asked him when I have seen him more serious than usual. 'Sometimes I think that we never shall,' he has answered."

"Surely you asked him what he meant by the Valley of Fear?"

"I did; but his face would become very grave and he would shake his head. 'It is bad enough that one of us should have been in its shadow,' he said. 'Please God it shall never fall upon you!' It was some real valley in which he had lived and in which something terrible had occurred to him, of that I am certain; but I can tell you no more."

Holmes steepled his long fingers. "And he never mentioned any names?"

"Yes, he was delirious with fever once when he had his hunting accident three years ago. Then I remember that there was a name that came continually to his lips. He spoke it with anger and a sort of horror. McGinty was the name—Bodymaster McGinty. I asked him when he recovered who Bodymaster McGinty was, and whose body he was master of. 'Never of mine, thank God!' he answered with a laugh, and that was

all I could get from him. But there is a connection between Bodymaster McGinty and the Valley of Fear."

"There is one other point," said Inspector MacDonald. "You met Mr Douglas in a boarding house in London, did you not, and became engaged to him there? Was there any romance, anything secret or mysterious, about the wedding?"

She met his gaze levelly. "There was romance. There is always romance. There was nothing mysterious."

"He had no rival?"

"No, I was quite free."

"You have heard, no doubt, that his wedding ring has been taken. Does that suggest anything to you? Suppose that some enemy of his old life had tracked him down and committed this crime, what possible reason could he have for taking his wedding ring?"

For an instant I could have sworn that the faintest shadow of a smile flickered over the woman's lips.

"I really cannot tell," she answered. "It is certainly a most extraordinary thing."

"Well, we will not detain you any longer, and we are sorry to have put you to this trouble at such a time," said the inspector. "There are some other points, no doubt; but we can refer to you as they arise."

She rose, and I was again conscious of that quick, questioning glance with which she had just surveyed us. What impression has my evidence made upon you? The question might as well have been spoken. Then, with a bow, she swept from the room.

"She's a beautiful woman—a very beautiful woman," said MacDonald thoughtfully, after the door had closed behind her. "This man Barker has certainly been down here a good deal. He is a man who might be attractive to a woman. He admits that the dead man was jealous, and maybe he knew best himself what cause he had for jealousy. Then there's that wedding ring. You can't get past that. The man who tears a wedding ring off a dead man's—What do you say to it, Mr Holmes?"

My friend had sat with his head upon his hands, sunk in the deepest thought. Now he rose and rang the bell. "Ames," he said, when the butler entered, "where is Mr Cecil Barker now?"

"I'll see, sir."

He came back in a moment to say that Barker was in the garden.

"Can you remember, Ames, what Mr Barker had on his feet last night when you joined him in the study?"

"Yes, Mr Holmes. He had a pair of bedroom slippers. I brought him his boots when he went for the police."

"Where are the slippers now?"

"They are still under the chair in the hall."

"Very good, Ames. It is, of course, important for us to know which tracks may be Mr Barker's and which from outside."

"Yes, sir. I may say that I noticed that the slippers were stained with blood—so indeed were my own."

"That is natural enough, considering the condition of the room. Very good, Ames. We will ring if we want you."

A few minutes later we were in the study. Holmes had brought with him the carpet slippers from the hall. As Ames had observed, the soles of both were dark with blood.

"Strange!" murmured Holmes, as he stood in the light of the window and examined them minutely. "Very strange indeed!"

Stooping with one of his quick feline pounces, he placed the slipper upon the blood mark on the sill. It exactly corresponded. He smiled in silence at his colleagues.

The inspector was transfigured with excitement. His native accent rattled like a stick upon railings.

"Man," he cried, "there's not a doubt of it! Barker has just marked the window himself. It's a good deal broader than any bootmark. I mind that you said it was a splay-foot, and here's the explanation. But what's the game, Mr Holmes—what's the game?"

"Ay, what's the game?" my friend repeated thoughtfully.

White Mason chuckled and rubbed his fat hands together in his professional satisfaction. "I said it was a snorter!" he cried. "And a real snorter it is!"

VI. A DAWNING LIGHT

The three detectives had many matters of detail into which to inquire; so I returned alone to our modest quarters at the village inn. But before doing so I took a stroll in the curious old-world garden which flanked the house. Rows of very ancient yew trees cut into strange designs girded it round. Inside was a beautiful stretch of lawn with an old sundial in the middle, the whole effect so soothing and restful that it was welcome to my somewhat jangled nerves. The only jarring note was the soaring Westinghouse-Tesla tower which I fancied hummed softly with the suppressed static energy beamed at it. It was ringed by a high fence—but I had no intention of venturing any closer than was necessary.

In that deeply peaceful atmosphere one could forget, or remember only as some fantastic nightmare, that darkened study with the sprawling, blood-stained figure on the floor. And yet, as I strolled round it and tried to steep my soul in its gentle balm, a strange incident occurred, which brought me back to the tragedy and left a sinister impression in my mind.

I have said that a decoration of yew trees circled the garden. At the end farthest from the house they thickened into a continuous hedge. On the other side of this hedge, concealed from the eyes of anyone approaching from the direction of the house, there was a stone seat. As I approached the spot I was aware of voices, some remark in the deep tones of a man, answered by a little ripple of feminine laughter.

An instant later I had come round the end of the hedge and my eyes lit upon Mrs Douglas and the man Barker before they were aware of my presence. Her appearance gave me a shock. In the dining-room she had been demure and discreet: the very image of feminine propriety. Now all pretence of grief had passed away from her. Her eyes shone with the

joy of living, and her face still quivered with amusement at some remark of her companion. He sat forward, his hands clasped and his forearms on his knees, with an answering smile upon his bold, handsome face. In an instant—but it was just one instant too late—they resumed their solemn masks as my figure came into view. A hurried word or two passed between them, and then Barker rose and came towards me.

"Excuse me, sir," said he, "but am I addressing Dr Watson?"

I bowed with a coldness which showed, I dare say, very plainly the impression which had been produced upon my mind.

"We thought that it was probably you, as your friendship with Mr Sherlock Holmes is so well known. Would you mind coming over and speaking to Mrs Douglas for one instant?"

I followed him with a dour face. Very clearly I could see in my mind's eye that shattered figure on the floor. Here within a few hours of the tragedy were his wife and his nearest friend laughing together behind a bush in the garden which had been his. I greeted the lady with reserve. I had grieved with her grief in the dining room. Now I did my best to meet her appealing gaze with an unresponsive eye.

"I fear that you think me callous and hard-hearted," said she.

I shrugged my shoulders. "It is no business of mine," said I.

"Perhaps some day you will do me justice. If you only realized—"

"There is no need why Dr Watson should realize," said Barker quickly. "As he has himself said, it is no possible business of his."

"Exactly," said I, "and so I will beg leave to resume my walk."

"One moment, Dr Watson," cried the woman in a pleading voice. "There is one question which you can answer with more authority than anyone else in the world, and it may make a very great difference to me. You know Mr Holmes and his relations with the police better than anyone else can. Supposing that a matter were brought confidentially to his knowledge, is it absolutely necessary that he should pass it on to the detectives?"

"Yes, that's it," said Barker eagerly. "Is he on his own or is he entirely in with them?"

I looked from one to the other: at Barker's commanding presence and Mrs Douglas's pleading eyes. "I really don't know that I should be justified in discussing such a point."

"I beg—I implore that you will, Dr Watson! I assure you that you will be helping us—helping me greatly if you will guide us on that point."

There was such a ring of sincerity in the woman's voice that for the instant I forgot all about her levity and confess I was moved only to do her will.

"Mr Holmes is an independent investigator," I said. "He is his own master, and would act as his own judgement directed. At the same time, he would naturally feel loyalty towards the officials who were working on the same case, and he would not conceal from them anything which would help them in bringing a criminal to justice. Beyond this I can say nothing, and I would refer you to Mr Holmes himself if you wanted fuller information."

So saying I raised my hat and went upon my way, leaving them still seated behind that concealing hedge. I looked back as I rounded the far end of it, and saw that they were still talking very earnestly together, and, as they were gazing after me, it was clear that it was our interview that was the subject of their debate.

"I wish none of their confidences," said Holmes, when I reported to him what had occurred. He had spent the whole afternoon at the Manor House in consultation with his two colleagues, and returned about five with a ravenous appetite for a high tea which I had ordered for him. "No confidences, Watson; for they are mighty awkward if it comes to an arrest for conspiracy and murder."

"You think it will come to that?"

He was in his most cheerful and *débonnaire* humour. "My dear Watson, when I have exterminated that fourth egg I shall be ready to put you in touch with the whole situation. I don't say that we have fathomed it—far from it—but when we have traced the missing dumb-bell—"

"The dumb-bell!"

"Dear me, Watson, is it possible that you have not penetrated the fact

that the case hangs upon the missing dumb-bell? Well, well, you need not be downcast; for between ourselves I don't think that either Inspector Mac or the excellent local practitioner has grasped the overwhelming importance of this incident. One dumb-bell, Watson! Consider an athlete with one dumb-bell! Picture to yourself the unilateral development, the imminent danger of a spinal curvature. Shocking, Watson, shocking!"

He sat with his mouth full of toast and his eyes sparkling with mischief, watching my intellectual entanglement. The mere sight of his excellent appetite was an assurance of success; for I had very clear recollections of days and nights without a thought of food, when his baffled mind had chafed before some problem while his thin, eager features became more attenuated with the asceticism of complete mental concentration. Finally he lit his pipe, and sitting in the inglenook of the old village inn he talked slowly and at random about his case, rather as one who thinks aloud than as one who makes a considered statement. For myself, I removed one my own Tiedeman's cigarettes, and joined him.

"A lie, Watson—a great, big, thumping, obtrusive, uncompromising lie—that's what meets us on the threshold! There is our starting point. The whole story told by Barker is a lie. But Barker's story is corroborated by Mrs Douglas. Therefore she is lying also. They are both lying, and in a conspiracy. So now we have the clear problem. Why are they lying, and what is the truth which they are trying so hard to conceal? Let us try, Watson, you and I, if we can get behind the lie and reconstruct the truth." He blew out a noxious cloud of pipe smoke.

"How do I know that they are lying? Because it is a clumsy fabrication which simply *could* not be true. Consider! According to the story given to us, the assassin had less than a minute after the murder had been committed to take that ring, which was under another ring, from the dead man's finger, to replace the other ring—a thing which he would surely never have done—and to put that singular card beside his victim. I say that this was obviously impossible.

"You may argue—but I have too much respect for your judgement, Watson, to think that you will do so—that the ring may have been taken

before the man was killed. The fact that the candle had been lit only a short time shows that there had been no lengthy interview. Was Douglas, from what we hear of his fearless character, a man who would be likely to give up his wedding ring at such short notice, or could we conceive of his giving it up at all? No, no, Watson, the assassin was alone with the dead man for some time with the electric lights fully lit. Of that I have no doubt at all.

"But the gunshot was apparently the cause of death. Therefore the shot must have been fired some time earlier than we are told. But there could be no mistake about such a matter as that. We are in the presence, therefore, of a deliberate conspiracy upon the part of the two people who heard the gunshot—of the man Barker and of the woman Douglas. When on the top of this I am able to show that the blood mark on the windowsill was deliberately placed there by Barker, in order to give a false clue to the police, you will admit that the case grows dark against him." He paused a moment to refill his pipe.

"Now we have to ask ourselves at what hour the murder actually did occur. Up to half-past ten the servants were moving about the house; so it was certainly not before that time. At a quarter to eleven they had all gone to their rooms with the exception of Ames, who was in the pantry. I have been trying some experiments after you left us this afternoon, and I find that no noise which MacDonald can make in the study can penetrate to me in the pantry when the doors are all shut.

"It is otherwise, however, from the housekeeper's room. It is not so far down the corridor, and from it I could vaguely hear a voice when it was very loudly raised. The sound from a shotgun is to some extent muffled when the discharge is at very close range, as it undoubtedly was in this instance. It would not be very loud, and yet in the silence of the night it should have easily penetrated to Mrs Allen's room. She is, as she has told us, somewhat deaf; but none the less she mentioned in her evidence that she did hear something like an anguished moan and a sob, followed by a door slamming half an hour before the alarm was given. Half an hour before the alarm was given would be a quarter to eleven. I have no doubt

that what she heard as a slamming door was the report of the gun, and that this was the real instant of the murder."

"But the moan and sob," I interjected, "what of those?"

Holmes shook his head. "Almost certainly not what she believed. No human cry, regardless of how desolate, can be heard so clearly—unless the perpetrator was booming out more loudly than the greatest ham on the London stage..."

"Cries of terror—or agony, perhaps?"

"No—it will not do, Watson. I believe we must look elsewhere for the agency of what Mrs Allen thinks she heard."

He paused again, smoking thoughtfully, his gaze far away. "We have now to determine what Barker and Mrs Douglas, presuming that they are not the actual murderers, could have been doing from quarter to eleven, when the sound of the shot brought them down, until quarter past eleven, when they rang the bell and summoned the servants. What were they doing, and why did they not instantly give the alarm? That is the question which faces us, and when it has been answered we shall surely have gone some way to solve our problem."

"I am convinced myself," said I, "that there is an understanding between those two people. She must be a heartless creature to sit laughing at some jest within a few hours of her husband's murder."

"Exactly. She does not shine as a wife even in her own account of what occurred. I am not a whole-souled admirer of womankind, as you are aware, Watson, but my experience of life has taught me that there are few wives, having any regard for their husbands, who would let any man's spoken word stand between them and that husband's dead body. Should I ever marry, Watson, I should hope to inspire my wife with some feeling which would prevent her from being walked off by a housekeeper when my corpse was lying within a few yards of her. It was badly stage-managed; for even the rawest investigators must be struck by the absence of the usual feminine ululation. If there had been nothing else, this incident alone would have suggested a prearranged conspiracy to my mind."

"You think then, definitely, that Barker and Mrs Douglas are guilty of the murder?"

"There is an appalling directness about your questions, Watson," said Holmes, shaking his pipe at me. "They come at me like bullets. If you put it that Mrs Douglas and Barker know the truth about the murder, and are conspiring to conceal it, then I can give you a whole-souled answer. I am sure they do. But your more deadly proposition is not so clear. Let us for a moment consider the difficulties which stand in the way:

"We will suppose that this couple are united by the bonds of a guilty love, and that they have determined to get rid of the man who stands between them. It is a large supposition; for discreet inquiry among servants and others has failed to corroborate it in any way. On the contrary, there is a good deal of evidence that the Douglases were very attached to each other."

"That, I am sure, cannot be true," said I, thinking of the beautiful smiling face in the garden.

"Well at least they gave that impression," said Holmes airily. "However, we will suppose that they are an extraordinarily astute couple, who deceive everyone upon this point, and conspire to murder the husband. He happens to be a man over whose head some danger hangs——"

"We have only their word for that."

Holmes looked thoughtful. "I see, Watson. You are sketching out a theory by which everything they say from the beginning is false. According to your idea, there was never any hidden menace, or secret society, or Valley of Fear, or Boss MacSomebody, or anything else. Well, that is a good sweeping generalization. Let us see what that brings us to. They invent this theory to account for the crime. They then play up to the idea by leaving this electric bicycle in the park as proof of the existence of some outsider. The stain on the windowsill conveys the same idea. So does the card on the body, which might have been prepared in the house. That all fits into your hypothesis, Watson. But now we come on the nasty, angular, uncompromising bits which won't slip into their places. Why a cut-off shotgun of all weapons—and an American one at

that? How could they be so sure that the sound of it would not bring someone on to them? It's a mere chance as it is that Mrs Allen did not start out to inquire for the slamming door. Why did your guilty couple do all this, Watson?"

"I confess that I can't explain it."

"Then again, if a woman and her lover conspire to murder a husband, are they going to advertise their guilt by ostentatiously removing his wedding ring after his death? Does that strike you as very probable, Watson?"

He had me there. "No, it does not."

"And once again, if the thought of leaving a bicycle concealed outside had occurred to you, would it really have seemed worth doing when the dullest detective would naturally say this is an obvious blind, as the bicycle is the first thing which the fugitive needed in order to make his escape."

"I can conceive of no explanation."

"And yet there should be no combination of events for which the wit of man cannot conceive an explanation. Simply as a mental exercise, without any assertion that it is true, let me indicate a possible line of thought. It is, I admit, mere imagination; but how often is imagination the mother of truth?

"We will suppose that there was a guilty secret, a really shameful secret in the life of this man Douglas. This leads to his murder by someone who is, we will suppose, an avenger, someone from outside. This avenger, for some reason which I confess I am still at a loss to explain, took the dead man's wedding ring. The vendetta might conceivably date back to the man's first marriage, and the ring be taken for some such reason.

"Before this avenger got away, Barker and the wife had reached the room. The assassin convinced them that any attempt to arrest him would lead to the publication of some hideous scandal. They were converted to this idea, and preferred to let him go. For this purpose they probably extended the bridge, which can be done quite noiselessly, and then rolled it back again. He made his escape, and for some reason thought that he

could do so more safely on foot than on the bicycle. He therefore left his machine where it would not be discovered until he had got safely away. So far we are within the bounds of possibility, are we not?"

"Well, it is possible, no doubt," said I, with some reserve.

"We have to remember, Watson, that whatever occurred is certainly something very extraordinary. Well, now, to continue our supposititious case, the couple—not necessarily a guilty couple—realize after the murderer is gone that they have placed themselves in a position in which it may be difficult for them to prove that they did not themselves either do the deed or connive at it. They rapidly and rather clumsily met the situation. The mark was put by Barker's blood-stained slipper upon the windowsill to suggest how the fugitive got away. They obviously were the two who must have heard the sound of the gun; so they gave the alarm exactly as they would have done, but a good half hour after the event."

"And how do you propose to prove all this?"

"Well, if there were an outsider, he may be traced and taken. That would be the most effective of all proofs. But if not—well, the resources of science are far from being exhausted. I think that an evening alone in that study would help me much."

"An evening alone!"

"I propose to go up there presently. I have arranged it with the estimable Ames, who is by no means wholehearted about Barker. I shall sit in that room and see if its atmosphere brings me inspiration. I'm a believer in the *genius loci*. You smile, friend Watson. Well, we shall see. By the way, you have that big umbrella of yours, have you not?"

"It is here."

"Well, I'll borrow that if I may."

"Certainly—but what a wretched weapon! If there is danger—"

"Nothing serious, my dear Watson, or I should certainly ask for your assistance. But I'll take the umbrella. At present I am only awaiting the return of our colleagues from Tunbridge Wells, where they are at present engaged in trying for a likely owner to the bicycle."

It was nightfall before Inspector MacDonald and White Mason came

back from their expedition, and they arrived exultant, reporting a great advance in our investigation.

"Man, I'll admeet that I had my doubts if there was ever an outsider," said MacDonald, "but that's all past now. We've had the bicycle identified, and we have a description of our man; so that's a long step on our journey."

"It sounds to me like the beginning of the end," said Holmes. "I'm sure I congratulate you both with all my heart."

"Well, I started from the fact that Mr Douglas had seemed disturbed since the day before, when he had been at Tunbridge Wells. It was at Tunbridge Wells then that he had become conscious of some danger. It was clear, therefore, that if a man had come over with a bicycle it was from Tunbridge Wells that he might be expected to have come. We took the electric bicycle over with us and showed it at the hotels. It was identified at once by the manager of the Eagle Commercial as belonging to a man named Hargrave, who had taken a room there two days before. This bicycle and a small valise were his whole belongings. He had registered his name as coming from London, but had given no address. The valise was London made, and the contents were English; but the man himself was undoubtedly Irish."

"Well, well," said Holmes gleefully, "Irish, eh? You have indeed done some solid work while I have been sitting spinning theories with my friend! It's a lesson in being practical, Mr Mac."

"Ay, it's just that, Mr Holmes," said the inspector with satisfaction.

"But this may all fit in with your theories," I remarked to Holmes.

"That may or may not be. But let us hear the end, Mr Mac. Was there nothing to identify this man?"

"So little that it was evident that he had carefully guarded himself against identification. There were no papers or letters, and no marking upon the clothes. A cycle map of the county lay on his bedroom table. He had left the hotel after breakfast yesterday morning on his bicycle, and no more was heard of him until our inquiries."

"That's what puzzles me, Mr Holmes," said White Mason. "If the fellow did not want the hue and cry raised over him, one would imagine

that he would have returned and remained at the hotel as an inoffensive tourist. As it is, he must know that he will be reported to the police by the hotel manager and that his disappearance will be connected with the murder."

"So one would imagine. Still, he has been justified of his wisdom up to date, at any rate, since he has not been taken. But his description—what of that?"

MacDonald referred to his notebook. "Here we have it so far as they could give it. They don't seem to have taken any very particular stock of him; but still the porter, the clerk, and the chambermaid are all agreed that this about covers the points. He was a man about five foot nine in height, fifty or so years of age, his hair a dignified white, a moustache, a curved nose, and a face which all of them described as fierce and forbidding."

"Well, bar the expression, that might almost be a description of Douglas himself," said Holmes. "He is just over fifty, with white hair and moustache, and about the same height. Though the white hair is certainly suggestive." He tapped at pursed lips with a finger. "Did you get anything else?"

"He was dressed in a heavy grey suit with a reefer jacket, and he wore a short yellow overcoat and a soft cap."

"What about the shotgun?"

"It is less than two feet long. It could very well have fitted into his valise. He could have carried it inside his overcoat without difficulty."

"And how do you consider that all this bears upon the general case?"

"Well, Mr Holmes," said MacDonald, "when we have got our man—and you may be sure that I had his description being Teslagraphed within five minutes of hearing it—we shall be better able to judge. But, even as it stands, we have surely gone a long way. We know that an Irishman calling himself Hargrave came to Tunbridge Wells two days ago with bicycle and valise. In the latter was a sawed-off shotgun; so he came with the deliberate purpose of crime. Yesterday morning he set off for this place on his bicycle, with his gun concealed in his overcoat. No one saw him arrive, so far as

we can learn; but he need not pass through the village to reach the park gates, and there are many cyclists upon the road. Presumably he at once concealed his cycle among the laurels where it was found, and possibly lurked there himself, with his eye on the house, waiting for Mr Douglas to come out. The shotgun is a strange weapon to use inside a house; but he had intended to use it outside, and there it has very obvious advantages, as it would be impossible to miss with it, and the sound of shots is so common in an English sporting neighbourhood that no particular notice would be taken."

"That is all very clear," said Holmes.

"Well, Mr Douglas did not appear. What was he to do next? He left his bicycle and approached the house in the twilight. He found the bridge extended and no one about. He took his chance, intending, no doubt, to make some excuse if he met anyone. He met no one. He slipped into the first room that he saw, and concealed himself behind the curtain. Thence he could see the bridge go back; and when the house was raised he knew that his only escape was through the moat. He waited until quarter-past eleven, when Mr Douglas upon his usual nightly round came into the room. He shot him and escaped, as arranged. He was aware that the electric bicycle would be described by the hotel people and be a clue against him; so he left it there and made his way by some other means to London or to some safe hiding place which he had already arranged. How is that, Mr Holmes?"

"Well, Mr Mac, it is very good and very clear so far as it goes. That is your end of the story. My end is that the crime was committed half an hour earlier than reported; that Mrs Douglas and Barker are both in a conspiracy to conceal something; that they aided the murderer's escape—or at least that they reached the room before he escaped—and that they fabricated evidence of his escape through the window, whereas in all probability they had themselves let him go by extending the bridge. That's *my* reading of the first half."

The two detectives shook their heads.

"Well, Mr Holmes, if this is true, we only tumble out of one mystery into another," said the London inspector.

"And in some ways a worse one," added White Mason. "The lady has never left these shores in all her life. What possible connection could she have with an Irish assassin which would cause her to shelter him?"

"And what," I added, "would an Irishman be doing with an American shotgun?" For I'm sure I was not the only one in that room to whom consideration of anarchists and Irish separatism had not abruptly suggested itself.

Holmes clapped his thin hands. "Capital, Watson, capital! I freely admit the difficulties. I propose to make a little investigation of my own tonight, and it is just possible that it may contribute something to the common cause."

"Can we help you, Mr Holmes?"

"No, no! Darkness and Dr Watson's umbrella—my wants are simple. And Ames, the faithful Ames, no doubt he will stretch a point for me. All my lines of thought lead me back invariably to the one basic question— why should an athletic man develop his frame upon so unnatural an instrument as a single dumb-bell?"

It was late that night when Holmes returned from his solitary excursion. We slept in a double-bedded room, which was the best that the little country inn could do for us. I was already asleep when I was partly awakened by his entrance.

"Well, Holmes," I murmured, "have you found anything out?"

He stood beside me in silence, his candle in his hand. Then the tall, lean figure inclined towards me. "I say, Watson," he whispered, "would you be afraid to sleep in the same room with a lunatic, a man with softening of the brain, an idiot whose mind has lost its grip?"

"Not in the least," I answered in astonishment.

"Ah, that's lucky," he said, and not another word would he utter that night.

VII. THE SOLUTION

Next morning, after breakfast, we found Inspector MacDonald and White Mason seated in close consultation in the small parlour of the local police sergeant. On the table in front of them were piled a number of letters and Teslagrams, which they were carefully sorting and docketing. Three had been placed on one side.

"Still on the track of the elusive bicyclist?" Holmes asked cheerfully. "What is the latest news of the ruffian?"

MacDonald pointed ruefully to his heap of correspondence.

"He is at present reported from Leicester, Nottingham, Southampton, Derby, East Ham, Richmond, and fourteen other places. In three of them—East Ham, Leicester, and Liverpool—there is a clear case against him, and he has actually been arrested. The country seems to be full of the fugitives with yellow coats."

"Dear me!" said Holmes sympathetically. "Now, Mr Mac and you, Mr White Mason, I wish to give you a very earnest piece of advice. When I went into this case with you I bargained, as you will no doubt remember, that I should not present you with half-proved theories, but that I should retain and work out my own ideas until I had satisfied myself that they were correct. For this reason I am not at the present moment telling you all that is in my mind. On the other hand, I said that I would play the game fairly by you, and I do not think it is a fair game to allow you for one unnecessary moment to waste your energies upon a profitless task. Therefore I am here to advise you this morning, and my advice to you is summed up in three words—abandon the case."

MacDonald and White Mason stared in amazement at their celebrated colleague.

"You consider it hopeless!" cried the inspector.

"I consider *your* case to be hopeless. I do not consider that it is hopeless to arrive at the truth."

"But this cyclist. He is not an invention. We have his description, his valise, his electric bicycle. The fellow must be somewhere. Why should we not get him?"

"Yes, yes, no doubt he is somewhere, and no doubt we shall get him; but I would not have you waste your energies in East Ham or Liverpool. I am sure that we can find some shorter cut to a result."

"You are holding something back. It's hardly fair of you, Mr Holmes." The inspector was annoyed.

"You know my methods of work, Mr Mac. But I will hold it back for the shortest time possible. I only wish to verify my details in one way, which can very readily be done, and then I make my bow and return to London, leaving my results entirely at your service. I owe you too much to act otherwise; for in all my experience I cannot recall any more singular and interesting study."

"This is clean beyond me, Mr Holmes. We saw you when we returned from Tunbridge Wells last night, and you were in general agreement with our results. What has happened since then to give you a completely new idea of the case?"

"Well, since you ask me, I spent, as I told you that I would, some hours last night at the Manor House."

"Well, what happened?"

"Ah, I can only give you a very general answer to that for the moment. By the way, I have been reading a short but clear and interesting account of the old building, purchasable at the modest sum of one penny from the local tobacconist."

Here Holmes drew a small tract, embellished with a rude engraving of the ancient Manor House, from his waistcoat pocket.

"It immensely adds to the zest of an investigation, my dear Mr Mac, when one is in conscious sympathy with the historical atmosphere of one's surroundings. Don't look so impatient; for I assure you that even

so bald an account as this raises some sort of picture of the past in one's mind. Permit me to give you a sample. *Erected in the fifth year of the reign of James I, and standing upon the site of a much older building, the Manor House of Birlstone presents one of the finest surviving examples of the moated Jacobean residence—*"

"You are making fools of us, Mr Holmes!"

"Tut, tut, Mr Mac!—the first sign of temper I have detected in you. Well, I won't read it verbatim, since you feel so strongly upon the subject. But when I tell you that there is some account of the taking of the place by a parliamentary colonel in 1644, of the concealment of Charles for several days in the course of the Civil War, and finally of a visit there by the second George, you will admit that there are various associations of interest connected with this ancient house."

"I don't doubt it, Mr Holmes; but that is no business of ours."

"Is it not? Is it not? Breadth of view, my dear Mr Mac, is one of the essentials of our profession. The interplay of ideas and the oblique uses of knowledge are often of extraordinary interest. You will excuse these remarks from one who, though a mere connoisseur of crime, is still rather older and perhaps more experienced than yourself."

"I'm the first to admit that," said the detective heartily. "You get to your point, I admit; but you have such a deuced round-the-corner way of doing it."

"Well, well, I'll drop past history and get down to present-day facts. I called last night, as I have already said, at the Manor House. I did not see either Barker or Mrs Douglas. I saw no necessity to disturb them; but I was pleased to hear that the lady was not visibly pining and that she had partaken of an excellent dinner. My visit was specially made to the good Mr Ames, with whom I exchanged some amiabilities, which culminated in his allowing me, without reference to anyone else, to sit alone for a time in the study."

"What! With that?" I ejaculated.

"No, no, everything is now in order. You gave permission for that,

Mr Mac, as I am informed. The room was in its normal state, and in it I passed an instructive quarter of an hour."

"What were you doing?"

"Well, not to make a mystery of so simple a matter, I was looking for the missing dumb-bell. It has always bulked rather large in my estimate of the case. I ended by finding it."

"Where?"

"Ah, there we come to the edge of the unexplored. Let me go a little further, a very little further, and I will promise that you shall share everything that I know."

"Well, we're bound to take you on your own terms," said the inspector; "but when it comes to telling us to abandon the case—why in the name of goodness should we abandon the case?"

"For the simple reason, my dear Mr Mac, that you have not got the first idea what it is that you are investigating."

"We are investigating the murder of Mr John Douglas of Birlstone Manor."

"Yes, yes, so you are. But don't trouble to trace the mysterious gentleman upon the bicycle. I assure you that it won't help you."

"Then what do you suggest that we do?"

"I will tell you exactly what to do, if you will do it."

MacDonald grumbled a while. "Well, I'm bound to say I've always found you had reason behind all your queer ways. I'll do what you advise."

"And you, Mr White Mason?"

The country detective looked helplessly from one to the other. Holmes and his methods were new to him. "Well, if it is good enough for the inspector, it is good enough for me," he said at last.

"Capital!" said Holmes. "Well, then, I should recommend a nice, cheery country walk for both of you. They tell me that the views from Birlstone Ridge over the Weald are very remarkable. No doubt lunch could be got at some suitable hostelry; though my ignorance of the country prevents me from recommending one. In the evening, tired but happy—"

"Man, this is getting past a joke!" cried MacDonald, rising angrily from his chair.

"Well, well, spend the day as you like," said Holmes, patting him cheerfully upon the shoulder. "Do what you like and go where you will, but meet me here before dusk without fail—without fail, Mr Mac."

"That sounds more like sanity."

"All of it was excellent advice; but I don't insist, so long as you are here when I need you. But now, before we part, I want you to write a note to Mr Barker."

The inspector failed to mask either his impatience or confusion. "Well?"

"I'll dictate it, if you like. Ready?

"*Dear Sir:—It has struck me that it is our duty to drain the moat, in the hope that we may find some—*"

"It's impossible," said the inspector. "I've made inquiry."

"Tut, tut! My dear sir, please do what I ask you."

"Well, go on."

"*—in the hope that we may find something which may bear upon our investigation. I have made arrangements, and the workmen will be at work early to-morrow morning diverting the stream—*"

"Impossible!"

Holmes ignored the interjection. "*—diverting the stream; so I thought it best to explain matters beforehand.*"

"Now sign that, and send it by hand about four o'clock. At that hour we shall meet again in this room. Until then we may each do what we like; for I can assure you that this inquiry has come to a definite pause."

Evening was drawing in when we reassembled. Holmes was very serious in his manner, myself curious, and the detectives obviously critical and annoyed.

"Well, gentlemen," said my friend gravely, "I am asking you now to put everything to the test with me, and you will judge for yourselves whether the observations I have made justify the conclusions to which I have come. It is a chill evening, and I do not know how long our

expedition may last; so I beg that you will wear your warmest coats. It is of the first importance that we should be in our places before it grows dark; so with your permission we shall get started at once."

We passed along the outer bounds of the Manor House park until we came to a place where there was a gap in the rails which fenced it. Through this we slipped, and then in the gathering gloom we followed Holmes until we had reached a shrubbery which lies nearly opposite to the main door and the steel bridge. The latter had not yet been rolled back, whilst the house sat firmly still upon its footings. Holmes crouched down behind the screen of laurels, and we all three followed his example.

"Well, what are we to do now?" asked MacDonald with some gruffness.

"Possess our souls in patience and make as little noise as possible," Holmes answered.

"What are we here for at all? I really think that you might treat us with more frankness."

Holmes laughed, glancing in my direction. "Watson insists that I am the dramatist in real life," said he. "Some touch of the artist wells up within me, and calls insistently for a well-staged performance. Surely our profession, Mr Mac, would be a drab and sordid one if we did not sometimes set the scene so as to glorify our results. The blunt accusation, the brutal tap upon the shoulder—what can one make of such a *dénouement*? But the quick inference, the subtle trap, the clever forecast of coming events, the triumphant vindication of bold theories—are these not the pride and the justification of our life's work? At the present moment you thrill with the glamour of the situation and the anticipation of the hunt. Where would be that thrill if I had been as definite as a timetable? I only ask a little patience, Mr Mac, and all will be clear to you."

"Well, I hope the pride and justification and the rest of it will come before we all get our death of cold," said the London detective with comic resignation.

We all had good reason to join in the aspiration; for our vigil was a long and bitter one. Slowly the shadows darkened over the long, sombre face of the old house. A cold, damp reek from the moat chilled us to

the bones and set our teeth chattering. There was a single bulb over the gateway and a steady glow in the windows of the fatal study. Everything else was dark and still.

"How long is this to last?" asked the inspector finally. "And what is it we are watching for?"

"I have no more notion than you how long it is to last," Holmes answered with some asperity. "If criminals would always schedule their movements like railway trains, it would certainly be more convenient for all of us. As to what it is we—well, *that's* what we are watching for!"

As he spoke the bright, yellow light in the study was obscured by somebody passing to and fro before it. The laurels among which we lay were immediately opposite the window and not more than a hundred feet from it. Presently it was thrown open with a whining of hinges, and we could dimly see the dark outline of a man's head and shoulders looking out into the gloom. For some minutes he peered forth in furtive, stealthy fashion, as one who wishes to be assured that he is unobserved. Then he leaned forward, and in the intense silence we were aware of the soft lapping of agitated water. He seemed to be stirring up the moat with something which he held in his hand. Then suddenly he hauled something in as a fisherman lands a fish—some large object which obscured the light as it was dragged through the open casement.

"Now!" cried Holmes. "Now!"

We were all upon our feet, staggering after him with our stiffened limbs, while he ran swiftly across the bridge and rang violently at the bell. There was the rasping of bolts from the other side, and the amazed Ames stood in the entrance. Holmes brushed him aside without a word and, followed by all of us, rushed into the room which had been occupied by the man whom we had been watching.

The electric light on the wall represented the glow which we had seen from outside. As we entered its light shone upon the strong, resolute, clean-shaved face and menacing eyes of Cecil Barker.

"What the devil is the meaning of all this?" he cried. "What are you after, anyhow?"

Holmes took a swift glance round, and then pounced upon a sodden bundle tied together with cord which lay where it had been thrust under the writing table.

"This is what we are after, Mr Barker—this bundle, weighted with a dumb-bell, which you have just raised from the bottom of the moat."

Barker stared at Holmes with amazement in his face. "How in thunder came you to know anything about it?" he asked.

"Simply that I put it there."

"You put it there! You!"

"Perhaps I should have said 'replaced it there'," said Holmes. "You will remember, Inspector MacDonald, that I was somewhat struck by the absence of a dumb-bell. I drew your attention to it; but with the pressure of other events you had hardly the time to give it the consideration which would have enabled you to draw deductions from it. When water is near and a weight is missing it is not a very far-fetched supposition that something has been sunk in the water. The idea was at least worth testing; so with the help of Ames, who admitted me to the room, and the crook of Dr Watson's umbrella, I was able last night to fish up and inspect this bundle.

"It was of the first importance, however, that we should be able to prove who placed it there. This we accomplished by the very obvious device of announcing that the moat would be dried tomorrow, which had, of course, the effect that whoever had hidden the bundle would most certainly withdraw it the moment that darkness enabled him to do so. We have no less than four witnesses as to whom it was who took advantage of the opportunity, and so, Mr Barker, I think the word lies now with you."

Sherlock Holmes put the sopping bundle upon the table beside the lamp and undid the cord which bound it. From within he extracted a dumb-bell, which he tossed down to its fellow in the corner. Next he drew forth a pair of boots. Then he laid upon the table a long, deadly, sheathed knife and a strange device which looked for all the world like a miniature harpoon such as is commonplace in the world's whaling fleets—save

this was a mere eighteen inches in length, with a pistol-grip and trigger. Finally he unravelled a bundle of clothing, comprising a complete set of underclothes, socks, a grey tweed suit, and a short yellow overcoat.

"The clothes are commonplace," remarked Holmes, "save only the overcoat, which is full of suggestive touches." He held it tenderly towards the light. "Here, as you perceive, is the inner pocket prolonged into the lining in such fashion as to give ample space for our strange spear-gun. The tailor's tab is on the neck—Neal, Outfitter, *Vale de Verme*, SLC. I have spent an instructive afternoon in the rector's library, and have enlarged my knowledge by adding the fact that *Vale de Verme* is now the generally accepted, though unofficial, term for an area to the south of the *Mare Nubium*—the site of the original lunar landing—in which the first mining colony on the Moon was established. SLC stands, of course, for the South Lunar Company. I have some recollection, Mr Barker, that you associated the mining districts with Mr Douglas's first wife; it was an error on all our parts to assume the mining was done here on Earth. It would surely not be too far-fetched an inference that the *VV* upon the card by the dead body might stand for *Vale de Verme*, or that this very valley which sends forth emissaries of murder may be that Valley of Fear of which we have heard. So much is fairly clear. And now, Mr Barker, I seem to be standing rather in the way of your explanation."

It was a sight to see Cecil Barker's expressive face during this exposition of the great detective. Anger, amazement, consternation, and indecision swept over it in turn. Finally he took refuge in a somewhat acrid irony.

"You know such a lot, Mr Holmes, perhaps you had better tell us some more," he sneered.

My friend smiled with little humour. "I have no doubt that I could tell you a great deal more, Mr Barker; but it would come with a better grace from you."

"Oh, you think so, do you? Well, all I can say is that if there's any secret here it is not my secret, and I am not the man to give it away."

"Well, if you take that line, Mr Barker," said the inspector quietly, "we must just keep you in sight until we have the warrant and can hold you."

"You can do what you damn please about that," said Barker defiantly.

The proceedings seemed to have come to a definite end so far as he was concerned; for one had only to look at that granite face to realize that no *peine forte et dure* would ever force him to plead against his will. The deadlock was broken, however, by a woman's voice. Mrs Douglas had been standing listening at the half opened door, unnoticed, and now she entered the room.

"You have done enough for now, Cecil," said she. "Whatever comes of it in the future, you have done enough."

"Enough and more than enough," remarked Sherlock Holmes gravely. "I have every sympathy with you, madam, and should strongly urge you to have some confidence in the common sense of our jurisdiction and to take the police voluntarily into your complete confidence. It may be that I am myself at fault for not following up the hint which you conveyed to me through my friend, Dr Watson; but, at that time I had every reason to believe that you were directly concerned in the crime. Now I am assured that this is not so. At the same time, there is much that is unexplained, and I should strongly recommend that you ask *Mr Douglas* to tell us his own story."

Mrs Douglas gave a cry of astonishment at Holmes's words. The detectives and I must have echoed it, when we were aware of a man who seemed to have emerged from the wall, who advanced now from the gloom of the corner in which he had appeared. Mrs Douglas turned, and in an instant her arms were round him. Barker had seized his outstretched hand.

"It's best this way, Jack," his wife repeated; "I am sure that it is best."

"Indeed, yes, Mr Douglas," said Sherlock Holmes, "I am sure that you will find it best."

The man stood blinking at us with the dazed look of one who comes from the dark into the light. It was a remarkable face, bold grey eyes, a strong, short-clipped, grizzled moustache, a square, projecting chin, and a humorous mouth—all surmounted by an uncombed mane of pure white hair. He took a good look at us all, and then to my amazement he advanced to me and handed me a bundle of paper.

"I've heard of you," said he in a voice which was not quite English and not quite American, but was altogether mellow and pleasing. "You are the historian of this bunch. Well, Dr Watson, you've never had such a story as that pass through your hands before, and I'll lay my last dollar on that. Tell it your own way; but there are the facts, and you can't miss the public so long as you have those. I've been cooped up two days, and I've spent the daylight hours—as much daylight as I could get in that noisy rat trap—in putting the thing into words. You're welcome to them—you and your public. There's the story of the Valley of Fear."

"That's the past, Mr Douglas," said Sherlock Holmes quietly. "What we desire now is to hear your story of the present."

"You'll have it, sir," said Douglas. "May I smoke as I talk? Well, thank you, Mr Holmes. You're a smoker yourself, if I remember right, and you'll guess what it is to be sitting for two days with tobacco in your pocket and afraid that the smell will give you away." He leaned against the mantelpiece and sucked at the cigar which Holmes had handed him. "I've heard of you, Mr Holmes. I never guessed that I should meet you. But before you are through with that," he nodded at my papers, "you will say I've brought you something fresh."

Inspector MacDonald had been staring at the newcomer with the greatest amazement. "Well, this fairly beats me!" he cried at last. "If you are Mr John Douglas of Birlstone Manor, then whose death have we been investigating for these two days, and where in the world have you sprung from now? You seemed to me to come out of the floor like a jack-in-a-box."

"Ah, Mr Mac," said Holmes, shaking a reproving forefinger, "you would not read that excellent local compilation which described the concealment of King Charles. People did not hide in those days without excellent hiding places, and the hiding place that has once been used may be again. I had persuaded myself that we should find Mr Douglas under this roof."

"And how long have you been playing this trick upon us, Mr Holmes?" said the inspector angrily. "How long have you allowed us to waste ourselves upon a search that you knew to be an absurd one?"

"Not one instant, my dear Mr Mac. Only last night did I form my views of the case. As they could not be put to the proof until this evening, I invited you and your colleague to take a holiday for the day. Pray what more could I do? When I found the suit of clothes in the moat, it at once became apparent to me that the body we had found could not have been the body of Mr John Douglas at all, but must be that of the bicyclist from Tunbridge Wells. No other conclusion was possible. Therefore I had to determine where Mr John Douglas himself could be, and the balance of probability was that with the connivance of his wife and his friend he was concealed in a house which had such conveniences for a fugitive, and awaiting quieter times when he could make his final escape."

"Well, you figured it out about right," said Douglas approvingly. "I thought I'd dodge your British law; for I was not sure how I stood under it, and also I saw my chance to throw these hounds once for all off my track. Mind you, from first to last I have done nothing to be ashamed of, and nothing that I would not do again; but you'll judge that for yourselves when I tell you my story. Never mind warning me, Inspector: I'm ready to stand pat upon the truth.

"I'm not going to begin at the beginning. That's all there," he indicated my bundle of papers, "and a mighty queer yarn you'll find it. It all comes down to this: That there are some men that have good cause to hate me and would give their last dollar to know that they had got me. So long as I am alive and they are alive, there is no safety in this world for me. They hunted me from the Moon to Chicago to California, then they chased me out of America; but when I married and settled down in this quiet spot I thought my last years were going to be peaceable—"

"The Moon!" exclaimed MacDonald. "Our Moon?"

Holmes flicked an impatient hand. "Mr Mac, I have already remarked to Dr Watson that the white hair is most suggestive: an unnatural white; the unfortunate side-effect of the journey to the Moon. Afflicting even the bravest of men." He indicated the extraordinary harpoon device. "And that, unless I am very much mistaken, is a pneumatic grappler of a kind common in our lunar mining colonies. It is, I understand, a very

adaptable tool, with many usages." He glanced at Douglas, his expressed enigmatic.

"You're right, Mr Holmes. Scowrers we called them." He smiled bleakly at some private joke. "No matter the fix, your scowrer will set you right. But I digress—" He paused a moment, sucking on his cigar like a starving man.

"I never explained to my wife how things were. Why should I pull her into it? She would never have a quiet moment again; but would always be imagining trouble. I fancy she knew something, for I may have dropped a word here or a word there; but until yesterday, after you gentlemen had seen her, she never knew the rights of the matter. She told you all she knew, and so did Barker here; for on the night when this thing happened there was mighty little time for explanations. She knows everything now, and I would have been a wiser man if I had told her sooner. But it was a hard question, dear—" he took her hand for an instant in his own, "—and I acted for the best.

"Well, gentlemen, the day before these happenings I was over in Tunbridge Wells, and I got a glimpse of a man in the street. It was only a glimpse; but I have a quick eye for these things, and I never doubted who it was. It was the worst enemy I had among them all—one who has been after me like a hungry wolf after a caribou all these years. I knew there was trouble coming, and I came home and made ready for it. I guessed I'd fight through it all right on my own, my luck was a proverb in the States about '77. I never doubted that it would be with me still.

"I was on my guard all that next day, and never went out into the park. It's as well, or he'd have had the drop on me with that scowrer of his before ever I could draw on him. After the bridge was rolled up—my mind was always more restful when that bridge was back and the house up on its stilts in the evenings—I put the thing clear out of my head. I never dreamed of his getting into the house and waiting for me. But when I made my round in my dressing gown, as was my habit, I had no sooner entered the study than I scented danger. I guess when a man has had dangers in his life—and I've had more than most in my time—there

is a kind of sixth sense that waves the red flag. I saw the signal clear enough, and yet I couldn't tell you why. Next instant I spotted a boot under the window curtain, and then I saw why plain enough.

"You'll have seen the Westinghouse-Tesla tower out back. It's pretty fair most of the time, but we're a ways from the city, and sometimes the power beams falter, so I've gotten into the habit of carrying a lighted candle on my rounds—just in case. The study lights were off, but there was a good light from the hall lights through the open door. I put down the candle and jumped for a hammer that I'd left on the mantel. At the same moment he sprang at me. I saw the glint of a knife, and I lashed at him with the hammer. I got him somewhere; for the knife tinkled down on the floor. He dodged round the table as quick as an eel, and a moment later he'd got his scowrer from under his coat. I heard him prime it; but I had got hold of it before he could fire. I had it by the barrel, and we wrestled for it all ends up for a minute or more. It was death to the man that lost his grip.

"He never lost his grip; but he got it butt downward for a moment too long. Maybe it was I that pulled the trigger. Maybe we just jolted it off between us. Anyhow, he got the business end of the clawed spike in the face, the mooring blade gone clean through his brain, and there I was, staring down at all that was left of Ted Baldwin. I'd recognized him in the township, and again when he sprang for me; but his own mother wouldn't recognize him as I saw him then. I'm used to rough work; but I fairly turned sick at the sight of him."

He threw the remains of his cigar in the open grate. "The pneumatics on those grapplers isn't too powerful—meant as they are for use in lesser gravity—but at that range it hardly mattered. Baldwin was dead as a man can be.

"I was hanging on the side of the table when Barker came hurrying down—a scowrer's pretty quiet when you trigger it: just a pop of air—but he'd heard it nonetheless. I heard my wife coming, and I ran to the door and stopped her. It was no sight for a woman. I promised I'd come to her soon. I said a word or two to Barker—he took it all in at a glance—and we waited for the rest to come along. But there was no sign of them.

Then we understood that they could have heard nothing after, and that all that had happened was known only to ourselves.

"It was at that instant that the idea came to me. I was fairly dazzled by the brilliance of it. The man's sleeve had slipped up and there was the branded mark of the lodge upon his forearm. See here!"

The man whom we now knew as Douglas turned up his own coat and cuff to show a brown triangle within a circle exactly like that which we had seen upon the dead man.

"It was the sight of that which started me on it. I seemed to see it all clear at a glance. There were his height and hair and figure, about the same as my own. No one could swear to his face, poor devil—but we had to disguise the scowrer's mark. I brought down this suit of clothes and a shotgun I'd brought with me from the States and kept hidden. Barker baulked when he saw my intention, and I'm not ashamed to admit the thought left me sick—but it had to be done! Wiring both triggers of the shotgun, I pressed the barrel right up against Baldwin's face and fired—" His voice choked off.

"Efficiently obliterating the wounds caused by his … scowrer," Holmes spoke quietly into the silence.

Douglas took a deep breath. "Exactly. In a quarter of an hour Barker and I had put my dressing gown on him and he lay as you found him. We tied all his things into a bundle, and I weighted them with the best I could find—scowrers are mostly aluminium and not so hefty, as you can see— and put them through the window. The card he had meant to lay upon my body was lying beside his own.

"My rings were put on his finger; but when it came to the wedding ring," he held out his muscular hand, "you can see for yourselves that I had struck the limit. I have not moved it since the day I was married, and it would have taken a file to get it off. I don't know, anyhow, that I should have cared to part with it; but if I had wanted to I couldn't. So we just had to leave that detail to take care of itself. On the other hand, I brought a bit of plaster down and put it where I am wearing one myself at this instant. You slipped up there, Mr Holmes, clever as you are; for

if you had chanced to take off that plaster you would have found no cut underneath it."

Holmes muttered a sotto voce "Ha!" and waved his hand in dismissal. My friend never enjoys it when he misses a point, no matter how subtle; less so when it is alluded to by another.

"Well, that was the situation. If I could lie low for a while and then get away where I could be joined by my 'widow' we should have a chance at last of living in peace for the rest of our lives. These devils would give me no rest so long as I was above ground; but if they saw in the papers that Baldwin had got his man, there would be an end of all my troubles. I hadn't much time to make it all clear to Barker and to my wife; but they understood enough to be able to help me."

"And so you took refuge in an old priest hole," said Holmes. "Quite remarkable."

"More than that, Mr Holmes. When I had this old place refitted with all the machinery I kept all the bolt-holes—I guess you heard how the locals approved me resurrecting and maintaining the old traditions: like the rebuilt bridge across the moat. I found three in all, and used them as unobtrusive access to the machine room down below. I knew all about this hiding place, so did Ames; but it never entered his head to connect it with the matter. I retired into it—to wait amid the pumps, boilers, elevators and transformers—and it was up to Barker to do the rest.

"I guess you can fill in for yourselves what he did. He opened the window and made the mark on the sill to give an idea of how the murderer escaped. It was a tall order, that; but as the bridge was rolled up there was no other way. Then, when everything was fixed, he rang the bell for all he was worth. What happened afterward you know. And so, gentlemen, you can do what you please; but I've told you the truth and the whole truth, so help me God! What I ask you now is how do I stand by the English law?"

There was a silence which was broken by Sherlock Holmes.

"The English law is in the main a just law. You will get no worse than your deserts from that, Mr Douglas. But I would ask you how did this

man know that you lived here, or how to get into your house, or where to hide to get you?"

"I know nothing of this."

Holmes's face was very white and grave. "The story is not over yet, I fear," said he. "You may find worse dangers than the English law, or even than your enemies from America. I see trouble before you, Mr Douglas. You'll take my advice and still be on your guard."

VIII. A Chase

At Holmes' insistence we awaited the dawn before leaving Birlstone
Manor; and Mrs Allen would not let any of us leave without
breakfasting to some degree. Indeed, Mrs Douglas had to be firm with
the kindly housekeeper who was determined to ply us all with a full meal.
Reluctantly, she agreed to pack some sandwiches for us—but would not
be swayed over the provision of strong tea and coffee. Finally, refreshed
if unshaven, we quit the manor grounds and headed towards the town's
small railway station. Douglas submitted himself fully to the custody of
Inspector MacDonald, whilst his determined wife—after many stubborn
words—was allowed to accompany us. I admit to feeling a little wretched
when I thought back over my immediate reactions to her, and how I had
considered her in any way complicit in her husband's murder. She was,
I now realised, an admirable woman: a credit to her fair sex, unswayable
when in the right, and a staunch companion. Douglas was indeed the most
fortunate of men. Barker also demanded to be allowed to accompany his
friend, and none of us felt able to deny this forceful man.

Only on one point did the American and inspector disagree: Douglas
insisted on carrying a large pistol—a repeater from his native shores—
which carried its ammunition in a vertical box magazine attached just
before the trigger guard. The guard itself formed part of a lever which
cocked and armed the weapon—rather in the manner of a Winchester
rifle—and altogether it seemed to me a bulky and unmanageable firearm;
if not for a tailored pocket inside his coat, he would have been reduced to
carrying it in his hand. MacDonald was, quite understandably, disinclined
to allow a man—who was for all purposes his prisoner—to be armed, but
after Holmes intervened, Douglas was allowed to retain the cannon.

"After all, Mr Mac," said Holmes, "are either you or Mr White Mason armed? Is Mr Barker? I know that neither Watson nor myself are."

The inspector's great brows drew down. "Armed? Man, are you saying we should be?"

My friend's expression was neutral, but I fancy I detected the faintest edge of unease about his eyes. "I trust that I am wrong, inspector—but it may be that Douglas's pistol will be of use to us before we reach London."

The railway station was a little under half a mile outside the tiny village. As we made our way towards it we encountered no other souls—shopkeepers yet abed, farmworkers in their fields well before first light—and perhaps it was as well. Six men and one woman, taking a stroll through the Surrey countryside at such an hour might engender more questions that we would comfortably answer. Douglas and his wife walked together, conferring intermittently and in low tones; Holmes, MacDonald, Barker, White Mason and I flanked them—yet not so close that we might eavesdrop on their desultory conversation. I believe none of us thought there was anything man or wife could say to our interest at this stage—and much it would be imprudent to overhear.

The station was deserted on our arrival. As we filed into the ticket-office, Holmes raised a commanding hand, holding us back as he walked through and thoroughly scrutinised the platform. Then a cursory gesture summoned us forward.

"I see there are seventeen minutes before the arrival of our train," spoke Holmes, gesturing at the wall-mounted timetable. "Perhaps, Mr Mac, it would be wise to have Mr and Mrs Douglas wait inside the stationmaster's office until then."

"What?" snapped Barker. "Is the man to be detained already?"

Holmes shook his head. "Precautions, Mr Barker. Your friend has invested too much time and effort in maintaining his invisibility to squander the advantage."

Douglas took Barker's shoulder. "Let it go, Cecil," said he softly. "He has the right of it: it's too soon to be dropping my guard."

Barker harrumphed loudly, but allowed MacDonald to usher the

Douglases into the stationmaster's cramped office, where at least they would have a cosy fire. Then White Mason, Barker, Holmes and I stood on the draughty platform, huddled into our coats; it looked as though it would be another sunny day—albeit a cold one. Holmes alone appeared unaffected by the weather; having lit one of his cannabis cigarettes while he waited.

"We must be alert," said he.

White Mason's cheerful expression never changed. "You're expecting trouble?"

"But why?" Barker drew up his collar and tugged at his hat-brim. "Baldwin is dead; the message sent out—"

Holmes grinned a skeletal smile. "Mr Barker, I believe we are dealing with men of the most mistrustful character. Suspicion is a way of life: of outsiders and most insidiously, of each other." He threw his finished cigarette towards the railway line below us. "Do you think that they would be content with something so simple as a note left with a body? It smacks of the melodramatic and has limited practicality. What if the note were lost, or overlooked? If some rustic bobby—and I mean no offence, Mr White Mason—trampled it to the floor, or tossed it aside, assuming it to be nothing? Or if it were simply not reported: an irrelevance carelessly annotated, and instantly dismissed from memory? How then would word get back?"

A tethered aerostat whined by overhead. We paused until the high-pitched drone conducted by the tethering cables dimmed; I took the time to collect my thoughts before speaking.

"The note was merely symbolic. A gesture. Baldwin—" and I found myself looking around the otherwise empty railway station uneasily "—would be expected to rendezvous with others of his kind."

"Hah! You have the gist of it, Watson! Once Baldwin had done his work he would flee—quite possibly by the very route you, Barker, suggested with your crude theatricals—"

A black scowl disfigured Barker's heavy face.

"—then he must meet up with a confederate at a time and a place

pre-agreed upon, to report success. Only then would these hard, twisted minds accept Douglas's death. I'm afraid all of your friend's clever improvisations may only have delayed the inevitable, Barker. As with the Hydra of myth—cut off one head, another two will replace it!"

Barker appeared abruptly shrunken: his hard-eyed bravado punctured. "Then what must we do, Mr Holmes?"

"We are ahead in the game—by how much I know not—but that is our one advantage. Once Douglas is in London, and under the aegis of Scotland Yard, I believe our man will be safe enough."

We had been joined on the platform by more travellers. A pretty young woman who, to judge by her dress, was a member of the professional class; two men in shapeless overcoats and equally formless hats who looked like labourers or farm workers; and three more scarcely out of boyhood in sharp, modern suits—talking in excited, staccato voices and smoking endless cigarettes. From the distance came the shriek of a locomotive whistle, made sharp and brilliant by the cold air. Everyone except the labourers grew expectant at the sound: obviously through experience or knowledge of the timetable they had judged their arrival more expertly than our own.

White Mason consulted his watch—a huge sphere of a timepiece— and grunted with satisfaction. "Perfectly on time. Shall I fetch Mr MacDonald and the Douglases?"

Holmes laid a restraining hand on his wrist. "Allow me, detective. Do you all board the train when it arrives and secure us a compartment. I shall join you presently." With that he left us on the platform and vanished inside the stationmaster's office.

The train arrived at the station, pulled I noted by one of the new compact turbine-electric locomotives; although only an 0-4-0+0-4-0, it was so much more efficient than the huge Reid-Ramsey prototypes from which all subsequent working locomotives derived. Its sleek, modern lines were in sharp contrast to the rake of ageing, clerestory-roofed carriages it hauled, and I wondered to what degree the designer had been influenced by the freight and passenger balloons which had become the railways' greatest competitor.

Barker quickly found an empty first-class compartment. White Mason and he settled themselves down whilst I stood by the door, looking towards the stationmaster's office and wondering where the deuce Holmes was. If they did not hurry he, MacDonald and the Douglases would miss the train entirely. The two labourers had made no effort to board the train: either meeting a passenger or awaiting some item of luggage, I assumed.

The guard blew his whistle, and Holmes was still nowhere to be seen. The carriage shuddered as the locomotive began to pull on its load, the only sound being the hiss of leaking steam. Barker was at my side—equally alarmed by events.

"Where are they?" he cried. "Has there been—?"

The office door flew wide; Holmes, the inspector and his charges appeared through it and sprinted across the narrow space of platform. Holmes tore the compartment door open and all four tumbled in—my friend last of all. He slammed the door shut behind him and laughed in what I considered an inappropriate delight.

"Most exhilarating! You must recommend such early-morning pursuits to your patients, Watson!"

"What was the meaning for such a display?" demanded Barker. He stood aside to allow Mrs Douglas to sit herself; her beautiful face was pale, but two bright spots burned high on her cheeks. Her husband seemed perplexed, whilst MacDonald stood gasping for breath. Holmes dropped open the window and looked towards the receding railway station before stepping back and pulling the window shut again.

"We have the drop on them, as you Americans say. I doubt they will be caught so easily a second time."

"Holmes," said I, "some kind of explanation, if you would be so kind?"

He laughed again, in high spirits after his sudden, violent exertion. "My apologies, friend Watson—I had no opportunity to acquaint you with my likely actions; and there were too many ears to hear, besides. Let us all sit and recover ourselves." We joined Mrs Douglas and White Mason, Holmes sliding the window tightly shut.

Taking out his pipe, my friend packed it with tobacco and began

to smoke in silence. Since it was obvious there would be no speedy explanation, I offered my own cigarettes—Douglas and MacDonald gratefully took one each—and we all waited on Holmes. The air of the compartment grew quite thick—thanks mostly to Holmes' ghastly tobacco which even the clerestory louvres failed to ventilate—and Mrs Douglas opened the window to allow the miasma to exit. Ashamed by the tacit rebuke, I extinguished my own half-smoked Bird's Eye, as did Douglas and the inspector; Holmes, however, puffed on oblivious, as he marshalled his thoughts before revealing them *a capite ad calcem*.

Eventually, he spoke. "You will, of course, have observed our fellow travellers on the platform this morning: the young lady Teslagraph operator, the labourers, and the three shop assistants out for a day in London to celebrate a birthday."

MacDonald winked in my direction with a laugh. "Ay, Mr Holmes—we all saw six other people waiting for the train."

"On the contrary, Mr Mac, you saw four awaiting this train—and two for Mr Douglas."

White Mason's broad face widened further with delight. "I'd be honoured if you'd share your reasoning with us, Mr Holmes."

My friend bowed his head at the compliment, taking full delight in it. He used the stem of his pipe to highlight his several points. "The girl removed her thick winter gloves for a few moments, to place a ticket in her reticule. I observed the mild spatulation on the fingertips of her right hand— an indication that she habitually depresses typing keys with that hand—but none on the left. However, there was a small burn across the back of that hand—a long and narrow cicatrice which might be caused by a hot wire. Hence she is not a typewritist—else both sets of fingertips would be broadened; Teslagraph operators have a small array of keys to tap, one-handed, whilst the small burn is typical of an occupational hazard amongst those new to the job: many Teslagraphs are often badly-earthed."

"Marvellous, Mr Holmes, marvellous." White Mason was clearly delighted; whilst I was pleased not to be cast in the role of Holmes' foil.

"And I suppose you deduced the shop-boys by the ink under their nails?"

Holmes threw his head back and barked a short laugh. "Capital! You see, Watson, the dangers of your romanticised fictions? I am cast forever as a Dupin who may fathom a person's role and motives from the creases in their trousers! Not at all, Mr White Mason, not at all. They were talking loudly enough for all to hear; I merely listened…"

It was my turn to smile. "Which leaves the labourers—who are, I imagine, anything but that?"

"They are certainly men used to the most gruelling of heavy labour, Watson. Life has beaten all softness from their flesh and hearts. But not in the fields that we know, I'll hazard. Their coats were big and shapeless, but not bulky enough to disguise the presence of the objects carried underneath, in poachers' pockets. Objects which by their dimensions suggested themselves to be more of your scowrers, Mr Douglas."

The American did not seem surprised: his reaction was muted. "My enemies are legion, Mr Holmes," said he with a trace of bitterness.

"In addition," continued Holmes, "even though their unsightly hats were jammed hard over their heads, I could still perceive tufts of badly-dyed hair. Hair which under the inexpertly smeared boot-blacking is as white as your own, Mr Douglas."

Barker leaned forward. "More of the dead Baldwin's stamp?"

"Precisely that. They have been awaiting word from their dead comrade—or a direct confirmation that Douglas is no more—I apologize for my directness, Mrs Douglas."

The admirable woman drew herself up, taking her husband's arm. "Not at all, Mr Holmes. I am grateful that you are so forthright."

He bowed his head. "Receiving neither word nor rendezvous they reasoned that Douglas lived still and would soon be fleeing Birlstone—most likely by train. And so—" here he paused again, his pale lips twitching "—they staked out the railway station. I believe that is the appropriate colloquialism, is it not? However, they arrived late on our heels, by which time Mr Mac had Mr and Mrs Douglas out of sight in the stationmaster's office. They could not be sure which train their prey

might take but would, I am sure was the plan, board it the very moment they saw him embarking; and then finish what the wretched Baldwin had so obviously failed to do. Again, Mrs Douglas—"

She waved his apology aside.

"—by delaying as long as possible—until the train was already in motion—we caught them by surprise."

"So?" Mrs Douglas's eyes were liquid with hope. "We have escaped them?"

"For now, madam." Holmes glanced out of the compartment window; I realised he was watching the supports of the tethered aerostat lines as they flicked past. The humour passed instantly, and he reached for one of the paper-wrapped bundles Birlstone Manor's insistent housekeeper had pressed upon us. "However, let us now see what the estimable Mrs Allen has provided for our breakfast."

It was a crude repast: thickly-cut slices of bread smeared with salty butter and wrapped around lumps of sharp local cheese, some eggs the housekeeper had somehow found time to hard-boil, and slabs of pork pie. Nevertheless it was quite delicious; I had quite forgotten my hunger until the first bite—and then I fell upon the meal with a gluttonous appetite. In addition, a large sweet, crisp apple had been packed for each of us—no doubt from a store laid up for the winter months—which complemented the cheese perfectly. Holmes did the simple meal full justice; whilst our two policemen chewed on stoically with the detachment of those used to eating at irregular hours, and often poorly. Mrs Douglas picked at her own, taking bird-sized pecks from her apple whilst ignoring the rest; her husband gave all the appearance of a man forcing down damp wallpaper; and Barker tore his food to shreds as though offended by its rustic simplicity.

Once we were done, Holmes consulted his watch. "They will be coming soon, Watson," said he quietly, "and we are ill-prepared. Oh, for the gift of foresight—then should we have left London armed and ready!"

"How will they reach us?" I asked. "Even should they in some wise

steal a train or locomotive, short of ramming this one and risking all on board, they could not stop us."

He laughed—though there was little humour in it. "In truth, my friend, I would not consider such actions beyond them. They are past subtlety; their only goal now is success—at any price! But no: they have another course—and one that will be no real challenge for whatever skills they may have acquired on the Moon—"

The train shuddered into motionlessness and Holmes leapt for the door. Flinging it wide he stepped down onto a brief platform: the station—nameless as far as I could see—was little more than a halt. Seated as I was by the opened doorway, I could see exactly as did Holmes: no one either alighted or boarded. Moments later the locomotive sounded a shrill whistle and I stepped aside for Holmes to re-enter our compartment—though he leaned his thin frame through the window for many seconds, until the anonymous station was accelerating to the rear. Eventually satisfied upon some point, he extricated himself from the window frame and slid the glass up. Beckoning me closer, he lowered his voice to a more conspiratorial tone.

"That was the last stop before London. We might expect our enemies soon." He indicated the aerostat line running above us. "Pressed—taken to the fullest limit of its speed—I believe one of those aerial freighters might overtake us."

I thought quickly. My experience of aerostats was limited to the larger species, and that the military kind. I understood that vessels such as the ill-fated *HMAS Keane* are capable of speeds in excess of seventy knots—though the full details are understandably kept secret by the government—whilst most aerial liners are content to cruise somewhere around the fifty mark. I could conceive of no reason why a tethered aerostat—its electric engines given full rein—should not match those performances. Only the restrictions placed on the machines by railway and canal companies preventing them from rocketing along their restraining cables at previously unheard of speed.

"Holmes—one could outpace this train, I'm sure. Particularly if any loaded freight were to be dumped…"

"Your thoughts accord with mine." He tapped a window, his fingers rapping out a staccato drumroll. Then he fell back against his seat, his lips quirking; his eyes twinkling with sudden mischief. "Well, we still have a lengthy journey before us," he said aloud, addressing the compartment in general, "and little to divert us beyond the English countryside in winter; therefore I feel it is time that I acquainted you with the true facts behind my good friend's melodramatic account of our recent cases. I have a fancy to one day set them down myself, recording the definitive interpretation of events—free of sentiment and emotional detour. To that end I must stimulate the muscles of a raconteur."

In all the years I have known Holmes, it would be fair to say I have never known him to be comfortable in the role of conversationalist: only when expounding on his deductions—and enjoying the fruits of his singular brain—was he anything but brusque or to the point. That morning, however, he had his small audience captive: contrasting my own—oft criticised—narrative style against what he considered the more authentic voice of the dealer in facts. Like a polished university lecturer he presented his case, assembled his facts and drew his conclusions, without once lapsing into pedantry; he even provoked an occasional smile or appreciative chuckle. In all, a praiseworthy performance; I only regret I was unable to record it verbatim—for I believe many have come to see my friend as a dry stick, with no room for frivolity in his difference engine of a heart. But I was occupied, surreptitiously watching out for our pursuers, as Holmes knew I would, whilst he distracted them.

I spotted the gaining aerostat easily: outlined against a clear sky, its rigid, mantle glinted in the winter Sun. The reception aerials by which it received its transmitted power were swept back at rakish angles—four in all; two on the dorsal surface, two on the ventral—providing it with a vaguely piscine appearance. It was still riding at regulation height as far as I could judge; but I knew the winches of these aerial freighters were capable of grounding a behemoth such as this in two minutes or less:

speed and efficiency were the currency by which the several companies who owned the tethered air fleets thrived or perished.

I glanced towards Holmes. He interpreted my glance in a second and acknowledged with a terse nod. Then his speech became quick and urgent as he explained to all what was happening. Mrs Douglas's emotions betrayed her for an unguarded second, as hands fluttered at her throat; but moments later she was controlled again. Douglas leaned forward to touch her cheek, and bravely she returned his reassuring smile; then he joined Holmes and me at the window. Barker and the two policemen stood close by.

As we watched, with a sickening sense of helplessness, the tethered aerostat overtook the train—its anchoring cables taut and straining against the dirigible's velocity. MacDonald and White Mason grasped the situation with admirable dexterity.

"They will try to halt the locomotive in some way," said the CID man. "Once motionless, we shall be helpless!"

"Calm yourself, Mr Mac," cautioned Holmes. "They can do nothing to the engine itself— unless these infernal scowrers are more deadly than I credit them to be…"

Douglas shook his head. "They might be used to intimidate; but at the range those jaspers must use them—and under the Earth's gravity—it would be a lucky shot indeed to do more than bounce ineffectually off the locomotive."

"And if I were one of the crew," I added, "I should be inclined to open the throttle if someone in an aerostat should begin waving any kind of weapon at me."

As if it had merely awaited my word, the train surged forward, flinging us all temporarily off balance. Holmes' expression was one of wry amusement.

"And now friend Watson adds clairvoyance to his legion of talents."

Douglas had produced the large repeating pistol. He cocked it by means of the trigger-guard lever. "Let me take a crack at them," he growled. "Those pneumatic claws are no match for honest iron!"

"You anticipate my thoughts, Mr Douglas." Holmes glanced up at the carriage's ceiling. "But we will need a much more advantageous spot from which to take pot-shots…"

"You can't mean the roof, Holmes?" I cried.

"Can I not? Where else do you propose? You are the army man, Watson—advise me…"

I had to acknowledge he was correct. But whoever took to the unsteady roof would not only be placing themselves at risk of being thrown to the racing ground below, but also provide an easy target for the desperate creatures in the stolen aerostat. "And what if they are armed with something more deadly than scowrers?"

But even as Holmes and I stood and debated, Douglas was already at the door. He swung it open, stepped down onto the footboard and—clinging against the horizontal grab irons which lay outside each carriage window—he edged himself towards the carriage-end. In moments he was gone.

MacDonald was all for following him, but Holmes held him back. "It is not for Scotland Yard's finest to go climbing around the roofs of first-class carriages. Nor you, Mr White Mason—nor indeed Mr Barker—" Douglas's friend looked about to protest loudly at that, but Holmes quelled him with a look. "I flatter myself that I retain a certain alacrity which will prove adequate to gaining the roof; whilst Watson here is as sure-footed as a mountain goat—"

I confess that news came as a surprise to me.

"—I cannot allow any of you to risk your lives—"

"Whilst he can apparently risk mine with little regard…," I could not help but interject.

"Ha! Again your bristly humour impales me! Come, Watson—you know you would never forgive me going it alone. *Audentes fortuna iuvat!*" And with that he too swung himself out of the gaping door and was lost to sight.

White Mason was rubbing his chin. "I have always imagined Mr Holmes to be a stolid, reasoning individual," said he, "but he has quite the impetuous streak."

"Ay—he exists to confound us," said MacDonald with a wry smile. I silently agreed.

"Watch over Mrs Douglas and Barker," said I, quietly. "If the three of us—well, let us say we do not prevail, those men might not be content with just Douglas. I fancy they would silence us all."

MacDonald nodded. "Understood, doctor. Take care yourself, now…"

With understandable trepidation, I approached the open door. It swung gently—propelled by the sway of the moving carriage. Clinging to the window strap with my left hand and the door frame with my right, I felt for the footboard which ran the length of the carriage with the toe of my boot. With both feet firmly on the wide step I released the strap and held onto the frame with both hands then, wishing I was once more the young medical officer who had taken command of a burning aerostat simply because he was too unseasoned to appreciate the risks, I let go with my right hand. Shuffling along the footboard towards the carriage rear, holding dearly onto each set of grab irons at each window I passed—often meeting the startled face of a fellow passenger—I eventually reached the end of the carriage. My right hand closed upon a rail which curved up to the roof. Clinging to it desperately, I let go of the last grab iron, shuffled the last few inches—with my eyes shut, I believe!—and swung myself flat against the rocking carriage's end.

There were two sets of basic iron steps—four in each—which began above a buffer and met near the apex of the roof. Each set was accompanied by a separate handrail. Should the carriage be stationary, accessing the roof would be simplicity itself; now, it would be a foolhardy—or desperate—individual indeed who attempted it. As two such individuals had preceded me, I could be no less reckless. Holding the rail in both hands, I took the steps carefully, being certain each foot was firmly placed before raising the other. I daresay the ascent took less than a minute; at the time it felt more like a lifetime.

I pulled myself flat onto the roof. Holmes and Douglas had seated themselves comfortably on the raised clerestory; if the American did

not hold a raised pistol, they would have been the sedate image of two gentlemen taking a moment of ease. As I pulled myself flat onto the carriage roof, Holmes glanced at me, grinning fiercely.

"Is this not revitalising, Watson? I envy our forebears who rode the rails in open waggons, enjoying the elements!"

I scuttled to his side in the most undignified manner. "Perhaps on that point we may agree to differ," I gasped, sitting myself on the clerestory. I am not ashamed to admit my breathing was as ragged as my heartbeat; I mopped my brow with a handkerchief.

"Stout Watson! Breathe deeply, my dear fellow, for our work is upon us." He indicated the aerostat cable—and the sleek construct which loomed overhead, pacing our train easily. Already it had begun to lower itself down its restraining cables. In the pilot's gondola, positioned amidships on the ventral surface, I could clearly see frantic activity: an access hatch hanging open, an indistinct figure framed within.

"They must wait for the ship to be as low in the air as possible," cried Douglas. The barrel of his huge pistol seemed attached to the dirigible by invisible cords, so steady was his aim. "They cannot hope to strike with any accuracy at a range greater than five yards."

I watched the freighter as its bulk neared inexorably. In those moments I felt some sympathy with the great whales: helpless to flee even as death—in the shape of a black whaling ship—approaches. "So close," I gasped. My breathing was settling at last.

"On the Moon, doctor, a man with a good aim and strong arm could easily manage ten times that distance!"

The sky was eclipsed as the aerostat reached the lowest limit of its tethering cables. Now it seemed to skim the landscape: a leviathan cruising the ether, our train no more significant to it than a shoal of parasitic fish. The rigid mantle looked close enough to touch. I felt the prickle of tears in my eyes.

"The ammonia employed as buoyancy," explained Holmes, blinking away his own irritation. "Even the most efficient seals may not prevent some trace escaping. At altitude of course it is of no consequence."

I was watching the gondola—now surely within the scowrer's range: through open hatch and the many windows I could clearly see the two putative labourers, now revealed for who they really were as they levelled their strange harpoon weapons.

"The Willabys!" cursed Douglas. He fired his repeater; I heard the shell ricochet off the gondola sides, and had the satisfaction of seeing both men inside shrink aside. "So they escaped the Devil's Bowl shoot-out too!" Outwardly cool, he levered another shell into place and took a second shot—but I perceived the whitened knuckles and bunching jaw muscles. A deep fury possessed the man; God help the Willabys if he took them alive.

This time the occupants of the gondola merely flinched as the bullet failed to hit a significant target. Even as Douglas levered a third shot into the chamber one raised his scowrer and fired. There was a sound somewhere between a sigh and a gulp, and a clawed harpoon struck the edge of the carriage roof. It failed to find purchase, however, and fell away. I heard a distant buzz—with a certain degree of surprise and chagrin, I realised the failed shot was being reeled back.

"You failed to inform us those harpoons were reusable, Mr Douglas!" Holmes was indignant.

"So I did, sir." Douglas fired again. "Consider me admonished."

Glass shattered in the gondola: the second of the Willabys was using the flat butt of his scowrer to smash out the windows. A moment later I heard the pneumatic sob of him firing—but his shot failed to even find the carriage. It rewound quickly.

"What can they hope to gain by hooking us like a salmon?" I cried. "Surely they do not mean to crawl across!"

"If both them scowrers get a good enough hold," growled Douglas, his American accent broadening in the excitement, "they can use 'em as anchors. While one lets out the aerostat's tethers, the other will be rewinding the scowrer's lines…"

"Ha!" Holmes clapped his hands. "They will haul their aerial mount close enough for them to simply leap the gap. They are inventive."

Belatedly a thought occurred to me. "Bridges, Holmes—and tunnels…!"

"Sadly, there are none before London, my dear doctor." He narrowed his eyes. "A detail of which I'm sure our friends are only too aware."

Another scowrer claw impacted upon the roof; this time it sank deep into the wood. There was a savage cry of triumph from the aerostat's gondola, followed by the whir of a rewinding line. And as incredible as it looked to my eyes, it was obvious the vast bulk of the rigid envelope was edging closer to the racing train. Buoyed as it was by ammonia vapour, all visual evidence to the contrary, the aerostat weighed practically nothing. Whilst its electric motors kept it apace of the train, it could be winched between running cable and carriage with no more effort than if it was a toy balloon.

Holmes was upon the straining line in a second. Drawing a knife from his pocket he attempted to cut through the scowrer cable—but fell back with a cry of frustration.

"Toughened aluminum line!" declared Douglas as he took a careful shot at the one holding the scowrer presently embedded in the roof. "Able to withstand the extremes of a lunar day—you're going to need more than just a pocket knife to cut it."

"Evidently!" Holmes was waspish with frustration.

I dodged just in time as the second scowrer fired its toothed harpoon into the edge of the clerestory roof bare inches from where I sat. Clearly, the aerostat was coming into range of those devilish tools. I turned and, seizing the thin line in both hands, I tugged as hard as I might. I was rewarded seconds later as the claws tore free of the wood—almost throwing myself bodily from the roof as it loosened. If Holmes had not floored me with an expert rugby tackle, I shudder to think what may have resulted.

The line ripped free of my grasp; the palms of both hands would certainly have been flayed had I not been wearing thick winter gloves. The clawed end dragged across the roof, ploughing shallow furrows where it passed. Holmes and I came uncertainly to our feet, expecting the

rewound line to be fired again directly. Douglas fired again—the hammer of his repeater snapping with a hollow rap on an empty chamber. With admirable cool, the American disconnected the empty magazine and threw it negligently aside, produced a pre-loaded one from his coat, and thrust it into place. He levered a bullet into place and fired—as calmly as if he was competing in a local shooting contest.

The second scowrer was fired again; once more its wicked barbs embedded themselves in the clerestory. I stooped to attempt another extraction, but Holmes' arm upon my shoulder stayed me.

"No, friend Watson—let them come as close as they dare!" By the light in his eyes I knew he had a plan—but it sounded an audacious one.

"If they gain this roof, the outcome will not be at all certain!"

"It will not come to that. Remember the Birlstone railway disaster…" He called out to Douglas: "Can you target the propulsive motors?" He pointed at the electrically-powered impulse motors, contained in plain boxes at the ends of the tethering cables: clamped securely around the running cable. The American smiled with confidence.

"Sir, as a boy I fought Johnny Reb; as a man I have faced down many a redskin. No man alive cannot but attest I hit anything I aim at!"

"Then I would obliged—!"

Douglas lowered the barrel of his repeater, levelling in carefully at the leading drive-box. All the while I watched the colossal aerostat loom ever closer overhead; the hatefully triumphant faces of Douglas's implacable enemies growing clearer with each heartbeat. There was a shot, followed a moment later by another. I dragged my attention away from the aerostat in time to see Douglas fire a third bullet into the motor's housing. The casing buckled and flew apart, exposing the electric impulse drive within.

"Do not miss, Mr Douglas," spoke Holmes.

I divined their intention: if Douglas shot apart the motor, the aerostat would quickly lose impetus—yet still be attached to the train by the scowrer lines. Weightless, it would be dragged in the train's wake faster even than the tethering cables could be paid out. The two men must release their harpoons or risk being snatched from the gondola to an uncertain fate. The American took his fourth shot.

What happened next far exceeded my expectations—although in my darkest moments I often credit Holmes with exactly foreseeing the outcome. As the bullet struck, the lead motor spewed sparks and flames and came to a halt with shocking abruptness. The aerostat wallowed like a baffled whale, its nose dipping sedately as the forward tethering cable ceased all motion. A moment later its tail also dropped, pulled by a motor still running full ahead. The entire dirigible twisted with misleading grace, its weightless bulk towed after the speeding train. But weightless though it may have been, it still had mass, and momentum; the abrupt changes in attitude and velocity drove slow ripples through the rigid mantle as it buckled. The rear motor ran directly into the stalled forward, provoking a further explosion of sparking metal and wiring. Inexorably, the aerostat sank ground-wards.

Even then the vessel may have been saved had the scowrer cables torn themselves free of the carriage roof, or the occupants of the gondola simply ejected their deadly tools. But neither of those events followed. Fate or bigoted determination dictated the proceedings. The aerostat drifted to the ground with a deceptive leisureliness, its mantle heaving as though it was constructed of nothing more inflexible than vulcanized rubber. Dragged after the train, pinned by its tethering cables, the aerostat struck the ground; the impact drove waves up through the crushing mantle. It split.

I saw a lone figure crawl out from under the collapsing frame. He stood uncertainly and took an unsteady step before clutching at his face and throat. Writhing horribly he fell to the ground; after a moment, he moved no more. The ammonia contained in the envelope: deadly when concentrated. I recalled the Birlstone railway disaster: more were killed by the released toxic gas than the crash itself.

The aerostat wreckage spread across the railway line, running cable, and many square yards of farmland beside. There would be no trains to or from London until it was cleared up safely. We managed to lever the

embedded scowrer lines free with great effort, coiling them up to recover their considerably battered launchers. MacDonald could add them to his evidence. Back in our compartment Mrs Douglas greeted her husband with tearful relief; Barker shook Holmes and myself by the hand; the two policemen stared at the three of us in mutual disbelief.

"Man," sighed MacDonald as he collapsed back into a seat, "I canna wait to read this adventure!"

PART TWO
THE SCOWRERS

The following, although firmly based upon John Douglas's account of his adventures on the Moon has been dramatized at the insistence of my editor, who believes the original, dry facts would be far below my readers' expectations

I. THE MAN

And now, my long-suffering readers, I will ask you to come away with me for a time, far from the Sussex Manor House of Birlstone, and far also from the year of grace in which we made our eventful journey which ended with the strange story of the man who had been known as John Douglas. I wish you to journey back some twenty years in time, and into the black void beyond our world by some quarter of a million of miles, that I may lay before you a singular and terrible narrative—so singular and so terrible that you may find it hard to believe that even as I tell it, even so did it occur.

Do not think that I intrude one story before another is finished. As you read on you will find that this is not so. And when I have detailed those distant events and you have solved this mystery of the past, we shall meet once more in those rooms on Baker Street, where this, like so many other wonderful happenings, will find its end.

It was the fourth of February in the year 1876, even on the arid wastes of our lunar companion; for although a lunar day is almost the length of a terrestrial month, convention had already dictated that Greenwich Mean

Time and the Julian calendar were the Moon's standard. Day and night were arbitrary terms that had nothing to do with the Sun's position in the lunar sky. Even though it had been a little more than twelve months since Gordon's Expeditionary Force had landed, planting the Union Flag in the name of the Queen-Empress, men had laboured long and hard to hew the bones of a crude settlement from the grey soil. A primitive, electrically-driven Atkinson & Philipson transport was slowly groaning its way up the steep gradients which led from the original landing site on the *Mare Nubium*—already an ordered port with reception areas and compressed gas ballistae for return Earth-shots—to the ice and ore mining sites near the southern pole and the mining centre of Victoria which lies at the head of the *Vale de Verme*: named by its discoverers for the strange outcroppings which litter its slopes—fossils of ancient volcanic activity—shaped like towering worm-casts. From this point the route sweeps downward to Albertstown, Helmdale, and towards the mysteries of the Moon's so-called Dark Side. The oft-travelled track had scarred the surface into the semblance of a permanent roadway; at regular intervals along the way were embarkation points, where long lines of hoppers awaited, piled with new and exotic ores: a hidden wealth, hints of which had brought a rude population and a bustling life to this harsh, unforgiving satellite.

From every corner of Earth had they come, all with the grandest expectations of the gold and gems they would surely find on his brave, new world. South Africans, Indians, Malays, British and other peoples of the Empire; with an even greater proportion from the United States and Canada: those lands where prospecting was the livelihood for so many. And like the majority had discovered in California and Dakota, the reality was so much more deadly. The simple daily fight to stay alive took precedence over the hunt for precious stones which the Moon rarely created, for its internal pressures were nothing compared to the neighbour around which it orbited. Disappointment was the most common currency in this most desolate corner of the Solar System.

For desolate it was! Little could the first selenauts who had traversed

it have ever imagined that the Earth's fairest prairies and most lush water pastures were valueless compared to this gloomy world of grey crater and airless desert. Above the dark and often frozen scars upon their flanks, the high, bare crowns of mountain and crater and un-eroded rock towered upon each margin, leaving a long, winding, tortuous valley in the centre. Up this the Atkinson & Philipson was slowly crawling: a blunt cylinder of aluminium, slung between broad, continuous steel tracks, both wider than the transport's crude body. A fine, silty rain ran continuously from the churning tracks, drifting slowly back to the ground.

Electric lamps glowed in the transport's tubular accommodation, a long, bare carriage in which some twenty or thirty people were seated. The greater number of these were workmen returning from their day's toil in the trenches which littered the lower part of the valley, their excursion suits—bulky, articulated bands of steel and aluminium padded by layers of insulation to safeguard the wearer from both the extreme heat of lunar day and the equally deadly cold of night—were scarred and smeared. Although each had removed their ponderous aluminium helmets, none strayed beyond the touch of their gauntleted fingers: the transport's stale, pressurized interior might yet fail and it would be death to the man who delayed in re-sealing his suit. At least a dozen, by their grimed faces and the oxide lanterns and pneumatic grapplers—the infamous scowrers—which hung from their clumsy suits, proclaimed themselves miners. These sat in a group and conversed in low voices, glancing occasionally at two men on the opposite side of the car, who wore the scarlet excursion suits and black caps of the British Lunar Expeditionary Company enforcers. Even though all of the companies in the *Vale* employed their own private team of enforcers, the BLEC, as befitted the largest employer, also fielded the largest private police force. Unmatched in their reputation for brutality and expediency. the Bleeker Boys—as they were unaffectionately dubbed—were feared by many and unloved by all.

Several women of the labouring class and one or two travellers who might have been small local storekeepers—for even in this remotest corner

of the Empire the basics of family life and rude commerce ran on just as in the sunniest village of Kent—made up the rest of the company, with the exception of one young man in a corner by himself. It is with this man that we are concerned. Take a good look at him; for he is worth it.

He is a fresh-complexioned, middle-sized young man, not far, one would guess, from his thirtieth year. He has large, shrewd, humorous grey eyes which twinkle inquiringly from time to time as he looks round through his goggles at the people about him. It is easy to see that he is of a sociable and possibly simple disposition, anxious to be friendly to all men. Anyone could pick him at once as gregarious in his habits and communicative in his nature, with a quick wit and a ready smile. And yet the man who studied him more closely might discern a certain firmness of jaw and grim tightness about the lips which would warn him that there were depths beyond, and that this pleasant, white-haired young man might conceivably leave his mark for good or evil upon any society to which he was introduced.

Having made one or two tentative remarks to the nearest miner, and receiving only short, gruff replies, the traveller resigned himself to uncongenial silence, staring moodily out of the porthole at the stark lunar landscape.

It was not a cheering prospect. Against the starlit sky there pulsed the red glow of pressure kilns on the crater sides. Great heaps of slag and dumps of cinders loomed up on each side, with the high shafts of the thermal converters towering above them, utilising every degree of heat to generate electric power. Huddled groups of low, metal domes, the thick mica portholes of which outlined themselves in a pallid, ghastly light, hunched here and there above the surface—like icebergs, only the merest fraction of what lay hidden below—and the frequent halting places were crowded with their slow-moving, excursion-suited inhabitants.

The mining valleys beyond the southernmost edge of the *Mare Nubium* were no resorts for the leisured or the cultured. Everywhere there were stern signs of the crudest battle for life, the rude work to be done, and the rude, strong workers who did it.

The young traveller gazed out into this dismal country with a face of mingled repulsion and interest, which showed that the scene was new to him. At intervals he drew from the roomy leather grip-sack slung about his excursion suit a bulky letter to which he referred, and on the margins of which he scribbled some notes. Once, from the same sack, he produced something which one would hardly have expected to find in the possession of so mild-mannered a man. It was a brass-framed pistol of the largest size, with a box magazine fitted forward of the trigger guard. As he unclipped the magazine and turned it slantwise to the light, the glint upon the rims of the copper shells within showed that it was fully loaded. He quickly reassembled the weapon and restored it to his leather sack, but not before it had been observed by a working man who had seated himself upon the adjoining bench.

"Hullo, mate!" said he. "You seem heeled and ready. A late model Volcanic repeating pistol, if I'm not mistaken—I recognise it by the magazine."

The young man smiled with an air of embarrassment.

"Yes," said he, "we need them sometimes in the place I come from."

"And where may that be?"

"I'm last from Chicago."

"A stranger in these parts?"

"Yes."

"You may find you need to carry iron," said the workman. "But I'd not recommend that particular cannon."

"Ah! is that so?" The young man seemed interested.

"You're not on Earth now, mate—the kick from that thing will likely knock you base over apex; and the shell could fair puncture a bulkhead. You wouldn't be wanting that, now."

"I'll endeavour to remember." The young man frowned. "But you imply I should go tooled up anyhow…"

"Have you heard nothing of doings hereabouts?"

"Nothing out of the way."

"Why, word is surely slow in reaching Earth—but you'll hear quick enough. What made you come here?"

"I heard there was always work for a willing man."

"Are you a member of the Labour Union?"

"Sure."

"Then you'll get your job, I guess. Have you any friends?"

"Not yet; but I have the means of making them."

"How's that, then?"

"I am one of the Eminent Order of Freemen. There's no town without a lodge, and where there is a lodge I'll find my friends."

The remark had a singular effect upon his companion. He glanced round suspiciously at the others in the car. The miners were still whispering among themselves. The two company enforcers were dozing. He came across, seated himself close to the young traveller, and held out his gauntleted hand.

"Put it there," he said.

A hand-grip passed between the two.

"I see you speak the truth," said the workman. "But it's well to make certain." He raised his right hand to his right eyebrow. The traveller at once raised his left hand to his left eyebrow. "Dark nights are unpleasant," said he.

"Yes, for strangers to travel," the other answered.

"That's good enough. I'm Brother Scanlan, Lodge 341, *Vale de Verme*. Glad to see you in these parts."

"Thank you. I'm Brother John McMurdo, Lodge 29, Chicago. Bodymaster, J. H. Scott. But I am in luck to meet a brother so early."

"Well, there are plenty of us about. You won't find the order more flourishing anywhere than right here in the *Vale*. But we could do with some lads like you. I can't understand a spry man of the Labour Union finding no work to do in Chicago."

"I found plenty of work to do," said McMurdo.

"Then why did you leave?"

McMurdo nodded towards the security men and smiled. "I guess those chaps would be glad to know," he said.

Scanlan groaned sympathetically. "In trouble?" he asked in a whisper.

"Deep."

"A penitentiary job?"

"And the rest."

"Not a killing!"

"It's early days to talk of such things," said McMurdo with the air of a man who had been surprised into saying more than he intended. "I've my own good reasons for leaving Chicago, and let that be enough for you. Who are you that you should take it on yourself to ask such things?" His grey eyes gleamed with sudden and dangerous anger from behind his goggles.

"All right, mate, no offence meant. The boys will think none the worse of you, whatever you may have done. Where are you bound for now?"

"Victoria."

"That's the third halt down the line. Where are you staying?"

McMurdo took out an envelope and held it close to the dim oxide lamp. "Here is the address—Jacob Shafter, Sheridan Tunnel. It's a lodging that was recommended by a man I knew in Chicago."

"Well, I don't know it; but Victoria is out of my beat. I live at Albertstown, and that's here where we are drawing up. But, say, there's one bit of advice I'll give you before we part: If you're in trouble in Victoria, go straight to the Union House and see Boss McGinty. He is the Bodymaster of the *Vale* Lodge, and nothing can happen in these parts unless Black Jack McGinty wants it. So long, mate! Maybe we'll meet in lodge one of these evenings. But mind my words: If you are in trouble, go to Boss McGinty."

Scanlan stood and fitted the bulky aluminium helmet to his articulated suit. He waved in a friendly manner before shuffling towards the transport's airlock, and McMurdo was left once again to his thoughts. Outside the flame-lit portholes of the frequent kilns were dazzling contrasts to the inky sky. During the dark phases of the Moon, earthly observers might look up

and see them as vivid sparks against the night: stars more brilliant than any other in the firmament. Against their lurid background dark, misshapen figures were bending and straining, twisting and turning, with the motion of winch or of windlass, to a soundless rhythm. The occasional Tesla tower flickered with the molten light—for the use of transmitted power was more common on the Moon than the more conservative Earth of that time—appearing as ruddy gossamer fingers plucking at the heavens.

"I guess hell must look something like that," said a voice.

McMurdo turned and saw that one of the red uniformed enforcers had shifted in his seat and was staring out into the cold, flame-edged waste.

"For that matter," said the other, "I allow that hell must be something like that. If there are worse devils down yonder than some we could name, it's more than I'd expect. I guess you are new to this part, young man?"

"Well, what if I am?" McMurdo answered in a surly voice.

"Just this, mister, that I should advise you to be careful in choosing your friends. I don't think I'd begin with Mike Scanlan or his gang if I were you."

"What the hell is it to you who are my friends?" McMurdo roared in a voice which brought every head in the transport round to witness the altercation. "Did I ask you for your advice, or did you think me such a sucker that I couldn't move without it? You speak when you are spoken to, and by the Lord you'd have to wait a long time if it was me!" He thrust out his face and grinned at the security man like a snarling dog.

The two enforcers, heavy, good-natured men, were taken aback by the extraordinary vehemence with which their friendly advances had been rejected.

"No offence, stranger," said one. "It was a warning for your own good, seeing that you are, by your own showing, new to the place."

"I'm new to the place; but I'm not new to you and your kind!" cried McMurdo in cold fury. "I guess you're the same in all places, shoving your advice in when nobody asks for it."

The enforcer shook his head. "I'll treat your manner as an effect of the flight from Earth—it takes men in many different ways. Some it drives completely mad. But I'd advise you to curb that mouth of yours…"

McMurdo slid his hand inside the leather grip-sack and laid a hold on his repeating pistol. "And I'd advise you not to call me mad!" he snarled.

"Maybe we'll see more of you before very long," said one of the enforcers with a grin. "You're a real hand-picked one, if I am a judge."

"I was thinking the same," remarked the other. "I guess we may meet again."

"I'm not afraid of you, and don't you think it!" cried McMurdo. "My name's Jack McMurdo—see? If you want me, you'll find me at Jacob Shafter's in Sheridan Tunnel, Victoria; so I'm not hiding from you, am I? Day or night I dare to look the like of you in the face—don't make any mistake about that!"

There was a murmur of sympathy and admiration from the miners at the dauntless demeanour of the newcomer, while the two enforcers shrugged their shoulders and renewed a conversation between themselves.

A few minutes later the transport rolled into an ill-lit huddle of crouching domes and discarded machinery, and there was a general clearing; for Victoria was by far the largest sites. McMurdo fitted the helmet to his excursion suit, checking the seals carefully as he had been shown. As the helmet locked in place, he heard the whine of motors starting up: the array of pumps starting to move the fluid which, depending on circumstances, either carried excess heat away, or warmed the suit internally. He was about to pass through the transport's airlock off into the darkness, when one of the miners accosted him.

"By gosh, mate! You know how to speak to the cops," he said in a voice of awe his own helmet failed to muffle. "It was grand to hear you. Let me carry your grip and show you the road. I'm passing Shafter's Tunnel on the way to my own shack."

There was a chorus of friendly "Good-nights" from the other miners as they exited the transport's airlock and shuffled down a crude ramp

of regolith and dust. Before ever he had set foot in it, McMurdo the turbulent had become a character in Victoria.

The moonscape had been a place of terror; but this place was in its way even more depressing. Down that long valley there was at least a certain gloomy grandeur in the Sun-dazzled rocks and black skies, while the strength and industry of man found fitting monuments in the hills which he had spilled by the side of his monstrous excavations. But Victoria showed a dead level of mean ugliness and squalor. Of actual human habitation there was no sign: the low domes were just the peaks of underground storage for the variety of machinery with which the place kept itself alive, or earned its keep. What might pass elsewhere as a broad trench was churned up by the traffic into a horrible rutted furrow of bared rock and gritty dust. The slatted aluminium side-walks laid across the scored lunar surface were narrow and uneven. The numerous electric lamps were fitful and unreliable, relying as they did on storage batteries and the inadequate thermo-electric power provided by distant heat-exchangers. Those lights which stayed alight served only to show more clearly a long line of manhole covers embedded in the rutted trench, unkempt and dirty. It was to these that McMurdo's companion guided him. He pressed his helmet against McMurdo's so that he might be heard.

"Here—city limits!" His voice was hollow with irony as he stooped awkwardly in his rigid suit, steel-ringed fingers encircling a handle which was counter-sunk in a manhole cover. He pulled it free, turning slowly; the cover raised itself. He indicated to McMurdo that he should climb inside.

It was a narrow fit: not much more than a hand's thickness on either side of the unyielding shoulders of McMurdo's suit. He climbed with little skill down a steel ladder—although he was glad to be out of the unscreened sunlight: even with the coolant sucking away what heat it could, he had felt the light of our native star on his back more fiercely than the sunniest of days on Earth—to be brought up short by another circular cover, blocking the shaft. They were within another airlock. McMurdo paused—looking up as best he could as his companion pulled down the manhole cover

above them and dogged it tight, plunging them into utter blackness. Only then did McMurdo stoop, clumsily feeling for the handle, and unseal the hatch below. They climbed down into a tunnel—some ten feet in diameter, its coarse black walls strung with more dancing lamps—and divested themselves of their cumbersome helmets once the inner hatch was again sealed. McMurdo felt through his booted feet rather the heard the muted throb of pumps, and fancied he felt the kiss of the lightest of breezes on his cheek: an air-handling system supplying both air and a comfortable temperature to the burrow. He fancied there was an odour to the atmosphere: a residue of the air's artificial origins in distant ionisation columns where water—from both thawed lunar ice and recycled waste— was split into its component elements.

"Lava tunnels," explained McMurdo's companion, "left over from the Moon's more active youth. The ground under the *Vale* is honeycombed with 'em—lucky for us. Saves us having to try building too much on the surface: we can all stay down here, like bloomin' rabbits!" He smiled and struck off along the tunnel.

"Got everything we need—dug out of the sides: houses, shops, pubs… Stick a train in and it'd be just like the Underground. Victoria's centre is just along here…"

As they approached the centre of the town the tunnel was brightened by a row of well-lit store-fronts—lying flush against the tunnel's sides, like a surrealist's dream—and even more by a cluster of pubs and gaming houses, in which the miners spent their hard-earned but generous wages.

"That's the Union House," said the guide, pointing to one pub which rose almost to the dignity of being a hotel: with a second floor hollowed from the tunnel's arching roof. "Jack McGinty is the boss there."

"What sort of a man is he?" McMurdo asked.

"What! Have you never heard of the boss?"

"How could I have heard of him when you know that I am a stranger in these parts?"

"Well, I thought his name was known clear across the Moon. It's been in the papers often enough."

"Earth doesn't have much call for the Moon's yellow sheets," McMurdo said gruffly. "What for?"

"Well," the miner lowered his voice, "over the affairs."

"What affairs?"

"Good Lord, mister! you are queer, if I must say it without offence. There's only one set of affairs that you'll hear of in these parts, and that's the affairs of the Scowrers."

"Why, I seem to have read of the Scowrers in back home in Chicago. A gang of murderers, are they not?"

"Hush, on your life!" cried the miner, standing still in alarm, and gazing in amazement at his companion. "Man, you won't live long in these parts if you speak in the open like that. Many a man has had the life beaten out of him for less."

"Well, I know nothing about them. It's only what I have read."

"And I'm not saying that you have not read the truth." The man looked nervously round him as he spoke, peering into the shadows as if he feared to see some lurking danger. "They name themselves after our universal grappling tools: scowrers, we call 'em." His thin smile was humourless and bitter. "No matter the fix, your scowrer will set you right, is the old saw. And if killing is the way to settle it, then God knows there is murder and to spare. But don't you dare to breathe the name of Jack McGinty in connection with it, stranger; for every whisper goes back to him, and he is not one that is likely to let it pass. Now, that's the tunnel you're after, that one branching off to the left. You'll find old Jacob Shafter's place about half a mile along it; 'tain't much of a place, even for the *Vale*, but Jacob's as honest a man as lives in this township."

"I thank you," said McMurdo, and shaking hands with his new acquaintance he plodded, grip-sack in one hand, helmet in the other, up the tunnel which led to the dwelling house. On Earth, half a mile in the clumsy excursion suit would have been close to impossible, but in the Moon's lesser gravity McMurdo found the going easier than he could have hoped for. He found Jacob Shafter's house identified by a simple basalt sign; at the sealed hatch he gave a resounding knock.

It was cracked and opened at once by someone very different from what he had expected. It was a woman, young and singularly beautiful. She was of the fair German type, her blonde hair—had he not known better—looked perfectly natural, with the piquant contrast of a pair of beautiful dark eyes with which she surveyed the stranger with surprise and a pleasing embarrassment which brought a wave of colour over her pale face. Framed in the bright light of the open doorway, it seemed to McMurdo that he had never seen a more beautiful picture; the more attractive for its contrast with the sordid and gloomy surroundings. A lovely violet growing upon one of those black slag-heaps of the mines would not have seemed more surprising. So entranced was he that he stood staring without a word, and it was she who broke the silence.

"I thought it was father," said she with a pleasing little touch of an accent McMurdo would come to recognise as Afrikaans. "Did you come to see him? He is down town. I expect him back every minute."

McMurdo continued to gaze at her in open admiration until her eyes dropped in confusion before this masterful visitor.

"No, miss," he said at last, "I'm in no hurry to see him. But your house was recommended to me for board. I thought it might suit me—and now I know it will."

"You are quick to make up your mind," said she with a smile.

"Anyone but a blind man could do as much," the other answered.

She laughed at the compliment. "Come right in, sir," she said. He followed her into a simple room hollowed from the dark lunar rock. Its walls had been roughly plastered and given a lime wash that reflected back the irregular light from a handful of wall lamps. From the positioning of an electric stove, a table rudely chipped from a slate-like material, several fold-away chairs and a broad dresser it was clear this one room served as kitchen, parlour and dining room. There was another closed hatch towards the rear. "I'm Miss Ettie Shafter, Mr Shafter's daughter. And I can see by your eyes that you are wondering what is such a child doing in this desolate place—"

He made to protest, but she help up a pale hand. "My mother's

dead, and I run the house. The blood of *voortrekkers* flows in my veins, sir—although now I think you may call us *botrekkers*." Her laugh was delightful—though he detected the hint of steel in her eyes. "You can sit down by the stove until father comes along—Ah, here he is! So you can fix things with him right away."

A heavy, elderly man in a scuffed excursion suit came plodding through the opened hatch. In a few words McMurdo explained his business. A man of the name of Murphy had given him the address in Chicago. He in turn had had it from someone else. Old Shafter was quite ready. The stranger made no bones about terms, agreed at once to every condition, and was apparently fairly flush of money. For three pounds a week paid in advance he was to have board and lodging.

So it was that McMurdo, the self-confessed fugitive from justice, took up his abode under the roof of the Shafters, the first step which was to lead to so long and dark a train of events, ending back on a far distant world.

II. The Bodymaster

McMurdo was a man who made his mark quickly. Wherever he was the folk around soon knew it. Within a week he had become infinitely the most important person at Shafter's. There were ten or a dozen boarders there, staying in rooms beyond the second hatch, hollowed out from the lunar crust; but they were honest foremen or commonplace clerks from the stores, of a very different calibre from the young American. Of an evening when they gathered together his joke was always the readiest, his conversation the brightest, and his song the best. He was a born boon companion, with a magnetism which drew good humour from all around him.

And yet he showed again and again, as he had shown in the surface transport, a capacity for sudden, fierce anger, which compelled the respect and even the fear of those who met him. For the law, too, and all who were connected with it, he exhibited a bitter contempt which delighted some and alarmed others of his fellow boarders.

From the first he made it evident, by his open admiration, that the daughter of the house had won his heart from the instant that he had set eyes upon her beauty and her grace. He was no backward suitor. On the second day he told her that he loved her, and from then onward he repeated the same story with an absolute disregard of what she might say to discourage him.

"Someone else?" he would cry. "Well, the worse luck for someone else! Let him look out for himself! Am I to lose my life's chance and all my heart's desire for someone else? You can keep on saying no, Ettie: the day will come when you will say yes, and I'm young enough to wait."

He was a dangerous suitor, with his glib tongue, and his pretty, coaxing ways. There was about him also that glamour of experience and of mystery which attracts a woman's interest, and finally her love. He could talk of the sweet valleys of County Monaghan from which his ancestors came, of the lovely, distant island, the low hills and green meadows of which seemed the more beautiful when imagination viewed them from this place of black rock and frozen shadow.

Then he was versed in the life of the cities of the North, of Detroit, and the lumber camps of Michigan, and finally of Chicago, where he had worked as a logger. And afterwards came the hint of romance, the feeling that strange things had happened to him in that great city, so strange and so intimate that they might not be spoken of. He spoke wistfully of a sudden leaving, a breaking of old ties, a flight into a strange world, ending in this dreary valley, and Ettie listened, her dark eyes gleaming with pity and with sympathy—those two qualities which may turn so rapidly and so naturally to love.

McMurdo had obtained a temporary job as bookkeeper for he was a well-educated man. This kept him out most of the day, and he had not found occasion yet to report himself to the head of the lodge of the Eminent Order of Freemen. He was reminded of his omission, however, by a visit one evening from Mike Scanlan, the fellow member whom he had met in the train. Scanlan, the small, sharp-faced, nervous, black-eyed man, seemed glad to see him once more. After a glass or two of whisky he broached the object of his visit.

"Say, McMurdo," said he, "I remembered your address, so I made bold to call. I'm surprised that you've not reported to the Bodymaster. Why haven't you seen Boss McGinty yet?"

"Well, I had to find a job. I have been busy."

"You must find time for him if you have none for anything else. Good Lord, man! you're a fool not to have been down to the Union House and registered your name the first morning after you came here! If you run against him—well, you mustn't, that's all!"

McMurdo showed mild surprise. "I've been a member of the lodge for

over two years, Scanlan, but I never heard that duties were so pressing as all that."

"Maybe not in Chicago."

"Well, it's the same society here."

"Is it?"

Scanlan looked at him long and fixedly. There was something sinister in his eyes.

"Isn't it?"

"You'll tell me that in a month's time. I hear you had a talk with company enforcers after I left the transport."

"How did you know that?"

"Oh, it got about—things do get about for good and for bad in this district."

"Well, yes. I told the hounds what I thought of them."

"By the Lord, you'll be a man after McGinty's heart!"

"What, does he hate the enforcers too?"

Scanlan burst out laughing. "You go and see him, my lad," said he as he took his leave. "It's not the enforcers but you that he'll hate if you don't! Now, take a friend's advice and go at once!"

It chanced that on the same evening McMurdo had another more pressing interview which urged him in the same direction. It may have been that his attentions to Ettie had been more evident than before, or that they had gradually obtruded themselves into the slow mind of his good Boer host; but, whatever the cause, the landlord beckoned the young man into his private room and started on the subject without any circumlocution.

"It seems to me, mister," said he, his Afrikaans accent much thicker than his daughter's, "that you are gettin' set on my Ettie. Ain't that so, or am I wrong?"

"Yes, that is so," the young man answered.

"Vell, I vant to tell you right now that it ain't no manner of use. There's someone slipped in afore you."

"She told me so."

"Vell, you can lay that she told you truth. But did she tell you who it vas?"

"No, I asked her; but she wouldn't tell."

"I dare say not, the leetle baggage! Perhaps she did not vish to frighten you avay."

"Frighten!" McMurdo was on fire in a moment.

"Ah, yes, my friend! You need not be ashamed to be frightened of him. It is Teddy Baldwin."

"And who the devil is he?"

"He is a boss of Scowrers."

"Scowrers! I've heard of them before. It's Scowrers here and Scowrers there, and always in a whisper! What are you all afraid of? Who are the Scowrers?"

The older man instinctively sank his voice, as everyone did who talked about that terrible society. "The Scowrers," said he, "are the Eminent Order of Freemen!"

The young man stared. "Why, I am a member of that order myself."

"You! I vould never have had you in my house if I had known it—not if you vere to pay me a hundred pound a veek."

"What's wrong with the order? It's for charity and good fellowship. The rules say so."

"Maybe in some places. Not here!"

"What is it here?"

"It's a murder society, that's vat it is."

McMurdo laughed incredulously. "How can you prove that?" he asked.

"Prove it! Are there not fifty murders to prove it? Vat about Milman and Van Shorst, and the Nicholson family, and old Mr Hyam, and little Billy James, and the others? Prove it! Is there a man or a voman in this valley vat does not know it?"

"See here!" said McMurdo earnestly. "I want you to take back what you've said, or else make it good. One or the other you must do before I quit this room. Put yourself in my place. Here am I, a stranger in the town. I belong to a society that I know only as an innocent one. You'll find

it through the length and breadth of the States and Britain, but always as an innocent one. Now, when I am counting upon joining it here, you tell me that it is the same as a murder society called the Scowrers. I guess you owe me either an apology or else an explanation, Mr Shafter."

"I can but tell you vat the whole vorld knows, mister. The bosses of the one are the bosses of the other. If you offend the one, it is the other vat vill strike you. We have proved it too often."

"That's just gossip—I want proof!" said McMurdo.

"If you live here long you vill get your proof. But I forget that you are yourself one of them. You vill soon be as bad as the rest. But you vill find other lodgings, mister. I cannot have you here. Is it not bad enough that one of these people come courting my Ettie, and that I dare not turn him down, but that I should have another for my boarder? Yes, indeed, you shall not sleep here after tonight!"

McMurdo found himself under sentence of banishment both from his comfortable quarters and from the girl whom he loved. He found her alone in the single room that same evening, and he poured his troubles into her ear.

"Your father is after giving me notice," he said. "It's little I would care if it was just my room, but indeed, Ettie, though it's only a week that I've known you, you are the very breath of life to me, and I can't live without you!"

"Oh, hush, Mr McMurdo, don't speak so!" said the girl. "I have told you, have I not, that you are too late? There is another, and if I have not promised to marry him at once, at least I can promise no one else."

"Suppose I had been first, Ettie, would I have had a chance?"

The girl sank her face into her hands. "I wish to heaven that you had been first!" she sobbed.

McMurdo was down on his knees before her in an instant. "For God's sake, Ettie, let it stand at that!" he cried. "Will you ruin your life and my own for the sake of this promise? Follow your heart! 'Tis a safer guide than any promise before you knew what it was that you were saying."

He had seized Ettie's white hand between his own strong brown ones.

"Say that you will be mine, and we will face it out together!"

"Not here?"

"Yes, here."

"No, no, Jack!" His arms were round her now. "It could not be here. Could you take me away?"

A struggle passed for a moment over McMurdo's face; but it ended by setting like granite. "No, here," he said. "I'll hold you against the world, Ettie, right here where we are!"

"Why should we not leave together?"

"No, Ettie, I can't leave here."

"But why?"

"I'd never hold my head up again if I felt that I had been driven out. Besides, what is there to be afraid of? Are we not free folks on a new, free world? If you love me, and I you, who will dare to come between?"

"You don't know, Jack. You've been here too short a time. You don't know this Baldwin. You don't know McGinty and his Scowrers."

"No, I don't know them, and I don't fear them, and I don't believe in them!" said McMurdo. "I've lived among rough men, my darling, and instead of fearing them it has always ended that they have feared me— always, Ettie. It's mad on the face of it! If these men, as your father says, have done crime after crime in the *Vale*, and if everyone knows them by name, how comes it that none are brought to justice? You answer me that, Ettie!"

"Because no witness dares to appear against them. He would not live a month if he did. Also because they have always their own men to swear that the accused one was far from the scene of the crime. But surely, Jack, you must have read all this. I had understood that every paper on the Earth was writing about it."

"Well, I have read something, it is true; but I had thought it was a story. Maybe these men have some reason in what they do. Maybe they are wronged and have no other way to help themselves."

"Oh, Jack, don't let me hear you speak so! That is how he speaks—the other one!"

"Baldwin—he speaks like that, does he?"

"And that is why I loathe him so. Oh, Jack, now I can tell you the truth. I loathe him with all my heart; but I fear him also. I fear him for myself; but above all I fear him for father. I know that some great sorrow would come upon us if I dared to say what I really felt. That is why I have put him off with half-promises. It was in real truth our only hope. But if you would fly with me, Jack, we could take father with us and live forever far from the power of these wicked men."

Again there was the struggle upon McMurdo's face, and again it set like granite. "No harm shall come to you, Ettie—nor to your father either. As to wicked men, I expect you may find that I am as bad as the worst of them before we're through."

"No, no, Jack! I would trust you anywhere."

McMurdo laughed bitterly. "Good Lord! how little you know of me! Your innocent soul, my darling, could not even guess what is passing in mine. But, hullo, who's the visitor?"

The door had opened suddenly, and a young fellow came swaggering in with the air of one who is the master. He was a handsome, dashing young man of about the same age and build as McMurdo himself, dressed in indoor clothing. A hand-held pneumatic grappling device was strung casually from his shoulder—a scowrer of the kind McMurdo would come to know so well. Under a flat black felt cap, which he had not troubled to remove, a handsome face with fierce, domineering eyes and a curved hawk-bill of a nose looked savagely at the pair who sat by the stove.

Ettie had jumped to her feet full of confusion and alarm. "I'm glad to see you, Mr Baldwin," said she. "You're earlier than I had thought. Come and sit down."

Baldwin stood with one hand resting on the grip the scowrer, looking at McMurdo. "Who is this?" he asked curtly.

"It's a friend of mine, Mr Baldwin, a new lodger here. Mr McMurdo, may I introduce you to Mr Baldwin?"

The young men nodded in surly fashion to each other.

"Maybe Miss Ettie has told you how it is with us?" said Baldwin.

"I didn't understand that there was any relation between you."

"Didn't you? Well, you can understand it now. You can take it from me that this young lady is mine, and you'll find it a very fine evening for a walk."

McMurdo sneered: he too was dressed only for the interiors. "Thank you, I am in no humour for a walk."

"Aren't you?" The man's savage eyes were blazing with anger. "Maybe you are in a humour for a fight, Mr Lodger!" He raised his scowrer; the grappling hook with its deadly arrow like tip glittered in the inconsistent lighting.

"That I am!" cried McMurdo, springing to his feet. "You never said a more welcome word."

"For God's sake, Jack! Oh, for God's sake!" cried poor, distracted Ettie. "Oh, Jack, Jack, he will hurt you!"

"Oh, it's Jack, is it?" said Baldwin with an oath. "You've come to that already, have you?"

"Oh, Ted, be reasonable—be kind! For my sake, Ted, if ever you loved me, be big-hearted and forgiving!"

"I think, Ettie, that if you were to leave us alone we could get this thing settled," said McMurdo quietly. "Or maybe, Mr Baldwin, you will take a turn down the tunnels with me. It's a quiet evening, and I mind there's some open space a ways to the left."

"I'll get even with you without needing to dirty my hands," said his enemy. "You'll wish you had never set foot in this house before I am through with you!"

"No time like the present," cried McMurdo.

"I'll choose my own time, mister. You can leave the time to me. See here!" He suddenly rolled up his sleeve and showed upon his forearm a peculiar sign which appeared to have been branded there. It was a circle with a triangle within it. "D'you know what that means?"

"I neither know nor care!"

"Well, you will know, I'll promise you that. You won't be much older, either. Perhaps Miss Ettie can tell you something about it. As to you,

Ettie, you'll come back to me on your knees—d'ye hear, girl?—on your knees—and then I'll tell you what your punishment may be. You've sowed—and by the Lord, I'll see that you reap!" He glanced at them both in fury, the deadly tip of his scowrer quivering. Then he dropped the grappler, turned upon his heel, and an instant later the hatch had slammed behind him.

For a few moments McMurdo and the girl stood in silence. Then she threw her arms around him.

"Oh, Jack, how brave you were! But it is no use, you must fly! Tonight—Jack—tonight! It's your only hope. He will have your life. I read it in his horrible eyes. What chance have you against a dozen of them, with Boss McGinty and all the power of the lodge behind them?"

McMurdo disengaged her hands, kissed her, and gently pushed her back into a chair. "There, there! Don't be disturbed or fear for me. I'm a Freeman myself. I'm after telling your father about it. Maybe I am no better than the others; so don't make a saint of me. Perhaps you hate me too, now that I've told you as much?"

"Hate you, Jack? While life lasts I could never do that! I've heard that there is no harm in being a Freeman anywhere but here; so why should I think the worse of you for that? But if you are a Freeman, Jack, why should you not go down and make a friend of Boss McGinty? Oh, hurry, Jack, hurry! Get your word in first, or the hounds will be on your trail."

"I was thinking the same thing," said McMurdo. "I'll go right now and fix it. You can tell your father that I'll sleep here tonight and find some other quarters in the morning."

From his room he fetched his clumsy excursion suit and donned it, for no sane man walked abroad—even in the tunnels—without such protection as it provided. It was not unknown for the air circulation to falter—or sometimes fail for long minutes.

The bar of McGinty's pub was crowded as usual; for it was the favourite loafing place of all the rougher elements of the town. The man was popular; for he had a rough, jovial disposition which formed a mask, covering a great deal which lay behind it. But apart from this popularity,

the fear in which he was held throughout the township, and indeed down the whole thirty miles of the valley and past the mountains on each side of it, was enough in itself to fill his bar; for none could afford to neglect his good will.

Besides those secret powers which it was universally believed that he exercised in so pitiless a fashion, he was a high public official, a municipal councillor, and a commissioner of transport, elected to the office through the votes of the ruffians who in turn expected to receive favours at his hands. Rates and taxes were enormous; the public works were notoriously neglected, the accounts were slurred over by bribed auditors, and the decent citizen was terrorized into paying public blackmail, and holding his tongue lest some worse thing befall him.

Thus it was that, after less than a year, Boss McGinty's diamond pins had become obtrusive, his gold chains weighty across a gorgeous vest, and his pub had expanded month by month, until it threatened to absorb one whole side of the Market tunnel.

McMurdo marched through the yawning hatch, pushed open the swinging door of the pub and made his way amid the crowd of men within, through an atmosphere blurred with tobacco smoke and heavy with the smell of spirits, so choked the local ventilation pumps could barely scrub it clear. The place was brilliantly lighted, and the huge, heavily gilt mirrors upon every wall reflected and multiplied the garish illumination. There were several bartenders in their shirt sleeves, hard at work mixing drinks for the loungers who fringed the broad, brass-trimmed counter.

At the far end, with his body resting upon the bar and a cigar stuck at an acute angle from the corner of his mouth, stood a tall, strong, heavily built man who could be none other than the famous McGinty himself. He was a white-maned giant, bearded to the cheek-bones, and with a shock of untamed hair which fell to his collar. His complexion was as swarthy as that of an Italian, and his eyes were of a strange dead black, which, combined with a slight squint, gave them a particularly sinister appearance.

All else in the man—his noble proportions, his fine features, and his frank bearing—fitted in with that jovial, man-to-man manner which he affected. Here, one would say, is a bluff, honest fellow, whose heart would be sound however rude his outspoken words might seem. It was only when those dead, dark eyes, deep and remorseless, were turned upon a man that he shrank within himself, feeling that he was face to face with an infinite possibility of latent evil, with a strength and courage and cunning behind it which made it a thousand times more deadly.

Having had a good look at his man, McMurdo elbowed his way forward with his usual careless audacity, and pushed himself through the little group of courtiers who were fawning upon the powerful boss, laughing uproariously at the smallest of his jokes. The young stranger's bold grey eyes looked back fearlessly through their glasses at the deadly black ones which turned sharply upon him.

"Well, young man, I can't call your face to mind."

"I'm new here, Mr McGinty."

"You are not so new that you can't give a gentleman his proper title."

"He's Councillor McGinty, young man," said a voice from the group.

"I'm sorry, Councillor. I'm strange to the ways of the place. But I was advised to see you."

"Well, you see me. This is all there is. What d'you think of me?"

"Well, it's early days. If your heart is as big as your body, and your soul as fine as your face, then I'd ask for nothing better," said McMurdo.

"By gosh! you've got an Irish tongue in your head anyhow," cried the pub-keeper, not quite certain whether to humour this audacious visitor or to stand upon his dignity. "So you are good enough to pass my appearance?"

"Sure," said McMurdo.

"And you were told to see me?"

"I was."

"And who told you?"

"Brother Scanlan of Lodge 341, *Vale de Verme*. I drink your health Councillor, and to our better acquaintance." He raised a glass with which

he had been served to his lips and elevated his little finger as he drank it.

McGinty, who had been watching him narrowly, raised his thick bleached eyebrows. "Oh, it's like that, is it?" said he. "I'll have to look a bit closer into this, Mister—"

"McMurdo."

"A bit closer, Mr McMurdo; for we don't take folk on trust in these parts, nor believe all we're told neither. Come in here for a moment, behind the bar."

There was a small room there, lined with barrels. McGinty carefully closed the door, and then seated himself on one of them, biting thoughtfully on his cigar and surveying his companion with those disquieting eyes. For a couple of minutes he sat in complete silence. McMurdo bore the inspection cheerfully, resting one hand on his suit helmet where he had placed it on a barrel, the other tucked in his leather grip-sack. Suddenly McGinty stooped and produced a scowrer of his own. The point was aimed unwavering at McMurdo's face.

"See here, my joker," said he, "if I thought you were playing any game on us, it would be short work for you."

"This is a strange welcome," McMurdo answered with some dignity, "for the Bodymaster of a lodge of Freemen to give to a stranger brother."

"Ay, but it's just that same that you have to prove," said McGinty, "and God help you if you fail! Where were you made?"

"Lodge 29, Chicago."

"When?"

"June 24, 1872."

"What Bodymaster?"

"James H. Scott."

"Who is your district ruler?"

"Bartholomew Wilson."

"Hum! You seem glib enough in your tests. What are you doing here?"

"Working, the same as you—but a poorer job."

"You have your back answer quick enough."

"Yes, I was always quick of speech."

"Are you quick of action?"

"I have had that name among those that knew me best."

"Well, we may try you sooner than you think. Have you heard anything of the lodge in these parts?"

"I've heard that it takes a man to be a brother."

"True for you, Mr McMurdo. Why did you leave Chicago?"

"I'm damned if I tell you that!"

McGinty opened his eyes. He was not used to being answered in such fashion, and it amused him. "Why won't you tell me?"

"Because no brother may tell another a lie."

"Then the truth is too bad to tell?"

"You can put it that way if you like."

"See here, mister, you can't expect me, as Bodymaster, to pass into the lodge a man for whose past he can't answer."

McMurdo looked puzzled. Then he raised the hand which had been resting in his grip-sack: it held a worn newspaper cutting.

"You wouldn't squeal on a fellow?" said he.

"I'll wipe my hand across your face if you say such words to me!" cried McGinty hotly.

"You are right, Councillor," said McMurdo meekly. "I should apologize. I spoke without thought. Well, I know that I am safe in your hands. Look at that clipping."

McGinty glanced his eyes over the account of the shooting of one Jonas Pinto, in the Lake Saloon, Water Street, Chicago, in the New Year week of 1874.

"Your work?" he asked, as he handed back the paper.

McMurdo nodded, returning cutting and hand back into his grip.

"Why did you shoot him?"

"I was helping Uncle Sam to make dollars. Maybe mine were not as good gold as theirs, but they looked as well and were cheaper to make. This man Pinto helped me to shove the queer—"

"To do what?"

"Well, it means to pass the dollars out into circulation. Then he said

he would split. Maybe he did split. I didn't wait to see. I just killed him and lighted out for the lunar mines."

"Why the lunar mines?"

"'Cause I'd read in the papers that they weren't too particular in those parts."

McGinty laughed. "You were first a coiner and then a murderer, and you came to these parts because you thought you'd be welcome."

"That's about the size of it," McMurdo answered.

"Well, I guess you'll go far. Say, can you make those dollars yet?"

McMurdo took half a dozen from his pocket. "Those never passed the Philadelphia Mint," said he.

"You don't say!" McGinty held them to the light in his enormous hand, which was hairy as a gorilla's. "I can see no difference. Gosh! you'll be a mighty useful brother, I'm thinking! We can do with a bad man or two among us, Friend McMurdo: for there are times when we have to take our own part. We'd soon be against the wall if we didn't shove back at those that were pushing us."

"Well, I guess I'll do my share of shoving with the rest of the boys."

"You seem to have a good nerve. You didn't squirm when I shoved this scowrer at you."

"It was not me that was in danger."

"Who then?"

"It was you, Councillor." McMurdo again withdrew his hand from the grip—this time it was closed around his Volcanic repeating pistol, cocked and ready. "I was covering you all the time. I guess my shot would have been as quick as yours."

"By gosh!" McGinty flushed an angry red and then burst into a roar of laughter. "We've had no such holy terror come to hand this many a year. I reckon the lodge will learn to be proud of you—" He broke off as the bartender entered the room. "Well, what the hell do you want? And can't I speak alone with a gentleman for five minutes but you must butt in on us?"

The bartender stood abashed. "I'm sorry, Councillor, but it's Ted Baldwin. He says he must see you this very minute."

The message was unnecessary; for the set, cruel face of the man himself was looking over the servant's shoulder. He pushed the bartender out and closed the door on him.

"So," said he with a furious glance at McMurdo, "you got here first, did you? I've a word to say to you, Councillor, about this man."

"Then say it here and now before my face," cried McMurdo.

"I'll say it at my own time, in my own way."

"Tut! Tut!" said McGinty, getting off his barrel. "This will never do. We have a new brother here, Baldwin, and it's not for us to greet him in such fashion. Hold out your hand, man, and make it up!"

"Never!" cried Baldwin in a fury.

"I've offered to fight him if he thinks I have wronged him," said McMurdo. "I'll fight him with fists, or, if that won't satisfy him, I'll fight him any other way he chooses. Now, I'll leave it to you, Councillor, to judge between us as a Bodymaster should."

"What is it, then?"

"A young lady. She's free to choose for herself."

"Is she?" cried Baldwin.

"As between two brothers of the lodge I should say that she was," said the Boss.

"Oh, that's your ruling, is it?"

"Yes, it is, Ted Baldwin," said McGinty, with a wicked stare. "Is it you that would dispute it?"

"You would throw over one that has stood by you since we landed on this hell-hole in favour of a man that you never saw before in your life? You're not Bodymaster for life, Jack McGinty, and by God! when next it comes to a vote—"

The Councillor sprang at him like a tiger. His hand closed round the other's neck, and he hurled him back across one of the barrels. In his mad fury he would have squeezed the life out of him if McMurdo had not interfered.

"Easy, Councillor! For heaven's sake, go easy!" he cried, as he dragged him back.

McGinty released his hold, and Baldwin, cowed and shaken, gasping for breath, and shivering in every limb, as one who has looked over the very edge of death, sat up on the barrel over which he had been hurled.

"You've been asking for it this many a day, Ted Baldwin—now you've got it!" cried McGinty, his huge chest rising and falling. "Maybe you think if I was voted down from Bodymaster you would find yourself in my shoes. It's for the lodge to say that. But so long as I am the chief I'll have no man lift his voice against me or my rulings."

"I have nothing against you," mumbled Baldwin, feeling his throat.

"Well, then," cried the other, relapsing in a moment into a bluff joviality, "we are all good friends again and there's an end of the matter."

He took a bottle of champagne down from the shelf and twisted out the cork.

"See now," he continued, as he filled three high glasses. "Let us drink the quarrelling toast of the lodge. After that, as you know, there can be no bad blood between us. Now, then the left hand on the apple of my throat. I say to you, Ted Baldwin, what is the offence, sir?"

"The clouds are heavy," answered Baldwin

"But they will forever brighten," responded McGinty.

"And this I swear!"

The men drank their glasses, and the same ceremony was performed between Baldwin and McMurdo.

"There!" cried McGinty, rubbing his hands. "That's the end of the black blood. You come under lodge discipline if it goes further, and that's a heavy hand in these parts, as Brother Baldwin knows—and as you will damn soon find out, Brother McMurdo, if you ask for trouble!"

"Faith, I'd be slow to do that," said McMurdo. He held out his hand to Baldwin. "I'm quick to quarrel and quick to forgive. It's my hot Irish blood, they tell me. But it's over for me, and I bear no grudge."

Baldwin had to take the proffered hand; for the baleful eye of the terrible Boss was upon him. But his sullen face showed how little the words of the other had moved him.

McGinty clapped them both on the shoulders. "Tut! These girls! These

girls!" he cried. "To think that the same petticoats should come between two of my boys! It's the devil's own luck! Well, it's the colleen inside of them that must settle the question; for it's outside the jurisdiction of a Bodymaster—and the Lord be praised for that! We have enough on us, without the women as well. You'll have to be affiliated to Lodge 341, Brother McMurdo. We have our own ways and methods, different from Chicago. Saturday night is our meeting, and if you come then, we'll make you free forever of the *Vale de Verme.*"

IV. Lodge 341, Vale de Verme

On the day following the evening which had contained so many exciting events, McMurdo moved his lodgings from old Jacob Shafter's and took up his quarters at the Widow MacNamara's in a poorly-maintained, ill-lit tunnel on the extreme outskirts of the town. Scanlan, his original acquaintance aboard the transport, had occasion shortly afterwards to move into Victoria, and the two lodged together. There was no other boarder, and the hostess was an easy-going old Irishwoman who left them to themselves; so that they had a freedom for speech and action welcome to men who had secrets in common.

Shafter had relented to the extent of letting McMurdo come to his meals there when he liked; so that his intercourse with Ettie was by no means broken. On the contrary, it drew closer and more intimate as the weeks went by.

In his bedroom at his new abode McMurdo felt it safe to reassemble the coining moulds and apparatus, and with examples of the various forms of company scrip with which all miners were paid, create stamps to match them all. The British Lunar Expeditionary Company was the major employer, with coins struck by the Royal Mint; but there were smaller, private companies ever keen to exploit the Moon and its resources, buying up parcels of land on the periphery of the *Vale* and offering handsome wages: the Birmingham Small Arms Company, Rae & Sturmash, Harland & Wolff, Aveling & Porter, Kynoch and Walker Brothers & Co. Under many a pledge of secrecy a number of brothers from the lodge were allowed to come in and see the sets, each carrying away in his pocket some examples of the false scrip, so cunningly struck that there was never the slightest difficulty or danger in passing it. With

such a wonderful art at his command, and his compact apparatus with its efficient micro-boiler able to stamp coins at the rate of several each minute, why McMurdo should condescend to work at all was a perpetual mystery to his companions; though he made it clear to anyone who asked him that if he lived without any visible means it would very quickly bring the law upon his track.

One company enforcer was indeed after him already; but the incident, as luck would have it, did the adventurer a great deal more good than harm. After the first introduction there were few evenings when he did not find his way to McGinty's pub, there to make closer acquaintance with 'the boys,' which was the jovial title by which the dangerous gang who infested the place were known to one another. His dashing manner and fearlessness of speech made him a favourite with them all; while the rapid and scientific way in which he polished off his antagonist in an 'all in' bar-room scrap earned the respect of that rough community. Another incident, however, raised him even higher in their estimation.

Just at the crowded hour one night, the hatch opened and a man entered in the scarlet suit of a British Lunar Expeditionary Company enforcer. There was a hush as he entered, and many a curious glance was cast at him; but the relations between enforcers and criminals are peculiar on the Moon, and McGinty himself, standing behind his counter, showed no surprise when the Bleeker Boy enrolled himself among his customers.

"A straight whisky; for the night is bitter," said the enforcer. "I don't think we have met before, Councillor?"

"You'll be the new captain?" said McGinty.

"That's so. We're looking to you, Councillor, and to the other leading citizens, to help us in upholding law and order in this township. Captain Marvin is my name."

"We'd do better without you, Captain Marvin," said McGinty coldly; "for we have our own means of policing the *Vale*, and no need for any imported goods. What are you but the paid tool of the capitalists, hired by them to club or shoot your poorer fellow citizen?"

"Well, well, we won't argue about that," said the other good-

humouredly. "I expect we all do our duty same as we see it; but we can't all see it the same." He had drunk off his glass and had turned to go, when his eyes fell upon the face of Jack McMurdo, who was scowling at his elbow. "Hullo! Hullo!" he cried, looking him up and down. "Here's an old acquaintance!"

McMurdo shrank away from him. "I was never a friend to you nor any other cursed copper in my life," said he.

"An acquaintance isn't always a friend," said the enforcer captain, grinning. "You're Jack McMurdo of Chicago, right enough, and don't you deny it!"

McMurdo shrugged his shoulders. "I'm not denying it," said he. "D'ye think I'm ashamed of my own name?"

"You've got good cause to be, anyhow."

"What the devil d'you mean by that?" he roared with his fists clenched.

"No, no, Jack, bluster won't do with me. I was an officer in Chicago before ever I came to this darned burned out cinder, and I know a Chicago crook when I see one."

McMurdo's face fell. "Don't tell me that you're Marvin of the Chicago Central!" he cried.

"Just the same old Teddy Marvin, at your service. We haven't forgotten the shooting of Jonas Pinto down there."

"I never shot him."

"Did you not? That's good impartial evidence, ain't it? Well, his death came in uncommon handy for you, or they would have had you for shoving the queer. Well, we can let that be bygones; for, between you and me—and perhaps I'm going further than my duty in saying it—they could get no clear case against you, and Chicago's open to you tomorrow."

"I'm very well where I am."

"Well, I've given you the pointer, and you're a sulky dog not to thank me for it."

"Well, I suppose you mean well, and I do thank you," said McMurdo in no very gracious manner.

"It's mum with me so long as I see you living on the straight," said the

captain. "But, by the Lord! if you get off after this, it's another story! So good-night to you—and good-night, Councillor."

He left the bar-room; but not before he had created a local hero. McMurdo's deeds in far Chicago had been whispered before. He had put off all questions with a smile, as one who did not wish to have greatness thrust upon him. But now the thing was officially confirmed. The bar loafers crowded round him and shook him heartily by the hand. He was free of the community from that time on. He could drink hard and show little trace of it; but that evening, had his mate Scanlan not been at hand to lead him home, the feted hero would surely have spent his night under the bar.

On a Saturday night McMurdo was introduced to the lodge. He had thought to pass in without ceremony as being an initiate of Chicago; but there were particular rites in Victoria of which they were proud, and these had to be undergone by every postulant. The assembly met under one of the half-buried domes, surrounded by titanic machinery and stored vehicles. Some sixty members assembled at Victoria, lost amidst the dome's lofty vastness; but that by no means represented the full strength of the organization, for there were several other lodges in the *Vale* who exchanged members when any serious business was afoot, so that a crime might be done by men who were strangers to the locality. Altogether there were not less than five hundred scattered over the entire settlement.

In the vast dome the men were gathered round a long table. At the side was a second one laden with bottles and glasses, on which some members of the company were already turning their eyes. Behind them reared one of the ceaseless atmosphere pumps: like a colossal church organ, reaching into the dome's shadowy apex, a nightmare maze of pipes and tubes; a slowly beating heart providing a basso profundo harmony to the night's proceedings. To the left were a squadron of battered Atkinson & Philipson transports, along with empty ore hoppers and two as yet pristine tractor units bearing Thomas Rickett badges. On the right was a chaos of mining equipment: pneumatic rams that were the modern

replacement to the more wasteful hydraulic mining methods familiar to McMurdo; impactor drills: yard-long cylinders composed of multiple barrels mounted on skeletal tracked frames—developed from the Gatling gun principle—which, powered by remote steam engines, spun at terrific speeds, spitting out steel-jacketed bullets at velocities that shattered the most reluctant Moon rock into dust; and wheeled storage batteries, each twice the height of a man, which served as the only source of power should the steam catastrophically fail.

McGinty sat at the head of the tables with a flat black velvet cap upon his shock of tangled white hair, and a coloured purple stole round his neck, so that he seemed to be a priest presiding over some diabolical ritual. To right and left of him were the higher lodge officials, the cruel, handsome face of Ted Baldwin among them. Each of these wore some scarf or medallion as emblem of his office.

They were, for the most part, men of mature age; but the rest of the company consisted of young fellows from eighteen to twenty-five, the ready and capable agents who carried out the commands of their seniors. Among the older men were many whose features showed the tigerish, lawless souls within; but looking at the rank and file it was difficult to believe that these eager and open-faced young fellows were in very truth a dangerous gang of murderers, whose minds had suffered such complete moral perversion that they took a horrible pride in their proficiency at the business, and looked with deepest respect at the man who had the reputation of making what they called 'a clean job.'

To their contorted natures it had become a spirited and chivalrous thing to volunteer for service against some man who had never injured them, and whom in many cases they had never seen in their lives. The crime committed, they quarrelled as to who had actually struck the fatal blow, and amused one another and the company by describing the cries and contortions of the murdered man.

At first they had shown some secrecy in their arrangements; but at the time which this narrative describes their proceedings were extraordinarily

open, for the repeated failure of the law had proved to them that, on the one hand, no one would dare to witness against them, and on the other they had an unlimited number of staunch witnesses upon whom they could call, and a well-filled treasure chest from which they could draw the funds to engage the best legal talent in the satellite. In ten months of outrage there had been no single conviction, and the only danger that ever threatened the Scowrers lay in the victim himself—who, however outnumbered and taken by surprise, might and occasionally did leave his mark upon his assailants.

McMurdo had been warned that some ordeal lay before him; but no one would tell him in what it consisted. He was led now by two solemn brothers into a triangular space formed by three ore hoppers. Beyond the crude partition he could hear the murmur of many voices from the assembly within. Once or twice he caught the sound of his own name, and he knew that they were discussing his candidacy. Then there entered an inner guard with a green and gold sash across his chest.

"The Bodymaster orders that he shall be trussed, blinded, and entered," said he.

The three of them removed his coat, turned up the sleeve of his right arm, and finally passed a rope round above the elbows and made it fast. They next placed a thick black cap right over his head and the upper part of his face, so that he could see nothing. He was then led through a gap in the parked hoppers into the assembly hall.

It was pitch dark and very oppressive under his hood. He heard the rustle and murmur of the people round him, and then the voice of McGinty sounded dull and distant through the covering of his ears.

"John McMurdo," said the voice, "are you already a member of the Eminent Order of Freemen?"

He bowed in assent.

"Is your lodge No. 29, Chicago?"

He bowed again.

"Dark nights are unpleasant," said the voice.

"Yes, for strangers to travel," he answered.

"The clouds are heavy."

"Yes, a storm is approaching."

"Are the brethren satisfied?" asked the Bodymaster.

There was a general murmur of assent.

"We know, Brother, by your sign and by your countersign that you are indeed one of us," said McGinty. "We would have you know, however, that in this new world we have certain rites, and also certain duties of our own which call for good men. Are you ready to be tested?"

"I am."

"Are you of stout heart?"

"I am."

"Take a stride forward to prove it."

As the words were said he felt two hard points in front of his eyes, pressing upon them so that it appeared as if he could not move forward without a danger of losing them. None the less, he nerved himself to step resolutely out, and as he did so the pressure melted away. There was a low murmur of applause.

"He is of stout heart," said the voice. "Can you bear pain?"

"As well as another," he answered.

"Test him!"

It was all he could do to keep himself from screaming out, for an agonizing pain shot through his forearm. He nearly fainted at the sudden shock of it; but he bit his lip and clenched his hands to hide his agony.

"I can take more than that," said he.

This time there was loud applause. A finer first appearance had never been made in the lodge. Hands clapped him on the back, and the hood was plucked from his head. He stood blinking and smiling amid the congratulations of the brothers. Before him stood McGinty, a steel rod clenched in his hand; an electrical cable, clad in aluminium shielding, tailed off in the direction of a giant battery. The tip smoked still from where it had seared McMurdo's flesh; they had marked him as their own

with an electric branding iron.

"One last word, Brother McMurdo," said McGinty. "You have already sworn the oath of secrecy and fidelity, and you are aware that the punishment for any breach of it is instant and inevitable death?"

"I am," said McMurdo.

"And you accept the rule of the Bodymaster for the time being under all circumstances?"

"I do."

The Bodymaster reached down and produced an unused, gleaming scowrer; with great ceremony he handed it across to McMurdo. "Then in the name of Lodge 341, *Vale de Verme*, I welcome you to its privileges and debates. You will put the liquor on the table, Brother Scanlan, and we will drink to our worthy brother."

McMurdo's coat had been brought to him; but before putting it on he examined his right arm, which still smarted heavily. There on the flesh of the forearm was a circle with a triangle within it, deep and red, as the branding iron had left it. One or two of his neighbours pulled up their sleeves and showed their own lodge marks.

"We've all had it," said one; "but not all as brave as you over it."

"Tut! It was nothing," said he; but it burned and ached all the same.

When the drinks which followed the ceremony of initiation had all been disposed of, the business of the lodge proceeded. McMurdo, accustomed only to the prosaic performances of Chicago, listened with open ears and more surprise than he ventured to show to what followed.

"The first business on the agenda paper," said McGinty, "is to read the following letter from Division Master Windle of Albertstown Lodge 249. He says:

"Dear Sir:—There is a job to be done on Andrew Rae of Rae & Sturmash, pit owners near this place. You will remember that your lodge owes us a return, having had the service of two brethren in the matter of the enforcer last fall. You will send two good men, they will be taken charge of by Treasurer

Higgins of this lodge, whose address you know. He will show them when to act and where.

Yours in freedom,
J. W. WINDLE D.M.A.O.F."

"Windle has never refused us when we have had occasion to ask for the loan of a man or two, and it is not for us to refuse him." McGinty paused and looked round the room with his dull, malevolent eyes. "Who will volunteer for the job?"

Several young fellows held up their hands. The Bodymaster looked at them with an approving smile.

"You'll do, Tiger Cormac. If you handle it as well as you did the last, you won't be wrong. And you, Wilson."

"And what shall I use for the deed?" asked the volunteer, a mere boy in his teens.

"It's your first, is it not? Well, you have to be blooded some time. It will be a great start for you. As to the means, you'll find it waiting for you, or I'm mistaken. If you report yourselves on Monday, it will be time enough. You'll get a great welcome when you return."

"Any reward this time?" asked Cormac, a thick-set, dark-faced, brutal-looking young man, whose ferocity had earned him the nickname of 'Tiger.'

"Never mind the reward. You just do it for the honour of the thing. Maybe when it is done there will be a few odd pounds at the bottom of the box."

"What has the man done?" asked young Wilson.

"Sure, it's not for the likes of you to ask what the man has done. He has been judged over there. That's no business of ours. All we have to do is to carry it out for them, same as they would for us. Speaking of that, two brothers from the Albertstown lodge are coming over to us next week to do some business in this quarter."

"Who are they?" asked someone.

"Faith, it is wiser not to ask. If you know nothing, you can testify nothing,

and no trouble can come of it. But they are men who will make a clean job when they are about it."

"And time, too!" cried Ted Baldwin. "Folk are gettin' out of hand in these parts. It was only last week that three of our men were turned off by Foreman Blaker. It's been owing him a long time, and he'll get it full and proper."

"Get what?" McMurdo whispered to his neighbour.

"The business end of a scowrer!" cried the man with a loud laugh. "What think you of our ways, Brother?"

McMurdo's criminal soul seemed to have already absorbed the spirit of the vile association of which he was now a member. "I like it well," said he. "'Tis a proper place for a lad of mettle."

Several of those who sat around heard his words and applauded them.

"What's that?" cried the white-maned Bodymaster from the end of the table.

"'Tis our new brother, sir, who finds our ways to his taste."

McMurdo rose to his feet for an instant. "I would say, Worshipful Master, that if a man should be wanted I should take it as an honour to be chosen to help the lodge."

There was great applause at this. It was felt that a new Sun was pushing its rim above the horizon. To some of the elders it seemed that the progress was a little too rapid.

"I would move," said the secretary, Harraway, a vulture-faced old greybeard who sat near the chairman, "that Brother McMurdo should wait until it is the good pleasure of the lodge to employ him."

"Sure, that was what I meant; I'm in your hands," said McMurdo.

"Your time will come, Brother," said the chairman. "We have marked you down as a willing man, and we believe that you will do good work in these parts. There is a small matter tonight in which you may take a hand if it so please you."

"I will wait for something that is worthwhile."

"You can come tonight, anyhow, and it will help you to know what we stand for in this community. I will make the announcement later. Meanwhile," he glanced at his agenda paper, "I have one or two more

points to bring before the meeting. First of all, I will ask the treasurer as to our bank balance. There is the pension to Jim Carnaway's widow. He was struck down doing the work of the lodge, and it is for us to see that she is not the loser."

"Jim was shot last month when they tried to kill Chester Wilcox of Helmdale," McMurdo's neighbour informed him.

"The funds are good at the moment," said the treasurer, with the bankbook in front of him. "The firms have been generous of late. Kynoch paid five hundred to be left alone. Walker Brothers sent in a hundred; but I took it on myself to return it and ask for five. If I do not hear by Wednesday, their winding gear may get out of order. There was an incident with an unsecured impactor last year before they became reasonable. Then the BLEC has paid its contribution. We have enough on hand to meet any obligations."

"What about Archie Swindon?" asked a brother.

"He has sold out and left the district. The old devil left a note for us to say that he had rather be a free crossing sweeper in London than a large mine owner under the power of a ring of blackmailers. By gosh! it was as well that he made a break for it before the note reached us! I guess he won't show his face in this valley again."

An elderly, clean-shaved man with a kindly face and a good brow rose from the end of the table which faced the chairman. "Mr Treasurer," he asked, "may I ask who has bought the property of this man that we have driven out of the district?"

There was a briefest consultation of accounts. "Yes, Brother Morris. It has been bought by the North British Satellite Mining Company."

"And who bought the mines of Todman and of Lee that came into the market in the same way last year?"

"The same company, Brother Morris."

"And who bought the ilmenite works of Manson and of Shuman and of Van Deher and of Atwood, which have all been given up of late?"

"They were all bought by the West Gilmerton General Mining Company."

"I don't see, Brother Morris," said the chairman, "that it matters to us who buys them, since they can't carry them out of the district."

"With all respect to you, Worshipful Master, I think it may matter very much to us. This process has been going on now since first landing. We are gradually driving all the small men out of trade. What is the result? We find in their places great companies like Harland & Wolff or the North British, who have their directors in London or Manchester, and care nothing for our threats. We can take it out of their local bosses; but it only means that others will be sent in their stead. And we are making it dangerous for ourselves. The small men could not harm us. They had not the money nor the power. So long as we did not squeeze them too dry, they would stay on under our power. But if these big companies find that we stand between them and their profits, they will spare no pains and no expense to hunt us down and bring us to court."

There was a hush at these ominous words, and every face darkened as gloomy looks were exchanged. So omnipotent and unchallenged had they been that the very thought that there was possible retribution in the background had been banished from their minds. And yet the idea struck a chill to the most reckless of them.

"It is my advice," the speaker continued, "that we go easier upon the small men. On the day that they have all been driven out the power of this society will have been broken."

Unwelcome truths are not popular. There were angry cries as the speaker resumed his seat. McGinty rose with gloom upon his brow.

"Brother Morris," said he, "you were always a croaker. So long as the members of this lodge stand together there is no power on this world or another that can touch them. Sure, have we not tried it often enough in the law courts? I expect the big companies will find it easier to pay than to fight, same as the little companies do. You said it yourself: the BLEC has already paid its due—and on time. That edifice is greater than all of the other businesses combined, yet is happy to contribute."

The old man's brow furrowed—as though dazed or struggling to recall

a thought. "Mr Chairman, I am not sure that this was meant to be our role—"

"Our role is what I say it is!" roared McGinty; then he visibly calmed himself. "And now, Brethren," he took off his black velvet cap and his stole as he spoke, "this lodge has finished its business for the evening, save for one small matter which may be mentioned when we are parting. The time has now come for fraternal refreshment and for harmony."

Strange indeed is human nature. Here were these men, to whom murder was familiar, who again and again had struck down the father of the family, some man against whom they had no personal feeling, without one thought of compunction or of compassion for his weeping wife or helpless children, and yet the tender or pathetic in music could move them to tears. McMurdo had a fine tenor voice, and if he had failed to gain the good will of the lodge before, it could no longer have been withheld after he had thrilled them with *I'm Sitting on the Stile, Mary,* and *On the Banks of Allan Water.*

In his very first night the new recruit had made himself one of the most popular of the brethren, marked already for advancement and high office. There were other qualities needed, however, besides those of good fellowship, to make a worthy Freeman, and of these he was given an example before the evening was over. The whisky bottle had passed round many times, and the men were flushed and ripe for mischief when their Bodymaster rose once more to address them.

"Boys," said he, "there's one man in this town that wants trimming up, and it's for you to see that he gets it. I'm speaking of James Stanger of the *Herald*. You've seen how he's been opening his mouth against us again?"

There was a murmur of assent, with many a muttered oath. McGinty took a slip of paper from his waistcoat pocket.

"'*LAW AND ORDER!*' That's how he heads it."

"*REIGN OF TERROR ON THE MOON—Eight months have now elapsed since the first assassinations which proved the existence of a criminal organization in our midst. From that day these outrages have never ceased,*

until now they have reached a pitch which makes us the opprobrium of the civilized worlds. Is it for such results as this that our new world welcomes to its bosom the poor and downtrodden who seek a life in the heavens, beyond any promise of an earthly Eden? Is it that they shall themselves become tyrants over the very men who have given them shelter, and that a state of terrorism and lawlessness should be established under the very shadow of the sacred folds of the Union Flag which would raise horror in our minds if we read of it as existing under the most effete monarchy of the East? The men are known. The organization is patent and public. How long are we to endure it? Can we forever live—'"

"Sure, I've read enough of the slush!" cried the chairman, tossing the paper down upon the table. "That's what he says of us. The question I'm asking you is what shall we say to him?"

"Kill him!" cried a dozen fierce voices.

"I protest against that," said Brother Morris, the man of the good brow and shaved face. "I tell you, Brethren, that our hand is too heavy in this valley, and that there will come a point where in self-defence every man will unite to crush us out. James Stanger is a man aged beyond his years. He is respected in the township and the district. His paper stands for all that is solid in the *Vale*. If that man is struck down, there will be a stir through this place which will echo back across the *Mare Nubium* and beyond, ending only with our destruction."

"And how would they bring about our destruction, Mr Standback?" cried McGinty. "Is it by the enforcers? Sure, half of them are in our pay and half of them afraid of us. Or is it by the law courts on Earth? We are very far from Earth, Brother—and on this black orb we are the law!" A general shout of angry satisfaction greeted his words.

"I have but to raise my finger," cried McGinty, "and I could put two hundred men into this settlement that would clear it out from end to end." Then suddenly raising his voice and bending his huge brows into a terrible frown, "See here, Brother Morris, I have my eye on you, and have had for some time! You've no heart yourself, and you try to take the heart out of others. It will be an ill day for you, Brother Morris, when

your own name comes on our agenda paper, and I'm thinking that it's just there that I ought to place it."

Morris had turned deadly pale, and his knees seemed to give way under him as he fell back into his chair. He raised his glass in his trembling hand and drank before he could answer. "I apologize, Worshipful Master, to you and to every brother in this lodge if I have said more than I should. I am a faithful member—you all know that—and it is my fear lest evil come to the lodge which makes me speak in anxious words. But I have greater trust in your judgement than in my own, Worshipful Master, and I promise you that I will not offend again."

The Bodymaster's scowl relaxed as he listened to the humble words. "Very good, Brother Morris. It's myself that would be sorry if it were needful to give you a lesson. But so long as I am in this chair we shall be a united lodge in word and in deed. And now, boys," he continued, looking round at the company, "I'll say this much, that if Stanger got his full deserts there would be more trouble than we need ask for. These editors hang together, and within days every rag and journal on Earth would be crying out for troops to be despatched forthwith. But I guess you can give him a pretty severe warning. Will you fix it, Brother Baldwin?"

"Sure!" said the young man eagerly.

"How many will you take?"

"Half a dozen, and two to guard the door. You'll come, Gower, and you, Mansel, and you, Scanlan, and the two Willabys."

"I promised the new brother he should go," said the chairman.

Ted Baldwin looked at McMurdo with eyes which showed that he had not forgotten nor forgiven. "Well, he can come if he wants," he said in a surly voice. "That's enough. The sooner we get to work the better."

The company broke up with shouts and yells and snatches of drunken song. The crude bar was still crowded with revellers, and many of the brethren remained there. The little band who had been told off for duty passed out of the vast dome and into the tunnels, proceeding in twos and threes so as not to provoke attention. The lighting strung along the curved sides flickered worse than if they had been ageing gas street lamps

back in London. The men stopped and gathered in a knot outside a crude store front close to the centre of the settlement: little more than a doorway and single porthole, their seals hanging ajar, signifying the place was in use. The words, *Lunar Herald* were printed in gold lettering above the door hatch. From within came the clanking of the printing press.

"Here, you," said Baldwin to McMurdo, "you can stand below at the door and see that the road is kept open for us. Arthur Willaby can stay with you. You others come with me. Have no fears, boys; for we have a dozen witnesses that we are in the Union Bar at this very moment." He slipped his suit helmet on and sealed it—the signal for all of the others to do the same.

It was nearly midnight, and the tunnel was deserted save for one or two revellers upon their way home. The party pushed open the door of the newspaper office, Baldwin and his men stamped in and up a metal stair which faced them. McMurdo and another remained below. From the shadows above came a shout, a cry for help, and then the sound of trampling feet and of falling chairs. An instant later an unsuited man rushed out on the landing.

He was seized before he could get farther, and his goggles snapped, toppling down to McMurdo's feet. There was a thud and a groan. He was on his face, and half a dozen hand scowrers were clattering together as they fell upon him. He writhed, and his long, thin limbs quivered under the blows. The others ceased at last; but Baldwin was hacking at the man's head, which he vainly endeavoured to defend with his arms. His white hair was dabbled with patches of blood. Baldwin was still stooping over his victim, putting in a short, vicious blow whenever he could see a part exposed, when McMurdo thundered up the stair—his unwieldy bulk made lighter and more agile by the lesser gravity—and pushed him back.

"You'll kill the man," said he. "Drop it!"

Baldwin looked at him through his helmet visor, his face set in amazement. "Curse you!" he cried, his voice muffled but still clear. "Who are you to interfere—you that are new to the lodge? Stand back!"

He raised his scowrer; but McMurdo aimed his own, newly-presented grappler.

"Stand back yourself!" he cried, loosening his mica visor to be more clearly heard. "I'll blow your face in if you lay a hand on me. As to the lodge, wasn't it the order of the Bodymaster that the man was not to be killed—and what are you doing but killing him?"

"It's truth he says," remarked one of the men.

"By gosh! you'd best hurry yourselves!" cried the man below. "Some of the portholes are undogging, and you'll have the whole town here inside of five minutes."

There was indeed the sound of shouting from the tunnels, and a little group of compositors and typesetters was forming in the hall below and nerving itself to action. Leaving the limp and motionless body of the editor at the head of the stair, the criminals battered their way through the nervy group, anonymous and protected in their suits, and made their way swiftly as they could along the lava tunnels. Having reached the Union House, some of them mixed with the crowd in McGinty's pub, whispering across the bar to the Boss that the job had been well carried through. Others, and among them McMurdo, broke away into side streets, and so by devious paths to their own homes.

IV. The Valley of Fear

When McMurdo awoke next morning he had good reason to remember his initiation into the lodge. His head ached with the effect of the drink, and his arm, where he had been branded, was hot and swollen. Having his own peculiar source of income, he was irregular in his attendance at his work; so he had a late breakfast, and remained at home for the morning writing a long letter to a friend. Afterwards he read the *Lunar Herald*. In a special column put in at the last moment he read:

"OUTRAGE AT THE HERALD OFFICE – EDITOR SERIOUSLY INJURED."

It was a short account of the facts with which he was himself more familiar than the writer could have been. It ended with the statement:

The matter is now in the hands of the enforcement agencies; but it can hardly be hoped that their exertions will be attended by any better results than in the past. Some of the men were recognized, and there is hope that a conviction may be obtained. The source of the outrage was, it need hardly be said, that infamous society which has held this community in bondage for so long a period, and against which the Herald *has taken so uncompromising a stand. Mr Stanger's many friends will rejoice to hear that, though he has been cruelly and brutally beaten, and though he has sustained severe injuries about the head, there is no immediate danger to his life.*

Below it stated that a detachment of BLEC enforcers—Bleeker Boys— armed with purpose-made Enfield CO_2 rifles, had been requisitioned for the defence of the office.

McMurdo had laid down the paper, and was lighting his pipe with a

hand which was shaky from the excesses of the previous evening, when there was a knock outside, and his landlady brought to him a note which had just been handed in by a lad. It was unsigned, and ran thus:

"I should wish to speak to you, but would rather not do so in your house. You will find me beside the flagstaff upon Miller Hill. If you will come there now, I have something which it is important for you to hear and for me to say."

McMurdo read the note twice with the utmost surprise; for he could not imagine what it meant or who the author of it was. Had it been in a feminine hand, he might have imagined that it was the beginning of one of those adventures which had been familiar enough in his past life. But it was the writing of a man, and of a well-educated one, too. Finally, after some hesitation—only those whose need was desperate ventured out during the lunar night—he determined to see the matter through.

Miller Hill is the prosaic name given to a spoil heap just to the north of Victoria, named after James Miller: the first miner to extract enough ore from the lunar rock to make steel smelting a possibility. The man had died shortly before he had been able to enjoy the fruits of his labours, and the BLEC had subsumed his claim. From the top of it one has a view not only of the surface domes and vents which delineate the straggling, grimy site, but of the whole *Vale*, with its scattered trenches, pneumatic mines and processing plants casting a thin pall of disturbed dust and crushed rock over the surface, slow to settle in the low gravity.

McMurdo toiled up the winding path hedged in with discarded boulders. The Sun was already up and casting dazzling highlights on the ragged valley sides. He felt its heat through both his suit's insulation and coolant system—the lunar day regularly peaks at two hundred and seventy-three Fahrenheit as there was no dense atmosphere to temper the Sun's rays—even as transformers within the armour stored the light in electrical cells to power its pumps. He was sweating before he came close on the desolate peak. Beside it was a simple cairn, commemorating the

life of James Miller, and next to that stood a man, the lamp depending from his excursion suit glowing a pale yellow. When he turned, raising his lamp to cast some light through his mica visor, McMurdo saw that it was Brother Morris, he who had incurred the anger of the Bodymaster the night before. The lodge sign was given and exchanged as they met. They touched helmets to transmit the sounds of their speech.

"I wanted to have a word with you, Mr McMurdo," said the older man, speaking with a hesitation which showed that he was on delicate ground. "It was kind of you to come."

"Why did you not put your name to the note?"

"One has to be cautious, mister. One never knows in times like these how a thing may come back to one. One never knows either who to trust or who not to trust."

"Surely one may trust brothers of the lodge."

"No, no, not always," cried Morris with vehemence. "Whatever we say, even what we think, seems to go back to that man McGinty."

"Look here!" said McMurdo sternly. "It was only last night, as you know well, that I swore good faith to our Bodymaster. Would you be asking me to break my oath?"

"If that is the view you take," said Morris sadly, "I can only say that I am sorry I gave you the trouble to come and meet me. Things have come to a bad pass when two free citizens cannot speak their thoughts to each other."

McMurdo, who had been watching his companion's face very narrowly through his visor, relaxed somewhat in his bearing. "Sure I spoke for myself only," said he. "I am a newcomer, as you know, and I am strange to it all. It is not for me to open my mouth, Mr Morris, and if you think well to say anything to me I am here to hear it."

"And to take it back to Boss McGinty!" said Morris bitterly.

"Indeed, then, you do me injustice there," cried McMurdo. "For myself I am loyal to the lodge, and so I tell you straight; but I would be a poor creature if I were to repeat to any other what you might say to me in confidence. It will go no further than me; though I warn you that you may get neither help nor sympathy."

"I have given up looking for either the one or the other," said Morris. "I may be putting my very life in your hands by what I say; but, bad as you are—and it seemed to me last night that you were shaping to be as bad as the worst—still you are new to it, and your conscience cannot yet be as hardened as theirs. That was why I thought to speak with you."

"Well, what have you to say?"

"If you give me away, may a curse be on you!"

"Sure, I said I would not."

"I would ask you, then, when you joined the Freeman's society in Chicago and swore vows of charity and fidelity, did ever it cross your mind that you might find it would lead you to crime?"

"If you call it crime," McMurdo answered.

"Call it crime!" cried Morris, his voice vibrating with passion. "You have seen little of it if you can call it anything else. Was it crime last night when a man was beaten till the blood dripped from his white hairs? Was that crime—or what else would you call it?"

"There are some would say it was war," said McMurdo, "a war of two classes with all in, so that each struck as best it could."

"Well, did you think of such a thing when you joined the Freeman's society at Chicago?"

"No, I'm bound to say I did not."

"Nor did I when I joined it at Merthyr. It was just a benefit club and a meeting place for one's fellows. Then I heard of this place—curse the hour that the name first fell upon my ears!—and I came to better myself! My God! to better myself! My wife and three children came with me. I started a dry goods store in Market Tunnel, and I prospered well. The word had gone round that I was a Freeman, and I was forced to join the local lodge, same as you did last night. I've the badge of shame on my forearm and something worse branded on my heart. I found that I was under the orders of a black villain and caught in a mesh-work of crime. What could I do? Every word I said to make things better was taken as treason, same as it was last night. I can't get away; for all I have in the world is in my store. If I leave the society, I know well that it means

murder to me, and God knows what to my wife and children. Oh, man, it is awful—awful!" He pulled away so McMurdo could hear his voice no more, but his heavy suit twitched as though the body within shook with convulsive sobs.

McMurdo shrugged his shoulders—though the other could not have seen it. They knocked helmets again. "You were too soft for the job," said he. "You are the wrong sort for such work."

"I had a conscience and a religion; but they made me a criminal among them. I was chosen for a job. If I backed down I knew well what would come to me. Maybe I'm a coward. Maybe it's the thought of my poor little woman and the children that makes me one. Anyhow I went. I guess it will haunt me forever.

"It was a lonely house, twenty miles from here, in the remotest tunnels yet discovered. I was told off for the door, same as you were last night. They could not trust me with the job. The others went in. When they came out their gauntlets were crimson to the wrists. As we turned away a child was screaming out of the house behind us. It was a boy of five who had seen his father murdered. I nearly fainted with the horror of it, and yet I had to keep a bold and smiling face; for well I knew that if I did not it would be out of my house that they would come next with their bloody hands and it would be my little Fred that would be screaming for his father.

"But I was a criminal then, part sharer in a murder, lost forever in this world, and lost also in the next. Though I am a good Welshman I am also Catholic; but the priest would have no word with me when he heard I was a Scowrer, and I am excommunicated from my faith. That's how it stands with me. And I see you going down the same road, and I ask you what the end is to be. Are you ready to be a cold-blooded murderer also, or can we do anything to stop it?"

"What would you do?" asked McMurdo abruptly. "You would not inform?"

"God forbid!" cried Morris. "Sure, the very thought would cost me my life."

"That's well," said McMurdo. "I'm thinking that you are a weak man and that you make too much of the matter."

"Too much! Wait till you have lived here longer. Look down the valley! See the cloud of that overshadows it! I tell you that the cloud of murder hangs thicker and lower than that over the heads of the people. It is the Valley of Fear, the Valley of Death. The terror is in the hearts of the people from the dusk to the dawn. Wait, young man, and you will learn for yourself."

"Well, I'll let you know what I think when I have seen more," said McMurdo carelessly. "What is very clear is that you are not the man for this place, and that the sooner you sell out—if you only get a penny for every pound the business is worth—the better it will be for you. What you have said is safe with me; but, by gosh! if I thought you were an informer—"

"No, no!" cried Morris piteously.

"Well, let it rest at that. I'll bear what you have said in mind, and maybe someday I'll come back to it. I expect you meant kindly by speaking to me like this. Now I'll be getting home."

"One word before you go," said Morris. "We may have been seen together. They may want to know what we have spoken about."

"Ah! that's well thought of."

"I offer you a clerkship in my store."

"And I refuse it. That's our business. Well, so long, Brother Morris, and may you find things go better with you in the future."

That same afternoon, as McMurdo sat smoking, lost in thought beside the stove of his sitting-room, the hatch swung open and its framework was filled with the huge figure of Boss McGinty's suit. He passed the sign, and then seating himself opposite to the young man he looked at him steadily for some time, a look which was as steadily returned.

"I'm not much of a visitor, Brother McMurdo," he said at last. "I guess I am too busy over the folk that visit me. But I thought I'd stretch a point and drop down to see you in your own house."

"I'm proud to see you here, Councillor," McMurdo answered heartily,

bringing his whisky bottle out of the cupboard. "It's an honour that I had not expected."

"How's the arm?" asked the Boss.

McMurdo made a wry face. "Well, I'm not forgetting it," he said; "but it's worth it."

"Yes, it's worth it," the other answered, "to those that are loyal and go through with it and are a help to the lodge. What were you speaking to Brother Morris about on Miller Hill this morning?"

The question came so suddenly that it was well that he had his answer prepared. He burst into a hearty laugh. "Morris didn't know I could earn a living here at home. He shan't know either; for he has got too much conscience for the likes of me. But he's a good-hearted old chap. It was his idea that I was at a loose end, and that he would do me a good turn by offering me a clerkship in a dry goods store."

"Oh, that was it?"

"Yes, that was it."

"And you refused it?"

"Sure. Couldn't I earn ten times as much in my own bedroom with four hours' work?"

"That's so. But I wouldn't get about too much with Morris."

"Why not?"

"Well, I guess because I tell you not. That's enough for most folk in these parts."

"It may be enough for most folk; but it ain't enough for me, Councillor," said McMurdo boldly. "If you are a judge of men, you'll know that."

The swarthy giant glared at him, and his gloved paw closed for an instant round the glass as though he would hurl it at the head of his companion. Then he laughed in his loud, boisterous, insincere fashion.

"You're a queer card, for sure," said he. "Well, if you want reasons, I'll give them. Did Morris say nothing to you against the lodge?"

"No."

"Nor against me?"

"No."

"Well, that's because he daren't trust you. But in his heart he is not a loyal brother. We know that well. So we watch him and we wait for the time to admonish him. I'm thinking that the time is drawing near. There's no room for scabby sheep in our pen. But if you keep company with a disloyal man, we might think that you were disloyal, too. See?"

"There's no chance of my keeping company with him; for I dislike the man," McMurdo answered. "As to being disloyal, if it was any man but you he would not use the word to me twice."

"Well, that's enough," said McGinty, draining off his glass. "I came down to give you a word in season, and you've had it."

"I'd like to know," said McMurdo, "how you ever came to learn that I had spoken with Morris at all?"

McGinty laughed. "It's my business to know what goes on in this place," said he. "I guess you'd best reckon on my hearing all that passes. Well, time's up, and I'll just say—"

But his leave-taking was cut short in a very unexpected fashion. With a sudden crash the hatch was flung open, and three frowning, intent faces glared in at them from under the peaks of police caps. McMurdo sprang to his feet and reached for his scowrer; but his arm stopped midway as he became conscious that two Enfield CO_2-rifles were levelled at his head. A man in a scarlet excursion suit advanced into the room, clutching a scowrer of his own. It was Captain Marvin, once of Chicago, and now of the Bleeker Boys. He shook his head with a half-smile at McMurdo.

"I thought you'd be getting into trouble, Mr Crooked McMurdo of Chicago," said he. "Can't keep out of it, can you? Suit yourself up and come along with us."

"I guess you'll pay for this, Captain Marvin," said McGinty. "Who are you, I'd like to know, to break into a house in this fashion and molest honest, law-abiding men?"

"You're standing out in this deal, Councillor McGinty," said the enforcer. "We are not out after you, but after this man McMurdo. It is for you to help, not to hinder us in our duty."

"He is a friend of mine, and I'll answer for his conduct," said the Boss.

"By all accounts, Mr McGinty, you may have to answer for your own conduct some of these days," the captain answered. "This man McMurdo was a crook before ever he came here, and he's a crook still. Cover him, Sergeant, while I disarm him."

"There's my scowrer yonder," said McMurdo coolly. "Maybe, Captain Marvin, if you and I were alone and face to face you would not take me so easily."

"Where's your warrant?" asked McGinty. "By gosh! a man might as well live in Russia as in Victoria while folk like you are running the law. It's a capitalist outrage, and you'll hear more of it, I reckon."

"You do what you think is your duty the best way you can, Councillor. We'll look after ours."

"What am I accused of?" asked McMurdo.

"Of being concerned in the beating of old Editor Stanger at the *Herald* office. It wasn't your fault that it isn't a murder charge."

"Well, if that's all you have against him," cried McGinty with a laugh, "you can save yourself a deal of trouble by dropping it right now. This man was with me in my pub playing poker up to midnight, and I can bring a dozen to prove it."

"That's your affair, and I guess you can settle it in court tomorrow. Meanwhile, come on, McMurdo, and come quietly if you don't want one of these across your head." He gestured with his scowrer. "A tidy little weapon, to be sure. You stand wide, Mr McGinty; for I warn you I will stand no resistance when I am on duty!"

So determined was the appearance of the captain that both McMurdo and his boss were forced to accept the situation. The latter managed to have a few whispered words with the prisoner before they parted.

"What about—?" he jerked his thumb upward to signify the coining plant.

"All right," whispered McMurdo, who had devised a safe hiding place under the floor.

"I'll bid you goodbye," said the Boss, shaking hands. "I'll see Reilly the lawyer and take the defence upon myself. Take my word for it that they won't be able to hold you."

"I wouldn't bet on that. Guard the prisoner, you two, and shoot him if he tries any games. I'll search the house before I leave."

He did so; but apparently found no trace of the concealed plant. When he had descended he and his men escorted McMurdo—now fully suited up, helmet in one hand—to Bleeker headquarters. It was away across the *Vale*, situated within the BLEC offices. The surface was nearly deserted; but a few loiterers followed the group, and emboldened by the anonymity afforded them by their suits, waved crude gestures at the prisoner.

Two held barely-legible placards: *LYNCH THE CURSED SCOWRER!* one declared. *LYNCH HIM!* echoed the second. They pointed as he was pushed into the police station, miming laughter. After a short, formal examination from the inspector in charge he was put into the common cell. Here he found Baldwin and three other criminals of the night before, all arrested that afternoon and waiting their trial next morning. Far below the BLEC offices, hacked from the coarse rock, the cell had but one harsh electric light which was never extinguished; the stale, recirculated air was rank and frigid. But for their excursion suits, which they were allowed to continue wearing, they might have frozen well before their trial.

But even within this inner fortress of the law the long arm of the Freemen was able to extend. Late at night there came a jailer with a straw bundle for their bedding, out of which he extracted two bottles of whisky, some glasses, and a pack of cards. They spent a hilarious night, warmed by the rough spirits, without an anxious thought as to the ordeal of the morning.

Nor had they cause, as the result was to show. The magistrate could not possibly, on the evidence, have held them for a higher court. On the one hand the compositors and pressmen were forced to admit that the light was uncertain, that they were themselves much perturbed, and that it was difficult for them to swear to the identity of the assailants—since

all were armoured crown to toe in suits—although they believed that the accused were among them. Cross examined by the clever attorney who had been engaged by McGinty, they were even more nebulous in their evidence.

The injured man had already deposed that he was so taken by surprise by the suddenness of the attack that he could state nothing beyond the fact that the first man who struck him wore a bronze-coloured suit. He added that he knew them to be Scowrers, since no one else in the community could possibly have any enmity to him, and he had long been threatened on account of his outspoken editorials. On the other hand, it was clearly shown by the united and unfaltering evidence of six citizens, including that high municipal official, Councillor McGinty, that the men had been at a card party at the Union House until an hour very much later than the commission of the outrage; besides there were any number of bronzed excursion suits to be found across the *Vale*.

Needless to say that they were discharged with something very near to an apology from the bench for the inconvenience to which they had been put, together with an implied censure of Captain Marvin and the Bleekers for their officious zeal.

The verdict was greeted with loud applause by a court in which McMurdo saw many familiar faces. Brothers of the lodge smiled and waved. But there were others who sat with compressed lips and brooding eyes as the men filed out of the dock. One of them, a little, dark-bearded, resolute fellow, put the thoughts of himself and comrades into words as the ex-prisoners passed him.

"You damned murderers!" he said. "We'll fix you yet!"

V. The Darkest Hour

If anything had been needed to give an impetus to Jack McMurdo's popularity among his fellows it would have been his arrest and acquittal. That a man on the very night of joining the lodge should have done something which brought him before the magistrate was a new record in the annals of the society. Already he had earned the reputation of a good boon companion, a cheery reveller, and withal a man of high temper, who would not take an insult even from the all-powerful Boss himself. But in addition to this he impressed his comrades with the idea that among them all there was not one whose brain was so ready to devise a bloodthirsty scheme, or whose hand would be more capable of carrying it out. "He'll be the boy for the clean job," said the oldsters to one another, and waited their time until they could set him to his work.

McGinty had instruments enough already; but he recognized that this was a supremely able one. He felt like a man holding a fierce bloodhound in leash. There were curs to do the smaller work; but some day he would slip this creature upon its prey. A few members of the lodge, Ted Baldwin among them, resented the rapid rise of the stranger and hated him for it; but they kept clear of him, for he was as ready to fight as to laugh.

But if he gained favour with his fellows, there was another quarter, one which had become even more vital to him, in which he lost it. Ettie Shafter's father would have nothing more to do with him, nor would he allow him to enter the house. Ettie herself was too deeply in love to give him up altogether, and yet her own good sense warned her of what would come from a marriage with a man who was regarded as a criminal.

One morning after a sleepless night she determined to see him, possibly for the last time, and make one strong endeavour to draw him from those evil influences which were sucking him down. She went to his house, as he had often begged her to do, and made her way into the rough, stone-carved room. He was seated at a table, with his back turned and a letter in front of him. A sudden spirit of girlish mischief came over her—she was still only nineteen. He had not heard her when she pushed open the door. Now she tiptoed forward and laid her hand lightly upon his bended shoulders.

If she had expected to startle him, she certainly succeeded; but only in turn to be startled herself. With a tiger spring he turned on her, and his right hand was feeling for her throat. At the same instant with the other hand he crumpled up the paper that lay before him. For an instant he stood glaring. Then astonishment and joy took the place of the ferocity which had convulsed his features—a ferocity which had sent her shrinking back in horror as from something which had never before intruded into her gentle life.

"It's you!" said he, mopping his brow. "And to think that you should come to me, heart of my heart, and I should find nothing better to do than to want to strangle you! Come then, darling," and he held out his arms, "let me make it up to you."

But she had not recovered from that sudden glimpse of guilty fear which she had read in the man's face. All her woman's instinct told her that it was not the mere fright of a man who is startled. Guilt—that was it—guilt and fear!

"What's come over you, Jack?" she cried. "Why were you so scared of me? Oh, Jack, if your conscience was at ease, you would not have looked at me like that!"

"Sure, I was thinking of other things, and when you came tripping so lightly on those fairy feet of yours—"

"No, no, it was more than that, Jack." Then a sudden suspicion seized her. "Let me see that letter you were writing."

"Ah, Ettie, I couldn't do that."

Her suspicions became certainties. "It's to another woman," she cried. "I know it! Why else should you hold it from me? Was it to your wife that you were writing? How am I to know that you are not a married man—you, a stranger, that nobody knows?"

"I am not married, Ettie. See now, I swear it! You're the only one woman on earth to me. By the cross of Christ I swear it!"

He was so white with passionate earnestness that she could not but believe him.

"Well, then," she cried, "why will you not show me the letter?"

"I'll tell you," said he. "I'm under oath not to show it, and just as I wouldn't break my word to you so I would keep it to those who hold my promise. It's the business of the lodge, and even to you it's secret. And if I was scared when a hand fell on me, can't you understand it when it might have been the hand of an enforcer?"

She felt that he was telling the truth. He gathered her into his arms and kissed away her fears and doubts.

"Sit here by me, then. It's a queer throne for such a queen; but it's the best your poor lover can find. He'll do better for you some of these days, I'm thinking. Now your mind is easy once again, is it not?"

"How can it ever be at ease, Jack, when I know that you are a criminal among criminals, when I never know the day that I may hear you are in court for murder? 'McMurdo the Scowrer,' that's what one of our boarders called you yesterday. It went through my heart like a knife."

"Sure, hard words break no bones."

"But they were true."

"Well, dear, it's not so bad as you think. We are but poor men that are trying in our own way to get our rights."

Ettie threw her arms round her lover's neck. "Give it up, Jack! For my sake, for God's sake, give it up! It was to ask you that I came here to-day. Oh, Jack, see—I beg it of you on my bended knees! Kneeling here before you I implore you to give it up!"

He raised her and soothed her with her head against his breast.

"Sure, my darlin', you don't know what it is you are asking. How could I give it up when it would be to break my oath and to desert my comrades? If you could see how things stand with me you could never

ask it of me. Besides, if I wanted to, how could I do it? You don't suppose that the lodge would let a man go free with all its secrets?"

"I've thought of that, Jack. I've planned it all. Father has saved some money. He is weary of this place where the fear of these people darkens our lives. He is ready to go. We would fly back together to Earth, return to Africa, where we would be safe from them."

McMurdo laughed. "The lodge has a long arm. Do you think it could not stretch from here to Pretoria or the Transvaal Republic?"

"Well, then, to the Americas, or to England, or to Germany—anywhere to get away from this Valley of Fear!"

McMurdo thought of old Brother Morris. "Sure, it is the second time I have heard the valley so named," said he. "The shadow does indeed seem to lie heavy on some of you."

"It darkens every moment of our lives. Do you suppose that Ted Baldwin has ever forgiven us? If it were not that he fears you, what do you suppose our chances would be? If you saw the look in those dark, hungry eyes of his when they fall on me!"

"By gosh! I'd teach him better manners if I caught him at it! But see here, little girl. I can't leave here. I can't—take that from me once and for all. But if you will leave me to find my own way, I will try to prepare a way of getting honourably out of it."

"There is no honour in such a matter."

"Well, well, it's just how you look at it. But if you'll give me six months, I'll work it so that I can leave without being ashamed to look others in the face."

The girl laughed with joy. "Six months!" she cried. "Is it a promise?"

"Well, it may be seven or eight. But within a year at the furthest we will leave the valley behind us."

It was the most that Ettie could obtain, and yet it was something. There was this distant light to illuminate the gloom of the immediate future. She returned to her father's house more light-hearted than she had ever been since Jack McMurdo had come into her life.

It might be thought that as a member, all the doings of the society would be told to him; but he was soon to discover that the organization

was wider and more complex than the simple lodge. Even Boss McGinty was ignorant as to many things; for there was an official named the Lunar Delegate, living in a comfortable apartment at the *Mare Nubium* landing field, who had power over several different lodges which he wielded in a sudden and arbitrary way. Only once did McMurdo see him, a sly, little rat of a man, with a slinking gait and a sidelong glance which was charged with malice. Evans Pott was his name, and even the great Boss of Victoria felt towards him something of the repulsion and fear which the huge Danton may have felt for the puny but dangerous Robespierre.

One day Scanlan, who was McMurdo's fellow boarder, received a note from McGinty enclosing one from Evans Pott, which informed him that he was sending over two good men, Lawler and Andrews, who had instructions to act in the neighbourhood; though it was best for the cause that no particulars as to their objects should be given. Would the Bodymaster see to it that suitable arrangements be made for their lodgings and comfort until the time for action should arrive? McGinty added that it was impossible for anyone to remain secret at the Union House, and that, therefore, he would be obliged if McMurdo and Scanlan would put the strangers up for a few days in their boarding house.

The same evening the two men arrived, each carrying his grip-sack. Lawler was an elderly man, shrewd, silent, and self-contained, clad in an old blackened excursion suit, which with the soft felt hat he wore constantly and ragged beard gave him a general resemblance to an itinerant preacher. His companion Andrews was little more than a boy, frank-faced and cheerful, with the breezy manner of one who is out for a holiday and means to enjoy every minute of it. Both men were total abstainers, and behaved in all ways as exemplary members of the society, with the one simple exception that they were assassins who had often proved themselves to be most capable instruments for this association of murder. Lawler had already carried out fourteen commissions of the kind, and Andrews three.

They were, as McMurdo found, quite ready to converse about their deeds in the past, which they recounted with the half-bashful pride of

men who had done good and unselfish service for the community. They were reticent, however, as to the immediate job in hand.

"They chose us because neither I nor the boy here drink," Lawler explained. "They can count on us saying no more than we should. You must not take it amiss, but it is the orders of the Lunar Delegate that we obey."

"Sure, we are all in it together," said Scanlan, McMurdo's mate, as the four sat together at supper.

"That's true enough, and we'll talk till the cows come home of the killing of Charlie Williams or of Simon Bird, or any other job in the past. But till the work is done we say nothing."

"There are half a dozen about here that I have a word to say to," said McMurdo, with an oath. "I suppose it isn't Jack Knox of Icehill that you are after. I'd go some way to see him get his deserts."

"No, it's not him yet."

"Or Herman Strauss?"

"No, nor him either."

"Well, if you won't tell us we can't make you; but I'd be glad to know."

Lawler smiled and shook his head. He was not to be drawn.

In spite of the reticence of their guests, Scanlan and McMurdo were quite determined to be present at what they called 'the fun.' When, therefore, at an early hour one morning McMurdo heard them treading down the stairs he awakened Scanlan, and the two hurried on their clothes. When they were dressed in their excursion suits they found that the others had stolen out, leaving the hatch open behind them. On the surface it was not yet dawn but in the burrows it was perpetual evening, and by the light of the dancing wall-lamps they could see the two men some distance down the tunnel. They followed them warily, treading noiselessly as they could in their boots.

The boarding house was near the edge of the town, and soon they were beyond its boundary where the lava tunnel ended in a sudden, rocky wall which was scaled by a steel ladder reaching to the arched roof and a hatch: the last exit to the surface. Here three men were waiting,

with whom Lawler and Andrews held a short, eager conversation. Then they all climbed the ladder into the airlock, dogging the tunnel hatch behind them. It was clearly some notable job which needed numbers. After allowing sufficient time for the five to have reached the surface, McMurdo and Scanlan followed.

McMurdo led. Once he had reached the outer hatch he cracked it slowly, raising it just enough for him to peer out across the bright lunar landscape. From his vantage he could see several faint trails spreading out; the strangers had taken that which led to the Crow Hill, a regolith formation resembling a huge corvid which overhung a processing plant: its products of steam, oxygen and hydrogen vital for the continuance—nay, the very existence—of Victoria. The plant was in strong hands which had been able, thanks to its energetic and fearless Scottish manager, Josiah H. Dunn, to keep some order and discipline during the long reign of terror.

A line of suited workmen were slowly making their way, singly and in groups, along the blackened path. McMurdo and Scanlan strolled on with them, keeping in sight of the men whom they followed. A thick grey cloud lay over them, and from the heart of it there grew a sickly, pallid glow, resolving as the cloud thinned into the entrance for the processing plant—towards which everyone was making. The crowd of workers trudged into the wide, pale-lit mouth of the huge airlock—sufficient to accommodate many times more the present number; McMurdo and Scanlan found themselves hemmed in, their quarry lost to view. The towering outer hatches swung closed; there was an expectant pause as the airlock was flooded with an atmosphere, ended by the pulsing of a green light above inner hatches—no less impressive than those on the outside— which laboriously cracked open. The workers unsealed their helmets, moving through the inner access; not one challenged the presence of two unfamiliar faces. All eyes stayed resolutely downcast; grimed faces sullen and detached. They even failed to react to the sudden scream of a steam whistle—though McMurdo flinched, and cursed himself for a frightened girl. It was the signal proclaiming the end of the night shift, and the commencement of the day's labour.

When they reached the open space which was the heart of the plant—cored out of the crow-shaped rock—there were already a hundred workers in place, with more following in despondent clumps. The strangers stood in a little group under the shadow of an engine house: Lawler easily identified in his black suit. Scanlan and McMurdo climbed a heap of slag from which the whole scene lay before them. Wide chutes hung from the high roof, disgorging endless landslides of blasted rock and boulders, mined from the coldest reaches of the lunar surface: those benighted pits where the Sun's heat never penetrates, and from the southern pole itself. Falling onto conveyors—anything that should miss shovelled back by stooped workmen—the rock was ground under colossal toothed rollers into rubble, and from there spilled into pits of fire. Hell itself could not be more dreadful. Any ice locked in the rubble vaporised into steam and boiled up into collecting ducts—along with any smoke or fine dust. The steam was condensed and stored as liquid water in the insulated tanks McMurdo and Scanlan saw in the furthest distance of that satanic hall; smoke and dust allowed to escape into the Moon's attenuated atmosphere. Elsewhere—though neither man could perceive them from their vantage—were the scission chambers: seething biological vats that saw water reduced to its elemental constituents of hydrogen and oxygen. Of the scorched rubble that remained, all was driven into heaps—such as the one McMurdo and Scanlan occupied—to be further smelted down in an effort to extract whatever elements might remain.

The plant supervisor, a great bearded Scotchman named Menzies, came out of the engine house and blew his whistle. All of the workers shuffled towards him to be instructed in their tasks of the day. At the same instant a tall, loose-framed young man with a clean-shaved, earnest face advanced eagerly towards the factory floor: the manager. As he came forward his eyes fell upon the group, silent and motionless, under the engine house. The men had retained their bulky helmets to screen their faces. For a moment the presentiment of Death laid its cold hand upon the manager's heart. At the next he had shaken it off and saw only his duty towards intrusive strangers.

"Who are you?" he asked as he advanced. "What are you loitering there for?"

There was no answer; but one stepped forward and raised what McMurdo recognised as a Colt revolver and shot the manager in the stomach. The hundred waiting miners stood as motionless and helpless as if they were paralysed. The manager clapped his two hands to the wound and doubled himself up. Then he staggered away; but another of the assassins fired a similar pistol, and he went down sidewise, kicking and clawing among a heap of clinkers. Menzies, the Scotchman, gave a roar of rage at the sight and rushed with an iron spanner at the murderers; but was met by two balls in the face which dropped him dead at their very feet.

There was a surge forward of some of the miners, and an inarticulate cry of pity and of anger; but a couple of the strangers emptied their six-shooters over the heads of the crowd, and they broke and scattered, some of them rushing wildly for the airlock. Only McMurdo and Scanlan watched as the murderers coolly threw their pistols onto a conveyor— to be crushed by the rollers and turned to slag in the fire-pits—before adding the bodies of the manager and Menzies.

When a few of the bravest had rallied, and there was a return to the factory floor, the murderous gang had vanished in the clouds of ejecta, without a single witness being able to swear to the identity of these men who in front of a hundred spectators had wrought this double crime.

Scanlan and McMurdo made their way back; Scanlan somewhat subdued, for it was the first murder job that he had seen with his own eyes, and it appeared less funny than he had been led to believe. The horrible screams of the dead manager's wife pursued them as they hurried to the town; even, it seemed, along the tunnel. McMurdo was absorbed and silent; but he showed no sympathy for the weakening of his companion.

"Sure, it is like a war," he repeated. "What is it but a war between us and them, and we hit back where we best can."

There was high revel in the lodge room at the Union House that night, not only over the killing of the manager and engineer of the Crow Hill

factory, which would bring this organization into line with the other blackmailed and terror-stricken companies of the district, but also over a distant triumph which had been wrought by the hands of the lodge itself.

It would appear that when the Lunar Delegate had sent over five good men to strike a blow in Victoria, he had demanded that in return three Victoria men should be secretly selected and sent across to kill William Hales of Stake Royal, one of the best known and most popular factory owners in Albertstown, a man who was believed not to have an enemy in the world; for he was in all ways a model employer. He had insisted, however, upon efficiency in the work, and had, therefore, paid off certain drunken and idle *employés* who were members of the all-powerful society. Coffin notices hung outside his door had not weakened his resolution, and so he found himself condemned to death.

The execution had now been duly carried out. Ted Baldwin, who sprawled now in the seat of honour beside the Bodymaster, had been chief of the party. His flushed face and glazed, bloodshot eyes told of sleeplessness and drink. He and his two comrades had spent the night before among the mountains. They were unkempt; their suits scored and smeared with dust. But no heroes, returning from a forlorn hope, could have had a warmer welcome from their comrades.

The story was told and retold amid cries of delight and shouts of laughter. They had waited for their man as he ridden back to his domed residence—for Albertstown has no lava tunnels—in a small, personal transport—little more than a skeleton frame on wheels—taking their station at the top of a steep hill, where his vehicle must be at its slowest. In his suit his movements were slow and uncoordinated; he had tried to lay his hand on a long wrench, and failed. They had pulled him out and shot him with their scowrers—the long, sharp anchoring tips easily piercing the gaps in his articulated suit. The air venting through the holes in his suit had sounded like screams for mercy. The screams were repeated for the amusement of the lodge.

"Let's hear again how he squealed," they cried.

None of them knew the man; but there is eternal drama in a killing,

and they had shown the Scowrers of Albertstown that the Victoria men were to be relied upon.

There had been one *contretemps*; for two figures had driven up while they were retrieving their blades from the silent body: electrical workers laying cable for an expanded lighting network. It had been suggested that they should kill them both; but they were harmless folk who were not connected with the mines, so they were sternly bidden to drive on and keep silent, lest a worse thing befall them. And so the blood-mottled figure had been left as a warning to all such hard-hearted employers, and the three noble avengers had hurried off into the mountains where unbroken nature comes down to the very edge of the scarred Moon face and the slag heaps. Here they were, safe and sound, their work well done, and the plaudits of their companions in their ears.

It had been a great day for the Scowrers. The shadow had fallen even darker over the *Vale*. But as the wise general chooses the moment of victory in which to redouble his efforts, so that his foes may have no time to steady themselves after disaster, so Boss McGinty, looking out upon the scene of his operations with his brooding and malicious eyes, had devised a new attack upon those who opposed him. That very night, as the half-drunken company broke up, he touched McMurdo on the arm and led him aside into that inner room where they had their first interview.

"See here, my lad," said he, "I've got a job that's worthy of you at last. You'll have the doing of it in your own hands."

"Proud I am to hear it," McMurdo answered.

"You can take two men with you—Manders and Reilly. They have been warned for service. We'll never be right in this district until Chester Wilcox has been settled, and you'll have the thanks of every lodge on the Moon if you can down him."

"I'll do my best, anyhow. Who is he, and where shall I find him?"

McGinty took his eternal half-chewed, half-smoked cigar from the corner of his mouth, and proceeded to draw a rough diagram on a page torn from his notebook.

"He's the chief foreman of the Iron Duke Company. He's a hard citizen, an old colour sergeant, veteran of many an African campaign: all scars and grizzle. We've had two tries at him; but had no luck, and Jim Carnaway lost his life over it. Now it's for you to take it over. That's the house—all alone at the Iron Duke Tunnel, same as you see here on the map—without another within earshot. It's no good by day. He's armed and shoots quick and straight with one of those infernal CO2-rifles; no questions asked. But at night—well, there he is with his wife, three children, and a hired help. You can't pick or choose. It's all or none. If you could get a box of explosive at the hatch—"

"What's the man done?"

"Didn't I tell you he shot Jim Carnaway?"

"Why did he shoot him?"

"What in thunder has that to do with you? Carnaway was about his house at night, and he shot him. That's enough for me and you. You've got to settle the thing right."

"There's these two women and the children. Do they go up too?"

"They have to—else how can we get him?"

"It seems hard on them; for they've done nothing."

"What sort of fool's talk is this? Do you back out?"

"Easy, Councillor, easy! What have I ever said or done that you should think I would be after standing back from an order of the Bodymaster of my own lodge? If it's right or if it's wrong, it's for you to decide."

"You'll do it, then?"

"Of course I will do it."

"When?"

"Well, you had best give me a night or two that I may see the house and make my plans. Then—"

"Very good," said McGinty, shaking him by the hand. "I leave it with you. It will be a great day when you bring us the news. It's just the last stroke that will bring them all to their knees."

McMurdo thought long and deeply over the commission which had been so suddenly placed in his hands. The isolated house in which Chester

Wilcox lived was about five miles off in an adjacent set of residential trenches, populated only by *employés* of the Iron Duke Company. That very night he started off all alone to prepare for the attempt. It was many hours before he returned from his reconnaissance. Next day he interviewed his two subordinates, Manders and Reilly, reckless youngsters who were as elated as if it were a deer-hunt.

Two nights later they met outside the town, all three armed with their scowrers, and one of them carrying a plain metal box containing the explosive which was used to blast ore-rich rocks into manageable pieces: an adaptation of terrestrial dynamite formulated specifically for the Moon. Rather than explode indiscriminately, lunamite—as it has jokingly become known—is a shaped charge which impels its force directly into the rock against which it is placed, fracturing it rather than scattering. It was two in the morning before they came to the lonely house. Lunar night had fallen recently, and the unearthly cold gnawed its way past their suit's heaters. The black sky was more congested with stars than could ever be appreciated from Earth now that the Sun's glare was gone; whilst overhead the home world had become a looming, blue and white three-quarter moon, casting the only light. Their miner's lamps were too limited in the gloom, and they carried powerful, battery-powered lights that threw a focused beam ahead of them; if the beam began to falter, the battery was recharged by simply cranking a dynamo by means of a folding handle. As an extra precaution Reilly's scowrer was anchored to a rocky outcrop close by the remote airlock access to Victoria through which they had emerged, the line paid out like Ariadne's thread behind them. It is true that all three men were not sorry when they located the first hatch that led down to the Iron Duke Tunnel, tied off the scowrer line, and were able to descend out of the cold and dark. Once in the unfamiliar burrow they chanced the removal of their helmets, both to see more clearly and enjoy the comparative warmth of the tunnel.

They had been warned to be on their guard against enforcers—for Wilcox had a small private army of his own; so they moved forward cautiously, with their scowrers cocked in their hands. But there was no

sound save the murmuration of distant pumps, and no movement but the gentle brush of air on their faces.

McMurdo listened at the entrance of the lonely house; but all was still within. Then he opened the box and removed three pyramidally-shaped copper-shelled charges from it; these he positioned against the hatch so that the blast would be directed inward, and not wasted blowing out into the tunnel. He attached chemical fuses which could burn even in the near vacuum of the lunar atmosphere, in this case lengthy ones to give them time to flee. When they were well alight he and his two companions returned back to the surface as swiftly as they were able, untying Reilly's scowrer line and retracing it—all of their lamps extinguished. They were many yards off, safe and snug behind a jagged ridge, before they felt the ground below them tremble with the force of the explosion. The lunar surface around the hatch cover, and beyond, shuddered before falling in on the collapsing house underneath. Their work was done. No cleaner job had ever been carried out in the blood-stained annals of the society.

But alas that work so well organized and boldly carried out should all have gone for nothing! Warned by the fate of the various victims, and knowing that he was marked down for destruction, Chester Wilcox had moved himself and his family only the day before to some safer and less known quarters, where his private enforcers should watch over them. It was an empty house which had been torn down by the lunamite, and the grim old colour sergeant of the war was still teaching discipline to the miners of Iron Duke.

"Leave him to me," said McMurdo. "He's my man, and I'll get him sure if I have to wait a year for him."

A vote of thanks and confidence was passed in full lodge, and so for the time the matter ended. When a few weeks later it was reported in the papers that Wilcox had been shot at from an ambuscade, it was an open secret that McMurdo was still at work upon his unfinished job.

Such were the methods of the Society of Freemen, and such were the deeds of the Scowrers by which they spread their rule of fear over the great and rich district which was for so long a period haunted by their

terrible presence. Why should these pages be stained by further crimes? Have I not said enough to show the men and their methods?

These deeds are written in history, and there are records wherein one may read the details of them. There one may learn of the stabbing of Bleeker Boys Hunt and Evans because they had ventured to arrest two members of the society—a double outrage planned at the Victoria lodge and carried out in cold blood upon two helpless and disarmed men. There also one may read of the shooting of Mrs Larbey when she was nursing her husband, who had been beaten almost to death by orders of Boss McGinty. The killing of the elder Jenkins, shortly followed by that of his brother, the mutilation of James Murdoch, the blowing up of the Staphouse family, and the murder of the Stendals all followed hard upon one another.

Darkly the shadow lay upon the Valley of Fear. The Sun arose to light the next lunar day like a beacon of hope; but nowhere was there any hope for the men and women who lived under the yoke of the terror. The clouds of dust and smoke ejected from the factories and processing plants thickened along the *Vale de Verme*; but never had the cloud above them been so dark and hopeless as in the year '76.

VI. DANGER

It was the height of the reign of terror. McMurdo, who had already been appointed Inner Deacon, with every prospect of someday succeeding McGinty as Bodymaster, was now so necessary to the councils of his comrades that nothing was done without his help and advice. The more popular he became, however, with the Freemen, the blacker were the scowls which greeted him as he passed along the tunnels of Victoria. In spite of their terror the citizens were taking heart to band themselves together against their oppressors. Rumours had reached the lodge of secret gatherings in the *Lunar Herald* office and of distribution of weapons among the law-abiding people. But McGinty and his men were undisturbed by such reports. They were numerous, resolute, and well-armed. Their opponents were scattered and powerless. It would all end, as it had done in the past, in aimless talk and possibly in impotent arrests. So said McGinty, McMurdo, and all the bolder spirits.

By the adopted Julian calendar it was a Saturday evening in May. Saturday was always the lodge night, and McMurdo was leaving his house to attend it when Morris, the weaker brother of the order, came to see him. His brow was creased with care, and his kindly face was drawn and haggard.

"Can I speak with you freely, Mr McMurdo?"

"Sure."

"I can't forget that I spoke my heart to you once, and that you kept it to yourself, even though the Boss himself came to ask you about it."

"What else could I do if you trusted me? It wasn't that I agreed with what you said."

"I know that well. But you are the one that I can speak to and be safe. I've a secret here," he put his hand to the armour plating above his breast, "and it is just burning the life out of me. I wish it had come to any one

of you but me. If I tell it, it will mean murder, for sure. If I don't, it may bring the end of us all. God help me, but I am near out of my wits over it!"

McMurdo looked at the man earnestly. He was trembling in every limb. He poured some whisky into a glass and handed it to him. "That's the physic for the likes of you," said he. "Now let me hear of it."

Morris drank, and his white face took a tinge of colour. "I can tell it to you all in one sentence," said he. "There's a detective on our trail."

McMurdo stared at him in astonishment. "Why, man, you're crazy," he said. "Isn't the place full of guards and enforcers and what harm did they ever do us?"

"No, no, it's no man of the district. As you say, we know them, and it is little that they can do. But you've heard of the Pinkerton's.?"

"I've read of some folk of that name."

"Well, you can take it from me you've no show when they are on your trail. It's not a take-it-or-miss-it government concern. It's a dead earnest business proposition that's out for results and keeps out till by hook or crook it gets them."

McMurdo poured himself a drink. "But some private bull from an American agency would have no jurisdiction here. It's likely the British government wouldn't welcome him any more than do we…"

Morris shook his head, unconvinced. "If a Pinkerton man is deep in this business, we are all destroyed."

"We must kill him."

"Ah, it's the first thought that came to you! So it will be up at the lodge. Didn't I say to you that it would end in murder?"

"Sure, what is murder? Isn't it common enough in these parts?"

"It is, indeed; but it's not for me to point out the man that is to be murdered. I'd never rest easy again. And yet it's our own necks that may be at stake. In God's name what shall I do?" He rocked to and fro in his agony of indecision.

But his words had moved McMurdo deeply. It was easy to see that he shared the other's opinion as to the danger, and the need for meeting it.

He gripped Morris's shoulder and shook him in his earnestness.

"See here, man," he cried, and he almost screeched the words in his excitement, "you won't gain anything by sitting keening like an old wife at a wake. Let's have the facts. Who is the fellow? Where is he? How did you hear of him? Why did you come to me?"

"I came to you; for you are the one man that would advise me. I told you that I had a shop on Earth before I came here. I left good friends behind me, and several emigrated to America to improve their lot. One of them is in the US telegraph service. Here's a letter he sent me that came up on the shot from Earth yesterday—thank the Lord our post is still unimpaired! It's this part from the top of the page. You can read it yourself."

This was what McMurdo read:

"How are the Scowrers getting on up there? We read plenty of them in the wires—though are sworn to secrecy. Between you and me I expect to hear news from you before long. Five big corporations and the two railroads have taken the thing up in dead earnest: they have ambitions for our closest neighbour, and think the British have forfeited all claim by their inaction. They mean it, and you can bet they'll get there! They are right deep down into it. Pinkerton has taken hold under their orders, and his best man, Birdy Edwards, is operating. The thing has got to be stopped right now."

"Now read the postscript."

"Of course, what I give you I should have no knowledge of; so it goes no further. It would mean my job, at the very least. But it's a queer cipher that you handle by the yard every day and can get no meaning from."

McMurdo sat in silence for some time, with the letter in his listless hands. The mist had lifted for a moment, and there was the abyss before him.

"Does anyone else know of this?" he asked.

"I have told no one else."

"But this man—your friend—has he any other person that he would be likely to write to?"

"Well, I dare say he knows one or two more."

"Of the lodge?"

"It's likely enough."

"I was asking because it is likely that he may have given some description of this fellow Birdy Edwards—then we could get on his trail."

"Well, it's possible. But I should not think he knew him. He is just a telegraph operator who has learned to decipher more of what goes through his hands than he should. He's just telling me the news that came to him by way of business. How would he know this Pinkerton man?"

McMurdo gave a violent start.

"By gosh!" he cried, "I've got him. What a fool I was not to know it. Lord! but we're in luck! We will fix him before he can do any harm. See here, Morris, will you leave this thing in my hands?"

"Sure, if you will only take it off mine."

"I'll do that. You can stand right back and let me run it. Even your name need not be mentioned. I'll take it all on myself, as if it were to me that this letter has come. Will that content you?"

"It's just what I would ask."

"Then leave it at that and keep your head shut. Now I'll get down to the lodge, and we'll soon make old man Pinkerton sorry for himself."

"You wouldn't kill this man?"

"The less you know, friend Morris, the easier your conscience will be, and the better you will sleep. Ask no questions, and let these things settle themselves. I have hold of it now."

Morris shook his head sadly as he left. "I feel that his blood is on my hands," he groaned.

"Self-protection is no murder, anyhow," said McMurdo, smiling grimly. "It's him or us. I guess this man would destroy us all if we left him long in the valley. Why, Brother Morris, we'll have to elect you Bodymaster yet; for you've surely saved the lodge."

And yet it was clear from his actions that he thought more seriously of this new intrusion than his words would show. It may have been his guilty conscience, it may have been the reputation of the Pinkerton organization, it may have been the knowledge that great, rich foreign corporations had set themselves the task of clearing out the Scowrers; but, whatever his reason, his actions were those of a man who is preparing for the worst. Every paper which would incriminate him was destroyed before he left the house. After that he gave a long sigh of satisfaction; for it seemed to him that he was safe. And yet the danger must still have pressed somewhat upon him; for on his way to the lodge he stopped at old man Shafter's. The house was forbidden him; but when he tapped at the window Ettie came out to him. The dancing Irish devilry had gone from her lover's eyes. She read his danger in his earnest face.

"Something has happened!" she cried. "Oh, Jack, you are in danger!"

"Sure, it is not very bad, my sweetheart. And yet it may be wise that we make a move before it is worse."

"Make a move?"

"I promised you once that I would go some day. I think the time is coming. I had news to-night, bad news, and I see trouble coming."

"The enforcers?"

"Well, a Pinkerton. But, sure, you wouldn't know what that is, nor what it may mean to the likes of me. I'm too deep in this thing, and I may have to get out of it quick. You said you would come with me if I went."

"Oh, Jack, it would be the saving of you!"

"I'm an honest man in some things, Ettie. I wouldn't hurt a hair of your bonny head for all that the world can give, nor ever pull you down one inch from the golden throne above the clouds where I always see you. Would you trust me?"

She put her hand in his without a word. "Well, then, listen to what I say, and do as I order you, for indeed it's the only way for us. Things are going to happen in the *Vale*. I feel it in my bones. There may be many of us that will have to look out for ourselves. I'm one, anyhow. If I go, by day or night, it's you that must come with me!"

"I'd come after you, Jack."

"No, no, you shall come *with* me. If this settlement is closed to me and I can never come back, how can I leave you behind, and me perhaps in hiding from the guards with never a chance of a message? It's with me you must come. I know a good woman in the place I come from, and it's there I'd leave you till we can get married. Will you come?"

"Yes, Jack, I will come."

"God bless you for your trust in me! It's a fiend out of hell that I should be if I abused it. Now, mark you, Ettie, it will be just a word to you, and when it reaches you, you will drop everything and come right down to the pick-up spot for the transport back to *Mare Nubium* and stay there till I come for you."

"Day or night, I'll come at the word, Jack."

Somewhat eased in mind, now that his own preparations for escape had been begun, McMurdo went on to the lodge. It had already assembled, and only by complicated signs and countersigns could he pass through the outer guard and inner guard who close-tiled it. A buzz of pleasure and welcome greeted him as he entered. The long room was crowded, and through the haze of tobacco smoke he saw the tangled white mane of the Bodymaster, the cruel, unfriendly features of Baldwin, the vulture face of Harraway, the secretary, and a dozen more who were among the leaders of the lodge. He rejoiced that they should all be there to take counsel over his news.

"Indeed, it's glad we are to see you, Brother!" cried the chairman. "There's business here that wants a Solomon in judgement to set it right."

"It's Lander and Egan," explained his neighbour as he took his seat. "They both claim the head money given by the lodge for the shooting of Crabbe over at Ice Ridge, and who's to say which fired the bullet?"

McMurdo rose in his place and raised his hand. The expression of his face froze the attention of the audience. There was a dead hush of expectation.

"Worshipful Master," he said, in a solemn voice, "I claim urgency!"

"Brother McMurdo claims urgency," said McGinty. "It's a claim that by the rules of this lodge takes precedence. Now Brother, we attend you."

McMurdo took the letter from his pocket.

"Worshipful Master and Brethren," he said, "I am the bearer of ill news this day; but it is better that it should be known and discussed, than that a blow should fall upon us without warning which would destroy us all. I have information that one of the most powerful and richest organizations on the Earth have bound themselves together for our destruction, and that at this very moment there is an American of the Pinkerton detective agency, one Birdy Edwards, at work in the valley collecting the evidence which may put a cable round the necks of many of us, and send every man in this room into a felon's cell. That is the situation for the discussion of which I have made a claim of urgency."

There was a dead silence in the room. It was broken by the chairman.

"What is your evidence for this, Brother McMurdo?" he asked.

"It is in this letter which has come into my hands," said McMurdo. He read the passage aloud. "It is a matter of honour with me that I can give no further particulars about the letter, nor put it into your hands; but I assure you that there is nothing else in it which can affect the interests of the lodge. I put the case before you as it has reached me."

"Let me say, Mr Chairman," said one of the older brethren, "that I spent a little time in the Californian gold fields and heard the name of Birdy Edwards, and that he is being the best man in the Pinkerton service."

"It's an unlikely thing, I know," said McGinty, "him being an American, and all. But does anyone know him by sight?"

"Yes," said McMurdo, "I do."

There was a murmur of astonishment through the hall.

"I believe we hold him in the hollow of our hands," he continued with an exulting smile upon his face. "If we act quickly and wisely, we can cut this thing short. If I have your confidence and your help, it is little that we have to fear."

"What have we to fear, anyhow?" McGinty growled. "No American shall have the right to dictate what happens on lunar soil. What can he know of our affairs?"

"You might say so if all were as staunch as you, Councillor. But this man has all the millions of the capitalists at his back. Do you think there is no weaker brother among all our lodges that could not be bought? He will get at our secrets—maybe has got them already. There's only one sure cure."

"That he never leaves the *Vale*," said Baldwin.

McMurdo nodded. "Good for you, Brother Baldwin," he said. "You and I have had our differences, but you have said the true word to-night."

"Where is he, then? Where shall we know him?"

"Worshipful Master," said McMurdo, earnestly, "I would put it to you that this is too vital a thing for us to discuss in open lodge. God forbid that I should throw a doubt on anyone here; but if so much as a word of gossip got to the ears of this man, there would be an end of any chance of our getting him. I would ask the lodge to choose a trusty committee, Mr Chairman—yourself, if I might suggest it, and Brother Baldwin here, and five more. Then I can talk freely of what I know and of what I advise should be done."

The proposition was at once adopted, and the committee chosen. Besides the chairman and Baldwin there were the vulture-faced secretary, Harraway, Tiger Cormac, the brutal young assassin, Carter, the treasurer, and the brothers Willaby, fearless and desperate men who would stick at nothing.

The usual revelry of the lodge was short and subdued: for there was a cloud upon the men's spirits, and many there for the first time began to see the cloud of avenging Law drifting up in that serene sky under which they had dwelt so long; and from such an unanticipated quarter. The horrors they had dealt out to others had been so much a part of their settled lives that the thought of retribution had become a remote one, and so seemed the more startling now that it came so closely upon them. They broke up early and left their leaders to their council.

"Now, McMurdo!" said McGinty when they were alone. The seven men sat frozen in their seats.

"I said just now that I knew Birdy Edwards," McMurdo explained. "I need not tell you that he is not here under that name. He's a brave man,

but not a crazy one. He passes under the name of Steve Wilson, and he is lodging at Albertstown."

"How do you know this?"

"Because I fell into talk with him. I thought little of it at the time, nor would have given it a second thought but for this letter; but now I'm sure it's the man. I met him on a transport when I went down to Albertstown on Wednesday—a hard case if ever there was one. He said he was a reporter. I believed it for the moment. Wanted to know all he could about the Scowrers and what he called 'the outrages' for a London paper—except his accent was no more English than my own. Asked me every kind of question so as to get something. You bet I was giving nothing away. 'I'd pay for it and pay well,' said he, 'if I could get some stuff that would suit my editor.' I said what I thought would please him best, and he handed me a five pound note for my information. 'There's ten times that for you,' said he, 'if you can find me all that I want.'"

"What did you tell him, then?"

"Any stuff I could make up."

"How do you know he wasn't a newspaper man?"

"I'll tell you. When got off the transport together, and I loitered a little, to watch what he'd do. I saw him enter the Teslagraph office; when he left, I went in myself. The operator recognised me at once, and became only too happy to share what he knew.

"'See here,' said he, 'I guess we should charge double rates for this.'

"'I guess you should,' said I. He had filled the form with stuff that might have been Chinese, for all we could make of it.

"'He fires a sheet of this off every day,' said the clerk, 'to the landing field on *Mare Nubium*. To go out on the first available shot back down to Earth.'

"'Yes,' said I; 'it's special news for his paper, and he's scared that the others should tap it.' That was what the operator thought and what I thought at the time; but I think differently now."

"By gosh! I believe you are right," said McGinty. "But what do you allow that we should do about it?"

"Why not go right down now and fix him?" someone suggested.

"Ay, the sooner the better."

"I'd start this next minute if I knew where we could find him," said McMurdo. "He's in Albertstown; but I don't know the lodgings. I've got a plan, though, if you'll only take my advice."

"Well, what is it?"

"I'll go to Albertstown tomorrow. I'll find him through the Teslagraph operator. He can locate him, I guess. Well, then I'll tell him that I'm a Freeman myself. I'll offer him all the secrets of the lodge for a price. You bet he'll tumble to it. I'll tell him the papers are at my house, and that it's as much as my life would be worth to let him come while folk were about. He'll see that that's horse sense. Let him come at ten o'clock at night, and he shall see everything. That will fetch him sure."

"Well?"

"You can plan the rest for yourselves. Widow MacNamara's is a lonely house. She's as true as steel and as deaf as a post. There's only Scanlan and me in the house. If I get his promise—and I'll let you know if I do—I'd have the whole seven of you come to me by nine o'clock. We'll get him in. If ever he gets out alive—well, he can talk of Birdy Edwards's luck for the rest of his days!"

"There's going to be a vacancy at Pinkerton's or I'm mistaken. Leave it at that, McMurdo. At nine tomorrow we'll be with you. You once get the door shut behind him, and you can leave the rest with us."

VII. The Trapping of Birdy Edwards

As McMurdo had said, the place in which he lived was lonely and very well suited for such a crime as they had planned. It was on the extreme fringe of the town and in a quiet, half-collapsed tunnel. In any other case the conspirators would have simply called out their man, as they had many a time before, and shot him if they could, stab him with their scowrers if they could not; but in this instance it was very necessary to find out how much he knew, how he knew it, and what had been passed on to his employers.

It was possible that they were already too late and that the work had been done. If that was indeed so, they could at least have their revenge upon the man who had done it. But they were hopeful that nothing of great importance had yet come to the detective's knowledge, as otherwise, they argued, he would not have troubled to write down and forward such trivial information as McMurdo claimed to have given him. However, all this they would learn from his own lips. Once in their power, they would find a way to make him speak. It was not the first time that they had handled an unwilling witness.

McMurdo went to Albertstown as agreed. The enforcers seemed to take particular interest in him that morning, and Captain Marvin—he who had claimed the old acquaintance with him at Chicago—actually addressed him as he waited at the station. McMurdo turned away and refused to speak with him. He was back from his mission in the afternoon, and saw McGinty at the Union House.

"He is coming," he said.

"Good!" said McGinty. The giant was in his shirt sleeves, with chains and seals gleaming athwart his ample waistcoat and a diamond twinkling

through the fringe of his bristling beard. Drink and politics had made the Boss a very rich as well as powerful man. The more terrible, therefore, seemed that glimpse of the prison or the gallows which had risen before him the night before.

"Do you reckon he knows much?" he asked anxiously.

McMurdo shook his head gloomily. "He's been here some time—six weeks at the least. I guess he didn't come into these parts to look at the prospect. If he has been working among us all that time with American money at his back, I should expect that he has got results, and that he has passed them on."

"There's not a weak man in the lodge," cried McGinty. "True as steel, every man of them. And yet, by the Lord! There is that skunk Morris. What about him? If any man gives us away, it would be he. I've a mind to send a couple of the boys round before evening to give him a beating up and see what they can get from him."

"Well, there would be no harm in that," McMurdo answered. "I won't deny that I have a liking for Morris and would be sorry to see him come to harm. He has spoken to me once or twice over lodge matters, and though he may not see them the same as you or I, he never seemed the sort that squeals. But still it is not for me to stand between him and you."

"I'll fix the old devil!" said McGinty with an oath. "I've had my eye on him this year past."

"Well, you know best about that," McMurdo answered. "But whatever you do must be tomorrow; for we must lie low until the Pinkerton affair is settled up. We can't afford to set the enforcers buzzing, today of all days."

"True for you," said McGinty. "And we'll learn from Birdy Edwards himself where he got his news if we have to cut his heart out first. Did he seem to scent a trap?"

McMurdo laughed. "I guess I took him on his weak point," he said. "If he could get on a good trail of the Scowrers, he's ready to follow it into hell. I took his money," McMurdo grinned as he produced a wad of five pound notes, "and as much more when he has seen all my papers."

"What papers?"

"Well, there are no papers. But I filled him up about constitutions and books of rules and forms of membership. He expects to get right down to the end of everything before he leaves."

"Faith, he's right there," said McGinty grimly. "Didn't he ask you why you didn't bring him the papers?"

"As if I would carry such things, and me a suspected man, and Captain Marvin after speaking to me this very day at the depot!"

"Ay, I heard of that," said McGinty. "I guess the heavy end of this business is coming on to you. We could put him down an old shaft when we've done with him; but however we work it we can't get past the man living at Albertstown and you being there today."

McMurdo shrugged his shoulders. "If we handle it right, they can never prove the killing," said he. "No one can see him come to the house after dark, and I'll lay to it that no one will see him go. Now see here, Councillor, I'll show you my plan and I'll ask you to fit the others into it. You will all come in good time. Very well. He comes at ten. He is to tap three times, and me to open the door for him. Then I'll get behind him and shut it. He's our man then."

"That's all easy and plain."

"Yes; but the next step wants considering. He's a hard proposition. He's heavily armed—and not for him some CO2-rifle: it'll be a six-cylinder if I'm not mistaken. I've fooled him proper, and yet he is likely to be on his guard. Suppose I show him right into a room with seven men in it where he expected to find me alone. There is going to be shooting, and somebody is going to be hurt."

"That's so."

"And it'll echo fine down these tunnels: the noise is going to bring every damned enforcer in the township on top of it."

"I guess you are right."

"This is how I should work it. You will all be in the big room—same as you saw when you had a chat with me. I'll open the hatch for him,

show him into the room beside the hatch, and leave him there while I get the papers. That will give me the chance of telling you how things are shaping. Then I will go back to him with some faked papers. As he is reading them I will jump for him and get my grip on his pistol arm. You'll hear me call and in you will rush. The quicker the better; for he is as strong a man as I, and I may have more than I can manage. But I allow that I can hold him till you come."

"It's a good plan," said McGinty. "The lodge will owe you a debt for this. I guess when I move out of the chair I can put a name to the man that's coming after me."

"Sure, Councillor, I am little more than a recruit," said McMurdo; but his face showed what he thought of the great man's compliment.

When he had returned home he made his own preparations for the grim evening in front of him. First he cleaned, gelled, and loaded his Volcanic repeating pistol, at the same time ensuring an extra two fully-loaded box magazines were close to hand. Then he surveyed the room in which the detective was to be trapped. By the Moon's Spartan standards it was a large apartment, with a long deal table in the centre, and the big stove at one side. There were no windows, but the entrance from the floor below was nothing more than a crudely-gouged arch; privacy ensured by a thick curtain. The apartment was very exposed for so secret a meeting. Yet the lodgings' distance from the main tunnel network made it of less consequence. Finally he discussed the matter with his fellow lodger. Scanlan, though a Scowrer, was an inoffensive little man who was too weak to stand against the opinion of his comrades, but was secretly horrified by the deeds of blood at which he had sometimes been forced to assist. McMurdo told him shortly what was intended.

"And if I were you, Mike Scanlan, I would take a night off and keep clear of it. There will be bloody work here before morning."

"Well, indeed then, Mac," Scanlan answered. "It's not the will but the nerve that is wanting in me. When I saw Manager Dunn go down at the plant yonder—and what they did to his bleeding corpse—it was just

more than I could stand. I'm not made for it, same as you or McGinty. If the lodge will think none the worse of me, I'll just do as you advise and leave you to yourselves for the evening."

The men came in good time as arranged. They were outwardly respectable citizens, their excursion suits clean and polished; but a judge of faces would have read little hope for Birdy Edwards in those hard mouths and remorseless eyes. There was not a man in the room whose hands had not been reddened a dozen times before. They were as hardened to human murder as a butcher to sheep.

Foremost, of course, both in appearance and in guilt, was the formidable Boss. Harraway, the secretary, was a lean, bitter man with a long, scraggy neck and nervous, jerky limbs, a man of incorruptible fidelity where the finances of the order were concerned, and with no notion of justice or honesty to anyone beyond. The treasurer, Carter, was a middle-aged man, with an impassive, rather sulky expression, and a yellow parchment skin. He was a capable organizer, and the actual details of nearly every outrage had sprung from his plotting brain. The two Willabys were men of action, tall, lithe young fellows with determined faces, while their companion, Tiger Cormac, a heavy, dark youth, was feared even by his own comrades for the ferocity of his disposition. These were the men who assembled that night under the roof of McMurdo for the killing of the Pinkerton detective.

Their host had placed whisky upon the table, and they had hastened to prime themselves for the work before them. Baldwin and Cormac were already half-drunk, and the liquor had brought out all their ferocity. Cormac placed his hands on the stove for an instant—it had been lighted, for there was a chill in the pumped air.

"That will do," said he, with an oath.

"Ay," said Baldwin, catching his meaning. "If he is strapped to that, we will have the truth out of him."

"We'll have the truth out of him, never fear," said McMurdo. He had nerves of steel, this man; for though the whole weight of the affair was on him his manner was as cool and unconcerned as ever. The others marked it and applauded.

"You are the one to handle him," said the Boss approvingly. "Not a warning will he get till your hand is on his throat. It's a pity there is no door to that archway."

McMurdo went and drew the thick curtain tight across the gap. "Sure no one can spy upon us now. It's close upon the hour."

"Maybe he won't come. Maybe he'll get a sniff of danger," said the secretary.

"He'll come, never fear," McMurdo answered. "He is as eager to come as you can be to see him. Hark to that!"

They all sat like wax figures, some with their glasses arrested halfway to their lips. Three loud knocks had sounded at the hatch downstairs.

"Hush!" McMurdo raised his hand in caution. An exulting glance went round the circle, and hands were laid upon their weapons.

"Not a sound, for your lives!" McMurdo whispered, as he went from the room, closing the curtain carefully behind him.

With strained ears the murderers waited. They counted the steps of their comrade down the rock steps. Then they heard him open the outer hatch. There were a few words as of greeting. Then they were aware of a strange step inside and of an unfamiliar voice. An instant later came the slam of the hatch and the turning of its dogging mechanism. Their prey was safe within the trap. Tiger Cormac laughed horribly, and Boss McGinty clapped his great hand across his mouth.

"Be quiet, you fool!" he whispered. "You'll be the undoing of us yet!"

There was a mutter of conversation from the next room. It seemed interminable. Then the door opened, and McMurdo appeared, his finger upon his lip.

He came to the end of the table and looked round at them. A subtle change had come over him. His manner was as of one who has great work to do. His face had set into granite firmness. His eyes shone with a fierce excitement behind his spectacles. He had become a visible leader of men. They stared at him with eager interest; but he said nothing. Still with the same singular gaze he looked from man to man.

"Well!" cried Boss McGinty at last. "Is he here? Is Birdy Edwards here?"

"Yes," McMurdo answered slowly. "Birdy Edwards is here. I am Birdy Edwards!"

There were ten seconds after that brief speech during which the room might have been empty, so profound was the silence. The hissing of a kettle upon the stove rose sharp and strident to the ear. Seven white faces, all turned upward to this man who dominated them, were set motionless with utter terror. Then, the curtains was torn from its hangings and a squad of Bleeker Boys—fully encased in their scarlet suits so that they resembled things more machine than man—stepped into the room, gleaming CO_2-rifles steady in their hands.

At the sight Boss McGinty gave the roar of a wounded bear and plunged for the archway, battering aside two suited enforcers. A levelled pistol—the match of the one now grasped firmly in McMurdo's steady hand—met him there with the stern blue eyes of Captain Marvin gleaming behind the sights. The Boss recoiled and fell back into his chair.

"You're safer there, Councillor," said the man whom they had known as McMurdo. "And you, Baldwin, if you don't take your hand off your pistol, you'll cheat the hangman yet. Pull it out, or by the Lord that made me—There, that will do. There are forty armed men in the tunnel outside—besides the sharpshooters before you—and you can figure it out for yourself what chance you have. Take their pistols, Marvin!"

There was no possible resistance under the menace of those rifles. The men were disarmed. Sulky, sheepish, and amazed, they still sat round the table.

"I'd like to say a word to you before we separate," said the man who had trapped them. "I guess we may not meet again so I'll give you something to think over between now and when you make your stand in the English Courts. You know me now for what I am. At last I can put my cards on the table. I am Birdy Edwards of the Pinkerton's Agency. I was chosen to investigate the dealings of the Scowrers and break up your gang, if I could. I had a hard and dangerous game to play. Not a soul, not one soul, not my nearest and dearest, not even the British Government, knew that I was playing it. Only Captain Marvin here—you can guess that he is also a Pinkerton's man, as are all the newly-appointed Bleeker Boys, and that neither is Marvin his given name—and my employers knew that. But it's over tonight, thank God, and I am the winner!"

The seven pale, rigid faces looked up at him. There was unappeasable hatred in their eyes. He read the relentless threat.

"Maybe you think that the game is not over yet. Well, I take my chance of that. Anyhow, some of you will take no further hand, and there are sixty more besides yourselves that will see a jail this night. I'll tell you this, that when I was put upon this job I never believed there was such a society as yours. I thought it was paper talk—that the Moon had somehow made its workers lax and unproductive—and that I would prove it so. They told me it was to do with the Freemen, but as John McMurdo I have been a member of the Chicago Lodge for nigh on three years, for reasons which have no bearing here. So I was surer than ever that it was just paper talk; for I found no harm in the society, but a deal of good.

"Still, I had to carry out my job, and I came to the Moon. When I reached this place I learned that I was wrong and that it wasn't a dime novel after all. So I stayed to look after it. I never killed a man in Chicago. I never minted a dollar in my life. Those I gave you were as good as any others; but I never spent money better. But I knew the way into your good wishes and so I pretended to you that the law was after me. It all worked just as I thought.

"So I joined your infernal lodge, and I took my share in your councils. Maybe they will say that I was as bad as you. They can say what they like, so long as I get you. But what is the truth? The night I joined you beat up old man Stanger. I could not warn him, for there was no time; but I held your hand, Baldwin, when you would have killed him. If ever I have suggested things, so as to keep my place among you, they were things which I knew I could prevent. I could not save Dunn and Menzies, for I did not know enough; but I will see that their murderers are hanged. I gave Chester Wilcox warning, so that when I collapsed the surface onto his dwelling he and his folk were in hiding. There was many a crime that

I could not stop; but if you look back and think how often your man came home the other road, or was down in town when you went for him, or stayed indoors when you thought he would come out, you'll see my work."

"You blasted traitor!" hissed McGinty through his closed teeth.

"Ay, John McGinty, you may call me that if it eases your smart. You and your like have been the enemy of God and man in these parts. It took a man to get between you and the poor devils of men and women that you held under your grip. There was just one way of doing it, and I did it. You call me a traitor; but I guess there's many a thousand will call me a deliverer that went down into hell to save them. I've had three months of it. I wouldn't have three such months again if they let me loose in the treasury at Washington for it. I had to stay till I had it all, every man and every secret right here in this hand. I'd have waited a little longer if it hadn't come to my knowledge that my secret was coming out. A letter had come into the town that would have set you wise to it all. Then I had to act and act quickly.

"I've nothing more to say to you, except that when my time comes I'll die the easier when I think of the work I have done in this valley."

McGinty spat, his eyes blazing with murderous fury. "You forget: we are all citizens of the British Empire—even here on this godforsaken rock! Our government will never allow some capitalist Yankee private detective to arrest us!"

The man calling himself McMurdo smiled cruelly. "You have forgotten why you are here … Bodymaster! You are an embarrassment to your government—one they took too long to deal with: for they could not acknowledge their error; nor their hand in it. But the U. S. has its own plans for this ball of rock so, for clearing up their mess and handing you over quiet—so that no one should ever hear of it—England will gratefully acquiesce to Washington's demands for American bases on the Moon. What do you think of that, Councillor? Maybe Congress should give us both a medal…"

McGinty's response was loud and inarticulate. He half-rose—but one

of the anonymous Bleeker Boys clubbed him back with the butt of his rifle.

"Now, Marvin," said the Pinkerton's man. "I'll keep you no more. Take them in and get it over."

VIII. Flight to the Far Side.

Yet the Scowrers had one last desperate throw. They were herded from the Widow MacNamara's lodging under tight supervision: each watched diligently as they walked heavily down the steps and crossed to the outer hatch. In the tunnel they were assembled into a loose clump, surrounded by the scarlet-suited Bleeker Boys. Once Marvin was content with the arrangements, the cowed ruffians were marched at a slow pace towards the town's centre. The man now revealed as Birdy Edwards followed behind—keen to see the men once and for all locked in the frigid BLEC gaol, but even more eager to meet up with his Ettie and fly from this atrocious world.

They had gone little more than ten yards and approaching a junction that would bring them closer to the more populous areas, when two suited figures stepped boldly into their path. Edwards recognised their unhelmeted faces instantly—Reilly and Manders, his accomplices in the failed murder of Chester Wilcox—and both held clusters of the pyramidal lunamite charges, short fuses already alight. Edwards had time to cry a brief warning before the two threw their bombs, and then pandemonium descended.

The prisoners broke ranks, jostling against startled enforcers. Blows were exchanged; Edwards heard several CO2-rifles being discharged—and then the charges detonated. The explosion, in such a limited space, impaired Edwards' hearing for many seconds. Swirling dust and smoke billowed about the tunnel, spiralling up towards the shattered roof through it—for the fall had exposed the burrow to the near-vacuum of the surface. Both Captain Marvin and his fellow Pinkerton groped for their helmets. Able to breathe again, they waded through the churning

miasma, only to find their way blocked by the caved-in tunnel roof. The broken, scarlet clad limbs hanging from the collapsed pumice and rock spoke of the fates of some enforcers; the protruding, worn legs of a scuffed suit indicated at least one Scowrer had met a similar end.

Edwards pressed his helmet against the other's. "We've been outmanoeuvred!" cried he, ears still ringing. "Seems I didn't have their full trust, after all!"

"We can only pray they were caught in the collapse too," spoke Marvin.

"No—this was planned: that McGinty is the very devil! They will be away by now. It's up to us to stop them!"

They retraced their steps past the Widow MacNamara's house; that worthy woman was standing at her hatch, demanding in a strident voice to be told what had happened for the explosion had penetrated even her poor hearing. Edwards scribbled a curt note ordering her to go inside, dog the hatch and put on her suit—for there was no telling how long before a rescue might arrive, nor what retribution might follow once those Lodge members not yet in custody learned of their comrades' fate. Continuing down the tunnel, they came at last to the ladder and airlock up which Edwards and Scanlan had followed the black-suited Lawler so many days earlier. In moments—their desperation lending them wings—they were upon the surface. The collapsed tunnel had brought the emergency services into action: teams of suited selenauts paced the circumference of the collapsed tunnel, testing the fractured crust with scowrers of their own, and guiding strange mechanisms—looking for all the world like wheeled Tesla aerials, except they were festooned with thick, insulated hoses—into place. As the two men passed, a dark grey material began to ooze from the hoses, spreading quickly across the splintered regolith, sealing it swiftly and effectively: a form of concrete made from local waste rock. Captain Marvin approached one of the workers—who responded to the Bleeker Boy insignia with a brisk salute—and told him of the Widow MacNamara's plight. Satisfied the woman was now in safe hands, both men continued their search for McGinty and his Scowrers.

In his urgency, Edwards forgot everything he had learned about walking in the Moon's lesser gravity: he bounded clumsily, stumbled often, and had to be restrained by Marvin.

"There will be nothing gained if you puncture your suit," the captain admonished him. Edwards reined himself in, though his face—if Marvin had been able to see it behind the thick mica visor—was strained with impatience and anxiety. What if McGinty remembered Ettie and sought her out? The man's habitually robust soul turned to water at the thought.

As they approached the surface above which lay the heart of Victoria, and its manifold airlocks, any one of which the Scowrers may have used to flee, Edwards discerned a chink of light to his left, along the point where the peak of one of the buried domes met the surface. He paused; as he watched the fissure widened into a trapezoid of bright light against which moved tenuous silhouettes. In that moment he recognised the dome as the one in where he had been so painfully initiated into the Scowrers; this could not be a coincidence. He pounded on Captain Marvin's arm to seize his attention. As the enforcer turned, there was movement with the trapezoid; a moment later two vehicles jostled out of the opened dome and onto the surface. Great lamps across the front of them blazed into life, pinpointing both Pinkertons. The vehicles turned towards them, dust spiralling from huge wheels. Whoever was driving meant to run them down! Edwards and the captain leapt aside; the vehicles missed them both by inches, scattering gritty dust across their prone forms.

Both men came clumsily to their feet, earnestly performing checks upon their suits to ensure neither had been punctured in the fall: even a pinprick would prove fatal if missed—leaking life-giving air, whilst allowing the heat of the lunar day past the insulation and coolant. The captain pressed his helmet against Edwards's.

"Those were the new Thomas Rickett tractors, if I'm any judge. They can run off transmitted power until they drop below the horizon, and then it's batteries."

"What is their range?" growled Edwards.

"On average, twenty miles—but each machine carries a multitude of spares as a precaution. They are used for exploratory work, after all."

"And they're headed south. To where, do you think?"

"The only way the trail goes is the Moon's far side—though what they might gain by holing up out there is beyond me."

"I've heard there's a good-sized crater back there in which the BLEC has already done a little exploratory digging. If they know it, there might be some place they can await sunrise."

"Then it's best we haul 'em back before that happens. My men are occupied rounding up the leavings of those Scowrers, and can't be distracted. So I guess it's just you and me."

Edwards patted the Volcanic pistol which was still safely stowed in his grip; his visored face was set in a righteous fury. "That sits well with me, friend."

They made for the dome. There was a hydraulic lift by which McGinty and his men had raised the tractors up from the deep base; the Pinkertons used this to descend and select for themselves a vehicle in which to give chase. The Rickett tractors were the newest of all the surface-travelling machines, and likely the swiftest—the very reason the fleeing Scowrers had chosen them. Edwards and the captain had no choice but to opt for an Atkinson & Philipson transport whose battered flanks and scuffed tracks spoke of better days. Edwards's preparations for his role as a miner on the run had included a thorough grounding in the operation of all such machinery he was likely to encounter and so when his eyes lit upon a tracked impactor drill he smiled dangerously to himself.

"Hitch that to the transport," he told Marvin, and while the captain dragged the drill across the floor and attached it to the transport's tow-bar, Edwards found a unit which would drive the spinning cylinders: a stationary steam engine, of which the boiler's highly-conductive sides could be exposed to the heat of the lunar day. With the captain's help they hoisted the machine up and bolted it in place across the Atkinson & Philipson's roof and ran the thickly-insulated hoses down to the impactor drill's inlet valves. During their chase across the Moon's surface the water

in the pressurised boiler would soak up the Sun's rays, heating it to a boiling point far above that enjoyed at normal atmospheric pressure. Once they ran into McGinty, Edwards intended to give the Bodymaster a demonstration of impactor drilling he'd likely never forget.

With the captain beside him in the driver's simple cabin—two unsprung seats surrounded by steel and aluminium, the only view of the exterior through several small mica windows which afforded no great visibility—Edwards spun the magneto handle. The transport whined as the motors began to turn; once Edwards released the brakes the vehicle shuddered and moved forward in a loud and surly growl. Clearly its engines were in a state of disrepair that matched the transport's general air of dilapidation. Guiding the brute via two handles which simply increased or decreased the velocity of the tracks on either side—powered by separate motors—Edwards drove the transport and its trailer onto the hydraulic lift. Captain Marvin disembarked to activate the lift, rejoining Edwards once they had gained the surface; the trapezoidal opening to the dome they left for others to seal: they had allowed McGinty and his men too wide a lead already.

It was a rough and harrowing ride across the Moon's ancient surface; one I will not attempt to fully describe, having no direct knowledge of the experience. Suffice it to say that the two Pinkerton's greatest luxuries were removing their bulky helmets and breathing the transport's own— albeit stale—air, and being sheltered from the Sun's heat. Edwards had both accelerator levers pushed to their maximum, yet still it felt to both men that the venerable Atkinson & Philipson merely crawled through the dust.

There is no twilight on the Moon, for the thin atmosphere could never refract and reflect the Sun's rays as is the way on Earth. Even more abruptly than at our own Equator, the Sun dips below the Moon's horizon, casting the land into bitter shadow. As sudden as the dousing of an electrical light, Edwards and the captain found themselves plunged from a moonscape of harshly-lit crags and rills and impenetrable shadow, to a Stygian world where the only light was supplied by a reflecting

Earth and distant stars. Should the Earth not be visible, or show as nothing more than a sliver of crescent, that stellar illumination counted as nothing. Edwards switched on the transport's light-beams: a pool of thin yellow shone upon the approaching surface for several yards all about, but made what lay beyond even blacker. At such times, Man's most primitive instincts come to the fore; populating the impenetrable with fantastic creatures and hideous beings, ready to prey upon a human species ill-equipped and unshaped for an alien world.

Neither man spoke as they rode through this ultimate night; perhaps they contemplated their chances of success—for neither could be sure where the Scowrers had fled, or the heading for the huge crater of which Edwards had heard only talk; or perhaps, as they listened to the grating whine of the transport's motors, the possibility they would be stranded far beyond rescue—for they had left no word of their intentions—and die on that most mysterious face of the Moon, never before seen by man,

But after a timeless trek across terrain which never seemed to change: lights. Two clusters of yellow beams—impossible to guess how far away—floated in the darkness. Edwards doused their own lamps, though he never slowed the transport's steady progress. It was true: twin sets of moving lights, dead ahead. Despite the Ricketts' greater speed, such was McGinty's misplaced confidence—false assurance that they would not be so swiftly followed—that the tractors had taken a leisurely drive. If the transport could remain undetected for just a while more, Edwards and the captain might yet lay the Scowrers by the heels.

Edwards turned their lights back on, but not so full as before. It meant they could not see the way ahead for more than a few feet—and of what passed to either side, little more than nothing—but it lessened the odds an observer in one of the Rickett tractors might glance back and discover their pursuers. For another hour all three vehicles tracked across the bleak rocks, the Atkinson & Philipson steadily gaining on its still blithely unaware prey; Edwards and Captain Marvin growing ever more tense as the moment of inevitable action neared.

"We are discovered!" cried the captain. Indeed, one of the fleeing sets

of lights had halted, even as the leading pinpoints seemed to accelerate. "They mean to make a stand of it!"

The nearer array of lights grew larger—and at much greater rate than Edwards would have thought. "They are coming at us!" he snarled when the truth became evident.

Marvin spat a derisory laugh. "Sure, they can't mean to ram us, Why, this vehicle is four times that tractor's weight!"

"I'm thinking they will have more of those lunamite bombs on board. Although they will be of little effect in the open, if a lucky pitch should roll one underneath us…"

The captain grasped his meaning. "Then we must strike first."

Edwards pulled back on the acceleration levers and stamped on the brakes. The transport came to an abrupt and shuddering halt. Both men snapped on their helmets and hastily quit the vehicle's cabin. The captain made for the impactor drill to the rear, whilst Edwards climbed onto the roof. According to the gauge on the steam engine, the boiler was just below its maximum pressure of thirty pounds to the square inch—most likely it had lost some heat once they had crossed into darkness. He pulled a toggle; within moments the boiler's naked sides were engulfed in a self-inflating balloon of reclaimed CO_2, enough to slow further radiated heat loss.

Something impacted against his excursion suit. He looked down in time to see a scowrer harpoon tumble gently to the roof. Its line jerked and rewound quickly. Edwards took cover behind the boiler; its lights blazing, the Rickett tractor stood not twenty feet away. Somewhere behind that dazzle, Edwards had no doubt, some of McGinty's upstanding lodge members were taking careful aim with their scowrers. He pulled his Volcanic pistol from his grip, aiming for one of the glaring lights. It refused to fire: seized by the cold, no doubt. Shrugging inside his suit—it had been a desperate throw, after all—he returned the repeater to the sack.

Two more scowrer harpoons spat past him—to either side of the boiler; one briefly embedded its anchoring tip in part of the boiler's external frame, but tumbled loose again. Edwards reached to the side of the enveloped boiler, pulled down on a lever that opened the steam to the connected hoses, and slid back—launching himself from the rear of the transport; he landed clumsily to the left of the impactor drill's unlimbered tow-bar. Signalling to the captain, he took hold on the drill's skeleton frame; together they rolled it out from behind the transport. They swung it out, until not only was it in full view of the Scowrers from the tractor, but they were also in view of the Pinkertons. Emboldened by the quarry's disappearance, five men stood before the Rickett, their deadly pneumatic grapplers raised. Edwards recognised them all, even hidden in their suits—for hadn't he had weeks in which to learn every idiosyncrasy of dress; each peculiar token and charm each man chose to decorate his suit. There was the secretary Harraway, Carter, Tiger Cormac, and standing off just a little were young Reilly and Manders, clutching hands full of lunamite charges. All five spotted him as one, and fired their scowrers; the deadly harpoons lanced through the thin atmosphere in eerie silence, too fast to track. Both Pinkerton men sheltered behind the drill's frame, and each arrowing point fell harmlessly against that instead.

As the scowrer's line speedily rewound, Edwards stepped up behind the impactor drill, swinging the cylinder of separate barrels to bear. He pulled another lever and depressed a black button. The compressed steam surged into the machine, spinning a turbine which drove the cylinder; and each barrel spat out their deadly slugs. Like the Gatling gun upon which it was based, the drill fired a staccato volley of steel—and in a heartbeat, all of the lights on the Rickett tractor shattered. No longer pinned by the beams, the Pinkerton's transport vanished into shadow; the Scowrers were blind—but all five remained illuminated in the yellow pool of light from the Atkinson & Philipson.

Edwards lowered the spinning barrels and fired once more. He did not release the black button until not only was each man mown down, but the tractor behind them was a riddled, unrecognisable wreck. There may not have been anyone left aboard—but he had to be sure. And in the end, he was merciful, by his own lights: the shells designed to pulverise rock

had slain them instantly—rather than left them in punctured suits, to die in slow agony from the cold and lack of air, as they would undoubtedly have done for him and Marvin.

If there was any remorse it may have been for Reilly and Manders, whose young souls had yet to grow the hard calluses of their comrades; but it was not the first time either Pinkerton had done a job before which another heart might have quailed. Only they could speak for their consciences.

Silently, they shut off the drill's steam supply and re-limbered it—starting to shiver as, now the moment of tension had passed, they grew aware of the cold—and drove around the destroyed tractor. The Scowrers had meant to stop them; but even though they had so singularly failed in that task, the delay had enabled McGinty and his rebel Freemen to increase their lead. The light spilling from their driving lamps was shrunken to a minute speck that could be dismissed by one who knew no better as an artefact of strained eyesight.

"He has the battery power," Edwards remarked. "I'm thinking this old girl is no match when it comes to stamina."

"We'll take him—even if we have to do it on foot…!"

Edwards nodded, though he knew he would be sorry if he never saw a certain pair of eyes and blonded tresses again. He maintained the lights at the lowest setting he dared: at full power they would be well-warned of rocky walls or dangerous rifts ahead, but the batteries would be drained much faster. The Rickett tractor had reserves enough for a return trip he guessed McGinty had no desire to make: the Councilman could afford to wash the moonscape in light.

The ground under their transport's tracks was rising with an increasing gradient: either the foot of a mountain, the peak of which was hidden in the darkness, or the ancient impact ejecta of a huge crater. Could it, Edwards considered, be the very crater of which he had heard? In which case McGinty and his men had reached their goal; they would likely know the lie of the land better than the Pinkerton detectives—it was here they would make a stand. Even the minute spark that was the distant

tractor was no longer visible; could the Rickett machine have already crested the crater rim and be descending into the crater itself? Or had they shaken their pursuers off and even now be back-tracking towards an ambush. Edwards crushed such thoughts from his mind: they were an enemy of decision. For right or wrong, he had his course.

An abrupt void swallowed the transport's light beams: they had reached the rim of the crater. A moment later the whole vehicle pitched forward as the nose passed the tipping point; the black sky spun away, and Edwards found himself staring at the parabolic drop inside the vast scar—all that remained of a huge impact which had occurred back when the Earth was still as lifeless as its satellite. The transport shook and groaned, its motors shrieking as though they had become packed with moon dust. The vehicle was drifting down at an angle, broadside to its direction of descent. Edwards eased back on the accelerator levers; the protesting motors settled. The transport continued to slide gently down the slope; grit rattled against its hull like hail against a metal sheet. Gradually it slowed as the slope lessened. Edwards opened up the left motor and the Atkinson & Philipson turned, once more orientated along its path.

For a moment the transport was poised above the floor of the unseen crater and clearly, not so far away, Edwards was gazing down upon the lights of the fleeing tractor. He pushed the accelerator levers to their maximum, keen that his murderous prey should not escape him.

After the tortuous route they had thus far endured, the comparatively smooth floor of the crater was a welcome luxury: almost like a flat Mare. Edwards was encouraged to dim the lamps further still, for the going was so fair. Even so, he knew the Rickett tractor had the turn of speed to beat the transport off until its batteries failed, unless McGinty stood and fought—and that, the Pinkerton man thought, he would never do. Not until the odds were stacked firmly in the Scowrer's favour.

And yet, as it became clear they were gaining on the tractor's lights, perhaps that was what the man intended. The Rickett was travelling slower with each moment, although it had not halted entirely. As they gained upon their quarry, the tractor becoming larger and clearer in their

restricted viewing panels, it was obvious the machine was in some form of distress: it cut to the left, its course under constant and hard correction. The left wheel assembly was either damaged or lacking power. Whatever the cause, Edwards felt obliged to offer a prayer to the Almighty: here was the break for which he had so yearned.

The transport overtook the wallowing tractor. Edwards spun his vehicle directly into the other machine's path; the tractor braked before it could strike the larger vehicle. Dust and stones slowly billowed from under the Rickett's spinning wheels as whoever drove it tried to reverse. After futile seconds in which the tractor merely spun upon its axis without making a foot in headway, its driver shut down the motors. The churned cloud of dust began to gently settle, as do excess salts in a saturated solution.

Edwards and Marvin clamped on their helmets, rushing from the transport's cabin—careful to exit from the right-hand side, using the large vehicle as cover. Edwards climbed to the roof, keeping flat, an unwavering eye on the tractor as he once again opened the steam valve on the boiler. The pressure was less than fifty per cent of maximum—some steam already exhausted by the brief fight earlier, and the water would certainly have cooled, despite the thick insulation.

Figures emerged from the Rickett tractor. Four in all: one encased in a suit so large it could only be McGinty himself; which marked the remaining three as Ted Baldwin and the two Willabys. Edwards felt a thrill of anticipation: he would enjoy being the man who finally did in the cruel but cowardly Baldwin. They fired their scowrers, but the Pinkerton man was already slipping off the roof and down the Atkinson & Philipson's side ladder. He raced as fast as he might to the drill assembly—no need to unlimber this time, for the tractor was already in easy range. Edwards stepped into place, opening the steam supply, his hand hovering over the black firing button as he swung the muzzle of the multiple barrels upon the four men.

And so he paused—for not a one moved, even though each had a rewound and primed scowrer raised and aimed. It was certain they had all divined the fate of their comrades, once it became clear to them just what it was the transport towed in its wake. McGinty and his men were many things, but they were never fools. They knew that the moment either of them triggered his scowrer, Edwards would fire the impactor drill, and it would be all over for them. The large figure which was McGinty lowered his scowrer; two of the others followed his lead but the fourth—it must be Ted Baldwin—kept his weapon raised.

"Make your gesture, Ted Baldwin!" cried Edwards—although he knew no one could have heard him. "'Tis all the same to me!" His thumb eased closer to the firing button, awaiting the merest hint that Baldwin meant to fire.

The drill platform shuddered, almost throwing Edwards free. He clung on with one arm looped around an upright. A moment later both transport and trailer were tossed carelessly up, a plume of dust and gas spewing around them; Edwards lost his hold and was flung to the ground. He struck the crater floor clumsily, a turtle flipped onto its back, and twisted in time to see the transport crash slowly back to the ground—an impact no less damaging for all its slow grace—and the drill platform topple slowly. From a disturbed pocket of gas lying just below the surface, or the timid descendant of the satellite's volcanic past, an unpredictable upwelling of pressurised vapour had vented on the surface, tossing the transport and drill assembly aside like children's toys. Even though it had lasted short moments, its effect was longer-lasting.

No longer under the threat of the drill, McGinty and his men sprang forward, pinning down Edwards before he could find his feet. One who could only be Ted Baldwin raised his scowrer, the anchoring tip brilliant in the lights from tractor and transport. He plunged the point down; luckily for Edwards, his strugglings made the other miss: the sharp edge glancing from the metal armour of his excursion suit. The Pinkerton man threw his weight against those holding him down, but he was helpless as a pinned beetle. Baldwin drew himself up from a second thrust—this time Edwards could not count on him missing.

Then the weight was gone. Edwards struggled part-way to his feet and glanced around. All four men had stepped away, looking towards

the fallen impactor drill: even though the assembly had fallen, the steam hoses were intact. Captain Marvin was hunched over the firing button; a short burst had distracted the Scowrers from the victim—badly-aimed though it was. Marvin fired again. The dust all around the men's feet churned and spat as shells ploughed the crater floor. Even though it was obvious to Edwards that reduced steam pressure had lost the rotating drill much of its power, its impactor shells could still easily rip through an excursion suit. The Scowrers evidently knew the same.

Edwards made it to his feet. The giant figure that was Boss McGinty saw his recovery and turned, raising his lance. He fired, but in his haste the shot went wide—ricocheting from a ring of Edwards's armour. Before McGinty could rewind his harpoon, the Pinkerton man closed with him. He pulled his Volcanic repeater from his grip-sack—even though it was still surely jammed. McGinty threw his suited arms around the American: encumbered in his suit he still had the strength to lift him bodily. Edwards raised his pistol, and brought the hilt down against McGinty's thick mica visor with all his strength. A fine crack appeared, and the Scowrer relaxed his grip, stepping back. Edwards pressed his advantage, swinging his gun once more like a mighty club. It contacted the mica; splinters flew off in graceful arcs. Edwards wished he could see the man's face in that moment: enjoy it as the cruelty and hideous rage dissolved into terror. McGinty stumbled as his nemesis took a final blow; the visor shattered. Shards of mica flew clear as the air inside evacuated with explosive force.

Boss McGinty, Bodymaster and terror of the *Vale de Verme*, collapsed to the crater floor, his excursion suit deflating like a withered balloon.

Edwards raised himself and looked around. Like a ghastly tableau in stark black and white, lit by the surface vehicle's lamps, Baldwin and the Willabys were immobile as Marvin trained the drill barrel upon them. Meekly they surrendered their pneumatic weapons under the threat of the drill's purposeful aim. Using the unbreakable line from one scowrer, Marvin lashed all three to the toppled drill platform; then he and Edwards surveyed the damage to the Atkinson & Philipson transport.

The vehicle was damaged beyond repair: both sets of tracks buckled, support struts snapped. The left wheel assembly of the Rickett tractor was severely battered—the result of transitioning the peak of the crater rim too swiftly and carelessly—with a simple repair the machine was made worthy. There remained ample battery power for their return.

But as the Pinkerton men corralled their prisoners on board, there was a mute detonation from the drill platform. The steam hose had finally split and a jet of vapour errupted—freezing to a cloud of minute ice crystals the very instant it contacted the Moon's thin atmosphere. Edwards and the captain were distracted for just a second, but it was enough for the Scowrers. All three broke loose, knocking their captors aside, and fled towards the spreading cloud. Edwards and Marvin shot with their scowrers, but neither man was an expert with the tool, and the lines flew wide of their targets. The three men vanished into the cloud. Edwards aimed the tractor's lights after the fleeing figures, but the beams reflected from the tiny particles; the frozen vapour blazed like it contained a thousand electric light bulbs. The cloud lasted for almost a minute, thinning as it expanded. Eventually it faded, but there was no trace of the Scowrers.

There is little more to tell. The Pinkerton men returned the tractor to Victoria, deciding that Baldwin and the Willabys would die soon enough: their suits held little remaining air; the shelter of the crippled transport would have prolonged their miserable lives for just a few hours more. Before the fateful meeting, Edwards had handed Mike Scanlan a sealed note to be left at the address of Miss Ettie Shafter, a mission which he had accepted with a wink and a knowing smile. Shortly after Edwards's return from the Moon's night, a beautiful woman and a much muffled man joined a return shot to Earth, and made a swift, unbroken journey out of danger. It was the last time that ever either Ettie or her lover set foot on the Moon or the *Vale de Verme*. Ten days later they were married in America, in Chicago—Edwards' true home—with old Jacob Shafter as witness of the wedding.

The trial of the remaining Scowrers was held back on Earth under a pall of secrecy—far from the place where their adherents might have

terrified the guardians of the law; far from the ears of the Press. In vain they struggled. In vain the money of the lodge—money squeezed by blackmail—was spent like water in the attempt to save them; for there would be no defence. An embarrassed government was read the cold, clear, unimpassioned statement of one who knew every detail of their lives, their organization, and their crimes. With equal coolness, those crimes were punished. Eight of Boss McGinty's chief followers met their fate upon the scaffold, cringing and whining when the last hour came. Fifty-odd had various degrees of imprisonment. At last they were broken and scattered. The cloud was lifted forever from the Moon. The work of Birdy Edwards was complete—but the world at large remained ignorant of the facts; if not for Edwards' own handwritten account, I would be as much in the dark as anyone.

And yet, as he had guessed, the game was not over yet. There was another hand to be played, and yet another and another. Ted Baldwin and the Willabys had by some means escaped the Moon's far side, hiding themselves in the *Vale* or close by; so had several others of the fiercest spirits of the gang. For ten years they were out of the world, and then came a day when they returned to Earth—a day which Edwards, who knew his men, was very sure would be an end of his life of peace. They had sworn an oath on all that they thought holy to have his blood as a vengeance for their comrades. And well they strove to keep their vow!

From Chicago he was chased, after two attempts so near success that it was sure that the third would get him. From Illinois he went under a changed name to California, and it was there that the light went for a time out of his life when Ettie Edwards died. Once again he was nearly killed, and once again under the name of Douglas he worked in a lonely canyon, where with an English partner named Barker he amassed a fortune. At last there came a warning to him that the bloodhounds were on his track once more, and he cleared—only just in time—for England. And thence came the John Douglas who for a second time married a worthy mate, and lived for five years as a Sussex county gentleman, a life which ended with the strange happenings of which we have heard.

PART THREE
THE DEVIL'S BOWL

I. Return to the Moon

Again I must request the indulgence of my readers as we leave one trial and spring back over the decades to what may, in retrospect, be considered a continuance. For although some twenty years might separate each case, at the heart still lay those dark events upon the Moon and the black, vengeful minds which had commissioned them.

The police trial passed with an almost indecent haste, as if the Yard—at the last—found something untoward in the case, and wished to wash their hands of it as soon as they may. The case of John Douglas was referred to the Quarter Sessions, at which—due in part to a lacklustre performance by the prosecution who were singularly unable to provide a single credible witness, but mostly to a deposition by Mr Sherlock Holmes, whose scalpel-sharp testimony presented a defendant who had been placed in the most trying of circumstances—he was acquitted as having acted in self-defence. Of the *Vale de Verme*, the Moon, and Douglas's previous *nom-de-guerre* Birdy Edwards the Pinkerton man, there was no mention.

"Get him out of England at any cost," wrote Holmes to the wife. "There are forces here which may be more dangerous than those he has escaped. There is no safety for your husband in England."

And so I considered a most curious adventure to be resolved. But there was to be a third act, one in which once again I was to play no part other than be the recorder of another's exploits. A little more than a

fortnight had elapsed since the John Douglas trial. It was late afternoon and I was sorting through the evening post at Baker Street, enjoying a cigarette and tea. Holmes had been out all day, and most of the previous night, for reasons he had not confided. I heard the front door slam and the sounds of hurried feet upon the stair—all accompanied by Holmes crying out impatiently for Mrs Hudson. He burst into our rooms, his colour bright, eyes feverish. He dropped his hat and stick carelessly and dropped into a seat facing me.

"From your general state of excitement," said I, "am I to conclude whatever mission you have been upon is either completed to your satisfaction, or about to be…?"

"Hah—you pierce me to the quick, Watson. Indeed, the errand which has most occupied me of late is done. The Birlstone case—"

"John Douglas and his wife are, to the best of my knowledge, gone from our shores…"

"And so they are—but still their presence haunts me. There are too many questions, Watson; too many hanging threads at which I am tempted to pluck…"

I put down the post and sat back.

"The Scowrers, for one example: why were they allowed *carte blanche* to govern or pillage as they saw fit? Parliament had its eyes and ears in that forsaken *Vale* in the form of the British Lunar Expeditionary Company … why did they not pass word back of how events were unfolding…?"

"Perhaps the Scowrers themselves were preventing it: ambushing any message back to Earth that would reveal their criminality."

Holmes lit his pipe. "Yet our American cousins knew well enough the truth. It is clear they had agents at large within our early settlements— and I would be a naïve fool to imagine that they have withdrawn them—even so they must still send back their reports through the same medium: documents carried aboard Earth-bound capsules, as susceptible to interception as any other message." Clouds of smoke thickened the air above his head. "No—it will not do!"

Regretting I might be fanning the flames of Homes' mania, I said: "Then do you detect the remote hand of any other?"

His thin lips quirked. "Part of my self-imposed task these past hours has included a visit to the South Lunar Company's offices on Pall Mall. The staff was only too pleased to assist me—although, of course, they withheld a great deal more than was vouchsafed. Nevertheless I was able to peruse some of their files covering the mid-'70s period. I am satisfied that many of the companies who profited from the Scowrers' heavy hands are quite genuine; some are trading still, others have either gone out of business or themselves become the subject of a take-over. I have not been able to prove to my own satisfaction that a single name, either mentioned in the Douglas/Edwards manuscript or listed in the BLC's records—or at least, those I was allowed to examine—exists merely as a front for another, more subtle interest."

"Then the government is guilty of nothing more than criminal lethargy?"

"The default position of any government, Watson, is to preserve the *status quo*." He leaned back further and stared at the ceiling. "Are you aware, friend Watson, that the British Lunar Expeditionary Company was dissolved less than two months after the Scowrers were put on trial; only to be replaced, with indecent haste, by the South Lunar Company? And, through that august body, not a single business—be it part of the Empire, or beyond—may not so much as express an interest in exploiting any fraction of the Moon's Britain territories without the SLC's express consent." He sighed. "It is a puzzle, to be sure. There are points of interest in our ex-Pinkerton's epistle, if the dialogue is reported with any accuracy. We still do not have the full story, Watson—and I mean to have it!"

I crushed out my cigarette. "How? The government will admit to nothing; if they felt open to scrutiny the original trial of the Scowrers would not have been held *in camera*. You have all you ever will from the SLC. Where else is there?"

Holmes came to his feet in a single fluid motion, crossing to the hearth. He leaned upon the mantel, fingers pressed to the bridge of

his nose. "Where else but the source, Watson: the Moon! All answers are sequestered there: the truth behind the Scowrers; how Ted Baldwin and his murderous associates survived certain death on the satellite's far side—!"

I confess to speechlessness. Holmes has always chased down his solutions with unquestioning vigour, regardless of where the trail might lead him. But the Moon? Finally, my tongue loosened. "You are proposing we visit the Moon, Holmes—?"

He turned his gaze upon me. "Ah—I confess to intemperance of language, Watson, and apologise if that misled you. Whilst I will certainly be journeying to our satellite, if fear you—my dearest friend—will not..."

Once again I was dumbstruck. Before I could protest, Holmes pressed ahead: "The voyage from our launching site at Kilima-Njaro to the *Mare Nubium* is fraught with its own, unique terrors, Watson. You saw how the hair of all who have undertaken it has been bleached: Douglas—or rather, Edwards—Baldwin, the Willabys... And the effects are not only physical—" He paused, his eyes focussing on some far-away horizon. "Ten years ago, the BLEC was inclined to be less particular in its choice of selenaut—you saw how Edwards mentioned many settlers in Victoria, Albertstown, *et cetera*, were of more mature years. In those heady times, when the expeditionary crews' prevailing criterion was to establish a robust infrastructure on which to build our first, sustainable lunar colony, I fancy the physical and mental well-being of those willing to carve a new corner of the Empire was of supreme unimportance.

"But all is changed! Now, only the finest physical specimens may challenge the rigours of space-shoots—"

"Of which you are clearly one—" I interjected. Holmes stared down at me, his expression unreadable.

"My dear fellow! Please believe that I argued your case both cogently and eloquently, but the minds of the SLC are more inflexible than some of our friends at Scotland Yard."

"Ah—another reason why you were at their Pall Mall office..."

"You are sharper than a needle this evening, Watson. It was over an interminable lunch with a Whitehall mandarin that I made my case, and he was perfectly amenable to the concept; but proved not to be the port-soaked fool I thought him when I mentioned your accompanying me. He had your life filed away in memory, Watson: your service in Afghanistan; the injuries you sustained on the ambushed *Keane* and your subsequent attack of enteric fever…Those very facts barred you from the shoot; no matter how recovered you may feel, he would not risk it. The SLC would not risk it. I am deeply sorry."

I lit another cigarette and sat quietly. So my friend was to go where mankind has dreamed of visiting since the days of Pythagoras—and I could not. I will not pretend that it was not a blow; since the very first, I have been at Holmes' side to record his extraordinary talents.

"Of course," he was saying, "it may be that they prefer to risk the life of a consulting detective who has—on more than one occasion—tweaked their noses, than my faithful Boswell." He dropped back into his seat; his eyes alight with a roguish twinkling. "After all, if I am gone, what is there to prevent you penning ever more lurid tales…?"

"A little unworthy of you, Holmes…"

"Indeed—and again I apologise—Ah, Mrs Hudson! At last!" Our worthy landlady had entered the room, her features composed in stern lines—mitigated by the relief so evident in her kindly eyes. Although she never sought to disguise just how great a trial she found in her wayward guest, her genuine affection for my friend was always more than its equal.

"I will be away for a few days, Mrs Hudson. There is a valise in my bedroom, not much larger than friend Watson's medical bag, already packed. Would you be good enough to have Billy bring it down for me?"

"Will you be travelling far, Mr Holmes?"

"Hah!" He glanced in my direction, face alight. "Far enough, Mrs Hudson—far enough! I need not stress, in my absence, that nothing is to be disturbed or touched in any way…?"

She glanced about the habitually untidy parlour, her expression eloquent, before quitting the room.

"You are leaving immediately?" I asked.

"I regret there is an urgency to my departure. Moon-shoots are not yet as mundane as train departures from Paddington: our satellite is a moving body; hence there must be an optimum period for any projectile flung in its direction. As an ex-military man you will of course be acquainted with the concept of deflection shooting: timing is all-important—Ah, Billy! This way—!" The boy had barely set foot in the room before Holmes had taken him by the arm and steered him towards his bedroom. A moment later both re-emerged—Billy carrying a bulky valise which wore its years badly, Holmes shrugging on a bulky overcoat.

"I cannot say how long I will be gone, Watson—a week at least, I imagine; if it is longer than a month I shall be surprised." He picked up hat, walking stick and a long thick scarf with which he muffled his face against the chilly air; then he was back off down the stairs, Billy in tow with his bag. I heard the door shut, and he was gone.

Mrs Hudson came back into the room, taking up my tea tray. She shook her head. "That must be the briefest leave-taking I have ever seen," said she. "Even for Mr Holmes."

I was moved to agree; though still stung by my exclusion from the adventure, I didn't risk speaking. Our estimable landlady vanished with the depleted tray and I was left to contemplate the unknowable period before Holmes' return. Lost in thought, time slipped me by; only Billy's return shook me from my study—some twenty minutes later—his face lit up with delight.

"Lord," said he, "that was a trek, and no mistake."

"No cabs to be had outside?"

"A good many, sir; but Mr Holmes insisted on walking up to Regents Park, with me totin' his blessed bag—that felt like there was an anvil in it—and then doesn't he just take a battered old Hansom back down to Hyde Park!" Despite his grumbling words Billy was clearly delighted: he knew there was work afoot; another mystery for the famous Sherlock Holmes.

I wondered at his choice of destination. Obviously he was boarding an aerostat there—but none of the dirigibles loading at Hyde Park field

ranged further than the French coast: all were strictly domestic flights. "I trust he tipped you well…"

Billy's grin widened as he produced a half-crown from his tunic. "And 'Mum's the word!' said he. Mum's the word!" He pocketed the coin. "Do you know what he's up to, doctor?"

I smiled back: the boy's enthusiasm was infectious. "As ever, Billy, I am as much in the dark as yourself. Perhaps more so." I dismissed him and returned to the evening post. In due course everything would become clear, I was certain; fretting would certainly never bring the conclusion any faster.

II. A Visitor

As was my habit whenever Holmes was either away or his caseload slack, I kept myself fully occupied. I had of late been establishing our new Farringdon practice with Stamford, my new brother-in-law. He was an amenable fellow, far more understanding of the demands on my time made by Holmes than *vice versa*. My wife Clemmie, by a supreme irony, tended to be as intolerant of my old friend and his irregular timetable as Holmes was of my other life. At the time I ascribed her behaviour to the natural jealously of a new bride towards any influence that drew her husband from her side; both her brother and I believed she would come to accept Baker Street as much a part of me as she would cricket on Sunday or a gentleman's club.

On the third day after Holmes' departure I received a curious visitor: not one of my own patients, nor Stamford's, and by his dress and comportment more likely to hire a private physician than frequent a hospital practice. It had been a long day—the Winter months still forcing their inevitable tragedies upon us—and Clemmie had been artlessly hinting that there was a concert she rather wished to visit that evening: Mathurin's Clockwork Symphony at the Crystal Palace; I had hoped to finish early. The newcomer was shown in without introduction: the last consultation of the day. His was a heavily built and massive frame, and there was a suggestion of uncouth physical inertia in the figure. My first reaction was that there was nothing wrong with the man that diet and exercise should not set right, but I was also struck by a strong sense of familiarity—although I am certain that we had never met before—and an almost palpable aura of entitlement and authority. As he eased himself into the chair facing me he offered nothing other than a level, commanding stare—not so much as a

card. Intrigued therefore, and before we exchanged a syllable, I elected to try Holmes' own methods upon the patient—for I sensed he would be less than forthcoming.

His huge body was dressed in clothing that, whilst of the finest cut and materials, was worn with a negligence suggesting either he cared little about his appearance, had no need to care, or was hated by his valet. His hat, which he dropped onto my desk, was of the finest silk whilst both ferrule and handle of his cane were of gold, polished to a gleam. The ferrule itself demonstrated little wear, which suggested the cane was new, or infrequently used. Above his unwieldy frame there perched a head so masterful in its brow, so alert in its steel-grey, deep-set eyes, so firm in its lips, and so subtle in its play of expression, that after the first glance one forgot the gross body and unhealthy colouration of the face and remembered only the dominant mind.

"I have the pleasure of addressing Doctor John Watson?" he asked at length.

"You do, sir. And you—?"

He allowed my question to hang. "Who I am is unimportant, doctor."

"Then I am afraid I cannot treat you…"

"Nor am I here on a question of my health."

"There we must beg to differ," said I. "As a doctor, I am concerned for the state of your liver."

His thin lips stretched into the ghost of a smile; he emitted a dry sound which I eventually recognised as a short laugh. "Excellent, doctor. You do not lack for medical skills; though your deductive reasoning—which you have tried to apply from the instant I sat—draws up short."

I sat forward in my chair. "Why are you here?"

"We must reverse the consultation process, doctor. I will ask: you will answer—"

"Now look—!"

He waved a large hand; the grey kid glove enclosing it as pristine as his cane's gold ferrule. "Do not fret yourself, sir. I wish only to know one thing: where is Sherlock Holmes?"

For a moment I was encompassed with fear. Was this one of Moriarty's men? Was Holmes correct in his analysis of the professor after all? I forced myself to relax. "Have you been to his lodgings in Baker Street?" I said, as off-handedly as I could.

"His landlady informs me only that he is absent."

"Then I'm afraid I cannot say," I replied.

"By which do you mean you are unwilling to say, or do you truly not know?"

"I do not know," I answered without hesitation.

My visitor stared at me a moment longer, his deep-set eyes drilled hard against my defences. This, I knew with all certainty, was a man to whom interrogation came as an innate gift. Then he stood—slowly and with no little effort. He took up his hat and bowed to me.

"Thank you, doctor. You have been most helpful." He trod heavily from my room, leaving me baffled and not a little concerned. Was he an enemy of Holmes? And if so, had I given anything away—no matter how trivial—by gesture or inflection? For I had no doubt that should mind-reading ever be proven a scientific fact, the man I had just faced would possess it to a frightening degree.

The encounter played upon my mind and I could not enjoy the symphony that evening—though I did admire Mathurin's clever use of multiple calliope banks. Afterwards, as we ate dinner, Clemmie enquired how I was—for she thought me unusually pensive. I tried to reassure her, saying it had been a trying day at the surgery with too many cases for which I could do nothing. She comforted me as best she could, though she would never be able to ease the weight which had settled over my heart that afternoon.

The days passed and some of my unease lifted as there was no sequel to the strange encounter; I began to convince myself that I had over-dramatized the interview—that the overweight gentleman had merely been a potential client who wished to consult Holmes, and did not feel able to confide in me further.

On the eighth day I received a Teslagram—delivered directly to me

at my surgery. It was from Holmes, informing me that he would be in his Baker Street rooms that evening, if I would care to visit and learn of his recent excursions. Naturally I was consumed by curiosity and asked the message courier to respond I would be there by seven at the latest. Clemmie was a little cool, being not in the least inquisitive about the Moon or what my old friend experienced whilst up there; but she agreed I must call on him—if only to assure myself he was well and in good spirits.

I arrived at 221B at a little past six forty-five. I let myself in, only to be met by Mrs Hudson herself at the foot on the stairs. Her face was lined with concern, and I immediately thought there must be something amiss with Holmes. She shook her head, "Though he is not himself, doctor," said she. "Wherever he has been, it has worked a change on him—in more than one way."

Alarmed I mounted the stairs to my friend's rooms. I knocked, and Holmes' familiar tones bade me enter. Inside all was gloom, for he had drawn every curtain and had but a single lamp burning—dimmed as much as possible. I made out his figure and advanced towards him—only to draw up with a gasp as he turned to greet me.

His hair had turned to a pure white.

I should, of course, have been prepared for it. Every other selenaut I had met or read about had been affected in this way, but I had simply never imagined it coming to Holmes. Swept back from his high, pale brow it gave him the air of a Dickensian spirit, doomed to haunt me until I should repent of my ways. His deep-set eyes twinkled at my hesitancy; his thin lip twitched.

"Fear not, my dear fellow—I am no ghost. I have but lately returned and had no time to refresh myself." He glanced in a mirror, his features disapproving. "Do you know I was helped to disembark at Hyde Park by a young lady who seemed to be under the misapprehension that I might be her grandfather...? Pah! Tomorrow I shall purchase a bottle of Alexander Ross's liquid hair-dye." He returned his attention to me.

"Now, Watson... Have you eaten yet? Mrs Hudson will be bringing

up a cold supper shortly. Sit, my dear fellow, sit—you look whiter than my new hair…"

He dropped into a chair, settled back and lit his pipe. Despite his landlady's fears, he seemed to me to be in the finest of spirits; although I was still attempting to reconcile the pallid creature before me with the Sherlock Holmes of but eight days ago.

"Other than the hair, you are well?" I asked, aware it was unlikely he would confess to it even if he were gravely ill. "Were you examined on your return?"

He puffed out a pall of foul smoke. "I assure you I am perfectly well."

"In this instance I think you had better bow to my expertise, Holmes. I would like to examine you…"

He waved a hand. "Any examination you would make of me would serve merely to appease your own private concerns, doctor. But—" he overrode my attempted objections, "—if it pleases you I will subject myself to your cold stethoscope tomorrow."

I confess to being less than happy with his suggestion, but knew it was most likely the best to be hoped for. I took out a cigarette and lit it.

"Then did you uncover all you wished to find?" I asked. "On the Moon?"

His face turned grave. "It is a deep business and does not reflect well, I regret to say, upon our government." He blew out a thick wash of pipe smoke and appeared to change the subject. "Whilst I was gone, did anyone enquire after me?"

"Indeed, yes." I told him of my curious visitor, including the small details I had observed, and my inconclusive deductions. Holmes nodded at each point, his eyes closed as if he sought to visualise the one I described.

"Bravo, Watson. You strike closer to the bull than you imagine, even if your conclusions are somewhat ethereal."

"You know him, then? Is he—?"

"A stooge of Moriarty?" His thin smile came and went like an adder's strike. "Not he. This is a creature who rarely ventures beyond his retreat—I suppose we are both to feel flattered: I that he is so solicitous;

yourself that he deigns to visit in person. You are correct in surmising he is a man of such lofty standing that his personal appearance may often be neglected. He is also, to my mind, of too languid a nature, with only his brain content to leave the comfort of his armchair."

"You clearly know him well."

"Better than myself—But here is Mrs Hudson with supper! Help yourself, Watson—and once we have eaten and supped our fill, I will give you the facts of my sojourn. Which you may later over-dramatize as you see fit…"

III. From Earth to the Moon

You will have already deduced (began Holmes), from remarks young Billy is certain to have made, that I followed the most indirect route possible—for I was, and am still, convinced that I would be followed. Even before my visit to the SLC offices on Pall Mall, perhaps so far back as our return from Birlstone, I have noted a small repertory company of faces appearing in the streets and places I frequented; I had to conclude that either they were the rankest amateurs of their craft, or it was intended that I observe them. I was being given notice. Therefore, it became incumbent upon me to at least attempt to lose them.

As you are aware I took a cab from Regents Park—immediately outside 221B would have been too easy—back down to Hyde Park, and the aerostat boarding field there. Billy heard my instructions to the cabby, and so too would the pair I observed close upon our heels. I had my scarf wound about my face as I departed—you may recall it—and so I did upon my arrival at Hyde Park; should the cabby ever be questioned, I departed as I had arrived. But under that scarf was a new face. You know I have some small skill in the appliance of theatrical make-up: my valise contained sufficient to effect an adequate disguise—with a thick mane of brown curls, a thin but ill-maintained moustache and florid imbiber's nose. Therefore, although Sherlock Holmes entered the cab at Regents Park, one Professor Stanley Morton stepped out at Hyde Park. Unless my followers were immediately behind my cab—and I am sure that they were not—I had eluded them. At least, for the moment.

If I may make a momentary digression, you will note that I used the name Stanley Morton. He is an alias—one of many—I have cultivated over the years, should ever I have need of him. Morton is a respected geologist and chemist who has—for a considerable time—been awaiting elevation to the position of Honorary Fellow of the Royal Society (he will never receive it, of course). When it was clear that you would not be permitted to accompany me, I gave my SLC interlocutor the impression that I had cooled on the idea. We finished luncheon and parted amicably—whereupon I returned to Pall Mall by a labyrinthine route and sought another interview with a young clerk who no more recognised the features of Sherlock Holmes than he would those of the fictional Professor Morton. The boy was of an impressionable nature: quickly dazzled by the professor's scientific credentials, and the discoveries he hoped for on the Moon—which he knew would accelerate his spurious invitation to the Royal Society. It was but a short time before I found myself the subject of a thorough physical examination—heart and lungs, blood taken for microscopical tests—upon the successful completion of which I left the SLC offices with full clearance, a boarding pass for the next available lunar shoot; even return aerostat tickets to Kilima-Njaro. I have to concede the process was most comprehensive. I must crave your indulgence for not revealing that one vital point, Watson—but in the light of that which you informed me, I believe your ignorance was your strongest armour against those who would have seen me frustrated.

From Hyde Park I caught an aerostat to Manchester; and from there a train down to Dover, where I purchased a ticket for a Channel crossing to Ostend—a ticket I had no intention of ever using. Thence I returned to London and on to New Brompton. A route which consumed both time and money, but I could not be sure I was no longer being shadowed— simply because I no longer espied those familiar faces in a crowd did not prove I was free of observation; only that the agency which pursued me no longer did so openly. However, the very fact that you were interrogated encourages me to believe I truly had escaped scrutiny.

Our vessel was the *HMAS Hyderabad*, en route to Bombay—with pick-ups arranged for Algiers, Cairo and Dar-es-Salaam. I will not trouble you with a description of travelling via aerostat for I am sure you are only too familiar with the sensations: the persistent drone of the engines, the

peculiar wallowing sensation so unlike that of a ship. My neat cabin was on the port side, its small porthole—no larger than my head—providing little in the way of a view; to appreciate the landscape over which we flew one had to sit in the dining room, where panoramic windows ensured a three hundred and sixty degree vista of the land and sea below. Each cabin came with its own steward—a mild inconvenience as I preferred to sleep without the encumbrance of the professor's guise upon my face; it became a necessary facet of his character that he would insist no one disturb him from the moment he retired to his emerging for breakfast.

The passengers on this particular voyage were very much what one might expect: a provincial governor and his wife returning to India after a spell in London; a member of the Egyptian consul who had struck up a friendship with both in the capital—and gave me every indication that he was conducting a discreet liaison with the governor's wife; an outwardly down-at-heel journalist working for *The Times* on his way to the Transvaal, who was clearly under the orders of the Foreign Office; an African family made rich through the ivory trade, pertaining to originate in Zanzibar, although their accent and customs revealed their true home as Kamerun; and an American who informed me he was a miner hoping to make his fortune in opals—although his watchful manner and the way in which his right hand would unconsciously stray to his hip indicated that his trade was in actuality more deadly: a pistol fighter, his type nearing extinction in his native land, fleeing the onset of civilization. In short, Watson, we were a well-met assembly, not a one of us entirely as we wished to be seen. By their actions throughout the flight to Dar-es-Salaam, I have no doubt they were neither seeking me, nor saw through my disguise. I was, I dared to believe, finally safe from observation.

The aerostat did not make landfall directly at Kilima-Njaro—all flights to within thirty miles of the mountain are strictly controlled by security forces under the remit of the SLC—but we were able to observe from a distance as our aerostat approached Dar-es-Salaam. Even at such a remove, the huge cannon was clearly visible: a great black welt rising from the slopes, its barrel hazy with distance and attendant cloud.

The American was gracious enough to commend the British on our achievements, ruefully admitting we had caught his fellow Americans on the hop, before adding "Though there ain't enough money in the world could get me inside one of them flying cannonballs!" On disembarking we all went our several ways. Upon identifying myself as Professor Morton to an official, I was ushered aside to a small but comfortable office where I was to await my connection to the Uhuru Gun: the Space Cannon on Kilima-Njaro.

The Dar-es-Salaam terminus is a large, impersonal edifice across which many souls stride in the self-important manner adopted by those involved in the most trivial of tasks: I was able to observe them easily through the glass of the office door. I was quite comfortable, for the African heat was kept largely at bay by an efficient cooling arrangement—no doubt modelled upon the system utilised upon the Moon, as described by John Douglas. At length I was joined by a white-haired worthy in the tunic of the SLC who inspected my documentation, enquired without interest after my intentions once landed upon our satellite, and finally led me to a highly-polished MotoCar driven by a native dressed in a white, tropical variety of the ubiquitous SLC uniform, and wished me well. Once I was seated, the machine lurched off across the rough African ground.

I was somewhat alarmed as it occurred to me I might be driven all the way to Kilima-Njaro in the MotoCar—and already the terrain grew harsh, testing the vehicle's suspension along with my own intestinal fortitude; but I need not have concerned myself. At the very periphery of the landing field was another tethered aerostat—smaller even than the one I had caught from Hyde Park—proudly bearing the SLC livery along with the company's motto: *Ad Astra Per Aspera*. I was to learn that the ordinary folk of the Moon's settlements have their own, more acerbic variation of the saying: *Ad Astra Per Alas Porci*: a comment, I am led to believe, on the shape and flying properties of the capsules fired from the cannon. I boarded this vessel, my only company the crew: I was the last to join on that particular shoot, the balance of the compliment had been awaiting firing time for a day or more. The journey to the mountain was completed in less than an hour, at an altitude which allowed me to observe Africa's wildlife in comfort—even though much of it fled at the sound of the hissing, whining engines—for the aerostat's gondola was little more than a glazed platform with armchairs placed at passengers' convenience. But once Kilima-Njaro begins to dominate the horizon—the Space Cannon more obvious with every mile—it commands all attention. A gondola attendant imparted to me some data on the great gun as we approached—most of which I had already gleaned elsewhere. Some three miles in length, an eastwards-facing cannon built into the side of Mount Kilima-Njaro, the Uhuru Gun is truly a marvel of our modern age, and worthy of every superlative lavished upon it. Designed to fire a cargo capsule of forty feet long by twelve feet in diameter beyond Earth's stratosphere, its colossal barrel cooled by glacial ice shipped by regular aerostat flights from within the Arctic Circle it is fitted with a steerable aiming telescope equipped with a forty inch refractor lens. Using a combination of explosive ignition, magnetic rifling and pneumatic pressure to achieve escape velocity, it is the most accurate gun in the world—which indeed it must be. For tethered at an altitude of 20,000 feet above the vast cannon, hovers the *HMAS Newton*: the platform from which Earth's selenauts take their first step to the Moon. But I will speak more of that shortly.

The mountain filled the forward view of the aerostat; I was surveying the ground below, for I could see no obvious landing spot. Indeed, the African landscape stretched on as plain and apparently virgin as it had been since the arrival of Europeans. In my defence, I can only posit I was distracted by my alien surroundings for I reasoned the apparent desertion only moments before the aerostat began to rise: directly upwards, its engines banked for it no longer required forward motion. Despite the version presented of me in your often romanticised editions of our adventures, Watson, I am not an infallible machine: I admit to making mistakes—or at least, failing to observe clearly all that might be seen. Once the Uhuru Gun had been built—other than access for a variety of maintenance crew—there was no need for selenauts to land anywhere within the precepts of the mountain; all would be handled on board the *Newton*: over three miles above the plains, and well away from the curious eye of foreign powers.

The ultimate stage of my journey—a silent, almost vertical ascent that shadowed the barrel of the gun so closely it might have been tethered—took a further twenty-five minutes. I was unable to appreciate the approach of the *Newton*—the fabled Flying Circus—for the bulk of the SLC aerostat obscured most of the sky above us. The gondola attendant distributed breathing apparatus—bitter-tasting cones of bronzed metal which enclosed both mouth and nose, attached to bottles of compressed air—minutes before the first view of the Flying Circus: accentuating that man is at the limits of his comfortable existence.

And then the aerostat is above the *Newton*'s landing deck, its nose lock engaged to a mast winch and is already being brought to "ground". I pride myself that I am above the general herd, Watson—indeed I will always be averse to cooing over the latest fashion like a nurse over her charge—whereas I am afraid Professor Morton is not. I made what I imagine were the requisite sounds of awe and appreciation; certainly my attendant gave all the appearance of being suitably encouraged by my response.

Only those who have observed the *Newton* at first hand may appreciate the science and compromise that inspires its construction—for a compromise it surely is: between man's engineering prowess and his frailty. The great Uhuru Gun is the best possible way for us to reach the Moon—and perhaps one day soon the Solar bodies beyond; I have seen many a learned treatise on the practicalities of using some form of rocket power, but in my own opinion such a mode of transport is filled with too much inherent danger. At least, for the present. So a gun-shot it is. But if any man living is aware of the limits of the human body, it will be you, Watson; and the tremendous speeds necessary to fire a body beyond our atmosphere and the pull of gravity. If a man were to be blasted directly off the Earth's surface, the acceleration would kill him instantly; but the further away from our sphere, that acceleration is incrementally less.

Three miles above our planet that delicate balance is reached: suspended within range of the Uhuru Gun's muzzle, held in place by the most sophisticated collusion of directional motors, tethers and hoists, each capsule containing its fragile crew awaits the firing of the gun below. Once the shell within the gun—the first stage, we may describe it—has ascended to the *Newton's* altitude it has lost some of its initial velocity but retains sufficient to escape gravity. A suspended projectile snares the shell, there is a transfer of momentum, the projectile is dragged aloft, and the launch is accomplished. It is a dangerous moment, Watson, and I fully comprehend why the SLC is so rigorous in its vetting of potential selenauts; it is a wonder to me that there were so few casualties when Gordon's expeditionary force was shot into space *en masse*.

My small aerostat alighted upon the open platform which comprises the bulk of the *Newton*. It became immediately clear to me why the dirigible was so much smaller than an average vessel: nothing very much larger would have traversed the labyrinth of cables suspending the platform from the overhead buoyancy mantle. This hydrogen-filled device is as far removed from the cigar shape with which we have all become familiar: it is in the form of a torus—a circle of highly-inflated, dull metallic material which has the apparent rigidity of aluminium, so expanded are the internal gas bags against the low atmospheric pressure. I was informed that this non-reflective material is silhouetted against the sky during daylight hours and illuminated by banks of electric bulbs at night, so that it is visible from the ground at all times. The manned capsule is suspended below this torus, and passes cleanly through the circular opening—yet another testament to the ingenuity and brilliant minds of the men who built our space-crossing navy.

Once disembarked from the company aerostat, I was led across a short landing field into a low building on the periphery, over which again blazed the legend *Ad Astra Per Aspera*. Within it was far warmer—for at 20,000 feet there is little heat in the air, despite the cloudless sky and ceaseless sunlight—and I was permitted to discard my breathing apparatus. All conveniences such as oxygen and heat are supplied from the ground far below, piped up alongside its stout mooring cables. It was here that I finally made the acquaintance of those who were to accompany me on the voyage up to the Moon. There were to be four of us on the trip: a James Ordway Taggart—a Scottish engineer whose shining face and tousled red locks belied one of the keenest scientific brains of the Empire; one Garrison Fitzbrian of Ireland—a former landowner who has turned his vast acreage over to the government as a proving ground for many projects, both secret and well-reported; David Nathaniel Jobson—a chemist whose laboratories based on the Sussex Downs have most recently completed successful experiments into combining aluminium with other, much rarer elements to forge compounds of startling durability; and of course myself: Professor Morton, whose most recent publication was a speculation upon the relationship between the Moon's regolith and ancient impact craters upon the Earth—such as the Canyon Diablo Crater in Arizona. We were all formally introduced, and then invited to sit for a brief induction speech—most of which was a repeat of information already imparted to me by magic lantern in London: how the projectile was to be controlled once it was beyond the atmosphere; the duration of the journey; how a safe landing would be accomplished on arrival at our destination… All merely designed to allay any fears that we—as men of the highest standing in our fields—would most likely be beyond anyway. Immediately afterwards each of us was enclosed in a bulky armoured suit which I reasoned, by their similarity to those described in the John Douglas testament, as essentially excursion suits: we would be wearing them until we landed upon the Moon. And then we were led to our projectile.

I had been hoping to see our Moon vehicle more clearly before stepping inside, but access was by a long, windowless tunnel which led directly from the building wherein we had received the rather pointless lecture to the capsule itself. I experienced a sensation of anti-climax as I was guided towards an overbearing chair set within an austere cylinder. Before and behind us was a plain bulkhead; not a single riveted join could I perceive: all was fused and polished to a smooth finish. Encased

in our suits we were then strapped securely each to his own chair, and so tightly that it was impossible to move; if it had not been that each armoured suit had a generous body cavity then breathing would have been singularly uncomfortable. Once our attendants were satisfied that none of us would be so much able as to raise a finger before encountering Moon-fall, they enclosed our heads in globular aluminium helmets—not unlike the heavier sort used by underwater explorers—which had a thin mica plate, similar to Isinglass, inserted at eye level so that we might at least see out. Once these had been clamped securely to our suits all I was able to hear was the thin whirr of motors somewhere within the suit and my own breathing. We might be able to breathe, and I was to discover the suits shielded us against the frigid void between worlds—the air we breathed also gently warmed—but we would be no more able to converse than fidget in our huge seats.

The attendants left our quarters, sealing the hatch with a dull report that I barely heard through my insulating helmet. Moments later I felt a sensation of swaying and knew the projectile was being hoisted into position: ready to be snatched away by our motive power. There was nothing for us to do but await the sudden, crushing lurch of the bullet; and that would come only when our destination had hauled itself across the African sky to a point where the shoot would take the briefest possible route. I knew that beyond the forward bulkhead the projectile contained a crew of two whose task it was to make small corrections to the flight by means of simple gas jets arranged along the capsule's outer shell, but beyond that our flight was determined entirely by the aim of the Uhuru Gun. Supposing there was no miscalculation or mechanical failure—and I had been assured that there had been far fewer accidents than even the most cynical engineer might suppose, a great comfort to me as I lay strapped to that colossal seat—the trajectories of Moon and capsule would perfectly intersect.

You know, Watson, that I am able to envelope myself in thought alone—become one with my mind—and so let slip the hours as though they are mere seconds; yet still boredom threatened to hang its black wings about me. I yearned for my pipe—a cigarette, at least; or the numbing chill of the cocaine needle. If there had been an outstanding case upon which I might turn my energies—But all I had was this open-ended, fruitless wait…

The abrupt launch did not go unheralded: we had already been forewarned that an instant before we were dragged away, a system of air sacs within our suits would inflate, creating a rigid cocoon against which any potentially damaging movement—be it wrist, foot or neck—was negated; I also understand that it has an effect upon the flow of blood which—under the action of abrupt, overwhelming acceleration—can be forced away from vital organs. The moment, when it came, was so immediate and unexpected that I admit to brief alarm. I felt encased in stone so utterly that even my heart could not force a beat. The disagreeable sensations were so all-consuming that the moment of launch quite passed me by: once the air sacs deflated, allowing me to fill my lungs once more and my distracted heart to recommence its labours, the projectile was already in flight—possibly far beyond the thin atmosphere and spearing through blackest space.

For the second time that day I was momentarily consumed by disappointment! Here was I, embarking on a momentous voyage beyond our home sphere, yet I had been unable to observe the vehicle that would be the author of that crossing; I had failed to appreciate the moment when I was shot from a cannon into the heavens and—it was abundantly clear— neither would I be able to witness the landing upon the Moon. I might have been travelling from Baker Street to Putney, my senses blanked, for all I could see.

The journey would take some eighteen hours, at speeds undreamed of even by our forefathers—who imagined that the comparatively sedentary pace of the first steam railways might crush the human body. Again I had little to do but take sanctuary within my thoughts; again I cursed myself that I had not the foresight to have made myself more familiar with the details of some obscure cases that even now elude solution—the French Gerumaine case, for example; or the disappearance of Prince Jacobi of

Austro-Hungary and his entire retinue in an open field last August. With nothing to distract me I might have made tremendous inroads into those events; as it was—

As with the imminent launch, we were warned of the Moon's approach by the air sacs within our suits once more violently inflating. The unimaginable velocity of our transit through space had to be countered by an equal braking force, else we would sail past our destination and be lost in the wastes between the far planets. The shell which had fired us into the skies was lost to us: most of its momentum transferred to our capsule, it would fall into an orbit from whence further deceleration must send it tumbling back to Earth. Whilst I and my fellow passengers were immobilised the projectile was turned so that the crew now faced the rear. A blunt section of the projectile which now formed the front of the vessel was blasted clear by the ignition of a single rocket. Following Newton's Laws that action slowed our projectile sufficiently for the Moon's gravity to pull us gently towards it, imposing even more braking.

Our air sacs deflated—and so too did those of the crew—allowing them to take control. Our projectile arced gently towards the lunar surface; the gas jets both altering its attitude so that it fell "backwards", but also slowing the descent. The jolt upon landing was no worse than the impact of a shunting locomotive on its train of coaches.

After that there was nothing we could but await whatever reception was usual in these circumstances. My fellows were eager to rid themselves of the obscuring helmets, but until we were freed of the shackles pinning us to our respective chairs we were helpless as specimen butterflies. At length the hatch was opened and removed, and an actinic light flooded our enclosure—no doubt far brighter to our under-exposed pupils than it was in actuality. More attendants, dressed no differently from the ones who had sealed us in on the *Newton*—for all he world as though we had been on a protracted and particularly violent fairground ghost train which had now reached its end—stepped inside and began to unseal our helmets. As our hearing was restored my fellows laughed and signalled their relief at a safe crossing; but their laughter died as my own helmet was

removed, to be replaced by a puzzled silence. The attendants pulled away; the cause of their consternation was only too obvious: Taggart, Fitzbrian and Jobson each one now bore a head of white hair—young Taggart's curls were the colour of fresh snow, the others' a little less pristine—but I wore a wig, of course. One which had steadfastly refused to blanch.

My disguise was uncovered.

IV. Moonbase Archie

I can only imagine the thoughts which possessed both attendants and my fellow passengers in these first moments: was I a spy? A saboteur? If either I was certainly a clumsy one since my disguise was so easily penetrated. In truth it was obvious that my wig would betray me the moment of arrival on the Moon—but I had seen little else I could do. Should I discard my entire make up before leaving *HMAS Newton*, and so allow my imposture to be exposed? To do so during the journey would be impossible. Thus I could no nothing but declare myself on arrival.

Taggart, Jobson and Fitzbrian were all released from their confining seats and led out of the projectile, whilst I was left to stew—trussed like a Christmas goose. I could hear a muted cacophony from beyond my cell: the hum and whirr of unfamiliar machinery, voices raised in command or acknowledgement, a deep, almost sub-aural drone which underlay all. At length I was joined once more by someone in obvious authority: a cadaverous gentleman somewhere in his late thirties, his own bleached hair thinning, a mournful white moustache overhanging the lower half of his face. He wore a black frock-coat with silver epaulettes and frogged buttons which gave him an air of a soon to be retiring theatre commissionaire, rather than the one of military command which I'm sure was his intent.

"Now, sir," he began without pause, "what are we to do with you?"

"If you would be so kind as to allow me to step free of this infernal chair," said I, "and to remove this restrictive suit, I would be glad to offer you my card…"

His moustache bristled at what he no doubt perceived my effrontery. "Your card, sir—?"

"My name is Sherlock Holmes. I can prove my claim easily—but only

if you allow me to rise and be quit of this tin can. It has been a long journey: I am suffering an understandable degree of discomfort, and my legs are beginning to cramp."

I do not know if my name meant anything to the fellow—or even if he believed me—but he quickly summoned two attendants who unstrapped me, helped me to my feet and out of the projectile. There was a brief ladder leading to the ground, but my enforced inactivity had left my limbs a little shaky, and again I required assistance reaching the floor. I was divested of my excursion suit—all the while closely monitored by another two burly men in tunics that boasted just a fraction less frogging than my friend with the moustache. Both held weapons which were close cousins to the air rifles used by the British Army's Air Rifle Companies, but larger and more brutally functional in design. The ease and familiarity with which they bore these guns was more compelling than any verbal threat.

Once out of the bulky armour I did my best to smooth the inevitable creases from my clothing and then—taking care not to give my armed colleagues any excuse to demonstrate their prowess or willingness—I produced a card. My friend with the moustache eyed the pasteboard with all of the distrust he could summon before handing it to one of the unarmed attendants. This worthy hurried away silently, leaving me to marvel at the tacit efficiency of the SLC: for of course all of the gentlemen were in that company's employ, and by association, the British government.

As we awaited whatever response should be forthcoming, I divested myself of the last, crumpled remnants of Professor Morton—the betraying wig and moustache, the disfigured nose—and acquainted myself with my new surroundings. John Douglas's description of the lunar colony in his day is now a quaint memory for I could clearly see the relentless evolution of both technique and environment. We stood under a lofty dome—but not a half-buried, plain metallic structure as has already been described to us: this was transparent throughout, comprised of a multitude of panes constructed of a material that must needs be

more durable than mere glass. The entire edifice rested upon elegant, arching struts—steel, aluminium, or a new alloy unfamiliar to me—and I was irresistibly reminded of the Crystal Palace. If the shade of Joseph Paxton should forsake its grave and voyage upward, I am sure it would be warmed by how influential his legacy has proven to be. The projectile which had brought me so far had obviously been drawn indoors from its initial landing—there was no obvious means of egress through the vaulted roof—and from the relaxed manner in which I saw all comported themselves and dressed, it was clear that life upon the Moon was not only considerably more comfortable—but a degree or two safer.

At length the attendant returned, this time accompanied by a personage whose plain dress and simple manner informed me of his lofty rank. Perhaps it has been your experience in the military, Watson, but I often find that the scale of decoration borne upon a man's breast is inversely proportional to his true position. So it was here. He was tall— easily having an inch or two on myself—but the extra flesh he bore upon that frame generated an impression of a shorter man. His thick hair was wild and ungroomed, reaching past his stiff collar; whilst his pleasant features radiated a *bonhomie* which was almost certainly the result of rigorous training, for it failed to penetrate his dark, watchful eyes.

"Mr Holmes!" cried the newcomer, extending both his hands. "If only we had known you were coming! But we have received no word!"

I returned his handshake. "I regret the deception, Mr—"

"Falburne. Josiah Falburne. I am assistant secretary to the director of Moonbase Archie, Mr Holmes…"

"Moonbase Archie…?"

I took his grand gesture to include not only the dome but what lay beyond. "That is the designation of this—what was once the original— landing site upon the Moon."

"Indeed. As I was saying, I regret the deception, Mr Falburne, but I felt it necessary. There have been occasions when I have found it best to travel swiftly, and anonymously; this is but one more."

He took me by the elbow, waving dismissively at the men in silver-

frogged tunics with his free hand. "That will be all, Houghton." The man with the mournful moustache—Houghton—bobbed a terse assent before leading his men away, grumbling at them pettily. "But what can have called the famous Sherlock Holmes away from London?" Falburne continued. "I am aware of no recent cases of murder—nor any event that is any manner inexplicable."

"The Scowrers," said I. Falburne jerked to a halt, his affability, for the moment, evaporated.

"Ah," was all he said.

"It was many years ago, I appreciate—but I have been made aware of certain matters over the past weeks, matter which still hang over the Empire's lunar colonies, and I thought it best to resolve them—to my personal satisfaction—on the spot. And with as much discretion as possible."

His smile returned. "Understood, Mr Holmes. Understood. But first you must refresh yourself: the long journey up from Earth is arduous and can drain the vitality of the most robust constitution."

I waved away the offer. "I ask only that you provide me with some simple accommodation for my stay…"

"There is nothing that may be described as grandiose on the Moon, Mr Holmes; even now. But I think you may be surprised—"

As he led me away from the landed projectile, housed in what I have come to think of as a hangar, similar in function to the great sheds wherein aerostats are stored, Falburne acted as though he was my official guide to this most remote corner of the Empire. We passed through a double door—an airlock, as Douglas described them—into a busier if no less impressive portion of the domed palace. It was full lunar day, and the overhead sun provided more than adequate lighting within; for the long lunar night I observed the arches were provided with many electrical lights. The lucid material of the many panes allowed an unobscured view of the Moon's surface: the undulating paleness of the *Mare Nubium*; more grand domes in the distance—though none reached the grandeur of the moonbase—and the skeletal spires of many Tesla transmitting masts. I observed no

individuals or transports out on the surface at that time, nor did I see much evidence around the moonbase. Falburne identified each dome for me: one provided appropriate suites for visiting dignitaries, another served as the satellite's SLC offices; a third fulfilled the function of embassies and consuls for those countries who have yet to lay any claim upon the Moon, but who still wish to exploit its many resources. Falburne maintained a steady monologue as he led me through the busy moonbase—barely a soul paid me any great interest, although many greeted my guide warmly—much of it inconsequential, all of it designed to inculcate within me a sense of awe and wonder at what Britain has achieved in such a brief span. I was impressed, and informed Falburne so, although I am not such a fool that I don't imagine the Americans or Germans would have attained any less if they had Britain's lead in space exploration.

We crossed the dome in what I estimated was a little under fifteen minutes, reaching an annexed dome that was like a miniature of the first, at a height of no more than two storeys. There was a platform attached to its external surface—reached by a set of open metal stairs leading to an interior door and a gantry on the far side of an external door—which served a loop of elevated rail, both ends of which curved away in what I judged to be a southerly direction.

"You have tethered aerostats," I remarked. Falburne beamed in delight.

"Of a sort, Mr Holmes, of a sort. But these are a little different from the ones with which you are familiar."

We mounted the stairs, halting at the clear wall in which there was another double-doored airlock. Falburne pressed a small button close to the doors; he turned to me.

"We should not have long to wait."

Out of curiosity, I reached out and touched a pane of the clear material. I had imagined it would be cold, as glass is always cold, doubly so as only a few inches beyond was an airless atmosphere; but it felt pleasurably warm to my fingers.

"Mica?" I enquired. Falburne appeared heartened as my knowledge.

"A form of glass, Mr Holmes, processed from unique silicates found

within the regolith —mica at such a necessary thickness would be too opaque. Our engineers—both here and working on Earth—have forged a glass that is stout enough to withstand the pressure differential, as well as collision from the small aerolites which continue to pepper the Moon's surface, whilst remaining transparent. Although it will not be obvious to you, the external surfaces are partially mirrored, to reflect solar radiation, and you will have already noticed that the material itself is more conductive than ordinary glass. To minimise the stresses of endless heating and cooling as the Sun rises and sets, the mixture of materials in every dome achieves an equilibrium—absorbing or radiating as each moment demands. It is quite the marvel, Mr Holmes."

"And lunar quakes? I understand they might last up to ten minutes."

"All of the major constructions rest upon sprung alloy rafts designed to absorb shocks far beyond any that have been recorded on the Moon. They float, do you see? Ah, here is our ride—"

Drifting towards us along the loop of elevated rail was a machine the like of which I had never before seen. It is best described as resembling two small aerostat mantles, placed aside each other, with the gondola section placed above and between the two. The twin hull thus created hung below the elevated rail, enclosing it, with four small Tesla receiving aerials protruding from them.

The vehicle drew abreast of our position. A doorway—adjacent to the airlock—opened in the raised gondola, followed a moment later by the dome's outer door. A seal inflated around the gap. Falburne was watching a pressure gauge carefully and only when the needle had risen to indicate normal pressure existed in the short gap between us and the gondola section did he open the inner door. We passed through the airlock and into the vehicle, Falburne closing the gondola's door firmly behind us. I stood in a blank space, lit only by a simple blue electrical lamp, reliant on Falburne's expertise. A moment passed as he once again assured himself that the door was sealed against outside's near vacuum, then he cracked a square hatch, indicating I should step through; I found myself in a compartment that would not disgrace a first-class carriage

on the Earth's most distinguished railway. Plush sofas lined the walls, which curved inward following the gondola's vaguely cylindrical outline. Several windows—or perhaps I would best describe them as portholes—punctuated the walls above the luxurious seating, providing an excellent view of the passing moonscape. The floor was carpeted in a pale blue matching the lamp outside; the walls were veneered with warmly-hued woods whilst all of the bare metal fittings were polished to a mirror gleam. But for all the luxurious appointments, I could not fail to see excursion suits—two at each of the gondola's opposing ends: a blunt reminder of the harsh realities beyond this pressurised cabin.

As I took advantage of a sofa, I felt the tug as the vehicle began to move—but I heard nothing. Falburne continued his induction tour: "The Moon has been a unique opportunity, Mr Holmes—the most hostile and unforgiving environment man has ever sought to tame. And yet, for all its strangeness, there is much that is familiar. The landscape around was forged as much by vulcanism as aerial bombardment; there is an atmosphere—albeit thin and unbreathable; the Sun heats us—though by a greater degree than any desert on Earth—and the nights are unimaginably cold; and gravity decrees there is still an up and a down. You might think that nothing of the machinery we enjoy on Earth will work on the Moon, yet— with subtle adjustments and a little imagination—it has been possible to recreate many of our familiar comforts. Sometimes, to improve...

"This rail car, for instance. On the Moon there are no railway or canal companies whose self-interests might be impugned so we are free to transport men and materials in any way we please or can imagine. Floating an aerostat can be problematical: lighter than air vessels cannot ride upon an atmosphere that is itself less dense than many buoyancy gases we might use; and there is nothing for a spinning blade to pull or push against. But that near vacuum will cause the smallest volume of gas to expand many times greater than it will under atmospheric pressure. Rigidity and lightness, Mr Holmes: the small pontoons upon which we ride are inflated to the rigidity of steel with hydrogen gas, whilst having none of the mass of equivalent structures formed from metal. Earth's tethered aerostats are moved by small induction motors; we use the same principle—but with much more powerful motors. This entire carriage, weight already at a minimum, floats upon a magnetic field which may propel it forward or backward—rapidly, and in silence."

"And to where does it propel us at present?"

"Tycho. You will know the crater…"

"Few do not: it is one of the most visible features of the Moon's face. And close by the mining area known as the *Vale de Verme*, I believe?"

"That was never an official term for the area, Mr Holmes; besides, the peculiar formations which led early settlers to christen it so are long gone."

"Indeed?"

"I regret they have fallen victim to the expanded operations." He leaned forward. "I wonder if your information may not be obsolete, Mr Holmes: to speak of the *Vale*—and you mentioned the Scowrers earlier…"

"Also long gone."

"Happily, yes. The days of the expeditionary camps were not cheerful ones, you must understand: it required a certain kind of man—hard, uncompromising—and that breed often includes criminality within its character. They are eradicated now."

"And yet they were allowed full rein for many months; their unchecked activities almost fatally compromised the Empire's future on the Moon. I am curious as to how that was allowed."

"Communications were poor back then, Mr Holmes; the British Lunar Expeditionary Company was unprepared for the extent of the Scowrer's reach, and the rapidity with which it spread—"

"They were lax, Mr Falburne! Complacent…!"

"Sir I hardly think—!"

"And neither did they—and therein lay their litany of mistakes. I do not suppose I am permitted to smoke on this vehicle? No? Then I shall endure…

"Let me tell you what I know, Mr Falburne; followed by what I surmise. You may confirm or deny any portion of what I about to say—but be prepared to defend your denials."

Falburne outwardly relaxed—though his eyes remained wary and his face pale. "Very well, Mr Holmes, we are alone and cannot be overheard: have your say."

I gave him a *précis* of John Douglas's account; save for the inclusion of the more notorious names such as Bodymaster McGinty and Ted Baldwin, I vouchsafed no other identities—though I do not fool myself into believing that Falburne was any more ignorant of the drama's full cast than was I. Once I was done he waited several seconds before speaking: it was clear he was considering his words carefully.

"Much of what you have said is a matter of public record and can be found at the SLC Pall Mall offices," he commented at length, "or indeed the archives of any reputable newspaper. The rest ... I know of your reputation, Mr Holmes so I will not stoop to questioning the authenticity of your sources, but the events you describe transpired years before I was in post, and I have no knowledge of them."

He had responded much as I suspected he would; I suppressed my smile. "You would have me believe that no fuller records exist—beyond those on Earth? Really, Mr Falburne, you do us both a disservice!"

His own smile was tight and fleeting. "As you prefer—but I can say no more."

"Then let me add the suppositions which I mentioned. I am aware that men in such deadly work as mining often form guilds and brotherhoods, and that these fraternal organisations often cross simple barriers of trade or workforce. I am also only too aware that businessmen often discourage such fraternities, fearing the unionisation of their men; and yet it seems that during the formative period of this colony, members of the Order of Freemen were given preferential selection when applying to leave Earth. Once here, they naturally swelled the ranks of the colony's greatest threat. Does that not strike you as odd?"

Falburne remained silent.

"You have claimed—and in this you are not alone—that through poor communications, Earth was unaware of the extent of the corruption and criminality of the Scowrers. In this I believe you are partially correct: McGinty and his kind controlled the entire *Vale*, the prevention of any unfavourable report reaching back down to Earth would be as nothing. Yet word did get out: rumours were commonplace—"

"The British government does not act upon unsubstantiated gossip—"

"In that you are wrong, Mr Falburne—and you insult us both by declaring it. The Empire has acted upon rumour—and less than rumour—many a time; and often saved lives by it. It will do so again. That it did not do so on this occasion is curious, do you not think? After all, the Americans put enough stock in a few anecdotes to investigate…"

"That the government of the United States saw fit to interfere in a British matter was unforgiveable! It was politics of the lowest kind: tantamount to the invasion of a friendly power on the flimsiest of excuses; followed by months of the highest diplomacy to restore some form of detente. One that remains on the shakiest of foundations…"

"Perhaps—but it goaded the British government into finally acting: we could not let the world—and specifically certain European powers—witness the Americans cleaning up a stink of our own creation…"

"Mr Holmes! The Scowrers were not a creation of the government—!"

I held up a placating hand. "Forgive me, I was too general. The Scowrers were a diseased organisation grown from the Freemen: a charitable society governed by lodges and run in a manner that would be familiar to many a businessman or peer of the realm. You might be conversant with many of their rituals yourself, Mr Falburne."

His face grew paler, and I knew I had struck a telling blow. "No government is a cohesive organism; there are always factions within factions. Rather than a unit, I would describe it more a loose confederacy of warring tribes, with little common currency; one of the few unifying elements is Freemasonry. There are, I would venture to suggest, more lodge members sitting in Parliament at any moment than there are from a single political party; a statistic which might sober us all.

"Freemasonry ran the Freemen, and the Freemen ran the Scowrers—or that was the plan. Through the Scowrers, and the network of lodges reaching back and up to the highest in Britain, the government would rule the lunar colonies without being observed to as so much raise a finger. Private enterprise would be welcomed—nay, actively encouraged—though few would be aware of how closely their business was to be observed.

"But the physical and mental stresses placed upon all who dared the lunar shoot were underestimated: the hair's bleaching is but an outward sign—in many the damage ran deeper. The men who first conquered the Moon—ay, and their women—were a tough and savage breed; they had to be. It was inevitable that with some—perhaps the worst of their kind—the mental disfigurement would manifest in the most brutal and debased way. Their original purpose was lost, distorted as their own minds had become—though some remembered it in the vaguest terms, but were shouted down; no longer did they exercise subtle control over the settlement for their masters in London, but total domination for themselves. Those very businesses which they were meant to guide from afar were terrorised and driven away, leaving a vacuum to be filled—albeit temporarily—by others deemed less suitable; even antithetical to the original design, for it allowed the incursion of manufactories owned by parties outside the Empire."

Falburne had regained himself a little: he tugged at his coat and collar. "Even if any of this were true, Mr Holmes—and I do not say it is—the government did indeed step in when it became clear the BLEC was not exerting sufficient control and that the Scowrers were beyond redemption."

"Belatedly, and only when most of the risk had been eliminated. The Pinkerton agents did you a great service, there. The resulting embarrassment to Britain would have been even greater than being perceived by the world as a prevaricator who could not agree how to deal with a few bullies in a distant colony."

I rested my head against the carriage's wall and stared up at the panelled roof as an overdue thought took me. "As for the Americans: perhaps

they perceived an echo of their own struggles against a colonial power a century earlier and sought to exploit it—for they are a romantic people."

"This is all conjecture, Mr Holmes—you have no proof."

This time I allowed myself a smile. "I have all the proof I require, but I agree: it cannot be tested in open court. We two know the truth of it—and that will have to suffice until another day." I felt the nudge of the single-railed vehicle braking. "But it would seem I have monopolised the entire journey, and now here we are. I thank you for your attention, Mr Falburne."

"You have been most diverting, Mr Holmes." He stood and made his way towards the exit. "Most diverting."

"Then I crave your indulgence in one more matter…"

"And that is?"

"Consider how Ted Baldwin and the Willabys not only survived for an unknown period on the Moon's far side, but made their way back to the *Vale de Verme*…"

V. TYCHO AND POLEHAVEN

We disembarked without recourse to excursion suits and once again I found myself standing under a stark lunar sky, shielded by a faceted dome of specialised glass. On all sides rose a barrier of local rock, upon which the clear roof was poised: we were within the Tycho crater itself. The single rail along which we had travelled emerged from the crater wall—through a multitude of airlocks, I was later informed—halting at a simple platform. We descended open stairs identical to those I had ascended at the Moonbase, to be met at the bottom by an open-topped electric cab, the driver again wearing a frogged tunic—a design to which I was growing increasingly familiar.

The crater has a diameter of fifty-three miles, and that area is already more than half-filled with the signs of an expanding city. Towering buildings that might equal, if not over reach those of New York City and Chicago dominated the view, most faced with stone quarried locally and based on traditional design so the overall impression was of the heart of London transported to an alien setting: both familiar and unsettling. The streets, however, were laid with a geometrical precision never to be found in a British city—in this it had more in common with the metropolises of the United States: conceived and executed from a drawing board.

All power seemed to be electrical in nature, providing lighting when necessary, and ensuring the air circulation ran constantly; yet I saw no large Tesla relay towers anywhere within the confines of the domed crater: only smaller receivers, either growing from building roofs or from the rears of the cabs and other motorised vehicles throughout the city. They were, Falburne was happy to point out, arrayed beyond the crater. There was a circle of ten placed just beyond the rocky circumference, each

tower capable of taking over instantly should either—or both—of its neighbours fail. Whilst on Earth a power failure might be inconvenient, upon the Moon, it would be catastrophic.

The cab halted outside a building which bore no form of identification and by its uniform design was indistinguishable from a hundred more. Falburne led me inside, explaining that it was a hostelry commonly used for visitors such as I, or permanent residents who had yet to establish for themselves suitable accommodation. I was shown a simple room: twelve feet square with a plain cot and a cheap rug upon the stone floor; one corner contained a plain writing desk and chair—ingeniously constructed from metal and stone due to the lack of wood—whilst another was occupied by a wash basin and mirror. Falburne demonstrated that hot water was available on demand through a mounted faucet: every building included a water tank within its topmost storey, and its contents were heated through a combination of the Sun's rays and immersible electrical heaters. Ingenious, eh, Watson—can you imagine Mrs Hudson's thoughts on such a device?

Falburne had to leave me then, but he promised to return in the morning and conduct me around the more industrialised sector beyond the crater: the place Douglas knew as *Vale de Verme*. He regretted he could not leave a cab at my disposal but assured me I would be free to wander anywhere within the crater city. "We have," said he, "no secrets here." By which disingenuous remark he revealed there would be secrets a-plenty.

Once alone I took pen and ink, committing my experiences to paper whilst they were still fresh, along with several observations and theories which I had yet to test. This *aide memoire* I then placed within my coat— despite all of Falburne's rhetoric and assurances, I was not about to leave my thoughts naked and available to anyone who might take a fancy to search my latest quarters—and took myself outside for an exploratory walk.

I realise that the term "outside" is purely relative and that beyond any of the buildings I was still contained within the domed crater; but I was

surprised how rapidly accustomed I became to thinking the regularly-arranged streets and the equally uniform architecture was truly open to the black sky and intense—though oddly diffracted—sunlight. I have failed to mention that the dome, with its multitude of half-silvered panes, sometimes acted in the manner of an imperfect prism and split the light passing through into its spectral components. At such times everything within the dome was briefly encased in a halo of rainbow hue; distracting—but not perhaps without a certain aesthetic charm.

I swiftly discovered that the city was efficient and functional: the quarter containing my hostelry held other buildings of similar purpose; elsewhere could be found a sector devoted entirely to offices—both for the SLC and other companies with a presence on the Moon— another quarter was of well-provided research facilities. Falburne was at least truthful when he said I was free to wander: I investigated three separate laboratories and was greeted cordially in each, my every question answered openly and in detail. My reputation preceded me—as did the details of my modest contributions to lunar exploration—and no door was closed. Even experimental notes and still embryonic hypotheses were freely discussed in my presence, and I am proud to admit that in each case I was able to offer insights of my own.

But much of the shine of those brief hours was lost when—among sheaves of protocols and hastily-jotted experimental observations—I noticed several sheets of what appeared to be invoices and requisitions either misplaced or jumbled amongst more important papers. I was about to edge them to one side—for I had no interest in whatever exorbitant price some Earth-based company was charging for reagents—when I noticed the authorizing signature on each. Although signature is quite the wrong word, for each instance was evidently from an inked rubber stamp, used to save time when the signatory is faced with a veritable mountain of paper to endorse. Rather than a name, the authorization came in the shape of a single letter: a large, copperplate *M*.

Ah—I know what you will say, Watson; by itself this is nothing: an initial, common enough, and might stand for Morris, or Micklewhite, or

Mattocks… But taken with all else, it is suggestive. We know Moriarty's reach extends to the Moon—through his astronomical expertise he holds a non-executive position on the board of the SLC, and you recall I mentioned the piece of moon rock in his study—it is a small step to imagine the professor reeling in his influences so that all SLC business— openly or by subterfuge—passes through his hands. And the Scowrers? Was there ever an organisation more suited to his methods than they? Corrupted and corrupting, they might stamp upon a nascent colony a vision far beyond that of the British government: Moriarty's vision…

Yet even as I saw this sigil, and similar thoughts vied in my brain I knew I still did not have the whole answer. What the Scowrers did would suit Moriarty no more than it did the Masonic plans which spawned them: for beyond everything he is a man of cold logic, of deliberation and order—the Scowrers stood for chaos, and he would not tolerate them. I concluded that he would more likely stand behind their destruction than wield them as a blunt instrument.

I returned to my rude quarters shortly after that, observing as I did so that nowhere had I seen any shops or stores, no restaurants or public houses. In my hostelry there was a small ground floor salon wherein residents could order basic meals. I dined on what I was assured was salmon that first night—although of a size beyond even the most outrageous angler's tale, attaining its leviathan stature in low gravity fish farms—and so concluded that dining out and other entertainments had yet to modify the city's Spartan ethic. In this I had greatly underestimated the human spirit's appetite for gaiety—but more of that later.

I passed a reasonable night on my cot—even though my pipe was still forbidden to me. Hookahs could be obtained, but they were imported and I deemed them an expensive luxury which I could likely forbear during my short stay. Sleep came swiftly and easily and I awoke early: refreshed and curious what the day might reveal. I enjoyed both the hot water and a plentiful breakfast of kedgeree; after which I settled myself in the salon, reading a newspaper that was three days old, awaiting my guide in the shape of Assistant Secretary Falburne.

He arrived at eleven, apologising if he had kept me waiting. I waved him off, more interested in seeing the colony than his excuses: he was no doubt a busy man, and I rated very low in his priorities. Again we travelled by electric cab, and back to the station to board another of the quasi-aerostat, one-rail carriages. This time I watched carefully through the portholes, marking the moments as we entered and exited the crate wall. A minute or so after quitting the crater we passed through a turnout on the single rail, turning away from the track on which we had arrived yesterday from Moonbase Archie.

Falburne was pensive at first, and not inclined to respond to my occasional attempt at conversation; but eventually he thawed and turned to me a grave and thoughtful countenance.

"You spoke yesterday of Baldwin and the Willabys," said he, "and of how they not only survived the Devil's Bowl, but escaped it—returning eventually to Earth."

"The Devil's Bowl?"

"The unofficial name given to a huge impact crater on the Moon's dark side, where the Pinkerton men made their stand."

"Ah—indeed. And have you an explanation?"

He fell silent again; I was convinced he knew, but was about to lie—and debated mutely with himself over how much truth to include.

"Their excursion suits held little air," said I to prompt him. "And the Pinkerton agents' transport was wrecked. It is inconceivable that any of the three could survive an appreciable time in this Devil's Bowl; for them to do so and *return* to the *Vale* is impossible."

He nodded. "Quite impossible."

"I have long held that to reach the truth—no matter how improbable it may appear— you must eliminate the impossible. In this instance, do we concede that cannot be done?"

"So it must seem—"

"Bah! You yield too quickly, Mr Falburne! Baldwin and his creatures fled into the crater, only to return; *ergo* it is not impossible. As unlikely as it may seem, it happened." I closed my eyes and thought, wishing I had recourse to some good, honest tobacco. "What is there, in that crater…?"

His delay in replying was suggestively long: his response carefully considered. "As far as we are able to ascertain, it is like any other crater which we have examined—very little to mark it as in any way different to Tycho, save in size."

"A potential home for another crater city?"

"The engineering challenges we faced with Tycho would be vastly magnified, for its diameter is some 1,600 miles; thirty times that of Tycho. We could harbour more than one city within its vast area, if it were possible."

"You have surveyed it thoroughly, I see."

"The SLC is thorough in all its endeavours, Mr Holmes!"

"Indeed." I allowed my attention to wonder, as though something through the opposite porthole caught my eye. "Have the German and American colonies shown any great interest in this colossal basin?"

"Both the United States and Germany settled areas in the northern hemisphere of the Moon, still in the earliest stages of colonisation. Even should they choose to travel in the most recent British surface vehicles— which on occasion we have loaned them—it would a long and dangerous drive to the Devil's Bowl."

"Indeed—but you have not answered my question. Have they?"

After another silence he nodded. "Both have sent expeditions into the uncharted regions of the dark side; it is our belief they have both mapped and sampled the Devil's Bowl…"

"Capital! But the British already knew of the crater during the Scowrer's time?"

"The first expeditions explored as far and as fast as they were able, Mr Holmes—you must already know that. We could not camp out on *Mare Nubium* indefinitely."

And then there was truly something outside the small windows to attract my attention: a raw landscape of ploughed rock, men and machines seething atop the exposed layers. I moved closer to a porthole to acquire a better view; Falburne glanced through the adjoining window.

"The Victoria collieries," he explained. "Where Bodymaster McGinty once ruled a camp of the same name with murder and intimidation, now diggers and drills plough far below the lava tunnels in which he hid. There—" he indicated a pit from which skeletal hints of old aluminium roof supports still clenched like a vast, dead hand "—there is the very dome—or the remains of it—where he presided over his mockery of a lodge. Now just another exploratory hole, the steel and aluminium that once cloaked it re-smelted and forged afresh."

I could picture it: the rough site that John Douglas had called home for many months, where he had found his first, late wife and much else besides: the tunnels in which colonists had lived like strange ants now little more than ruts and trenches; the domes, refineries and factories ploughed under; rocky walls and slag heaps reduced to dust and crushed flat under the wheels and tracks of the machines which had scraped the regolith clear and plundered the megaregolith deep below—leaving a wide, tiered pit. And overall was a grey miasma, almost the equal of any London fog: the disturbed dust of the lunar soil, thrown into the thin atmosphere, never allowed to settle.

"This is the *Vale de Verme* now," spoke Falburne, "swallowed by the expanding operations. The days of which you spoke were meant as an establishing period: the ores, water and gases mined were primarily used to build shelters and more machinery for to exploit whatever riches we might later discover. All of the workers now live at the southernmost tip of the *Vale*, in a fresh settlement christened Polehaven: our destination. You may find it crude and unsavoury, but I can assure you it is far and above what those wretches experienced in Boss McGinty's day."

Our one-railed vehicle sped on through a landscape far more satanic than any Blake might have conceived. Drilling and excavating machinery tore up the exposed rock; things like legless giants scooped up the debris in twin arms that ended in toothed buckets; this was deposited in open waggons coupled into long trains running on conventional tracks which wound through the pits and open collieries on the way to its destination. And everything seemed powered by a dual system of water, heated to

steam by electrical dynamos, driving great pistons which rarely leaked any waste vapour into the cloudy atmosphere.

I saw no human figure in that strange landscape, commenting upon it to Falburne. "There is little point for anyone to exit their machines," he explained. "One of those diggers may do the work of an entire crew, and more swiftly. And it is far safer for the men involved to be enclosed within a sealed and pressured cabin than be outside and risk a puncture to his excursion suit."

I approved of his concern; though I privately noted that with such machines—each operated by a single man—it would be possible to operate with a greatly reduced workforce. The irony did not escape me that for all his bluster and cruelty, Bodymaster McGinty would never have tolerated such a decimation of his membership.

Our carriage completed its silent journey in an hour and ten minutes—such was its speed. Through a window I noted the moment it passed out of the dust-choked exterior and into a clear, well-lit interior. It slowed to gentle halt, and minutes later Falburne and I were once more treading the polished floor of an artificial dome: this time a much smaller affair with few windows: the lighting provided by a network of electrical lamps. Figures in the familiar frogged tunic scurried about us on errands; though again, often pausing to greet Falburne who introduced me—at my request—simply as Professor Morton. The place had the air of a busy, if provincial, aerostat terminal.

"Is this Polehaven?" I enquired.

"Indeed no: this is known simply as Terminus One; Polehaven is another thirteen miles to the south, and presently not connected to the one-rail system. From here on we must take ground transport."

He led me to an enclosure wherein awaited several wheeled and tracked vehicles: all transports of a variety of sizes, for none was equipped with any form of digging or moving accessories. Waiting for us by an eight-wheeled machine about the size of a terrestrial railway carriage was a driver who saluted smartly before opening a hatch in the main body of the machine. We boarded and the hatch—an ingenious interlocking,

twin-door device— sealed behind us. There was plush seating, adequate for a dozen souls to rest in comfort, all within easy view of an array of small portholes—although vision through each was restricted to a very narrow field. The machine's engines started with a loud whine; with none of the gentleness of the one-rail carriage, the transport lunged forward, turned, and exited through a double airlock.

We were driven over rough ground which had yet to feel the cut of excavation; it must be, I conjecture, very much as the Moon first was before man claimed it. yet the atmosphere was still hazy with mined dust: the horizon—so clear up at Moonbase Archie—blurred into the sky, itself no longer the pristine black of my initial acquaintance.

"This is one of the new Thomas Humber machines," Falburne expounded. "Fully electric, extracting its power from the Tesla-Westinghouse transmission network integrated throughout the SLC territories. Many companies such as Humber and Lanchester that, back on Earth, might have struggled to exist in a market of bicycles and horse-carriages, have found new life designing and building machinery for us. And what they and we have learned through obstacle and resolution can only benefit us back on Earth."

"I have seen the towers," I admitted. "But from where is the electricity generated?"

"Stations buried deep inside the megaregolith, far below the extremes of heat and cold. Steam turbines heated by hydrogen gas provide us with all the electricity we need."

"Indeed—" The Humber lurched heavily to the left; a quick glance through the nearest porthole revealed a landscape of sharp-edged boulders, a rutted track picked carefully between them.

"*Terra Gigantum*," remarked Falburne as he clung to a dangling strap; I followed his sage example. "I sometimes believe those who first described those selenographic features not visible from Earth had more imagination than learning…"

"We touched upon the German and American settlements yesterday," said I once the vehicle's precipitous motions had eased a little. "The

newspapers back on Earth are bristling for some form of minor conflict—though they rein in short of calling for war. How are relationships between your respective colonies?"

"Cordial, for the most part." He paused, once again marshalling his thoughts. "I will not deny there are tensions—though nothing as extreme as the yellow press would have you believe. Governments of Earth may posture and bluster, but up here we all have a common enemy: the Moon herself. Though we all—American, German and British—may squabble frequently over borders and mineral rights, we will render aid and assistance even more readily. There is even a nascent lunar alliance—with representatives from the SLC and Germany's *Gesellschaft Nordmond*, along with the USA's Lunar Secretary, Haslett Flyte: whose authority derives straight from the White House—though it is presently a non-executive body with no true administrative or legal standing; and our respective Earth-bound governments have so far failed to recognise its existence."

"Excellent, Mr Falburne—you give me hope for mankind's future!"

He smiled broadly, warmed by my praise. "Thank you, Mr Holmes. And now, if you would care to glance through your nearest porthole, I believe we are approaching Polehaven: named—I'm sure you will have inferred—for its position on the lunar South Pole."

Even though my forward view was restricted I could see we were certainly approaching something not natural to the lunar surface. A blaze of light, perched upon the curved horizon, as though a previously unrecorded sun was about to rise.

"Polehaven is a city of light, Mr Holmes: for the Sun is a fickle creature at the Poles— even more so than she is on Earth—her heat and light begrudgingly bestowed upon us. So the inhabitants of Polehaven are as equally profligate with their expenditure of light and warmth."

"Then it is a curious place to establish a new settlement," I observed. "Were there no other, more amenable sites to be found?"

"Most of the ice is to be found at the Poles: the source of our liquid water and hydrogen —and a little of our oxygen." Falburne's smile grew

shrewd. "We are the South Lunar Company; where else should we locate the Moon's newest, most vibrant city?"

In that final sentence, Watson, he told me more than I had learned since arriving on the Moon; so much more than he had meant, I'm sure. The *Mare Nubium* was selected for the initial landing site because it is level; the *Vale de Verme* because of the lava tubes which were swiftly utilised as dwelling places whilst more permanent structures could be erected, also it had ice in deep gulleys and ravines where the Sun never reached, and a plentitude of oxides in the surface. But these were mere stepping-stones, Watson; toe-holds. By its very name it is clear Moonbase Archie is but the first of many, and a new settlement, placed directly on the southern Pole would be central to future expansion. Do you see? No—?

The British Empire, through the South Lunar Company, means to annex and settle the whole of the southern lunar hemisphere. The Devil's Bowl is a vital element in that expansion, for by its very size it commands a great proportion of that face of the Moon forever hidden from Earth. Is it any wonder there are tensions between the colonial powers?

As we neared Polehaven the glow coalesced into a vast glasshouse, its countless panes alive with the light from within. That it was intended as a sister construction to Moonbase Archie could not be doubted now I saw its entirety: once again it was as if the Crystal Palace had been reconstructed on the Moon's surface, but taking full advantage of the lesser gravity it was made on an even grander scale.

Once inside, however, the resemblance to the moonbase was shattered: whereas that building was a quiet, efficient machine populated by the tacitly industrious, Polehaven was a blaze of rude noise, garish light and bibulous humanity. No longer did I wonder at the lack of entertainment at Tycho: for here it all was, writ large. There were eating houses for every palette and pocket, alehouses and public bars, theatres which ran from simple music hall to the highest opera. Polehaven was the home of every soul who pitted their lives daily against the Moon and her treasures: miner, manufactory worker, driver, metalworker… Not for them the quiet, dry existence of Tycho; this new city ran hot with the same vitality and zest

which they brought to their work. And as in London, where the wretched of Whitechapel and Soho might rub shoulders with stockbroker or backbencher, I spotted many a SLC tunic in the crowd, along with those more soberly-suited such as Falburne and myself. Merely by catching a one-rail carriage, and following it with a journey in a large Humber or Lanchester, any soul could ensure themselves of whatever entertainment they desired—far from the sterile constraints of crater or moonbase.

But least I create the impression that Polehaven was some kind of industrial Gomorrah, I should add that beyond the teeming life of its central streets, the city boasted housing for the workers' families which would not shame the grandest house in Bloomsbury. As in Tycho, some effort had been made to dress every building in a veneer of Earthly normality, but underneath were homes and apartments, the spaciousness and cleanliness of which made the noblest of efforts by such as Salt or Akroyd look paltry and mean-spirited. The days of Bodymaster McGinty were gone indeed, in every respect: the first settlers, huddled in their crude burrows, could never have dreamed of such comfort and safety.

Falburne took me to a well-provided restaurant where we dined on beef and a variety of vegetables whose freshness I would have unhesitatingly vouched for—but they were, apparently, frozen on Earth and maintained in that state until needed; a development of the methods sailing ships once used for the transportation of meat from the Antipodes. Afterwards we took in a recital at what he proudly claimed to be the best opera house outside Italy—with acoustics unsurpassed anywhere. That may have been true, but I regret the performers on show were, at best, mediocre—although that is to be expected until world-class artists can be persuaded to endure the moon shoot, with all it subsequent maladies. I was being given the best treatment, of course; my questions and observations had already given Falburne cause to fret, and he would be doing his best to impress me—at least until word came back from Earth: for it is certain that the first projectile home, subsequent to my arrival, contained a message for his masters on Pall Mall.

But his best efforts were to be undermined. He had evidently left

word where he could be contacted if necessary, for part-way through the recital a boy in the ubiquitous SLC tunic approached us apologetically and murmured in Falburne's ear. He glanced at me a moment before indicating we should leave; for my part, I was not disappointed. A small electric cab was awaiting us at the opera house's door and the driver spared no time in whisking us away—endlessly squeezing a huge air horn to clear the street ahead of pedestrians.

"There has been an accident," Falburne explained. "Someone has been fatally injured in *Terra Gigantum*; the body has been brought here for preliminary investigations."

"How did they die?"

"That is uncertain at present."

"Then it is fortunate I am at hand…"

He said nothing to that, only smiled in a tight, strained manner.

The cab drew to a halt outside a many-storeyed, nondescript building, above the entrance to which hung a familiar blue lamp—save that the expected word *Police* was replaced by *SLC*. Falburne led us inside where I endured the curious stares of many in the usual tunics, some of whom were armed with the large airguns I had witnessed on my arrival at the moonbase. We descended a flight of stairs; I reasoned we were heading for a mortuary, a guess confirmed by the swelling aroma of carbolic which almost masked underlining, less clinical scents. Falburne pushed through a pair of plain steel doors and I found myself in a low room, lit by cold electrical lamps, with the familiar post mortem table close to the centre. Another was already in the mortuary: a short, balding man in shirt-sleeves, in the act of rolling back his cuffs. On the table before him was an excursion suit, containing the body of the dead worker.

The short man glanced up at our arrival, nodding a greeting to Falburne before frowning at myself.

"Dr Richards," said Falburne, "may I introduce Mr Sherlock Holmes of London. Mr Holmes, this is Dr James Richards whose many roles include that of pathologist."

The doctor looked at me anew, pale brows drawn down. "Mr Holmes,"

said he in a low, Welsh voice. "Of course I have heard of you—but is it not a long way to come for such a simple case?"

"Mr Holmes was with me when I was summoned, nothing more."

I stepped close to the prostrate form, looking at the scored and pitted suit carefully: it bore the hallmarks of many years' hard work and subsequent abuse. "How was he found?"

"Out in *Terra Gigantum*—a prospecting party came across him lying at the foot of one of the formations out there. He was already dead; it is likely he fell off the rock, puncturing his suit." Dr Richards reached towards the suit, about to unseal it. I held up a hand, glancing back towards Falburne.

"If you might indulge me?"

Richards also looked to Falburne. "If Dr Richards does not object," said the assistant secretary. The pathologist shrugged and stepped back.

"As you wish, sir—I am familiar with your methods—but I'm sure there is nothing here that could interest you."

I thanked him and bent closer to the body. "The suit has certainly seen some use: there is a great deal of wear about the helmet seal and the gauntlets' fingertips; also around the knees, suggesting the person is in the habit of kneeling."

"That is not unusual," said Richards. "Dropping to one knee or another to investigate something upon the ground is something of an occupational hazard: it is difficult to rise again, you understand."

"Indeed." I ran a finger across the chest plate, disturbing an accumulation of dust. I smelled it carefully: it reminded me of gunpowder, with a stronger hint of sulphur than I would have expected. "The armour appears to be greatly stressed: as though straining against internal forces— What of this scoring?" I asked, pointing to the legs where there was a peculiar pattern of lines, radiating up and away from the boots. Richards looked at it dismissively.

"It could be anything…"

"It could be, but almost certainly will prove not. And this—?" I indicated a symbol revealed when I had brushed at the dirt: two black

bars above and below a white field upon which was a black eagle. "The flag of Prussia, if I am not very much mistaken." I stepped back. "This man is German."

Neither man spoke. "Come, come, gentlemen: a German workman, found dead within SLC territory and you thought the fact unworthy of note…?"

Falburne sighed. "It is unfortunate, Mr Holmes—but we would prefer not to take the issue further. It is too delicate. Once Dr Richards has completed a preliminary post mortem examination, we shall alert the *Gesellschaft Nordmond* and allow them to collect the remains."

"Unfortunate indeed. But you were about to remove the helmet when I interrupted you, Dr Richards—pray proceed."

The pathologist leaned down and cracked the helmet seal. For a moment the great bowl would not move: I noted the metal was bent slightly out of shape; then it came free with a screech and Richards placed it carefully to one side. The features of the unfortunate German were frozen in a rictus of fear or agony, his skin a livid red.

"Is that colouration usual in cases of punctured suits, doctor?" I asked. He shook his head, either baffled or reluctant to commit himself.

"Might I suggest you re-pressurise the suit to determine where the puncture might be?"

"Is that necessary?" asked Falburne. "Surely the German authorities should be the ones to investigate?"

"Before returning this unfortunate to the *Gesellschaft Nordmond* it would be wise to accommodate yourself with the facts, gentlemen. I might tell you that I believe this individual died neither from a single puncture to his suit nor out in *Terra Gigantum*—though I suspect you are already aware of that. We are in a period of unprecedented international tensions; if you do not wish to intensify them, please do as I ask and confirm my hypothesis."

VI. The Devil's Bowl

As the re-pressurisation test could not be conducted within the confines of the mortuary at Polehaven, Falburne returned me to my hostelry at Tycho to await word. He spoke little on the journey, but sat always at a distance from me, his face drawn and grey; what so distracted him I could not know, but I was able to make a fair deduction. The German's death was not such a simple accident, and once the *Gesellschaft Nordmond* was involved events would take an ugly turn. For myself I was glad of the silence, for it gave me the opportunity to arrange my own thoughts. Even though the lie I had been told—for it was a lie—was a simple one, and therefore of the easiest to maintain, it collapsed to dust at the lightest touch. How had the SLC prospecting team so fortunately chanced upon the body of a single man in such an expanse, unless they had been looking for it—in which case: why? And where was the man's own transport?—he could not have walked all the way from the German colony in the northern hemisphere. Lunar protocol since the earliest days has dictated that no man ventures alone onto the surface; so where was his companion—or companions? A name once again figured in my conjectures, a name that had become the hub of lunar exploration: the Devil's Bowl.

I sat upon my bed as the night passed, again mourning the lack of tobacco, assembling what I knew against what I could deduce, testing both with extrapolations of the available data. When the Tycho morning dawned—signified by the fading up of the hostel's internal lighting system—I was confident I had an answer of sorts.

There was a terse knock upon my door just as I finished shaving. I opened the door to find Houghton—the moustached functionary who

had so warmly greeted my arrival at the moonbase—standing there. He saluted quickly.

"Mr Falburne's compliments, Mr Holmes, but he'd be grateful if you would be good enough to accompany me to his offices at Moonbase Archie."

"Morning, Houghton," I greeted him cheerfully, throwing on my coat. "There is nothing I would enjoy more."

Throughout the cab journey to the one-rail station—and in the carriage subsequently—Houghton was a model of rectitude, either ignoring my queries or fielding them with a mumbled "I wouldn't know, sir." If I had not known otherwise, I would have wagered the man did not know of a deceased German found the night before in likely compromising circumstances. At the moonbase he conducted me through the complex to an airy office on the third floor. With a "If you would just wait here, sir," he gestured to an array of armchairs before closing the door behind him.

Disdaining the chairs, I took the opportunity to investigate Falburne's office. One wall was composed entirely of local glass, with an excellent view of the *Mare* beyond. The remaining three were of glazed steel and aluminium, draped with thick grey curtains which both muffled the voices of those within and prevented the gaze of those without. His desk and chair were again of a variety of alloys—the sprung chair surprisingly comfortable—whilst the desk had been darkened by a chemical process to a colour approximating matured oak. The surface of the desk was sparse and neat, comprising a bound blotter with inkwells and pens, a personal Teslagraph, and a silver-framed print of a young lady: a sweetheart, most likely, for he wore no wedding ring. The wall immediately behind the desk was mounted by rows of plain shelving, dotted variously with volumes of SLC procedure and law, and selenography; treatises on mineralogy and off-Earth mining; and a slim manila folder—carelessly hidden and in evident haste between two weighty volumes—in which several sheets of correspondence had been stashed. I flipped through them quickly: all were of little importance—nothing of a confidential nature, so I suffered

no guilt at perusing them—though I was amused by one memorandum, timed and dated for the previous evening, which briefly warned of my interest in John Douglas and the Birlstone mystery. Significantly all were marked with that fateful sigil *M*. There being nothing else to interest me, I sat in one of the armchairs—noting they were less comfortable than Falburne's simple chair—and awaited the man.

He arrived some thirty minutes later, apologetic and flustered. He did not appear to have rested that night—or done so badly; certainly he had not shaved. He sat himself heavily in his chair, palming at his ruffled hair. He took a deep breath before speaking. "I'm sure I do not need to tell you things have gone badly, Mr Holmes."

"The Germans?"

"They are accusing the British of murdering their man—his name was Gunther Koenigsmann, by the by—or of sheltering his killer. They are refusing to believe he was found, in all innocence, in *Terra Gigantum*."

"As they should, for we both know he was not…"

"Mr Holmes—!"

"I may be able to assist you, Falburne—I will do all I can to prevent an escalation in the tensions between us and Germany—but you must be honest with me. In that lies your only hope."

He composed himself. "Very well…"

"What was the result of the re-pressurisation test?"

"As you suggested, there were multiple punctures in the excursion suit. Far too many to be result of a fall from even a great height, in lunar gravity."

"And the extraordinary lividity of Koenigsmann's features?"

"Dr Richards has several theories—"

"It is carbon monoxide poisoning—the symptoms are quite unique."

"He was poisoned by carbon monoxide in a punctured suit? Surely that is mutually contradictory…?"

"On the contrary, taken with that singular pattern of lines, radiating up from his feet, it leads only to one set of conclusions."

"And they are?"

"That Koenigsmann did not die out on *Terra Gigantum*, your team did not find him there, and that he was not murdered."

Falburne collapsed back against his chair. "You can prove this?"

"Conclusively. Can you arrange for a representative from the *Gesellschaft Nordmond* to be present when I present my case?"

"A Maximilian von Grunshafen presented his credentials this morning: come to claim Koenigsmann's body—and deliver his company's message. He shall hear of it."

"Excellent. Have you a conference room?"

"There is a small seminar room on the ground floor." The office door opened and Houghton entered; I had not seen Falburne summon him in any way, and I confess my pride was pricked that I had missed it. "Escort Mr Holmes to room 10, if you please; I will join you there shortly."

I was led to a room that could have been the twin to Falburne's office, save that it boasted just a single long table flanked by a dozen chairs. I took one of them. Falburne appeared after seven minutes accompanied by two others. The man on his right was a ramrod-stiff Prussian in military uniform, his white hair cropped close, who required no introduction, for it could be none other than *Herr* Maximilian von Grunshafen; the second figure I had already met: David Nathaniel Jobson: the alloy expert. Falburne introduced me by my true name and I greeted them both. Von Grunshafen snapped a curt bow; Jobson amused to discover that I had been the same Professor Morton whose disguise had caused so much alarm on our arrival.

As they joined me at the table I remarked: "I am unclear as to why you are with us, Mr Jobson."

Falburne answered before the other could speak. "Mr Jobson is probably the best qualified amongst us with regard to the Devil's Bowl. If you have any questions regarding it, he is your man."

"Well then," said I, "perhaps you may assist me. Naturally I acquainted myself with all available data on the Moon before arriving but there is one item on which I have found little in the way of hard facts: transitory lunar phenomena…"

Falburne was amused. "Anomalous lights; luminescent emissions; patterns or shadows which persist for days before vanishing? *Fata Morgana*, Mr Holmes—sprites…"

"And what of *outgassing*?" I asked.

It was Jobson who spoke. "The causes are poorly understood: it may be caused by rocks grinding together under the Earth's pull, or through residual volcanic activity; it may even be gases, trapped under the regolith, violently released by an unknown trigger. It is, as I said, very difficult to study. I am surprised you have learned of it, Mr Holmes."

"Mr Falburne is familiar with the actual incident to which I refer— but it took a great deal of research to find any detailed letter or paper in a scientific journal. I learned the actual term for it but a week ago."

"Outgassing is vanishingly rare," said Falburne, his tone reluctant. "There was a tractor caught in one, three years ago. It was crippled, and the crew had to be rescued. The conclusion was that the tractor itself triggered the eruption through weight or vibration."

"Though what has this to do with a murdered man?" muttered the German. "And should the Director not be present? Is this matter not too important for—" His pause was calculated "—an assistant?"

"Involving the Director will bring these proceedings directly under the purview of Her Majesty's government," said I. "For the moment I believe it is in the best interests of us all to keep matters as informal as possible."

Von Grunshafen shrugged his agreement.

"As to a murdered man," I continued, "nothing. But if you refer to Koenigsmann, then let me reassure you: he was not murdered."

He was dismissive. "You are English. I would not expect you to say differently."

"You know my reputation, *Herr* von Grunshafen. I stand for the truth—whatever it might be."

The German grunted before relapsing back into gruff silence.

"I have already warned Mr Falburne that I expect full honesty from him today, it goes without saying that I want nothing less from you, Mr

Jobson, or you *mein herr*. It is said that truth is the first casualty of war; well, here truth is a victim of a war neither declared nor acknowledged. Within this room, we shall have an amnesty."

All three gave me frank looks which ran from open hostility to amusement.

"Your man—Koenigsmann—was found dead by a number of British selenauts, his body brought in to Polehaven. They claim to have found him somewhere in *Terra Gigantum*—a report which you dispute, *Herr* von Grunshafen."

"*Naturliche*. He was murdered—"

"I have already said such was not the case, *mein herr*. However you are right to question the veracity; Koenigsmann was found nowhere near *Terra Gigantum*, but out in the Devil's Bowl."

There was no verbal response to my claim, but Falburne and the German stiffened; their eyes narrowing perceptibly.

"You are not surprised—ah well, I had expected no less. Obviously you, von Grunshafen, would be only too aware of the location of one of your spies—"

The German shouted me down, his face congested with fury. I waited until he had himself once more under control. "My apologies: perhaps spy is too strong a word; but do you deny Koenigsmann was out in the Devil's Bowl at your order?"

"I will admit to nothing."

"As you please—although I did request total honesty. However he was not alone: there would have been at least one other, if not more, along with the transport so evidently overlooked in the version of events given to us by Mr Falburne. I cannot speak for the exact actions, but I shall tell you what I am satisfied is a logical interpretation:

"Koenigsmann and his team leave their transport and spread out, taking whatever readings or measurements are required. It is still lunar night across the Bowl, so they are confident they will not be spotted. There is one of your *outgassings*, Mr Jobson, and poor Koenigsmann is unfortunate enough to be caught in it.

"You will recall the scoring on his suit, Falburne: radiating up from his feet, along with the multiple punctures and the lividity of his features. I submit that a huge pocket of gas, mostly, if not entirely composed of carbon monoxide, erupted under the wretched man's feet, from deep below the regolith. The fine dust and grit—propelled at high velocity—both scored and punctured his suit. Still under considerable pressure, the gas injected itself through the punctures before it could dissipate. So the poor man suffocated."

"I will have to verify this account with the body," spoke von Grunshafen.

"Do as you must, *mein herr*—I guarantee you will find his condition equates with my explanation."

"And his team?" asked Jobson. "What of them? Why did they not take his body back north?"

"I imagine they had to flee. Many transitory phenomena have been reported to be of a luminous nature, it is not unreasonable to speculate this was the same: visible for miles across the Bowl—especially in the dark. The SLC post hidden out there would have investigated—"

It was Falburne's turn to flush and bluster. "Look here—!"

"You are too direct a man for the duplicitous hand fate has dealt you, Falburne. You have admitted that the SLC has surveyed and mapped the Devil's Bowl in its entirety; and it is clear how large a part in the future of the Moon's colonisation the Bowl is due to play." I caught von Grunshafen's expression at those words: an arched eyebrow that revealed a great deal. I would have liked the opportunity to uncover exactly how much of the SLC's plans were known to him. Behind the comic opera Prussian posturing lies a keen brain, I am sure. "Then there was the tractor damaged by an outgassing three years ago," I continued. "From where came its rescuer? Are the machines equipped with some form of communications like portable Teslagraphs? I thought not. Then how fortunate another SLC vehicle should be passing, just as it was most needed.

"The Bowl was being explored less than two years after the first

landings on *Mare Nubium*, and Ted Baldwin and the Willabys not only escaped into its heart and survived, but returned; eventually making their way back to Earth. There was shelter, and evidently transport, even then. Given its importance to the SLC's future, I cannot conceive of anything less than a small settlement, discreetly placed."

Falburne drew a deep breath. "As a representative of the South Lunar Company I am unable to comment but—" another pause "—I can agree that we do have a … presence within the Bowl: a permanent survey base. It is, after all, an extremely large crater…"

Jobson drummed his fingers on the table top. "Then are you suggesting that the outgassing—acting like a maroon—alerted the staff at this SLC base and they investigated; so swiftly the *Gesellschaft Nordmond* team must flee without retrieving their fellow's body?"

"Succinctly put."

There was another period of silence, but this time a reflective one as the agents of two governments considered what I had placed before them. Von Grunshafen was the first to speak: "*Herr* Sherlock Holmes, your reputation is well known in the German states; now I see that is also well deserved. It is clear that a tragic accident was almost turned, by manic distrust, into something much worse. It is a matter of shame when civilised men allow themselves to be caught up in a wrong-headed fever." He stood and bowed to each of us in turn. "*Herr* Falburne, I am satisfied here; I will claim Koenigsmann's body and have him repatriated to Prussia. *Auf wiedersehn.*"

As the German left the seminar room, Falburne also stood, holding out a hand. "Thank you, Mr Holmes," said he. "You did me a great service this morning."

"Perhaps. For myself I feel as though I have colluded in some tawdry political drama that casts a poor light on us all." I took his hand briefly then allowed him to go. Jobson would have left too, but I detained him further.

"I am curious," said I, "why an expert on alloys should also be so knowledgeable about a portion of the Moon of which so few have heard."

He smiled easily. "It is the future, Mr Holmes: new metals; new alloys. England must be at the forefront…"

"Obviously there is more than one settlement in the Devil's Bowl: you highlighted that yourself. For the SLC team to reach the outgassing so fast that the Germans fled in disarray, their home must have been minutes away—and what is the likelihood of that? As likely as a survey team happening across a body within a vast landscape—or the weight of one man accidentally triggering an outgassing."

"Why Mr Holmes, what are you saying?"

"The Bowl is riddled with SLC outposts, all buried away from prying eyes. What are they guarding, Mr Jobson? What is out there?"

He considered a moment. "There are many wonders on this satellite, Mr Holmes: elements rarely found on Earth; isotopes which we have barely begun to understand, or uncovered a use…

"The Bowl is rich in thorium: a rare element that when combined with magnesium can be used to create stronger casings for our Moon-shoot projectiles, or more durable supports and shields for our city domes. There may even be implications for future use in—" He interrupted himself, his ready smile a little embarrassed. "But I drift into wild speculation; you are interested only in facts."

"Thank you, Mr Jobson: you have provided me with the puzzle's final piece—it is for me to decide how it fits." I came to my feet. "And now I fear I must leave the Moon; London calls me—I cannot neglect her cry."

VII. Home

"And there you have it, Watson." Holmes spread himself across the seat, savouring his pipe. "Ah," he added, "I have missed these simple luxuries…"

"And your return?"

"More direct than my voyage out, for I no longer had need for circumspection. I was put upon the next return shoot to Earth; I believe poor Falburne was relieved to wave me off. The projectile is fired from the Moon by a simple gas sling-shot—compressed gasses buried away from extremes of temperature—for the lunar escape velocity is but a fraction of the Earth's. Incredibly, our vessel home was configured as a balloon: the projectile attached to an envelope inflated to the rigidity of steel. Upon arrival at Earth the balloon acted as a brake, allowing for a gentle descent—the volume of gas within it gradually reducing under the pressure of Earth's atmosphere. We landed not twenty miles from Kilima-Njaro—an impressive feat of accuracy! From there I returned to London by the most direct route."

I allowed the facts to settle, scarcely believing that Holmes had ridden to the Moon and back with all the ease of catching a train to Liverpool. "You are content, then, that you have your answers?"

"I am answered as fully as I may be—of that I am sure. We have been swimming in dark waters these weeks, Watson, their blackness concealing a depth I have but lately come to appreciate. That I have reached any definite conclusion is a blessing."

"The Scowrers?"

"Initially agents of the Crown—though controlled by the most subtle means—their purpose degraded by the stresses of the conditions.

Whilst life upon the Moon is more comfortable than it was in the eighteen-seventies, the journey—both to and fro—is still unsettling: the confinement; the reckless velocities… I find myself still prone to mental lapses: imagine the impact on a lesser mind than my own."

"And the Devil's Bowl?"

"The initial surveys would have revealed the thorium—at which point I imagine the utmost secrecy would have been placed upon the findings. It is likely even McGinty was not fully aware of the Bowl's new importance—only that within it were stations where he might hide. Obviously Ted Baldwin and some of the others also knew of them. At the remaining Scowrers' trials nothing was revealed for either they truly did not know about the Bowl's secrets, or they maintained silence through misguided loyalty, or fear.

"When the South Lunar Company was created it effaced any trace of the Bowl from official records as surely as it had effaced the Scowrers. But clearly it is a secret too big to be kept, for obviously the Germans know the Bowl has something of importance within it; and it is likely the Americans suspect, too. The truth must out soon."

"The trial of John Douglas:" said I. "He was cleared too easily…"

"Excellent, Watson. This man of so many names and guises was another potential embarrassment: found guilty, he might garner the attention of the Press; found innocent he would quietly fade from memory—especially if he were to leave the country."

"Which he has."

"Precisely." Holmes frowned suddenly, as though a dark thought had just occurred. "Although I was also followed…" He rallied, waving his pipe to dispel the gloom. "This leaves merely our mysterious *M*."

"The professor?"

"That is my conclusion, Watson. It aligns with the facts. Moriarty has found his way into the South Lunar Company. Indeed—" he pulled loudly on his pipe, brow furrowed "—I wonder if he may not already *be* the South Lunar Company…"

"To what end?"

"That is my final question, doctor: to what end indeed? The SLC—for all that it is evidently rife with deception and misdirection—is not inherently criminal. Well…" he tapped out his pipe and rose, "that must wait for another day and more facts—not mere idle speculation. I have always found travel tiring, Watson: I am for my bed." So saying, he retired to his room; from whence he would not emerge for two days.

Epilogue: An Unseeing Dupe

Two months passed by, and the case to some extent faded from the minds of public and Press alike. Talk once again fell to speculation on the expanding American and German lunar colonies: Parliament had recently pressed both foreign governments on an assurance that neither of the great powers would interfere in any way with the Empire's legitimate holdings—"The Moon is big enough for us all," spoke the Prime Minister. An assurance which had yet to be received. Meat and drink to the more sensationalist dailies, whose ever-more provocative headlines called for both German and United States to withdraw swiftly from the British Moon. Then one morning an enigmatic note was slipped into the letter box of 221B. Watson opened it and read the single line aloud:

Dear me, Sherlock. Dear me!

There was neither superscription nor signature. I was moved to laugh at the quaint message; but Holmes showed unwonted seriousness. He snatched the sheet of paper from me and studied it long, his brow clouding.

"Devilry, Watson!" he barked, and collapsed onto the chaise-longue. "I have been as blind as a mole: believing my humble burrow the entire world—even as I scurry eagerly into the trap!" He glanced again at the note then, with a groan, leapt up and paced the rooms, his wiry frame vibrant with angry energy.

"I charge you, Watson, whenever you chose to edit this wretched episode into another of your sensationalist books, do not think to present me as the faultless reasoner: the scientific detective who unfailingly—

hah!—unfailingly unmasks his nemesis through observation and deduction... I have been a fool, Watson! An unseeing dupe!"

Alarmed, I took the slip of paper from Holmes' fingers and looked again, wondering what just what it was that distressed my friend so. The hand was spidery, in a deep violet ink; the paper seemed un-extraordinary. "I don't see it—"

"The notepaper, Watson! The watermark. The Greek ἔ...!"

For a second I was not with him; then I recalled: "My God, Holmes! Porlock—!"

"There is no Porlock. Nor was there ever! Always it was he! *He*—and not once did I so much as suspect. I have been the proverbial donkey, Watson, and those—" he waved a thin hand at the note "—those were my carrot!" He returned to the chaise-long, his normally pale features almost white. "And I fear through my incompetence I have doomed John Douglas!"

He relapsed into a dark brood from which I was unable to rouse him. I was left to read my newspaper as he smoked his revolting pipe in silence; I could not tell from his expression if he was thinking or merely sunk in an impenetrable study. Holmes spoke not a word until evening when Mrs Hudson knocked on the door to announce there was a gentleman who wished to see him, and that the matter was of the utmost importance. Close at the heels of his messenger came Cecil Barker, of the fortress Manor House. His face was drawn and haggard.

"I've had bad news—terrible news, Mr Holmes," said he.

Holmes stirred himself and gazed long and deeply at the man. "I feared as much," said he.

I rose, folding the newspaper, and showed the stricken Barker to a chair, offering him a brandy which was refused with an abrupt shake of the head. "You have not had a Teslagram, have you?"

"I have had a note from someone who has."

Barker took a quivering breath. "It's poor Douglas. They tell me his name is Edwards; but he will always be Jack Douglas of Benito Canyon to me. He and Mrs Douglas started out together for South Africa in the *RMAS Palmyra* three weeks ago."

"So I believe."

"The aerostat reached Cape Town last night. I received this 'gram from Ivy—Mrs Douglas—this morning." He dug inside his coat for a crumpled slip of yellow paper and held it in shaking fingers. "*Jack fallen overboard in storm shortly after leaving Khartoum. Most likely over Kurdufan. No one knows how accident occurred. Ivy Douglas.*"

"Ha! It came like that, did it?" said Holmes bitterly. "I had no doubt it would be well stage-managed."

"You mean that you think there was no accident?" Barker's expression was of a man who had already guessed the answer.

"None in the world."

"He was murdered?"

"Surely!"

"So I think also. These infernal Scowrers, this cursed vindictive nest of criminals—"

"No, no, my good sir," said Holmes. "There is a master hand here. It is no case of sawed-off shotguns and ice grapples. You can tell an old master by the sweep of his brush. This crime is from London, not from the Moon."

"But for what motive?"

Holmes stood and walked to the mantelpiece. He stuffed his pipe with tobacco and lit it before speaking. "Because it is done by men who cannot afford to fail, whose whole unique position depends upon the fact that all they do must succeed. A great brain and a huge organization have been turned to the extinction of one man. It is crushing the nut with the trip hammer—an absurd extravagance of energy—but the nut is very effectually crushed all the same."

I confess I shook my head. "Professor Moriarty again," said I, tired of the name.

"In part," replied Holmes. "But not alone. Though for too long I thought so. Indeed, so was I meant to believe." His laugh was bitter. "The ubiquitous *M*. The truth was before me, but I chose not to see it."

I was taken aback. "Holmes? Have you abandoned your absurd fantasies at last?"

His face twitched in a semblance of a smile. "Not at all, Watson. This whole sorry business—and its tragic ending—only convinces me the more. Moriarty is the spider whose web lurks deep and dark, whose motives are often murky and unclear; but he not alone."

A new fear stirred in my breast at those words: had Holmes' imaginings begun to spiral beyond control? Was he now seeing foes in every shadow? "Then who?"

"I can only say that the first word that ever came to us of the business was from the as we now are all too aware, fictional, Porlock. A source which, until now, had been faultless: crimes nipped in the bud, information as to where goods and contraband might be stashed... All the actions of a disaffected *employé*; one who I came to trust—and there was my downfall!"

I glanced at Barker, who seemed lost amongst Holmes' rhetoric; used as I was to my friend's circumlocution, at least I was keeping up. "You were being fed titbits," I offered. "Crumbs which could be tried and tested."

"I was a salmon being played, Watson—played by one of England's finest anglers. If every tip beforehand proved to be reliable, why then should not that last message: that Douglas was about to be murdered?"

"It was true," I reasoned. "Douglas's life was in danger. Only the help and vigilance of his friends—" here I glanced again at the forlorn Barker "—along with his native wit saved the man." In return he gave me a tired, grateful smile.

"Hah!" Holmes threw up his arms in dismissal. "Oh, the information was true indeed—as far as I allowed myself to believe it. But I approached it from the wrong angle, just as I was expected to. My own narrowness of mind assured me that the hapless Porlock was trying to warn me of his master's plots, when all this time it was that very cool brain—willing to sacrifice insignificant threads of his empire to convince me or, perhaps, employing me to unwittingly hamper his enemies—who called the tune."

"Very well, if it was not—" I hesitated to use the name Moriarty least I give more credence to Holmes' theories than I believed "—this criminal mastermind who threatened Douglas, then who?"

Holmes pulled his face into a ghastly grim. "You strike to the very heart of it, Watson! Who indeed?" He stood and began to pace, stabbing the air with his pipe to emphasise each of his points. "Douglas was an American; an agent of the Pinkerton Agency. He found himself on the Moon at the very moment England's first colony uncovered a great secret—a secret out in the Devil's Bowl—which even now the United States and Germany would sell their collective souls to possess. In brief, John Douglas may have seen and learned too much." In a final flourish he waved at the dire headlines shouting from the newspaper I had draped across the arm of my chair. "Think, Watson, think! No matter what credit you give to my beliefs, there is one indisputable fact about the professor you cannot deny: he is a member of our government!"

I simply stared back in disbelief. Even for Holmes, this was a wild accusation. "Are you saying our own government—the government of the Empire—on the word of one man tracked down and killed John Douglas...?"

"As McMurdo he chased McGinty to that damned Bowl; what may he have seen out there that he did not commit to paper? A Prussian, alone on the Bowl, dies by a phenomenon described as 'vanishingly rare'... It fits, Watson—unsavoury and fantastic as it may be; it fits."

"No." I shook my head, unwilling to credit what I was hearing. "This won't do, Holmes—"

"And your visitor, Watson, whilst I was gone: the one who was so concerned as to my safety and whereabouts. Did I not say it was done by those who cannot afford to fail? Those who above all else, must succeed? You say the government would not act on the word of a single man, but there is one man who at certain times *is* the government!" His eyes glowed with feverish light. "A British ship, Watson, over British possessions... Do not think that, when there is no turning back, even the Empire cannot be capable of the most ruthless tactics."

"And you are quite clear whom you are accusing? You told me once that any attempt to confront Moriarty with his alleged crimes would bring the full weight of the British judiciary upon the accuser; but this..."

I drew a breath; I felt dizzy. "Holmes—it would be treason..."

His anguished expression gave me all the answer I needed. "My dear fellow, I am all too aware of everything..." He sat, drew up his knees and hunched over them. "You heard me warn this man at Birlstone Manor House that the coming danger was greater than the past. In truth, it was far greater than even I anticipated. It is quite possible—" and here he raised his great head and stared blindly at the hearth "—that I led the agents of Douglas's demise directly to him."

Barker beat his head with his clenched fist in his impotent anger. "Do not tell me that we have to sit down under this? Do you say that no one can ever get level with this?"

"No, I don't say that," said Holmes, and his eyes seemed to be looking far into the future. "I don't say that the soul of John Douglas will find no justice; nor his widow. But you must give me time—you must give me time!" His voice dropped and I alone barely caught his last words: "For now it has become a family matter..."

We all sat in silence for some minutes while those fateful eyes still strained to pierce the veil.

A NOTE ON EDITION AND PLACEMENT

The *Valley of Fear* is a unique Holmes novel, written to retrospectively fit Professor Moriarty into the previously-established timeline outlined within *The Final Problem*. While it was first serialised in London's *Strand Magazine,* the first publication of the novel was in New York. For this reason its first full edit is the American edition, and the British edition that followed was an entirely independent edit which differed in some significant respects.

The US version is perhaps the most heavy-handed of edits, with some considerable changes, particularly in relation to secret society that the Pinkerton Birdy Edwards infiltrates. Identified in *The Strand* version as the Ancient Order of Freemen (having been based on the Ancient Order of Hibernians), some American editions instead called them the Eminent Order of Freemen, which we have retained to further distance the Scowrers from The Molly Maguires and their Irish origins. We have used hindsight to take the best of both editions, so the very British title of Worshipful Master has been retained in favour of 'Eminent Bodymaster', and we have kept Americanisms in relation to Birdy Edwards' experiences, and Britishisms elsewhere.

The dating used in *The Valley of Fear* was very specific, referencing the years 1876 and, by extension, 1888. This is compounded by the Moriarty references, and also to the first written appearance of Billy the Page. Which brings us to our mash-up, Vallis Timoris. There is, of course, no such valley in Mike's book—he chooses instead to call it the *Vale de Verme*—retaining the VV of the fictional Vermissa Valley. The origin of this disparity is a result of commissioning and promoting the book a whole year before it was written. Vallis means Valley or Hollow of Terror, and so we assume it refers to the Devil's Bowl rather than the *Vale de Verme* itself.

Transplanting the story from an American valley to a Lunar Mining Colony ruled by the British Empire wasn't straightforward. Much of the alternate timeline created by Professor Moriarty was worked out well in advance of this volume, but our original placement of the first Lunar proved a struggle—the British Empire landed on the Moon in 1875 and yet the Valley flashback was to show a fully functioning mining colony less than 12 months later. NASA couldn't have managed that, so how could the British Empire?

Well necessity, they say, is the mother of invention. The only way such a colony could exist was if it was launched at the same time as the Moon was colonised—or before. As it happens, this odd requirement led to the decision that the Moon wasn't landed on by a single capsule *à la Apollo 11*, but rather that a full-blown Colonial Expedition would have landed *en masse* upon the Lunar surface. This, we concluded, is exactly what a British military expedition would have planned. So, for more than a year before the lunar expedition the Empire fires torpedo after torpedo at the Moon, perfecting its Moon-shoots long before any men are sent ahead, and each torpedo would contain the supplies needed to supply an entire company of men, along with the tools the British Sappers would need to scour the lunar surface and establish a forward base or two.

General Gordon therefore arrives on New Year's Day in 1875, and by the following year a full-blown mining operation—based on the coal mines of the 1870s—is up and running when Birdy Edwards begins his investigation.

SHERLOCK HOLMES AND THE PULP TRADITION

by Adrian Middleton

Pulp as a fiction medium is often considered to have followed the dawn of the great detective by several years, and its figurative use for action-oriented popular literature is often—and erroneously—dismissed when talking about Sherlock Holmes. *The Valley of Fear* was the last of the long-form Holmes novels, written at the dawn of the Great War at a time when the pulp format was in its prime. It is the first Holmes novel to tie up some of the loose ends that preceded it, setting the character of Sherlock Holmes within a self-contained timeline of fictional events. As such it is the first proper pulp novel written by Sir Arthur Conan Doyle, and if you had been expecting one of his sedate detective mysteries you may have been sadly disappointed.

The pulp format—based on 10 x 7 in (254 x 178 mm) magazines printed on cheap, chemically treated woodpulp—had grown out of a paper-making process introduced in the 1880s (at exactly the same time the first Sherlock Holmes stories appeared, and the time in which the novel is set). The high acid content and the typically serrated edges of the paper, coupled with coal-tar based inks made it ideal for mass-produced magazines, whose lurid four-colour covers and tendency to brown over time reinforced the idea that the content was aimed at a lower class readership than its predecessors, enabling the evolution of the earlier Penny Dreadfuls, Boys' Papers and Dime Novels into a more substantial periodical.

Higher quality magazines like *The Strand*, *Pearson's* and *Harper's*—aimed at the middle classes—were already popular on both sides of the

Atlantic, and the popularity of Sherlock Holmes pushed their circulations to the limit. However, it wasn't until *The Golden Argosy*, Frank Munsey's popular fiction periodical founded in 1882, underwent changes of format—becoming *The Argosy* in 1888 and adopting the pulp format in 1896—that that these cheaper magazines were able to cater for a wider audience whose growing literacy fuelled its demand for tales of mystery and adventure. With greater circulations, these early pulps—such as *The Popular Magazine* (1904) and the *Blue Book* (1905)—achieved incredible circulations, attracting advertising revenue which would later be diluted by post-war paper shortages and the emergence of movie industry. Indeed the movie industry was to draw heavily upon pulp stories—and upon Holmes himself—as it evolved.

Quickly cornering the popular fiction market, the pulps exploded during the years leading up to the first world war, supplanting the Dime Novel format as they moved into multi-genre fiction, particularly Detective, Sport, Western and, by 1923, horror (in the form of *Weird Tales*), and 1926, science fiction (Hugo Gernsback's *Amazing Stories*). The early writers of adventure fiction and scientific romance (Conan Doyle among them, along with the likes of H. G. Wells and Rider Haggard)—more commonly published in the so-called Slicks (smaller circulation, better paper and a middle-class audience)—had inspired a new wave of writers such as Edgar Rice Burroughs, Raymond Chandler, Dashiell Hammett, William Hope Hodgson, Robert E Howard, Jack London, H P Lovecraft, Abraham Merritt and Sax Rohmer, who were kept popular by the medium well into the 1950s. The downside of this growth was that the pulps didn't pay well, and many writers focused more on output than quality, leading to a faster pace, a heavier reliance on cyphers and tropes, and dismissal in some quarters as less literary or meritorious.

In Britain, *The Strand* and its contemporaries continued to reign until the second world war, with only a couple of cheaper papers (*Adventure-Story Magazine* and *Mystery-Story Magazine*) in circulation. *The Strand* and its competitors, therefore, filled the popular gap occupied by their pulp cousins on the other side of the Atlantic. For Britain's most popular authors, therefore, the demands of the American pulp market were the most significant driver of popularity, and in the case of Sherlock Holmes, Lippincott's *Monthly Magazine of Philadelphia* was the first publisher of the second Holmes novel, *The Sign of Four*, in February 1890. Indeed, despite Holmes being London-based, the influence of the US upon his adventures was significant—three of the four Holmes novels, for example, involved an American dimension. A year before Holmes' own debut, in 1886, the New York Weekly had introduced the detective's pupil, Nick Carter, who quickly evolved into Manhattan's great detective. Several tales within the Holmes canon reflect the more visceral nature of the American pulps, and the shift in emphasis from detection to adventure can be charted through the order in which Doyle's stories are published. Baritsu, boxing, the use of a riding crop and pistol-whipping all emerge in later stories, and the final volume of Holmes tales, collected in *The Case-Book of Sherlock Holmes*, was often considered a weaker entry as a result of this shift.

Perhaps the most pulp-oriented Holmes story was *The Valley of Fear*, serialized in *The Strand* between September 1914 and May 1915. Published against the backdrop of World War One, it immediately preceded the first appearance of Street & Smith's *Detective Story Magazine*, which replaced *Nick Carter Weekly*. The rising popularity of detective fiction had a marked impact on Doyle. As the last story recounted by Watson without reference to Holmes's retirement, Valley focused more on the hard-boiled working-class back-story of the Pinkerton Birdy Edwards than upon the middle-class mystery that Holmes seeks to resolve, and consciously returns to the detective's heydey, throwing in Professor Moriarty (in spite of his presence not advancing the plot) for good measure. It was, in many ways a prototype, using tropes that would become popular just five years later with the arrival of Henry Mencken's *Black Mask* in April 1920. As America embraced the violent age of Prohibition and the Great Depression, many British writers—Doyle and Hemingway among them—reflected the change, even as new British novelists like Agatha Christie were moving away from them. Holmes

then, stands between two different and contradictory styles, and it is *The Valley of Fear* that straddles them most plainly.

Conan Doyle's Moriarty may have inspired the likes of Nikola and Fu Manchu, but in Valley he reclaims his creation as the master villain beloved of detective stories—the shady background supervillain—who, despite a lavish description, cannot be brought to account.

There follows a disassociated murder mystery—quite grisly by Watson's accounts (not often we see a victim whose head has been blown off with a shotgun)—that wouldn't be out of place in an Agatha Christie novel, and yet we are swiftly drawn from rural Sussex to a story about a distant American mine and a Pinkerton investigation into a secret society (based on the Molly Maguires) whose lawless reign over Vermissa Valley repeats the trick first used in *A Study in Scarlet*—telling a Western frontier story from the relative safety of civilized old England. But the outcome of the story—the hero dying, the villains escaping—creates a more dramatic world than the easy wins which are often Holmes' trademark.

But of course, *Vallis Timoris* isn't quite *The Valley of Fear*. As a mash-up it touches upon one of the other great tropes beloved of period pulp—Science Fiction. It is not just a matter of transplanting Vermissa Valley to the Moon, but of creating a credible fictional world in which such a location makes perfect sense in the alternate history we have created. Not just credible to the early SF readers of the 1920s, but to a modern post-1969 audience already familiar with the Lunar landings, with knowledge of what the Moon is like, and with expectations of scientific accuracy. With a healthy dose of pulp fiction thrown in for good measure.

ABOUT THE AUTHOR AND OTHER CONTRIBUTORS

Mike Chinn: Mike has been a Holmes fan since childhood and has written horror, fantasy and science fiction for years, publishing over 40 short stories and editing several anthologies. He has also scripted SF and Fantasy comics (*Stargazer* and *The Beano*) as well as two how-to books on writing for comics.

Mike's latest collection of short stories, *Give Me These Moments Back*, was published in March 2015 by The Alchemy Press.

Guy Adams: Guy worked as an actor and comedian for ten years before deciding it was time to settle down into a sensible, secure career. Then he decided to be a writer instead. He is the author of far too many books. Including: spy-fi series *The Clown Service*; weird western trilogy, *Heaven's Gate* and the strange crime/fantasy hybrid that is the *Deadbeat* series. He's written new adventures for Sherlock Holmes, adapted old Hammer movies and somehow wrote a biography of Leonard Rossiter. He also writes comics, predominately for *2000 AD* but is also the co-creator of Goldtiger with artist Jimmy Broxton.

He lives in Spain with his partner and their two grown-up boys. Joe is a songwriter and musician, Dan is a chef. Every night can be a cabaret dinner in his house, soon Guy will be happily fat and deaf.

Darrel Bevan: Darrel is a portrait and figure illustrator who, due to colour blindness, specialises in graphite illustration—mainly on

black and white images. When he isn't producing photo-realistic pencil drawings, he teaches.

Sir Arthur Conan Doyle (1859 – 1930): Scotsman, doctor, sportsman, whale hunter, war correspondent and the world-renowned author responsible for the creation of Sherlock Holmes, Doyle was a social crusader who didn't shy from the realms of science fiction or, as it was known in his heyday, scientific romance. After starting his career with such tales, he became distracted by the adventures of Holmes, returning to the genre with the fantastic adventures of Professor Challenger. He never knew what steampunk was, but we are sure he wouldn't have given a damn.

Adrian Middleton: Writer, editor, publisher, local historian and the son of a real-life detective, Adrian is the creator of the Moriarty Paradigm, and willingly accepts the accusation that he is—for now—a Doyle plagiarist. When he isn't editing, he also writes original science fiction, fantasy and adventure stories.

ENDNOTE

I am a member of that ageing band who remembers Douglas Wilmer playing Holmes in the BBC's mid-1960s TV series (he would later hand the role over to the inimitable Peter Cushing—Nigel Stock played Watson in both iterations – whilst taking on the mantel of Sir Dennis Nayland Smith in two Fu Manchu movies). I was around 10 years old at the time, but I'm certain that I was already aware of the Great Detective: like Tarzan or Superman, everyone knows Sherlock Holmes. I enjoyed Rathbone & Bruce in *The Hound of the Baskervilles* and *The Adventures of Sherlock Holmes*, although it would be some years before I finally bought my copy of *The Penguin Complete Sherlock Holmes*; still more before television produced what I consider to be my Sherlock Holmes: Jeremy Brett.

I can't say I've read much beyond the Conan Doyle canon, other than a few anthologies edited by the likes of Charles Prepolec, Mike Ashley and Michael Reaves & John Phelan, but even that small selection demonstrates the hold Holmes still has on the public imagination, and how the character may slip between the cracks into unfamiliar genres. From straightforward Conan Doyle pastiche to modern crime fiction and even the weird and supernatural, the lodger at 221B Baker Street has coolly deduced his way through it all. It was inevitable that Holmes would eventually get Steampunked.

I don't think I really knew what I was letting myself in for when I answered Fringeworks' email for Sherlock Holmes fans interested in writing for a new project. I'd certainly never written any Steampunk before. But when I was offered to chance to reimagine *The Valley of Fear*, with a large slice of the action set on the Moon, I seized it gleefully. Told

that I could Pulp it up a little, I went for it (and more than a little, in the end). Although it's unlikely Conan Doyle would have written anything like the scene with Holmes, Watson and Douglas on the carriage roof, my inspiration came from imperfect memories of the railway chase in the film adaptation of *The Seven Percent Solution*. The scenes on the Moon were from an appropriate mash-up of how lunar colonies were imagined back in the 1960s (suitably retro-engineered), Edwardian scientific romances (where astronauts wore nothing more robust than modified diving suits), a touch of Dan Dare, with visuals filtered through classic movies such as *The First Men in the Moon* and Disney's *Twenty Thousand Leagues Under the Sea*. And just for good measure, I threw in a little sniff of government conspiracy (as an impressionable youth, some of my favourite fiction was by Alistair MacLean).

And since I can't resist little in-jokes, it had to be Moonbase Archie.

Scientific accuracy did suffer along the way, I admit—resulting in the inevitable calls for change and clarification from editor Adrian Middleton. But in the end I think we compromised on something that, whilst highly improbable, isn't entirely impossible. As well as Adrian, for his editorial work, his vision of the new Steampunk Holmes and for knowing more about Conan Doyle's creation and the 19th century world than I ever will, I'd like to thank Damon Cavalchini for his work on the cover and the typesetting, and Sir Arthur Conan Doyle, without whom this book would most certainly not exist.

MIKE CHINN, 2015
Birmingham, England

MORIARTY PARADIGM

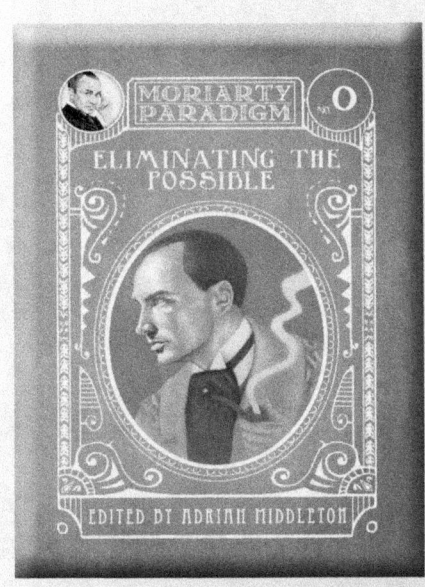

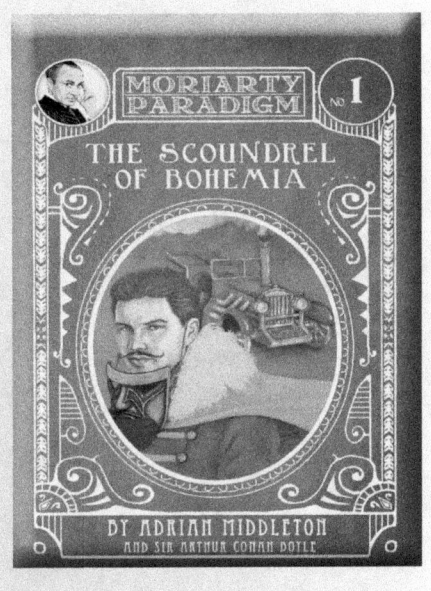

COMING SOON:

THE YELLOW FAÇADE

SIGN OF V

A STUDY IN STEAMPUNK

FIND OUT MORE ABOUT FRINGEWORKS BY SCANNING THE QR CODE BELOW

WWW.FRINGEWORKS.CO.UK

www.ingramcontent.com/pod-product-compliance
Lightning Source LLC
Chambersburg PA
CBHW051332020726
47501CB00007B/2051